No Time

Spirit Creek Series, Book Two

BRENDA SINCLAIR

To Nita
Happy Reading!
Brenda Sinclair

No Time is a work of fiction. All names, characters, places and incidents are the product of the author's imagination or are used fictitiously. Any resemblance to actual events, locales or persons, living or dead, is entirely coincidental.

ISBN 978-0-9919492-8-1

DEDICATION

To my three wonderful grandchildren: Cassidy, Ashton and Dakota.

ACKNOWLEDGMENTS

A huge thank you to Victoria Chatham, Doreen Logeot, Ellen Jorgenson, and Sharon Vierboom for beta reading and providing constructive critiques.

Thank you to Ted Williams for his excellent line editing and for his patience in catching my mistakes. And thank you to the exceptionally-talented Su Kopil from Earthly Charms at http://www.earthlycharms.com for the beautiful cover.

Thanks again to the friendly folks in Miles City, Montana including the hotel proprietors, the waitresses at the various eating places, grocery store clerks, and everyone who provided directions and answered my inquiries during my two visits to your fine town. I enjoyed myself immensely while completing my research, once in early May and again a few years later during a chilly October.

During both visits to Miles City, I checked out the Range Rider Museum over on West Main Street. What a lovely facility! The knowledgeable folks working there patiently answered my questions and often volunteered additional information and insights into the topic at hand. Thank you so much! Readers, if you find yourselves in Miles City and you're of a mind to shake hands with history, wander on over and spend a few hours walking through the various interesting displays. You won't be disappointed.

Thank goodness, I also dropped by the Miles City Library and talked with the very helpful and well-informed librarians. The Montana room upstairs is a goldmine for someone like myself doing research on the area history. And the rolls of microfilm, especially the old newspapers from my era of interest, were invaluable. I'm certain your town is understandably proud of that library.

NO TIME

CHAPTER 1

Spirit Creek, Montana
Saturday, April 5, 1890

"Are you certain?" whispered Miss Ellie Thomas, slumped on the uncomfortable ladder-back chair across from Doctor Benjamin Johnson's small metal desk. The room's antiseptic reek combined with the shocking diagnosis sent Ellie's stomach flip-flopping. She swallowed hard and met the doctor's eyes.

He nodded. "Positive."

Ellie had convinced herself the frenzy surrounding her wedding plans while keeping abreast of her school teaching duties caused her persistent malaise. Although twenty-five, she trembled in her shoes like a panicky child. What she'd just learned changed everything. "When will the…" she croaked.

"You're at least two months along," confirmed Doc Benjamin.

Ellie blinked away the tears filling her eyes. One night several weeks ago, she and Franklin had been overcome with passion. He was so gentle, it being her first time. But they agreed not again until they'd exchanged the wedding vows.

Only once. But apparently, that was all it had taken.

"Miss Thomas, many people would disagree with me, but I believe bringing a new life into the world is a good thing, no matter the circumstances."

Although sunshine streamed through the lace-covered window, a chill ran up Ellie's spine. Doc Benjamin couldn't be more wrong; this was a terrible thing. Single. Pregnant. As Spirit Creek's schoolteacher, her reputation would be ruined.

"Are you not engaged to Sheriff Smith?" Doc Benjamin set his stethoscope on the desk and met her eyes.

"Yes, he proposed on New Year's Day," whispered Ellie, glancing at the magnificent family heirloom on her finger. Sunlight caught the emerald brilliance of his mother's ring. The dear woman would be rolling in her grave if she was aware of Ellie's condition.

"That's good then," acknowledged the doctor, dipping a quill pen into the bottle of ink on his desk and scratching notes on his patient's chart.

"Franklin is a wonderful man." Her hand shook, fingers fiddling with the braid of fiery-red hair resting atop her shoulder.

"He's an excellent lawman and proudly serving his community," observed Doc Benjamin, leaning back in his chair.

"I love Franklin and I couldn't be happier." Ellie closed her eyes for a moment and recalled how her betrothed wrapped her in a crushing embrace against his muscular chest, how her arms encircled his narrow waist while she lost herself in his kisses. Her eyes flew open with the realization those actions had gotten her into this mess in the first place. She loved Franklin, but she should have been stronger. Neither of them had planned what happened, but it was too late to rethink their lapse in judgment now.

Doc Benjamin leaned forward in his chair. "Your happiness shows. I wish you and Franklin only the best."

"Thank you." Ellie smiled weakly. She'd taught school for years, having replaced Maggie Wentworth as schoolteacher after she married the sheriff, now the late William Burns. Ellie had almost given up on the idea of marriage and children of her own, until Franklin Smith moved to town. He'd courted her relentlessly, and she'd agreed to be his wife. But was she prepared for the enormous responsibility of motherhood?

"I'd like to examine you every month to check on your baby's progress," said Doc, standing.

Ellie rose from her chair. "I promise to come by regularly."

She quickly peeked into the mirror hanging near the door. While she adjusted her small hat, she considered the scandal that awaited her beyond the safety of the clinic doors. If she and Franklin stuck to their original wedding date, another two months would pass before she'd become a married woman. She'd be over four months along by then and most-likely showing. She couldn't wait that long.

Doc Benjamin opened the office door and Ellie exited the clinic. For a moment, she considered heading home to her room in back of the schoolhouse to indulge herself in a good cry. Instead, she reconsidered and headed toward Franklin's house.

The long skirts of her simple calico dress rustled as she strode down the wooden sidewalk, and the inch-high heels of her black, buttoned-up boots tapped out a rhythmic staccato as she hurried toward her destination. The afternoon breeze whispered in her ears, and the birds sang a little sweeter. Children's laughter wafted through the air from behind a fence. Ellie had never heard a more beautiful sound.

* * *

Sheriff Franklin Smith sat on a rickety old chair on the back veranda of the house he rented from local rancher, Luke Carlyle. He wiped his calloused hands on the soiled rag he'd used while cleaning his pistol before tossing the cloth aside. He reached over and patted his old flop-eared hound on the head. "Good dog, Captain."

Franklin checked his pocket watch. Ellie should be dropping by soon. "I wonder if Ellie plans to bake a batch of cookies when she arrives?" he asked the dog stretched out at his feet, because no lawman worth his salt would be caught talking to himself.

He stood and grabbed his Stetson off the small metal table nearby.

"Franklin!" Luke Carlyle rounded the house and strode toward him.

The sheriff's heart almost stopped. No lawman should allow a man to sneak up and surprise him like that. Luke, owner of the Diamond C Ranch and the area's wealthiest rancher, was a bit of a prankster, and Franklin hated to admit it, but he'd almost scared him to death. Franklin would get him back though. He always did. He stood hands on hips and glared at his good friend, while his heartbeat returned to normal.

"I'm glad I found you at home." Luke paused a second to catch his breath. "We've got big problems again."

"Now what?"

"They're back."

"Who's back?"

"The cattle rustlers…disappeared last fall...they've returned." Luke crossed the back yard to where the lawman stood and bent down to ruffle Captain's ears.

"Damnation!" exclaimed Franklin.

"Although someone spooked them last September, I suspected the gang suffered from a serious case of stupid, believing if they laid low for awhile all would be forgotten. My patience has paid off." Luke whipped off his Stetson, wiped his brow with his handkerchief and stuffed it back into his pocket. "We'll catch them in the act this time."

"That's a damn certainty," said Franklin, sticking his Stetson on his head. "You're sure it's the same gang?"

"You recall me mentioning a couple weeks ago that our new ranch hand, Bobby, seemed a little odd? Big guy, didn't miss any meals? But no ambition and as talkative as a wall?"

"Yep. Said you wouldn't trust him as far as you could toss him."

Franklin frowned. "Has he done something to justify your suspicions?"

"He snuck out of the bunkhouse last night, and Mike discreetly followed him off the Diamond C," replied Luke.

"Mike Armstrong, your foreman's son?"

Luke nodded and settled his Stetson back in place.

"What did this Bobby fellow do?"

"Met up with our former ranch hand, Frenchy, near the Circle M Ranch. We suspected he was part of the gang who disappeared last fall."

"Frenchy is working for the Maxwells? How the hell did that happen?"

"Asked myself the same question. I dropped by to see old Buddy Maxwell over on the Circle M this morning. Buddy recently hired his nephew, Russ Maxwell, from Texas to help his son, Cody, run the ranch. Buddy was looking a little peaked, now that I think about it."

"Is he ailing? Or just getting up in years?"

"Couldn't say, Franklin. Maybe a bit of both. Anyway, Buddy and Cody warned Russ that there were rustlers in the area, but Russ wasn't told we suspected a fellow who goes by the name Frenchy of being involved with them." Luke paced the ground in front of Franklin. "Russ unknowingly hired the man to help with branding season."

"So what makes you think they're rustling again?"

"Mike overhead them talking. He couldn't hear the entire conversation but he distinctly caught the words 'cattle' and 'hidden' before Bobby and Frenchy parted ways."

"Hot damn. Let's send a telegram to the lawmen up in Miles City and get this show on the road." Sheriff Smith grabbed his newly-cleaned pistol and shoved it into the leather holster riding his hip.

"My thoughts exactly." Luke grinned from ear to ear. "I'd wager those varmints have stolen over twenty head from me already. Time to put an end to this, once and for all."

The two men charged down the boardwalk heading toward the telegraph office. Franklin surmised that if a looker-on observed them hurrying as they were, the person might suspect he'd challenged Luke to a foot race. "Do you suppose Frenchy is the ringleader? He could be working for someone." The sheriff glanced at the rancher.

"Whether he is or not, we're capturing every last one of them," vowed Luke. "Ever since my father started the Diamond C operation by driving that first thousand head of Longhorns from Texas to Montana over twenty years ago, the Carlyle family has been plagued off and on by rustlers. It's just a part of ranching. But there's nothing I detest more than a dishonest man, and rustlers sit atop my list."

"Can't say I disagree with you." The sheriff quickened his pace to keep up.

"A less-civilized man might consider resorting to the old days' methods when local law didn't exist. Cattle and horse thieves were just strung up in the nearest tree. Problem solved."

"Not on your life, Luke. We're doing this proper by bringing in two or three more lawmen. We'll arrest them all well and legal. Won't be a judge alive discovering grounds to dismiss the charges. The whole lot will rot in jail for a good many years."

"What if they catch wind of our plans again?"

Franklin yanked open the telegraph office door and the two friends entered. "That ain't happening. We'll demand the Miles City lawmen respond immediately." Franklin fired off an urgent telegram to his colleagues in the neighboring town, advising them that the gang of rustlers had returned. He'd as much as ordered them to get their behinds to Spirit Creek.

When the sheriff headed toward the door, Luke dropped several coins on the elderly telegraph operator's desk. "You keep this business to yourself. Not a word to anyone."

The sickly old telegraph operator's arthritic fingers scooped up the monetary insurance that he'd keep mum. "What business?" he cackled with a rotten-toothed grin, adding a wink. "I didn't hear about nobody's business today."

Franklin and Luke strode out the door and stepped into the alley alongside the building to ensure their conversation wasn't overheard.

"I doubt that ailing old man warned the rustlers last September. It's purely miraculous he's still alive. Someone else must have sounded the warning, but not this time." Franklin shook Luke's hand.

"The moment you hear from them…."

"You'll be the first to know," interjected Franklin.

"Thank you. Appreciate it." Luke touched his hat brim and strode across the street toward the feed store where the sheriff noticed Thunder, Luke's stallion, stood tied to the hitching rail.

* * *

As Ellie passed alongside The Spirit Creek General Store, she glanced into one of the front display windows and stared at the image of the smiling young woman reflected back at her. No tell-tale bump yet, of course, but she'd heard women discussing an expectant woman's glow. Her hand lightly touched her cheek. Was she glowing at this very moment?

Elizabeth Waverly, the proprietor's wife, stood slightly stooped in one corner of the display area arranging a grouping of men's sturdy work boots. She spotted Ellie and waved, and Ellie extended a greeting to her through the clear glass pane.

Wilma Wallace, the liveryman's wife, stepped out of the store, holding her little girl wrapped in a knitted pink blanket. The infant shrieked like a banshee, and Ellie smiled. Would her baby be a girl, too? She really didn't care as long as the child was born healthy.

"Hello, Mrs. Wallace," greeted Ellie.

The baby's mother caught the small fist flailing wildly outside the blanket, gently planted a kiss on the small hand before tucking it back inside. "Good day, Miss Thomas. You must excuse me. I'm late heading home to nurse the boss here."

"I won't keep you then."

"Pleasure seeing you." Wilma smiled and then hurried across the street, looking both ways to avoid being hit by any passing wagons or horses.

Ellie sighed as she continued on her way. Just thinking about her handsome, six-foot-tall fiancé, the father of her child, incited a surge of flutters in her heart. Franklin must be told, of course. But how would he react to her news? Shocked? Elated? Angry? Ellie erased any doubts from her mind. Only happy thoughts today.

She turned down Franklin's street, feeling her lips crinkle at the edges. She suspected her eyes were twinkling with joy. A child of her own. Despite the uncertainty of Franklin's reaction to her situation, she couldn't contain her excitement.

Ellie spied Franklin's next-door neighbor's wife on her hands and knees weeding a flowerbed and she leaned over the short picket fence. "Good morning, Lily. How's the newspaper business these days?"

Arthur MacDonald recently opened the town's first newspaper, *The Spirit Creek Chronicle*, and Ellie visualized her own headlines: Unwed Schoolteacher Thrilled to Learn She's With Child. Wouldn't the gossips be shocked?

Lily waved. "Hello, Ellie. Everything is going very well, thank you. Arthur is planning a grand opening, perhaps in autumn when everyone isn't so busy."

"That sounds like an excellent idea."

Lily returned to her work.

Humming a silly tune she'd recently taught her school children, Ellie started up the front walk to Franklin's home where she spotted Robert James Rutherford knocking on her fiancé's front door. The lawyer stood rocking on the balls of his feet, not having spotted her approaching yet.

Ellie blanched when he turned toward her, his broad smile displaying a perfect set of pearly-white teeth. When he removed his silk-banded bowler, his pale-blond hair reflected sunlight like a beacon. As usual he was impeccably dressed in woolen trousers, starched white shirt, fitted waistcoat, stylish frock coat and polished boots.

"May I help you?" Ellie forced herself to return his smile while she slowly climbed the front steps.

"Good day, Miss Thomas. I'm delighted to cross paths with you again." Mr. Rutherford clasped his bowler in his hand.

"Likewise," she offered. As Ellie turned the handle on the heavy wooden door, Mr. Rutherford stepped closer to her and she inhaled a bay rum soap scent. She turned to speak to him but was distracted by a small cut on his chin where, most likely, he'd nicked himself shaving this morning. She almost reached out and touched the spot but caught herself.

"Franklin…Sheriff Smith…mustn't be at home." Ellie fanned her warm face with her small reticule, totally embarrassed by how flustered she suddenly felt.

Whenever she encountered the man, his hazel eyes hypnotized her in a wizardly spell and she'd just stare at him, dumbstruck. For some reason, the clean-shaven, professional gentleman sent her pulse racing and his smile warmed her heart every time. A totally scandalous reaction to the fellow, considering she was engaged to another man!

A stray tendril fell across her forehead and broke the spell. As she tucked her hair behind her ear, she recovered her senses and strode into the house. Setting her reticule, hat and gloves down on the entryway table, she silently pleaded, *please just speak your piece and leave.*

Mr. Rutherford fumbled a sealed envelope out of his coat pocket and almost dropped his hat while he stepped across the threshold. "I've prepared a document according to Sheriff Smith's instructions, and the papers await his signature."

Ellie's head whipped up and she met his eyes. "What papers?" Mortified that she'd blurted the inquiry, she added with a wave of her hand, "I'm sorry. That's absolutely none of my business."

"Nothing secretive." Mr. Rutherford smiled. "Sheriff Smith updated his Last Will and Testament."

"Oh…" Ellie stared at the lawyer, surprised by his statement. "I've never known anyone who wrote a will. Of course, I've never known anyone owning sufficient possessions to need one. I always considered a will a document solely required by the wealthy."

"Now that's where you're mistaken, Miss Thomas." Mr. Rutherford's expression turned serious. "I would encourage everyone to write out a will. Even meager possessions must be disposed of by some means when something unfortunate happens."

"Well, I can't imagine why Franklin would bother with a will. But it appears that he has. Considering he's a lawman working in a dangerous profession and all, I suppose it makes sense for him to…" She stopped mid-sentence, realizing that she'd been rambling.

"May I leave the document in your capable and trustworthy care?"

The lawyer handed her the envelope.

"Certainly…I'll see that Sheriff Smith…receives this." Ellie stammered and reached for the envelope with slightly shaking hands. She clutched it to her bosom as if her life depended on its safe-keeping.

"I'd hoped to catch Mr. Smith at home to finalize this. But have him peruse the document in its entirety before returning it in person to my office. A witnessed signature where I've indicated with an X is required at that time." Mr. Rutherford popped his bowler onto his head, touched the brim, and turned to leave.

"Thank you for dropping by with the papers." Ellie closed the door behind him and slumped back against it. An eternity passed before her heartbeat returned to normal.

"Get over this silliness," she scolded herself, as childhood infractions in the Boston orphanage that was home until her eighteenth birthday flashed through her mind. She felt like a total ninny. She was a grown woman and a respectable citizen. There was no need to feel so flustered around a litigator.

Could past unpleasant memories of her own and the other orphans' encounters with the law explain why she always became so frazzled around this small-town lawyer? Or was it the man himself?

Ellie tossed Mr. Rutherford's envelope onto Franklin's hallway table. The papers could wait. Her news couldn't.

She wandered into the kitchen and dragged a chair out from the table. While she sat absently twisting a tattered handkerchief in her hands, she reviewed the morning visit to Doc Benjamin in her mind. When she first heard the news, she'd believed her life was ruined. Now, having become accustomed to the idea, she couldn't wait to share the news with Franklin.

But would her betrothed be pleased? They'd discussed marriage but never children. Or had Franklin considered children a foregone conclusion, her being a teacher and all?

Ellie leapt to her feet and headed for the pantry. A batch of fresh-baked cookies never failed to elevate Franklin's mood.

"Are you here, Ellie?" Franklin inquired from the back doorway.

"Yes, I am and I need to tell you something." Ellie gasped. Before she realized what was happening, Franklin had swept her up in his arms and captured her lips with a warm kiss.

"Franklin Smith, put me down," scolded Ellie, when they finally came up for air.

"In a minute." Franklin prevented further protest with another lengthy kiss.

Ellie savored her betrothed's kisses, secretly relishing the few minutes delay to organize her thoughts. But this news couldn't be delayed indefinitely.

Finally, Franklin set Ellie on her feet.

"What did you want to discuss?" He strode across the floor, washed his hands at the sink, and dried them on a tattered brown towel.

"It's not so much…something to discuss…" Ellie bit her lower lip, telling herself not to cry.

And then a more worrisome notion popped into her head.

Since learning she carried Franklin's child, Ellie's concern centered solely on her reputation as Spirit Creek's schoolteacher. Not until this second had she considered the possible ramifications for Franklin. Would impregnating the local schoolteacher jeopardize Franklin's career? Diminish his standing in the community? She wasn't so concerned for herself. The majority of her life she carried the title of 'foundling' raised in a Boston orphanage, a child nobody wanted and nobody claimed. But Franklin worked hard all his life, and although he never admitted it, she suspected he hailed from a reputable family. Would Franklin face disciplinary action?

"Don't tell me you've come to your senses, and you no longer intend to marry me." Franklin feigned a frown but his twinkling eyes betrayed him.

Ellie smiled at his joke. She'd practiced the words in her head for the past hour, but suddenly her mouth felt clogged with cotton. Just tell him. There's nothing to worry about, she encouraged herself. But in her experience, when she thought those words there was something troubling just waiting around the corner.

She swallowed hard and thrust her shoulders back.

"Exactly the opposite, my darling, I must marry you for certain." Ellie met Franklin's eyes and whispered, "I'm going to have a baby."

* * *

Sheriff Franklin Smith didn't frighten easily, an admirable trait in a lawman. But for a moment Ellie's blunt announcement scared him witless. The unexpected news hovered in the air like an unseen wraith leaving a cold chill in its wake. Had he heard her correctly?

"Are you sure?" He frowned. "There was only that one time…"

"Doc Benjamin confirmed my condition this morning."

Franklin couldn't wipe the smile off his face. "Honey, that's…that's wonderful."

"Are you truly pleased?"

"I'm going to be a papa," he whispered in disbelief. And then he reached for her hand. "We should get married tomorrow."

Ellie burst into tears.

"Damnation." Franklin groaned with the realization he'd uttered the curse word aloud. But this was hardly the reaction he'd expected from Ellie. Wouldn't an unwed woman with child insist on a wedding as soon as one could be arranged? An immediate marriage was the first thought that entered his mind. For the life of him, he couldn't imagine what he'd said or done wrong.

"Why are you crying?" He rubbed her back.

"I had hoped you'd suggest moving up the wedding date, and I know you're going to be a wonderful father." Ellie smiled and touched his arm. "But how do we explain the urgency to the community without raising suspicions?"

"Oh, hang the suspicions. Let's just do it." Franklin lifted Ellie off her feet and swung her around the small kitchen.

"The good citizens of Spirit Creek can cipher—at least some of them anyway—and when this child arrives no one will be fooled, Franklin," warned Ellie, hugging his neck and hanging onto his shoulders for dear life as he twirled her about the room.

When he set her down finally, she dabbed her eyes with her handkerchief. Happy tears no doubt. At least, he hoped so. He couldn't love this woman more.

"Who cares what anyone thinks." Franklin cupped her tear-stained face in his hands. "I love you to the moon and back. Marry me as soon as possible."

"Yes," Ellie whispered. "I'll marry you, Franklin, tomorrow, in a week, whenever you want."

* * *

Franklin and Luke strolled across the churchyard after Sunday services, both appeared deep in thought. Luke hoped no one suspected the importance of their verbal exchange.

"I heard again from that fellow named Jimmy George Barkley, the Miles City deputy who contacted us last fall." Franklin's eyes darted around the vicinity to ensure their conversation remained private. "Barkley will travel to Spirit Creek in person, accompanied by another two deputies, at the earliest possible date."

"When will that be?" growled Luke.

"Not certain. Hopefully, within the next few days. But we're waiting until these reinforcements arrive before we set our plans in motion." The sheriff stood arms crossed.

Luke glared at the lawman. "I'm not known for my patience. Just doing nothing seems downright wrong."

"Can't be helped."

"Ever heard of this Barkley fellow?" inquired Luke.

"No. But Sheriff Bob Sanders is a former Texas Ranger now employed in Miles City. I'd trust the man with my life. Bob vouched for Barkley. As soon as Barkley and the others arrive in town, you'll be the first to know." Franklin touched his Stetson, acknowledging Luke's wife as she approached holding their four-month-old baby boy in her arms, their three older children at her heels.

"Is anything wrong?" Maggie met her husband's eyes.

"Nope," answered Luke, abruptly. He assisted his family into their carriage and then leapt onto the bench seat. "At least, not yet," he added as an afterthought.

Franklin exchanged a knowing look with Luke, and then sauntered away.

CHAPTER 2

Next morning, after sharing a hearty breakfast with his wife, Luke Carlyle pecked Maggie on the cheek and promptly headed down to the horse barn on the Diamond C Ranch. The familiar scent of horses and clean hay greeted him, and he inhaled deeply. Several of his prized Morgan horses nickered and bobbed their heads in greeting as Luke's boots tapped out a steady rhythm marking his progress to the birthing stall in back.

"Good morning, Mike." The stall door's metal hinges squeaked as Luke entered and swung the door shut again. He patted the mare's neck and whispered into her ear.

"Won't be long now, sir." Mike Armstrong, in his capacity of assistant foreman and head horseman, oversaw all the horseflesh on the Diamond C Ranch. This morning he was smiling like a proud papa-to-be.

"Good girl, Twilight, you're doing fine," encouraged Luke. Twilight bobbed her head to acknowledge her owner's words. She circled the straw-lined stall and then lay down. A minute later, she struggled to her feet again.

"Twilight has birthed half a dozen colts." Mike removed the blanket from the mare's back. "She knows what she's doing."

"I'll leave her to it then." Luke patted the young horseman on the back. "Let me know…"

"How-do, gentlemen!"

Luke nearly jumped out of his favorite boots. He whipped around, cursing under his breath. Distracted by his concern over the mare's laboring, he hadn't heard the sheriff enter the barn. "Dammit, Franklin, are you of a mind to scare me to death?"

"Figured you heard us walk in," drawled Sheriff Smith, chuckling.

Luke considered them even now. Franklin hadn't mentioned that Luke nearly gave him heart failure when he'd hollered at him outside his house a few days ago. But Luke figured he'd surprised the man, judging by the way Franklin stared daggers at him.

Luke leaned over the top rail of the birthing pen and shook hands with the sheriff.

"Brought someone you'll be eager to meet, Luke."

A tall skinny fellow stepped out of the shadows, and Luke's heart dropped like a lead weight to his stomach. "Holy Heat in Hades," he muttered, thrown back in time. Was he imagining things?

"This gentleman is Deputy Jimmy George Barkley, one of the Miles City lawmen we've been waiting for."

Luke barely heard the introductions, distracted by the young fellow's likeness to one of his favorite old ranch hands. Several seconds passed before he found his voice. "Pleased to meet you, Deputy Barkley." Luke stuck out his hand. Even in his confused state, Luke noticed the deputy's expensive garb. The mayor of Miles City stuffed his deputies' pay envelopes a lot fuller than Spirit Creek's mayor, Randy Barker, did. Or else the fellow hailed from a wealthy family. That new-looking Smith and Wesson revolver of his probably cost more than Luke's had.

"Call me Jimmy George. Pleased to meet you, Mr. Carlyle." The deputy smiled and shook the rancher's hand.

"Call me Luke," he stated, unable to pry his eyes off the young man. Noticing Franklin's expression, Luke figured the sheriff realized what he was thinking.

* * *

"I'm getting the impression something's wrong, sir." Jimmy George doubted either of these gentlemen had crossed paths with him before he hired on as a deputy sheriff in Miles City. But the rancher's intense scrutiny unnerved him.

"Nothing's wrong. But you're the spitting image of one of the Diamond C cowhands," observed Luke.

"What's the fellow's name?" Jimmy George stood hands on hips.

"Third." Luke and Franklin answered in unison.

Jimmy George frowned. "Third? That some sort of nickname?"

"Don't rightly know his real name. He showed up on the Diamond C, accompanied by two other fellows, about twenty years ago. An extensive career in bar brawling had addled the poor man's brains so that he couldn't recollect what his name was or where he hailed from."

"And this happened about twenty years ago?" Jimmy George felt sweat beading on his brow, and he hoped the other men wouldn't notice.

"Give or take a year."

"My pa disappeared twenty-three years ago, just fell off the face of the earth." Jimmy George spat the words. "Left Ma with a ten-year-old boy and a roof over our heads, but little else."

"Where do you hail from?" asked Luke.

"Virginia City." Jimmy George removed his Stetson, wiped his brow, and scratched his head. "Pa hated mining, set his sights on ranching. He left Ma and me to go in search of suitable ranch land. Told Ma to keep sewing her quilts and taking in washing, and he'd send for us when he got settled."

"And she never heard from him again," guessed Sheriff Smith.

"Not a word. She died a couple years later of fever." Jimmy George dropped his head, studied his boots for a moment, pretended to wrangle his emotions under control.

A little white lie popped into his head, a stroke of genius to his way of thinking. And it might ward off any unwelcome questions about his upbringing. "A local preacher raised me as his own flesh and blood, but I swore someday I'd learn what became of Pa." He hoped the men couldn't see in his eyes that, truthfully, Jimmy George couldn't have cared less what had happened to the old man. And if they discovered he'd been raised by a whore in a Virginia City brothel in exchange for chopping wood and dumping slop pails and the like, they'd probably be shocked.

"What did your ma tell you about him?" inquired Luke.

"Good man deep down, but cursed with a powerful fondness for liquor and fist fighting." Jimmy George reckoned he should throw in a bit of the truth.

Luke smiled. "That's about right."

"Sounds like Third for sure," added Smith.

Luke turned his attention back to the birthing pen. "Mike, would you kindly go fetch Third for me? He's splitting wood out behind your pa's cabin."

"Will Twilight be all right without me for a minute?" Mike hesitated and then moved forward.

Jimmy George recognized exceptional horseflesh when he saw it, and he understood the young man's reluctance to leave the mare. He'd noticed an incredible stallion out in the corral on the way into the barn. For a second, Jimmy George imagined himself flying across the rangeland with that magnificent beast beneath him. What he wouldn't do to own that animal!

"I'll stay with her. Don't worry." Luke slapped the young man's shoulder.

Mike nodded and strode out of the barn.

"You figure this Third fellow could be my pa?" Jimmy George shifted on his feet. Would meeting his old man face to face after all these years prove a blessing or a curse? This was the last thing he expected when he'd arrived in town earlier this morning. Hells bells, he didn't need another complication in his life.

"One way to find out." Luke patted the mare's neck before she lay down again. "Good girl, Twilight. You're doing fine."

"I understand you're distracted with this mare and all, Luke. But when can we…get down to business?" The sheriff whispered the last part.

"I appreciate your careful choice of words, Franklin. Our new ranch hand is working out on the range, but sometimes barns can grow ears. No sense taking chances."

"We're not letting these scoundrels escape again," added Jimmy George. He expected to meet up with a couple other scoundrels of his acquaintance in a few weeks, and this rustling business had better be wrapped up before then.

"We'll have a palaver in my study once we settle this matter with Third," assured Luke.

An old cowhand lumbered into the barn. "What in tarnation is so dang important? This whippersnapper drags me away from my chores but won't tell me why."

Luke smiled. "There's someone here you should meet."

Third glanced toward Jimmy George and visibly paled. Gnarled fingers reached out and grabbed hold of a stall railing for support.

"Third, this is Jimmy George Barkley, a deputy out of Miles City," explained Luke.

Jimmy George waited for some sign of recognition from the old man. Not much fazed Jimmy George, but those were his blue eyes, his too-large ears, his same hair color if you looked past the gray streaks in the sideburns and trimmed beard. For his age, the man could still be considered handsome.

"Howdy young feller," croaked Third. His eyes never left Jimmy George as he added, "Howdy Sheriff."

"Like looking in a mirror, Third, about thirty years ago?" Luke stepped up beside the old fellow.

"There's a mighty powerful resemblance," whispered Third.

"My pa, Walter George Barkley, disappeared from Virginia City twenty-three years ago. Are you him?" Jimmy George stood feet spread. Damn, the resemblance rattled him; there wasn't a doubt in his mind. This broken down old cowhand was his pa all right.

"Don't rightly know. Can't remember a dang thing about my past." Third tugged on his beard.

Jimmy George visualized the jumbled thoughts ricocheting around in the man's head, the conflicting emotions evident on his pa's face. "Ma's name was Edythe Jane Barkley. My parents married in Boston then moved to Virginia City. Does any of that sound familiar?" Jimmy George stepped closer. He decided aging might suit him, if he kept his good looks like his pa had.

"Sorry, boy, I can't say that it rings any bells." Third's voice caught. "After a humdinger of a bar brawl one night, I woke up two days later without any recollection of most of my life."

Clearly, the man's situation left his nerves a little raw to this day, but his son remained unaffected. Jimmy George stuffed his hand into a waistcoat pocket, dug through an envelope of papers and extracted an old photograph. "These folks are my parents on their wedding day." He handed the faded and wrinkled picture to Third.

The old fellow's arthritic hands trembled as he studied the images. A smile slowly creased his leathered face, and he glanced up at Jimmy George. "That's me. I'd swear on a stack of bibles piled as high as this barn." Third passed the photograph to his boss. "Tell me what you see, Luke."

The rancher studied the photograph. "Handsome woman your ma," he observed aloud.

"Thank you, sir," mumbled Jimmy George. His mother was the only reason he even carried the dang picture in the first place. To his way of thinking, she was the only person in the entire world who'd ever loved him. Perhaps showing these men the picture would prove a mistake. Was he getting himself into a situation that would uncover more of his past than was wise?

"Nice looking fellow she married, all done up in his Sunday duds." Luke grinned and glanced at Third. "And take a gander at that belt buckle."

"Mighty fine buckle," added Third, turning toward Jimmy George. "Son, you're looking at your pappy as sure as I'm standing here." Third opened his coat and pointed to the tarnished horse's head belt buckle that was currently holding up his dungarees. The buckle appeared identical to the one in the picture. "One of the few things I do remember: won this dang thing off a feller during a card game. His pa had ordered it custom-made for his son's twenty-first birthday. Always felt a mite guilty taking it from him, but I won it fair enough."

"So, you're claiming it's one of a kind?" asked Jimmy George.

"Only one in the world, far as I know." Third beamed.

"Suppose we ought to start calling you Walter now," drawled Luke, smiling. "Appears that's your right and proper name."

"Walter Barkley," whispered Third. "I've gotta wear this name like a new pair of boots for a while, son, afore it'll take shape and start feeling right."

"I never thought I'd see the day…" Jimmy George shook his head. Would finding his pa add another complication to his life? His wife's recent death created enough turmoil. And soon there would be other matters requiring his attention.

"Me neither, son." Third extended a trembling hand.

Jimmy George stared at the man, his pa. The old fellow just stood there, waiting for his grown son to shake his hand. But Jimmy George recalled all the nights his ma had cried herself to sleep and all the years he had struggled as a child to survive.

"You sonofabitch." Jimmy George reacted before he could stop himself. His fisted hand laid a haymaker on the old man, sending him sprawling onto his backside in a straw-lined stall.

Sheriff Smith rushed over and hauled the old fellow to his feet. "Did he hurt you, Third?" asked the lawman.

"I'm fine," grumbled Third, straightening his old felt hat and rubbing his jaw. "Didn't see that coming."

"As if the man's brains aren't addled enough…" Luke fisted Jimmy George's shirt in his hands and slammed him against a stall, the inertia cracking the young man's head against a post.

Jimmy George almost took a swing at the wealthy rancher, but caught himself. A deputy sheriff wouldn't go around laying into every man who crossed his path. The sole exception being his useless, long-lost father.

"Now, Luke, I probably deserved that." Walter Barkley stared into his son's eyes. "I can understand you hating me for deserting your ma and you. But I swear, all these years I had no idea who I was. Didn't know if I was single or married. Didn't know where I'd come from. Didn't know a damn thing."

"Did you at least attempt to find us? Did you make inquiries?" asked Jimmy George, sneering.

"Nope. Didn't rightly know where to start. Showed up here as broke as a man could be. Just set to working and saving my money, hoping someday I'd wake up and know who I was." Third shrugged his shoulders. "It just never happened. I got accustomed to answering to Third, just another cowhand working and living on the Diamond C Ranch. If you hadn't shown up here today, I'd probably have gone to my grave not knowing any different."

Jimmy George shifted from one foot to the other. "Is he telling the truth?" he demanded, glaring at Luke.

"God's honest truth." Luke met Jimmy George's eyes. "My father, Matthew Carlyle, told me years later that he'd made inquiries about Third for several months after he showed up here. Sent telegrams all over Hell's half acre asking for any information about a missing fellow fitting your pa's description."

"And…"

"Never heard a word back. Matthew never mentioned it to Third; he didn't want to get his hopes up." Luke stood feet spaced apart, hands on hips.

Jimmy George returned to his pa's side, shaken by this unexpected development. Perhaps the old fool wouldn't involve himself in his son's life. Turning to face the sorry excuse for a man, he said, "Well, then, like it or not, I guess I've got my pa back."

Walter Barkley beamed. "Son, I hope I'm not too much of a disappointment."

"Fact is, I'd figured you for dead years ago." Jimmy George hoped that didn't sound too harsh. Would anyone suspect he hadn't rightly cared a whit if his pa was alive or dead?

"For what it's worth, I'm real pleased to meet you, son." Walter Barkley limped closer and extended his hand once more.

After a moment's hesitation, Jimmy George shook hands with his pa. Better show some semblance of reconciliation with the old fool. "I hope your jaw heals up real soon," he added for sincerity's sake.

"So do I, boy." Third looked his son in the eye. "Got questions for you, son."

"I'll answer them if I can." Jimmy George forced a smile.

"First question," said Third beaming. "Who in tarnation taught you how to throw a punch?"

Jimmy George couldn't admit it was a Virginia City whore named Dottie.

* * *

A half hour later, Jimmy George joined Franklin and Luke in the Diamond C's main house to finalize their plans to capture the gang of rustlers.

"Can I get you a drink, gentlemen?" offered Luke, pointing to the small table laden with several bottles of spirits in his study.

"Thank you kindly, Luke. But not when I'm here on official business," stated Franklin emphatically.

"Me, neither, thank you," added Jimmy George. What he wouldn't give for a shot or two of that fine whiskey sitting there, but he reminded himself he was a lawman here to discuss business.

"What's the plan?" began Luke.

Jimmy George opened his mouth to put forward a suggestion, but closed it again when a woman swept into the room through the open doorway. Her simple calico dress and auburn hair, worn braided on top of her head, took nothing away from her stunning good looks. A coffee pot, cups, sugar and cream huddled together on the metal tray she carried.

"Gentlemen, can I interest anyone in a hot cup of coffee?"

She stopped in her tracks when she saw him, but smiled a welcome that would have warmed any man's heart as she placed the tray on Luke's desk.

"Maggie, this fellow is Jimmy George Barkley, one of the Miles City deputies here to aid in the capture of the rustlers. Deputy Barkley, this is my wife, Maggie Carlyle." Luke made the introductions.

"Pleased to meet you, Deputy Barkley," said Maggie, extending her hand. "My, you surely do resemble…"

"Yes, we've just discovered that the deputy is Third's son," stated Luke. "Our mystery ranch hand is Walter George Barkley from Virginia City."

"He's been Third for so long, I don't know as I'll adjust to his new name," exclaimed Maggie.

Damn, she was one fine-looking female. Jimmy George shook her hand and added, "I don't know as I'll adjust to having a pa again."

"And how are you, Sheriff?" asked Maggie, turning her attention to Franklin Smith.

"Better every day. Ellie and I have moved up our wedding date, and I couldn't be happier," said Franklin beaming.

Jimmy George almost scoffed aloud but caught himself. Only a dang fool looked forward to tying himself to one woman for the rest of his days. He'd learned that lesson the hard way.

"My heavens, this is sudden. Whatever prompted such a decision?" asked Maggie.

"We're just so darn in love, we couldn't wait until June. Once all this rustling business is finished up, we'll get hitched as soon as possible." Franklin rubbed his hands on his denims.

"Well, we look forward to attending your nuptials." Maggie glanced toward her husband who nodded his head in agreement. "Luke, if you wouldn't mind pouring the coffee, I'll leave you gentlemen to your planning. By the way, while executing this capture, please include a strategy to ensure everyone remains safe, especially my husband." Maggie dipped her head and strolled toward the door.

Luke followed.

"Thank you for your thoughtfulness, Mrs. Carlyle." Deputy Barkley admired her from behind. Damn shame she was a married woman. Of course, that had never gotten in his way of thinking before. But he had no inclination to partake in a bedroom romp with this rancher's wife, knowing he'd be as good as dead if he did.

Luke brushed his wife's cheek with a kiss and closed the door behind her.

* * *

Next afternoon, Luke and Maggie traveled into Miles City with

Ned, Mike and several ranch hands riding ahead of the buggy. Luke and his Diamond C crew were eager to meet with the lawmen and other ranchers and their hands to finalize plans for the capture of the rustlers. Bobby and a few other ranch hands who couldn't be included to prevent raising suspicions worked on the range.

After the children were dismissed from classes, Maggie strode up the two wooden steps outside the Spirit Creek schoolhouse. This building was as familiar to her as her own parlor; Maggie had arrived in town over eight years ago, leaving behind her privileged life in Philadelphia to teach children out West. A decision she'd never regretted. She rapped soundly on the door and stepped inside.

"Maggie, what a lovely surprise!" Ellie Thomas stepped out from behind the teacher's desk and greeted her visitor with a warm hug. The women wandered between the two rows of desks in the classroom and entered the teacher's private quarters in back. The sparsely-furnished, ten-foot-square room held a bed, table and two chairs, small woodstove, and two small cabinets. "Come in, sit down, and we'll have tea."

"Don't go to any bother, Ellie." Maggie removed her shawl and bonnet and tossed them onto the small quilt-covered bed. She cautiously lowered herself onto one of the rickety wooden chairs. "The school committee hasn't replaced this furniture, I see."

"Isn't it a wonder? Every morning while drinking my coffee, I expect to find myself suddenly flat on my bottom on the floor." Ellie laughed nervously. "I'm looking forward to becoming Franklin's wife for the new furniture alone."

"The two of you are very well-suited," observed Maggie, taking note of Ellie's shaky hands, as she filled the tea kettle and placed it back on the tiny woodstove. The teacups rattled as Ellie set them on the small wooden table.

"Another schoolteacher marrying the sheriff..." Ellie appeared lost in thought, and perhaps didn't realize she'd spoken aloud.

"The same thought crossed my mind a time or two," admitted Maggie. While teaching in Spirit Creek, she'd fallen in love and married her first husband, the local sheriff, who'd been killed while stopping an attempted bank robbery. "Ellie, something is wrong."

Finally, the young school teacher met her predecessor's eyes.

Maggie wagged her finger at the young woman, as soon as she attempted to argue. "Franklin informed us you've moved up your wedding date, citing how much you were in love and all that nonsense. But I'm not buying it."

"You don't believe we're in love?" Ellie paled.

"Oh, I *know* you're in love. But your nervousness just reinforces my suspicions...." Maggie's insinuation hung in the air.

"You're right. I'm going to have a baby. I'm so ashamed, but at the same time, I'm so happy." Ellie's eyes misted.

"Oh, my, I'd hoped I was wrong." Maggie slumped back in her chair.

"The minute I told Franklin, he insisted we move up the wedding date." Ellie sniffled. "Perhaps I should have left town, not shame his name this way."

"Shame *his* name? Ellie, you didn't get in the family way all by your lonesome. Your Mr. Smith shares equal responsibility." Maggie patted the distraught woman's hand.

"A schoolteacher is expected to provide an example, set a high standard in the community. Instead, everyone will consider me no better than some floozy working on her back in Darby's saloon." Ellie blew her nose in her handkerchief. "At least those ladies know something about preventing a baby from starting."

Maggie almost mentioned her new friend Belle's past predicament, but thought better of it. The young woman was thrown out of Darby's establishment the minute she started showing, but Luke's ranch hand, Third, married the soiled dove. Living close by on Luke's ranch, Maggie and Belle had become the best of friends despite their vastly different backgrounds.

"Ellie, what's the worst that can happen? The School Committee can't fire you, you've already given notice. You'll be married long before you're showing, and the child will be born in wedlock," reasoned Maggie.

Ellie acknowledged each statement with a nod while she poured boiling water into the teapot and set it on the table to allow their tea to brew.

"As I see it," continued Maggie, grinning, "the worst that can happen…the baby looks like his father and not you."

Ellie's jaw dropped and then she spluttered, "Maggie Carlyle...I…I have half a mind to tell Franklin what you said."

"Go right ahead. He'll probably agree with me." Maggie laughed and poured the tea. "This child was conceived in love, and he or she couldn't have chosen a better set of parents."

"But the townspeople will think so poorly of me." Ellie dabbed her eyes with her handkerchief.

"Let the old biddies count on their fingers." Maggie sipped her tea. "I was with child when I married Luke. The old gals whispered behind their hands, speculating when my baby would arrive. Willie was conceived six weeks or so before William died, but Luke loves that child as his own."

"They'll be whispering about me soon enough."

"Let them. Ellie, nobody is perfect. We all make mistakes, but life goes on. Before long someone new will catch their attention, and you'll be all but forgotten. Now, I must drop in on Elizabeth or she'll disown me." Maggie finished her tea, hugged the bride-to-be, and then grabbed her shawl. In truth, she must move up her plans for the secret quilting bee for Ellie's surprise bridal gift. "Take care of yourself. And best of luck with the little one you're carrying. Regardless of what you think, this child is not a mistake."

"Thank you, Maggie. I feel better already." Ellie hugged her friend warmly.

"No one will hear about this from me. You tell folks when you're ready."

The two women locked arms and walked through the classroom and out the schoolhouse door. Stepping into the late morning sunshine, Maggie adjusted her bonnet to shield her eyes and prevent a new crop of freckles.

"Bye, Maggie, and thank you for being such a good friend." Ellie waved as Maggie closed the gate.

Ellie's future couldn't look brighter, thought Maggie.

* * *

"Thank you, Reverend. We appreciate this." Luke removed his Stetson and shook hands with Reverend Gerald, as he strode into the church.

Last autumn, the meetings to discuss the capture of the rustlers were held either in Luke's study, at the jailhouse, or around Sheriff Smith's kitchen table. This time, the reverend had readily agreed to Luke's request that the lawmen and cattlemen meet at the church. If that wouldn't convince the rustlers the authorities weren't on their trail, nothing would.

Soon, several local ranchers and a motley collection of ranch hands wandered into the church, removed their hats, and settled into a seat. The pews were almost filled.

Sheriff Smith and the Miles City lawmen stood upfront. Deputy Ernest Jones dashed inside, dragged his Stetson off, and strode up the center aisle. Ernest was Florence and Earl's fifth oldest child, and Ernest had trained as a deputy under Franklin. The young lawman dreamed of becoming a Pinkerton Detective one day.

"Welcome, everyone!" Luke raised his voice, to be heard above the noise of exchanged greetings, laughter and conversations. Everyone silenced and he continued, "Firstly, gentlemen, in case we're questioned, let's claim the purpose of this meeting was to discuss Ronald Waverly's recent suggestion, in his capacity of School Committee Chairman."

The idea was met with a few blank expressions.

"For you fellows who live in more outlying areas and may not have heard, Ronald proposed a new, larger schoolhouse be built to accommodate the needs of the constantly growing community," explained Luke.

"So I reckon that part of yer story will be true if'n his idea is under consideration by town council," reasoned Ned.

"It's on the agenda for their next meeting," stated Robert Morgan.

"So that will be our cover story," reiterated Luke.

A rumble of agreement to the idea rolled throughout the room.

Luke glanced sideways. "Then I'll turn this meeting over to Sheriff Smith."

"Thank you, Luke." Sheriff Smith gazed around the room. "Let's get down to it."

Two hours later, the lawmen and ranchers had finalized what was in their minds a foolproof plan. A large sheet of newsprint courtesy of Arthur MacDonald from the newspaper office was tacked onto two flat boards, displaying their strategy. Unless a fellow had attended the meeting, even a college degree wouldn't help him decipher the collection of circles, lines and squiggles. But every man had been drilled on his part in their plans and had sworn he was ready.

"I believe we've covered everything," concluded Sheriff Smith, standing hands on hips at the front of the church.

The ranchers' and ranch hands' heads were nodding, and the Miles City deputies and Ernest Jones muttered their agreement as well.

Deputy Barkley added, "I can't think of any scenarios we haven't considered."

"Me neither," added Ernest.

"Then there's only one more step to take. Gentlemen, everyone stand please and raise your right hand," instructed Sheriff Smith. To keep everything all well and legal, he deputized every man present.

"Keep your eyes open to any clue that the rustlers are up to no good. As soon as you suspect something, put into action our plans to alert everyone," said Luke. "Let's hope we can carry this off without incident." Just prior to adjournment, Reverend Gerald stood and every man bowed his head. The clergyman offered a prayer that the capture would go as planned, and then the men headed off to collect horses, wives, children, and buggies. Soon, a steady stream of ranch folk headed out of town in all directions, destined for home.

CHAPTER 3

Thursday, April 10, 1890

The Diamond C ranch hands turned in at nine o'clock as usual and pretended to fall asleep in case tonight was the night. The men lay in their beds, trying to control their breathing while their hearts raced in anticipation. Bedsprings creaked as men shifted position and settled again. The sound of an owl's hoot drifted in through the bunkhouse's open window. A couple of the men actually dozed off and snored softly. The other men stilled and hoped Bobby wouldn't realize they weren't asleep.

Sure enough, just after eleven o'clock Bobby snuck out of bed, pulled on his clothes, saddled up, and rode away from the ranch.

The deputized ranch hands leapt out of their own beds, rousing their sleeping bunkmates, and moved into action. Mike saddled his gelding and raced toward town to alert the lawmen and set their plan in motion while Scotty headed for the Circle M to warn the Maxwell clan.

Luke's ranch foreman slipped into the kitchen of the main house. Spotting Luke seated at the kitchen table, he whispered, "Bobby's gone. That varmint rode outta here ten minutes ago."

"Let's go, Ned." Luke plucked his Stetson off the peg at the back door and strapped his pistol to his hip just in case. Having tucked Maggie and the children into bed hours ago, he quietly left the house, knowing if he woke her she'd lie awake waiting for his safe return.

"Hopefully, the other ranchers remembered their late night bed checks as instructed. I'd bet a year's wages other ranch hands are missing," mumbled Third, helping the men saddle their horses and load their guns.

"Aren't ya coming, Third?" asked Ned.

"Hell, no. I'm too old for this business. Be more hindrance than help," he proclaimed. "You fellers be careful now."

Ned, Luke and the ranch hands who'd been deputized by the

sheriff quickly saddled their horses. A few minutes later, they thundered across the valley leading away from the ranch to meet up with their fellow ranchers, Franklin Smith and the Miles City lawmen at the appointed location.

Luke's stallion raced across the open range. Astride Thunder, Luke felt ten feet tall. But he wasn't foolish enough to believe himself invincible. Tonight's business was dangerous, and he'd keep his wits about him. Luke silently prayed every man involved would come out of this unscathed, and every rustler would find himself behind bars in Miles City awaiting an immediate date with a judge at the court house.

An owl hooted from a nearby cottonwood tree, and Luke jumped at the sudden noise. Grinning in the dark, he silently cursed the creature. Crickets serenaded the men as they rode past the creek that meandered throughout the Diamond C. The night magnified every sound and even Thunder appeared uncharacteristically skittish as if the horse sensed the importance and danger of their mission.

"Mother Nature appears to be on our side tonight." Luke stared up at the sky where the full moon was mostly shrouded by dark clouds helping them avoid detection.

"Gonna need all the hep we can git, Sonny Boy," answered Ned, riding alongside him.

Saddle leather creaked under Luke's weight, and his heart was beating so loudly he felt certain Ned could hear it in the still night. "We have to make this work," pledged Luke.

"Don't fret, Sonny Boy. We'll git 'em this time," whispered Ned.

Every action had been planned to the last detail, and everyone was prepared and eager to end the rustling spree. By one-thirty in the morning, every lawman and deputized rancher and ranch hand was accounted for and standing in his designated place, nervously awaiting Sheriff Smith's signal to set the plan in motion.

Luke crouched low over the saddle and patted Thunder's neck. All he could do now was hurry up and wait.

As he listened to his own breathing, his thoughts turned to Maggie. Although their union began as a marriage of convenience, they'd fallen deeply in love, and both of them were committed to a lifetime together. He prayed his good friend, Franklin, would be equally happy when he married Ellie. Maggie confided the reason for the change in wedding date, and Luke believed Franklin would make an excellent father.

Luke smiled, recalling the bleary-eyed feedings at 2 a.m., endless messy diapers, and incessant wailing if cutting a new tooth. He'd endured it all with Catherine when his daughters were infants. And he'd been experiencing everything again with Maggie since the new baby arrived last December.

"Franklin, old buddy, you have no idea what you're in for," he whispered aloud.

When the signal came, Luke and everyone else leapt into action.

The lawmen shouted orders and startled the rustlers with the sudden appearance of two dozen men charging toward them on horseback. In a second, every rustler lit out in a different direction while the stolen cattle scattered, bawling and stampeding in a cloud of dust.

"Can hardly see a damn thing!" shouted someone. Luke didn't recognize the voice and he couldn't determine if the complaint came from one of the lawmen or a rustler.

"Over here. Two of them slipped into a crevice between these rocks," warned another man.

In the midst of the melee a barrage of shots were fired.

"Keep your heads down. The buggers are shooting at us," advised someone.

"I didn't sign up for no shooting," complained another.

"Then keep your damn head down."

"I've got one." The words were accompanied by a muffled thump. Someone either fell off his horse or was pulled out of his saddle.

"Get some handcuffs on him."

"I need a hand over here. This bugger's as big as a buffalo and smells worse than one."

"Where are you? I'm on the way."

"Ouch, you're standing on my arm. Help me handcuff this bastard."

"I'm trying, dammit. Hold him still."

When the dust settled, six rustlers were in handcuffs, including Frenchy and Bobby. Most of the stolen cattle were discovered hidden nearby in a secluded area. The stolen animals that the rustlers had stampeded in an effort to escape would be rounded up tomorrow come daylight.

The ranchers quickly accounted for every one of their hired hands, and it appeared no one caught any of the bullets that buzzed past them like bees on a hot summer day. A couple of hands volunteered to stay with the animals overnight. The ranchers agreed to meet up in the morning and sort the animals by brands and then herd their own cattle home.

Jimmy George and the two other deputies he'd brought from Miles City hauled away the last of the rustlers who were cussing and swearing that there'd been a terrible mistake. In spite of the fact they'd been caught red-handed, every one of them claimed he was innocent.

Finally, someone inquired about Sheriff Smith.

"Reckoned he was with Luke," said Ned.

"He rode right beside me." Luke swung around, half expecting the local lawman to materialize. "Where'd he go?"

"Did he head to town with the other lawmen?" inquired Robert Morgan, Luke's closest neighbor and lifelong friend.

"Wasn't with them," confirmed Luke. "I said a thank you and goodbye to each of those Miles City fellows, one at a time. They were the only lawmen I talked to."

"Then where'd the sheriff git to?" asked Ned.

"He's out here somewhere," added Wilber Simpson, another neighboring rancher.

"Something's wrong, boys." Ned lumbered over to his horse.

Luke mounted Thunder. "Search the area. Franklin's out here somewhere, and he's probably wounded. Hurry up, time's a wasting."

Earlier this evening Luke had welcomed the dark clouds that covered the full moon. Now, he cursed the black night, barely able to see three feet in front of himself. Efforts to call Franklin's name met with silence.

"He's out here, gentlemen. Keep looking," insisted Luke, hearing the worry in his own voice. They had to find the lawman, knowing he was injured.

Fifteen minutes later they located Sheriff Smith's horse. The lawman's body lay crumpled on the ground a dozen feet away. Judging by the blood stain on Franklin's white shirt, the bullet struck the sheriff in the heart, killing him instantly. No pain. He probably never knew what hit him. Luke shivered with the realization that he'd been riding alongside Franklin. If the bullet had flown by a few feet closer, Luke could have been the man lying there dead. Thank goodness, Fate hadn't made Maggie a widow again. Luke was alive and thankful for it.

But the fact his good friend's death came quickly would be little comfort to the man's fiancée.

* * *

The clouds had moved on, and Luke stood in the moonlight atop the schoolhouse steps, collecting his thoughts. As owner of the Diamond C Ranch, he'd been required to inform the next of kin of the death of a loved one on a few occasions, but it never got any easier. Especially when the deceased was someone he considered a close friend.

How was Ellie going to survive this?

Franklin, Ellie, Luke and Maggie had celebrated many occasions together: birthdays, holidays, community events. Ellie frequently babysat his children who called her Aunt Ellie. Franklin and Ellie had looked forward to marriage and parenthood, but a stray bullet had ended all their dreams in a second.

When he'd almost reached town, he'd decided he should have stopped at the ranch and brought Maggie with him. Ellie would need her friend when she heard about Franklin's passing. He woke Elizabeth Waverly instead, and she assured him she'd meet him here shortly.

After a minute, Luke took a deep breath and knocked loudly to wake the inhabitant. He couldn't wait for Elizabeth or put this off any longer.

Ellie Thomas cracked the door, wearing a plain cotton wrapper over her nightdress. Recognizing Luke, she flung the door wide open.

"Luke! Where's Franklin?" she asked, attempting to peek around Luke. "Did you capture those terrible men?"

Luke stood alone, cowboy hat in hand. He forced himself to meet Ellie's eyes, knowing his silence would tell her something had happened.

"Oh God, no," she whispered, wavering on slipper-clad feet. "Is Franklin hurt?"

"I'm sorry, Ellie. It's bad news." Luke's words hung in the air. Would Ellie realize that the expression could only mean one thing? There was no easy way to deliver such a message. Would it have been kinder to just say right off that Franklin was dead?

"No," she whimpered like a small animal in distress.

Luke cringed, unprepared for her heart-wrenching reaction. He could swear he heard her heart break. And he caught her in his arms when she fainted.

He carried Ellie through the classroom into her living quarters and gently laid her on the small metal bed. The springs barely creaked beneath her slight weight. He sat on a rickety chair nearby, and waited. A minute later her eyes fluttered and opened. She blinked and then met his eyes.

Better just get it said. "There was gunfire…from the rustlers. We caught them in the act. But…"

Ellie's eyes glazed over. She remained silent and appeared totally stunned.

"Franklin died quickly; he didn't suffer. I'm sorry, Ellie." Luke twisted his hat in his hands. There was no response from the poor woman. Had anything he'd said registered with her?

Ellie rolled her head side to side like a person suffering delirium from a high fever. Or enduring unimaginable pain. She'd loved Franklin, and the sheriff had admitted to Luke that he'd loved Ellie, almost since the day they'd met. No two people seemed better suited. The two of them finished each other's sentences like married folk would.

"Elizabeth Waverly's on her way over to collect you and keep you at her place for a couple days," said Luke, rising to his feet, recalling how distraught he'd felt after his first wife passed. "You shouldn't be alone."

Just then, a knock at the door startled him, and Elizabeth poked her head inside Ellie's small room. "How's she doing?" she whispered, tossing her shawl onto a chair. The bedsprings protested when she sat on the edge of the bed.

"Fainted straight away when I told her, but she came to within a minute. Sat up, stared into space for a spell, and then she flopped back on the pillow. Been rolling her head back and forth for a while. Dealing with the pain, I suppose." Luke worried the cowboy hat in his hand, feeling useless, but Elizabeth would handle things.

"You run along home now, Luke. I'll take care of the poor thing." Elizabeth patted the schoolteacher's shoulder. "Those two young people never got the opportunity to start their lives together. Absolute shame it is."

Ellie stilled her head and tear-filled eyes met Elizabeth's. "Yes, we did. What will I do now?" The distraught young woman sobbed uncontrollably.

"Everything will be all right in time, dear. You'll get through this," cooed Elizabeth. "But soothing words aren't going to help right now are they, girl?"

* * *

Ellie remembered speaking with Doc Benjamin last night shortly after arriving at Elizabeth's home in back of the store. She recalled Elizabeth speaking with Reverend Gerald. And in preparation for the burial, Ronald told Ellie he would arrange for the coffin. Doc must have given her laudanum since most of the remainder of the night and this morning remained a blur.

Ellie recalled donning a black dress and a veiled, black hat, borrowed from someone. Or had Elizabeth procured them at her general store? If questioned with a gun to her head, she couldn't have explained how she came to be standing at Franklin's gravesite. Her surroundings continually faded in and out; she felt in a fog. Her eyes filled with tears. Reverend Gerald should be officiating at their wedding, not her betrothed's funeral. Elizabeth stood beside her, one arm wrapped around Ellie's shoulders. How would she have managed without Elizabeth and Ronald?

Reverend Gerald began the burial service, but the majority of his words never infiltrated Ellie's clouded brain. She recalled other mourners, fellow citizens of Spirit Creek, speaking fondly of her fiancé. For the most part, Ellie stood like a statue, her mind floating in a cloud of confusion intermingled with moments of unbearable pain.

"Let's get you home, Ellie." Elizabeth nudged her forward.

"No," stated Ellie emphatically. "I require a few moments alone with Franklin, please."

Elizabeth met her eyes and nodded in agreement. "You should say your goodbyes in private, dear."

The kind-hearted matron wandered away leaving Ellie standing there, and she had never felt so alone in her life. Not even when she was abandoned outside an orphanage as a child had she felt this lonely. This disconsolate. And she was carrying a child who would never know its father. Ellie collapsed in a puddle on the ground, weeping inconsolably. In the distance, she heard footsteps rush toward her.

"Let her be," commanded Elizabeth.

The footsteps retreated.

Ellie couldn't say how long she'd sat on the ground, crying. The cloud that had enveloped her lifted a while ago, and she could think clearly again. She should have discovered herself floating in a pond from all the tears she'd shed. But aside from the soggy spots on the front of her dress and the soaked handkerchief in her hand, her surroundings remained unchanged.

Franklin wouldn't approve of such a display. He'd insist she soldier on and face the future with strength. But what the future held for her was anyone's guess. Ellie heaved a sigh. She slowly clambered to her feet, steadied herself, and took a few steps back. At Elizabeth's nod, several men began shoveling dirt into her beloved's grave.

Elizabeth gently grasped her elbow and led her toward the gate. "Let me take you home, Ellie."

"Home," she whispered. Spirit Creek was the only true home she'd ever known. One could hardly consider an orphanage a home, even if you'd grown up living there for twelve years.

Where would home be now?

Ellie refused to tarnish Franklin's good name. She should flee from Spirit Creek and relocate somewhere far away. The townsfolk must never learn her secret: Franklin Smith and Ellie Thomas conceived a baby out of wedlock.

CHAPTER 4

Monday, April 21, 1890

Ellie had avoided the reading of Franklin's will and settling of his affairs for days now. But Mr. Rutherford approached her after Sunday services yesterday and insisted the matter required her immediate attention. He emphasized that every effort would be made to ensure the whole business was handled as painlessly as possible, but she doubted that would happen. Ellie had cried an ocean of tears since Franklin's passing, and still her eyes welled at the mere thought of him.

Sunshine and warm breezes accompanied her on the walk to the law office. She stood outside, her hand resting on the shiny brass door latch. She wore the same black dress, black stockings and boots, and veiled black hat Elizabeth had provided for the burial. Grief weighed her down like boulders strapped to her shoulders.

"You can do this," she encouraged herself aloud.

Against her better judgment, she opened the door and stepped across the threshold. She paused for a moment while her eyes adjusted to the dim interior, and then she spotted the familiar young woman behind the wooden desk a ways beyond the entryway.

"Good morning, Miss Thomas." Janie Jones rose from her chair behind the secretary's desk and hurried over to Ellie's side. "Please accept my condolences on your loss. Sheriff Smith was a fine gentleman, and everyone appreciated his tireless work as sheriff. The entire town is in shock."

"Thank you, Janie." Ellie smiled at Florence Jones' fourth oldest child. She was pleased the girl had found employment; she'd been one of her favorite students. There were so few jobs for a decent woman in the small town, but Spirit Creek was growing rapidly with a new business opening almost every month.

The law office operated out of an old house and Ellie gazed about the entryway. Two metal cabinets stood to the left of Janie's desk. Three pegs attached to the wall by the front door awaited customers' outer clothing and hats. Two ladder-back chairs stood in front of a tall window covered in lacy, cream-colored curtains. Ellie assumed Mr. Rutherford utilized the second floor for his living quarters.

"Mr. Rutherford is expecting you." Janie strode across the room and slid open a set of wooden pocket doors revealing a substantial office space within the former parlor.

Ellie took a deep breath and followed Janie inside.

Sunshine streamed through three side-by-side windows and dust motes danced in the air. Occupying the majority of the room, a huge mahogany desk was situated in front of the windows, sitting atop a colorful, floral-patterned Axminster rug. The desk top was buried beneath mounds of books and papers. A small table to the right displayed an assortment of teacups, a sugar bowl and cream jug. Several crystal glasses and tall bottles of spirits occupied a larger table. Watercolor landscapes decorated one wall, and the lawyer's silk-banded bowler hung on the top peg of the mahogany coat tree standing by the door.

Mr. Rutherford rose from a leather upholstered chair and rounded his desk, almost tripping over his feet in his haste. "Good morning, Miss Thomas. Please accept my sincere condolences once again." He shook her hand and then motioned her toward the small wooden chair facing his desk. "May I offer you a cup of coffee or tea?"

Ellie released her breath, unaware she'd been holding it. "Thank you, but no," she answered, graciously.

She settled herself in the uncomfortable chair and adjusted her skirts. Her heart fluttered in her chest and her palms sweated profusely. Mr. Rutherford disrupted her capacity for rational thought every time she was anywhere near him. Why did she feel so flustered in this man's presence? She met his intoxicating eyes and he smiled at her. You're in mourning, she reminded herself. *Please, God, give me the strength to behave in a respectable manner.*

* * *

Robert Rutherford escaped behind his desk, settled back in the chair, and observed his newest client. Miss Ellie Thomas was undoubtedly the most beautiful woman he'd ever met. Red-rimmed eyes confirmed she was mourning her late fiancé, and her sad expression tugged at his heartstrings. If he could transfer her pain to himself, he gladly would. He'd loved Ellie since the day they were introduced almost a year ago, despite the fact she'd been involved with the sheriff romantically.

Now, she was free.

He hated that his heart soared at the possibility of a future some day with this remarkable woman, and his body reacted in the most inappropriate way whenever he thought of her as his wife. But she was grieving, and at present he must remain the consummate professional.

Ellie clasped her hands in her lap. "Why would you leave Boston to practice law in a small frontier town like Spirit Creek?"

Robert shifted in his chair, unnerved by her unexpected inquiry. Would she think less of him if he told her about his past? He must take the risk, in case she learned of it from another source. "There was an unfortunate incident in Boston. None of my doing, of course."

"Certainly," muttered Ellie, doubt evident in her voice. She avoided his eyes.

"Honestly, Miss Thomas. The situation had nothing to do with me." Robert leaned forward, rested his arms on his desk.

Why was it so important that she believed him? Because her opinion of him mattered, and he desperately hoped she'd fall in love with him in the future. "My twin brother is a very dangerous man constantly in trouble with the law, and he'd been involved in an armed bank robbery. Hoping to avoid prison, he claimed I'd done the dastardly deed."

Ellie shifted forward in the chair. "I hope you set the bounder straight."

"Eventually, I cleared my name, but by then my reputation had suffered irreparable damage. My employer believed in my innocence all along, but he insisted I strike out on my own to some distant place, preventing my brother's further interference in my life. Richard Rutherford resides in a Boston prison, and I pray he remains there." Robert felt his face redden. "That sounded rather harsh, but my disreputable brother caused me years of heartache."

"I understand your uncharitable feelings toward him. I hope you'll be very happy in Spirit Creek. Heaven knows, everyone complains about traveling all the way to Miles City whenever in need of a lawyer's services." Ellie blushed. "Not that someone like myself has ever required such a thing."

"Well, today you do." Robert smiled, grabbed his reading glasses off the desk and stuck them on his face. He reached for the sheaf of papers and attempted to still his shaking hands. "Shall we begin?"

* * *

Ellie leaned back in her chair, comfortable in Mr. Rutherford's presence for the first time since she'd known him. The warm-hearted fellow appeared genuinely concerned with her well-being, and his easy manner, infectious smile, and soft voice while sharing his history in Boston encouraged her to relax. She almost felt immune to those penetrating eyes.

She hadn't a clue as to what a will might reveal. Her thoughts flew to her friend Maggie and all the heartache she'd endured when her husband's sudden death revealed his secret gambling loans at the bank, resulting in the foreclosure on her home. But Franklin wasn't her husband, and thus, her circumstances were quite different from Maggie's. Surely a fiancée couldn't be held liable for debts. Taking a deep breath, she braced herself for anything unpleasant.

The lawyer perched his glasses on the end of his nose and began, "Being of sound mind…"

"What exactly does that mean?" inquired Ellie.

"It means Mr. Smith knew what he was doing."

"Of course, Franklin knew what he was doing! He wasn't a feeble-minded old man," blurted Ellie, defending the man she'd loved.

Mr. Rutherford removed his glasses. "Perhaps I'll summarize the contents of the late Mr. Smith's Will, and we'll ignore the legal jargon."

"That would probably be best. I doubt I'd understand a word of it anyway." Ellie hoped the lawyer would just say his piece and allow her to leave before she embarrassed herself with a tearful display.

"Firstly, Mr. Smith requested that in the event of his untimely death, Miss Ellie Thomas or Mrs. Ellie Smith, his wife—he believed you'd be married before his passing, but he included both names as a precaution—and any children resulting from your union be permitted to continue tenancy in the house he currently rented from Mr. Carlyle until it was your decision to leave." Robert glanced up from the document. "Mr. Carlyle has agreed to this stipulation."

"That won't be necessary. I couldn't afford the first month's rent." Ellie laughed nervously. She didn't add that she planned on being long gone before her secret revealed itself.

"Secondly, there's a substantial sum of money in Mr. Smith's estate. His parents were well-to-do citizens of San Francisco and the owners of several businesses when they passed away suddenly two years ago in a tragic carriage accident. Naturally, they left their entire estate to their only son, Franklin. Mr. Smith sold the businesses and secreted his true worth from everyone but his legal counsel, in hopes of being accepted in the community simply as one their own."

"Precisely how much money is *a substantial sum*?" inquired Ellie. If she inherited several hundred dollars, she could leave Spirit Creek and start anew, and her worries would be over. She would claim widowhood, which was close enough to the truth, and no one would learn her shameful secret. Once the baby was born and the money ran out, she would find a job. Simple enough plan, except she hated the thought of leaving Spirit Creek. She couldn't see herself living anywhere else.

Mr. Rutherford passed a sheet of paper across the desk. "These sums represent the current balances in Franklin Smith's San Francisco and Spirit Creek bank accounts."

Ellie plucked the paper off the desk and glanced at the bottom line. She felt herself pale, and the room swam before her eyes. The paper slipped from her fingers and fluttered to the floor. Ellie's backbone turn to jelly and she slid unceremoniously off the chair onto the floor just before everything went black.

Moments later, Ellie heard a murmur of voices in the distance.

"Wake up, Miss Thomas! Do we have smelling salts, Miss Jones?"

"I believe we do, sir."

From the far reaches of her mind, Ellie heard Janie's footsteps race out of the room and return a moment later. And then Ellie's nostrils were assailed. She moaned and twisted her head to avoid the insult to her senses.

"She's coming around." The secretary sighed, relief evident in her voice. "Mr. Rutherford, whatever happened?"

"Miss Thomas received a bit of a shock." Robert lifted Ellie into his arms and crushed her against his chest for an inappropriate length of time. Finally, he set her down on the chair.

Ellie's head swam and she wavered in her seat. Robert gently bent her body forward to prevent another fainting episode.

Janie passed Ellie a handkerchief, bending over and looking upward. "Are you feeling well enough to sit up, Miss Thomas?" she inquired, nearly standing on her head in order to meet the other woman's eyes.

If Ellie hadn't felt so mortified at having fainted, she may have laughed at the picture Janie made. "Yes, I believe so," she answered, slowly straightening herself. "I'll be fine in a minute."

"Thank goodness. You gave poor Mr. Rutherford such a fright. I've never heard a gentleman utter such a sound in my life." Janie righted herself, patted her chest. "I thought you'd died on the spot."

"I apologize for the disturbance."

"No need for apologies, Miss Thomas. Totally my fault. I should have prepared you for the full extent of your inheritance." Robert patted his brow before returning his handkerchief to his pocket. "Miss Jones, thank you for responding so quickly. You may return to your work."

"Yes, thank you, Janie," added Ellie, clasping the other woman's hand for a moment.

"You're both welcome." Janie left the room, sliding the pocket doors closed behind her.

Robert smiled at her from across the desk. "Now, let me explain the financial plan I've prepared for you. You'll want for nothing the remainder of your years. Franklin insisted I oversee your finances, protect your security, and ensure your happiness."

Ellie pinched her hand to ensure she wasn't dreaming, flinching with the slight pain. She'd gone from an almost penniless schoolteacher to an enormously wealthy woman. "Whatever will I do with so much money? I'd return every penny in a heartbeat in exchange for more time with Franklin."

The lawyer's pained expression surprised Ellie. Had he believed she would value Franklin's money ahead of the man himself? No, it must be something else, but for the life of her she couldn't imagine what it might be.

Ellie rose to leave. "My mind cannot process any further talk of dollars and cents today."

"I understand completely. Perhaps in a few days you'll feel up to another meeting." Mr. Rutherford escorted her to the front door of his office.

"Thank you for understanding." Ellie smiled, choosing not to reveal her plans to withdraw a sum of the money from Franklin's local bank account and leave Spirit Creek at the earliest opportunity.

"Please keep in touch, Miss Thomas."

Ellie slipped out the door without another word. She might be planning to deceive the man and leave town, but she wouldn't outright lie to him, assure him she would return any time soon.

She stood on the boardwalk outside the law office. A team of horses pulling a wagon rumbled down the street, and the sound of children's laughter floated on the air, which meant morning recess time at the school.

Angela Jones had completed her studies at the Spirit Creek School last June, and she dreamed of training as a teacher. With Ronald Waverly's blessing, Angela stepped in as teacher while Ellie overcame her initial grief. Angela would be in her glory stepping in as teacher if only for a short while. Perhaps even longer once Ellie left town, if a permanent replacement couldn't be hired immediately.

Angela and Agnes' parents, mother and father of twelve, could never afford higher education for any of their scholarly children, but Luke Carlyle had found a way around it, hiring the Jones girls and providing an education in lieu of financial payment.

Agnes Jones worked for Luke last year while Maggie was expecting and earned the opportunity to attend nursing school. But she'd chosen to marry Mike Armstrong and train locally as a midwife instead. Thanks to Luke Carlyle's generosity and her twin sister's marriage, Angela would benefit from her sister's hard work and attend normal school back East in the fall.

But none of that was Ellie's concern. First and foremost, she must plan her escape from Spirit Creek before her condition became known. A dozen decisions raced through her mind, competing for attention. She prayed she could withdraw a reasonable sum of Franklin's funds from the Spirit Creek Bank without encountering resistance from Mr. Peterman. She had tendered her resignation when she and Franklin moved up the wedding day, but the school committee had asked her to stay on until the end of May when a new teacher would be hired for the fall. She'd agreed to their stipulation since she'd planned on being a married woman and hopefully with loose-fitting dresses, she wouldn't be showing yet. Now, she would inform the committee of her newest change of plans, and hopefully, within a fortnight she sadly could put Spirit Creek behind her.

* * *

On Tuesday afternoon, Ellie Thomas sat ramrod straight at her desk, marking her students' arithmetic tests. She couldn't be more pleased with the results. Not for a moment did she praise her own abilities as a teacher for their exceptional performance. Tomorrow morning, all accolades would be extended to her industrious students.

Last night, Ellie secreted away her few possessions in a small travel trunk, a gift from a wealthy classmate at normal school. Mr. Rutherford must have advised the banker of her inheritance. She'd withdrawn three hundred dollars from Franklin's account at the bank without a bit of fuss and her plans to leave town were in place. The Deadwood Stage passed through Spirit Creek on route to Miles City every Monday, Wednesday and Friday. By this time tomorrow, she'd be gone.

She'd arranged a private meeting with Ronald Waverly, the School Committee chairman, to tender her resignation effective immediately, and she expected his arrival any minute.

"Hello. Anyone here?" called a familiar male voice from outside the schoolhouse.

"Yes, Mr. Waverly." Ellie dashed to meet her employer at the door. "Please come in. I appreciate you taking the time away from the store to meet with me."

"No bother. The missus can handle things for a few minutes." Mr. Waverly dragged his hat off his head, and then settled himself atop one of the larger desks. "Now, Miss Thomas, I know what you wanted to discuss with me."

"You do?" Ellie felt her cheeks warming.

"Of course. You tendered your resignation when you set your wedding date. But with Sheriff Smith's untimely death, you're concerned about your status as schoolmarm." Mr. Waverly smiled. "Please rest assured your position is not in jeopardy. In fact, I insist you stay on as our teacher. You've done an exceptional job over the years."

"Sir, that's not why I asked to meet with you. I'm leaving Spirit Creek; I plan to catch the Deadwood Stage tomorrow. There are just too many painful memories here." Ellie dabbed her eyes with her handkerchief, hoping her little white lie wasn't evident on her face.

"Miss Thomas, that's impossible." Mr. Waverly stood, towered over her. "We're at a crucial stage in the children's school year. Your students eagerly returned to class after the winter closure. Their education remains of utmost importance; the children must come before any personal considerations. Until I'm able to secure a commitment from another equally-qualified young lady, and she presents herself in town to commence teaching, I insist you fulfill your contract of employment with us."

Ellie blanched. "But that could take months!"

"I apologize for any inconvenience, but I must insist you continue teaching until a suitable replacement can be found." Mr. Waverly frowned. "I do recall receiving a letter from a young lady just a week ago, Miss Ivy Something-or-other, inquiring about a position as schoolteacher. Her credentials appeared quite suitable. I suppose I could send her a telegram today, and perhaps your plans won't be delayed for too long. Everything will depend on Miss Ivy's arrival."

"That would be wonderful! Thank you for your help, Mr. Waverly!" exclaimed Ellie. At least, all was not lost. If this girl accepted the position and arrived within the month, her reputation may be saved. "Please summon my replacement immediately and let me know when she's expected here."

"That I'll do. Enjoy the remainder of your day, Miss Thomas." Mr. Waverly plopped his hat on his head and showed himself out.

Ellie watched from the window as Mr. Waverly strolled out of the school yard. Not much hope of enjoying the remainder of a day he'd just thoroughly ruined. She'd intended to leave tomorrow. Now, she could be stuck here for two weeks, three weeks, longer.

She burst into tears.

CHAPTER 5

Tuesday, April 29, 1890

Ellie paced the floor of her private room in back of the schoolhouse. The steady clicking of her buttoned fancy boots on the wooden planks matched her thundering heartbeat. The days had dragged by, but finally Mr. Waverly sent word with one of her students that he'd be dropping by this evening with an update on her replacement. She hadn't eaten a bite of supper and her stomach protested the decision with a loud growl.

After the day she'd endured, she prayed for good news. Mayor Randy Barker hired Jimmy George Barkley from Miles City as Spirit Creek's new sheriff, replacing Franklin. Last Friday, the widowed sheriff had arrived in town: lock, stock, and six-year-old son. The child's distaste for book learning became evident within minutes of his arrival in class yesterday. Edward Barkley was an absolute hellion. She'd suffered through the two most horrendous workdays of her life. But this afternoon she'd sent a note home with the child, requesting his father meet with her at his convenience to discuss Edward's disruptive behavior.

"Miss Thomas, are you here?" called Mr. Waverly from the entrance.

Ellie had left the schoolhouse door ajar, anticipating her visitor's arrival. "Come in, sir. I'll be right out." She took a deep breath, pasted a pleasant smile on her face, and swept into the schoolroom with skirts swishing in her haste.

"Good evening, sir. Hasn't it been a lovely spring day today?" she commented, extending her hand to her employer.

"A winner for sure, miss." Mr. Waverly smiled and shook hands with her. "I come bearing good news for you. I've heard from Miss Ivy Paterson. You'll be delighted to hear that she's accepted the position."

"Oh, thank goodness. I'll purchase a ticket for tomorrow's stagecoach, sir. Thank you." Ellie beamed and shook her employer's hand again with renewed enthusiasm.

"Whoa now, Miss Thomas. Please allow me to finish." Mr. Waverly extracted his hand from her grasp. "Miss Paterson has agreed to sign a contract for employment beginning in September…"

"What?" Ellie's heart stopped for a moment. Not until September?

"Even if Miss Paterson left California today, she'd arrive in Spirit Creek perhaps a week or two before school finished. Makes no sense for her to come before September."

Ellie rapidly ciphered in her head. Her dresses were already becoming uncomfortably tight and she wrapped a shawl around herself most days, hoping everyone assumed she was chilled from grieving. A month from now, she'd most certainly be showing. "Couldn't Angela Jones step in for a few weeks and finish the school year."

"Angela is not a trained teacher. Besides, you signed a contract. I understand you're grieving your young man. If you need someone to talk to, my Elizabeth wouldn't mind you bending her ear a bit." Mr. Waverly smiled. "But I must insist you stay on as teacher and complete the school year."

"I'll carry on the best I can. I may not appear grateful, but I am, truly." Ellie grimaced with her little white lie. She didn't feel one iota of appreciation, fearing the man's stubbornness and her expanding waistline would soon result in her ruination in the eyes of the entire population of Spirit Creek.

"I'll see myself out then." Mr. Waverly lumbered out through the door, closing it behind him as Ellie staggered back to her private quarters.

She slumped onto a kitchen chair, dropped her head onto her crossed arms resting on the table, and sobbed her eyes out.

* * *

"Thank you kindly for keeping my boy, Mrs. Waverly."

"No problem at all, Sheriff Barkley. I don't mind a handsome young lad eating my cookies or small feet dirtying my floors." Elizabeth laughed, beaming. She ruffled Edward's hair.

The youngster glared at the storekeeper's wife.

"You behave, boy," ordered Sheriff Jimmy George Barkley as he tipped his Stetson to the woman and charged out of the general store.

Jimmy George strode toward the schoolhouse, miffed that the schoolmarm summoned him to discuss Edward. How had she worded her note? *His son's disruptive behavior*. Hell and damnation, the boy lost his ma less than six months ago, and then his pa uprooted him from his home and his friends. Of course, the kid was disruptive.

Jimmy George couldn't have cared less.

At times, he felt a little disruptive himself. But four or five shots of that rotgut Darby called whiskey usually fixed him right up. "Damned woman is just wasting my time." He kicked a stone in his path clear across the road. After reading the cryptic telegram the old fellow at the telegraph office dropped off at the jailhouse this afternoon, his son's behavior was the least of his problems.

Jimmy George stomped up the wide wooden steps leading to the schoolhouse, arriving unannounced. Dusk had settled in and a cool breeze ruffled his collar-length hair when he removed his Stetson. He pounded on the door.

His knock wasn't answered.

Jimmy George smiled to himself. "Now maybe something might be wrong," he postulated aloud. He was getting the hang of this law-keeping business. Wasn't that a hoot! He tried the door, discovered it unlocked, and ventured inside.

"Hello. Is there anybody here?" he hollered and then stood just inside the door, listening. He heard a muffled noise coming from somewhere in back. Sounded like a woman sobbing. Was she hurt? Or ill? He decided to investigate.

Jimmy George found the schoolmarm in the living quarters, seated at the kitchen table, sobbing loud enough to rouse the drunks passed out at Darby's saloon. No wonder she hadn't heard him come in.

He hated crying women. His late wife had bawled her eyes out about anything and everything. The sound grated on his nerves, but he supposed as the new sheriff he best show a measure of compassion for the woman. "I'm the new sheriff, Jimmy George Barkley. Are you hurt or ailing, Miss Thomas? Is there anything I can do?"

The woman just continued the annoying blubbering.

"I apologize for intruding." Jimmy George twirled his Stetson in his hands. "Miss, perhaps you should tell me what's wrong."

The woman continued to sob, even louder if that was possible.

Jimmy George tossed his hat on the table, plucked the schoolmarm off the chair, and then sat down with her wrapped in his arms. He inhaled her lily-of-the-valley scent. As he tightened his embrace, he brushed one hand across her soft, plump bosoms. By accident. Almost.

They remained seated there for several minutes until Miss Ellie Thomas cried herself out. Jimmy George hated the sound of a bawling female more than anything, but he'd held his tongue. Blessedly, the room finally remained silent. Thank goodness for small mercies.

"I understand you were engaged to Franklin Smith. Please accept…my sympathy…and all," stammered Jimmy George, losing himself in her beautiful eyes.

"We'd planned the most wonderful wedding and now Franklin's gone," wailed Ellie.

After a minute, she regained her composure and clambered off his lap.

Jimmy George needed to get the hell out of here. "I didn't mean to intrude on your grief, ma'am. I've come to apologize for Edward. I blame my son's behavior on the fact that his ma died six months ago, and the boy hasn't anyone to teach him what's proper," he explained, standing when he finished his rehearsed piece.

Jimmy George hoped his logic would pass muster since the schoolmarm wasn't thinking straight at the moment. Edward didn't have a ma, but he imagined proper behavior was taught over a number of years. Being without a ma for six months didn't really explain his son's total disregard for rules. Thinking on it, Jimmy George reckoned the kid was a chip off the old block since he held no regard for rules himself.

Of course, he'd seldom been around when his son was growing up, and he supposed his mousy little wife had done her best. But you really couldn't expect much from someone as useless as she'd been.

The schoolmarm met his eyes and Jimmy George could almost see the cogs working in her head. What was she thinking about so intently? Had she even heard a word he'd said about Edward?

"I'm with child," she whispered the confession out of the blue. Her hand flew to her mouth. "Goodness, I spoke that thought aloud, didn't I?"

"Yes, ma'am. I'm afraid you did," confirmed Jimmy George, understanding now why she was fit to be tied, sobbing and carrying on.

Smith was dead and Miss Thomas here was pregnant. Jimmy George didn't blame her late fiancé for rushing the wedding night. He'd require a nightly dunking in a horse trough filled with ice-cold water to keep his hands off her luscious body. What he wouldn't give for just one night of splendor inside her. His manhood sprang to attention the second the thought entered his mind. So the unmarried schoolteacher was pregnant. He'd bet every one of his bank accounts that Spirit Creek's gossiping old biddies would love nothing better than to hear this little tidbit.

"You cannot imagine how ashamed I am, and I hate the thought of leaving Spirit Creek. But I clearly have no other choice, and no time to lose if I'm going to keep my secret." Ellie's fingers twisted her sodden handkerchief. "But the school committee chairman is forcing me to continue teaching."

"I suppose being a schoolmarm doesn't pay a lot either, and you can't afford a ticket out of here," reasoned Jimmy George. "At least you'll keep your job until your middle starts to expand and the secret's out."

* * *

Ellie almost explained that she could easily afford a ticket to anywhere in the world, but she considered it wise to hold back that information. This man appeared kindly and genuinely concerned for her, but he was a complete stranger nonetheless.

The new sheriff scratched his head. "I don't recall counselling unmarried schoolteachers in the family way as being part of my job description when I signed on."

"There must be something I can do, instead of just waiting for the new teacher to arrive." Ellie chewed on her lower lip.

"There's a new schoolteacher on the way?"

"Yes, but Miss Paterson won't arrive here before August most likely, to start teaching come September. Meanwhile, I must complete this school year."

Jimmy George chuckled. "Perhaps I should marry you and solve both our problems. Your kid would have a name, and my son would have a new ma."

Instantly, Ellie thought of her friend, Maggie Carlyle, and her marriage of convenience with Luke that had worked out so well. Was the new sheriff standing here Ellie's destiny? Could she marry a total stranger?

The handsome man appeared kind-hearted. Being gainfully employed as the town sheriff, he could provide for her. After her baby arrived, she could always divorce him if things didn't work out. With the funds Franklin bequeathed to her, even alone, she could easily support herself and the child.

Jimmy George was Third's son. Third had rescued the pregnant Belle from one of the saloons. She couldn't recall which one. But Third had proven himself a wonderful husband and father.

Six feet of solution to Ellie's problem stood before her. She grimaced, hating herself for turning her back on Franklin's memory so soon after his passing. And for no better reason than saving her own reputation. Considering what she was about to agree to, a loveless marriage to a complete stranger was all she deserved.

"I'll marry you," whispered Ellie. Recalling the terms of Franklin's will, she added, "And I have a house we can all move into as well."

* * *

Jimmy George could have plucked his revolver out of the holster and shot himself. Hadn't the damn woman realized he was only joking? Hell and damnation, how had he gotten himself into this fix?

He glared at Miss Thomas, and then he remembered the soft

curves he'd felt beneath that simple calico dress when she'd occupied his lap a few moments ago. In his experience, redheaded women always worked a fellow over real good in bed. Perhaps being married to this beauty wasn't such a bad idea after all. His manhood throbbed in anticipation of the wedding night.

And she'd mentioned moving to a house. That would get him and Edward out of that damn hotel, away from prying eyes. He could use that to his advantage also. If his plans worked out, he wouldn't be around long enough to see the kid born anyway. In the meantime, he'd have a woman's body in his bed every night and someone to watch over his son.

"I'd be right honored to marry you, ma'am," he declared.

Thursday, May 1, 1890

Ellie sat at the Carlyle kitchen table, worrying her handkerchief in her hands.

"The man moved to town a week ago, Ellie. You don't know him from Adam." Luke started buttoning his waistcoat in the wrong hole and unbuttoned what he'd done. He tugged at the garment in frustration and then started again.

"I don't have a choice…" began Ellie, shifting in her chair.

Luke glared at her. "Franklin isn't cold in his grave, and you're up and marrying Jimmy George Barkley?"

"I have to," whispered Ellie, sighing loudly.

"She's carrying Franklin's baby," Maggie reminded her husband.

Luke flopped onto the chair next to his wife. "So you've told me. I can understand Ellie's predicament but still..." Luke folded his arms across his broad chest and glared at each woman in turn.

"When Franklin was killed, I planned to leave town at the earliest opportunity. Ronald Waverly informed me that I've signed a contract, however, and he's insisting I stay on as schoolteacher until my replacement, a Miss Ivy Paterson, arrives to teach in September. I could easily be showing before the end of May!"

"That would get the gossips' tongues wagging." Luke's expression softened and he trailed his fingers up and down his wife's arm.

Ellie noticed the simple act of affection, envious of the love between Luke and Maggie. Would her marriage of convenience turn out as well? "Let me explain why Jimmy George was at the school in the first place. When Mayor Barker hired him as our new sheriff, he arrived with a very troubled six-year-old son."

Luke straightened in his chair. "Barkley never mentioned a son to anyone that I know of. Unless he told Mayor Barker before he hired him. I wonder if there's something more he hasn't told us?"

"Well, he mentioned his wife had died six months ago," said Ellie.

"Barkley's wife died recently?" Luke remembered how torn up he'd been when he'd lost Catherine. Barkley seemed to have put his wife's death behind him already. Unless he did his grieving in private and pasted on a brave face in public. "I never heard mention of that neither. I wonder if he told Mayor Barker."

"Well, I sent a note home imploring the man to meet with me to discuss his son's disruptive behavior," continued Ellie.

"How did a note about bad behavior end up in a marriage proposal?" Luke slid forward on the chair, turning his full attention to Ellie's story.

Ellie filled in the details leading to the proposed marriage of convenience.

"At least he's a chivalrous devil," conceded Luke.

"I'm marrying Sheriff Barkley to form a family to serve both our purposes," whispered Ellie.

"I've used that argument myself." Luke grinned broadly.

"The same as what you did for Maggie, Jimmy George's proposition was the most unselfish thing anyone's ever done for me." Ellie sighed and blew her nose.

"I dare say the whole business makes sense." Luke scratched his head. "He's a lawman and that alone speaks for his character I suppose."

"The baby will come early. But at least by marrying Jimmy George, I'll ensure my child is born in wedlock." Ellie couldn't fathom being married to a complete stranger, but she hoped someday the four of them would become a loving family like her friends shared.

"And Edward Barkley couldn't hope for a better mother." Maggie hugged Ellie.

"Thank you for that lovely sentiment." Ellie tightened the embrace. She couldn't ask for a better friend and confidante. "I'll try my best to be a good stepmother. Edward's a very troubled boy, no doubt a result of his ma's recent death."

Maggie patted Ellie's hand. "I'm hopeful your marriage will be everything that Luke and I share."

"I'd like nothing better," admitted Ellie.

"Well, we promise to attend your wedding." Maggie walked Ellie out to the buggy she'd rented at the livery and waved as her friend headed back to town.

CHAPTER 6

Saturday, May 10, 1890

Following Jimmy George and Ellie's sudden marriage a week ago, Ronald Waverly somewhat reluctantly permitted Angela Jones to finish out the school year under Ellie's direction. Ellie agreed to meet with Angela every Friday at four o'clock to plan the next week's lessons and tests. By all reports, Angela had been doing a wonderful job and the children loved her. Ronald seemed pleased with the arrangement.

After the 'I do's' were spoken, Jimmy George and Edward moved into Franklin's house with Ellie, and Angela moved into the teacher's quarters in back of the schoolhouse to begin teaching on Monday morning. Someone had removed all of Franklin's possessions from the house, and Ellie suspected Elizabeth Waverly was responsible for that thoughtful act. Ellie couldn't have done it, his loss still too recent and her emotions much too raw.

For the past week, Ellie concentrated on being a housewife. Moving into a house previously occupied by a bachelor, with a man who'd been a widower with a young son, meant she'd washed and ironed clothes and bedding and curtains and linens until her hands were red and cracked. She recalled Maggie praising petroleum jelly and Ellie bought two jars at the general store. While there, despite her troubled mind, she had the forethought to instruct Elizabeth to change the name on her account to Mr. Jimmy George Barkley and Mrs. Ellie Barkley.

As well, she'd prepared three meals a day, baked bread and pies and cookies until she almost swooned from the heat in the kitchen. She hadn't burned the biscuits since her wedding night, but no one even noticed. Nothing she accomplished pleased her new husband.

Apple pie again, he whined.

You starched my work shirts, he complained.

Where are my favorite old boots, he asked one morning after a night of heavy drinking, having totally forgotten he'd thrown them out himself the day before after he'd purchased a costly new pair at the general store.

And she hadn't the foggiest notion how he'd paid for them on a sheriff's salary. Probably put them on their account at the store. In which case, Ellie knew she'd be paying for them from the funds Franklin left her.

Ellie tossed the last of the laundry she'd washed yesterday onto the kitchen table and started folding it, growing angrier by the minute. Jimmy George entertained himself in the saloon most every night, carousing with the women, gambling with the men, buying a round of drinks whenever it crossed his mind to do so. Certainly, he'd never intended for her to learn of such things, but she'd overheard two gentlemen talking about the new sheriff while she stood out of sight behind a rack of clothing at the general store. Evidently, Jimmy George intended to spend his paychecks on his own fun, because so far he'd contributed a mere pittance toward household expenses.

Fortunately, she'd never breathed a word about her inheritance from Franklin. Even Luke and Maggie hadn't been told. At the rate Jimmy George was going, she could well imagine how quickly he'd spend her into the poorhouse. And bless Franklin's heart for leaving her so financially well cared for. Every bill she ran up at the general store was promptly paid at the end of every week on her behalf by Mr. Rutherford from her substantial bank account. Even if they'd been curious, to their credit, neither Ronald nor Elizabeth had questioned her about the arrangement.

She stuffed the folded clothes into the bureau drawers of the furniture Franklin crafted with his own hands, so lovingly, for her. She took a deep breath, refusing to shed another tear. A person couldn't live on what ifs.

All week long Jimmy George crashed through the front door every night well after midnight, bragging about what a wonderful evening he'd had. Pretending she was asleep was impossible; the noise the drunken fool made would wake the dead. Fortunately, like most children, Edward proved himself an extremely sound sleeper.

While lost in her musings, she punched down the risen batch of bread she'd started this morning. She allowed each batch an extra rising time for the sole purpose of expending her pent up anger. This strategy produced lighter bread while proving exceptionally therapeutic.

She grimaced as she recalled every night, no matter how drunk, her new husband insisted on his marital rights. The bread received another punch. His sour breath and unwashed body almost made her gag. Punch. Punch. If she hadn't spent that blissful night in Franklin's arms and came to the marriage bed a virgin, she might have believed that Jimmy George's sweaty exertions were all there was between a man and a woman. But she knew better.

She was beyond caring what he did to her body, but she fervently prayed that his rough excuse for lovemaking never hurt her baby. When she'd shed her clothes to bathe this morning, she noticed the clear evidence of the life growing inside her, She lovingly caressed the pronounced bump several times a day. Her baby. Her last remnant of Franklin.

Ellie started shaping the bread into loaves and setting them into the buttered tin pans for the final rising. As she worked, she considered why such a dear sweet man like Franklin was taken from her. And what had she done to deserve Jimmy George Barkley? The answer seemed clear. She'd fornicated with Franklin and conceived his child. God was punishing her for that sin by snatching away her beloved man and giving her a despicable replacement. Proof, there was hell on earth.

Ellie tossed a clean tea towel over the loaves of bread and left them to rise before baking. "Did you really do the right thing by marrying Jimmy George?" she asked herself aloud, washing her hands in the tub of soapy dishwater and then drying them on a new kitchen towel.

Ellie didn't love Jimmy George, and he certainly didn't love her. She doubted he even liked her very much. He frequently complained about being saddled with a frumpy wife carrying another man's brat. How had she ever thought him kind-hearted and selfless? Considering his low opinion of her, why had he offered to marry her in the first place? She would never understand the man.

Ellie poured herself a cup of coffee from the pot warming on the woodstove and seated herself at the kitchen table. She took a sip, once again lost in her thoughts. She'd had no time to mourn Franklin before she'd dived into this marriage. And she'd only done it to save her reputation. What had she been thinking? The townsfolk weren't stupid. Once the baby arrived the gossips would do the ciphering and realize it was Franklin's child. To make matters worse, she'd taken on the added responsibility of caring for another woman's child. For the most part, Edward had ignored all of her motherly efforts. He complimented her on her cookies twice but nothing more. Was he just following his pa's poor example?

She prayed every day for the strength to keep up the pretence of their arrangement. Most of the townsfolk seemed to accept the union as a true marriage. She'd heard people speculate that Jimmy George and Franklin might have been acquaintances, both being lawmen. Perhaps they'd been mistaken in their belief that she was engaged to Franklin. Maybe they'd heard wrong and she was engaged to this Jimmy George fellow. She certainly wouldn't tell them otherwise.

But she couldn't share her unhappiness with anyone. Even Maggie, despite knowing the reason behind the marriage, believed Ellie was content.

Taking a moment, she placed a hand on her middle. Anticipating the joy of someday holding this baby in her arms seemed the only thing keeping her sane. She would endure Jimmy George and anything else thrown in her path to protect her unborn child.

"There is no sacrifice I won't make for you," she whispered to her unborn child.

"Did you say something?"

Ellie swung around and discovered her new stepson staring at her while Captain sat on the floor beside his new master. With his tongue lolling, the silly hound appeared to be smiling. She was glad Captain and Edward enjoyed each other's company so much. Franklin would be pleased that someone was caring for his beloved dog.

"Edward, I was just talking to myself." Ellie tousled his pale blond hair. For once, he didn't move away from her touch. "Would you like a glass of milk and some cookies?"

"Yes, ma'am."

Ellie smiled at his standard reply. The past two days, her every question and request immediately had elicited a *yes, ma'am* from him.

A minute later, Edward gulped down half his milk and reached for his second cookie. While Ellie stitched a ripped pocket on her husband's work shirt, Edward finished his afternoon snack. She startled and stuck her finger with the needle when she looked up to find Edward's nose almost touching her cheek. An odd expression appeared on his face, and then he raced back to his chair.

"Is something wrong, Edward?"

Silence.

"Do you miss your ma? Am I a poor substitute?" Ellie straightened in her chair. She now considered this little boy her own. Something was bothering her usually boisterous son, and she intended to discover what it was.

"I was just lookin'," mumbled Edward.

"Looking at what?" probed Ellie. Did Edward consider her freckles particularly interesting? His own face was covered in them so why the sudden interest in hers?

"There's nothing on your face. That's good," answered Edward.

"What do you mean?"

"No bruises or nothin'." Edward reached for his third cookie and took a huge bite.

"Why would there be bruises on my face?" Ellie's breath caught. Jimmy George had pushed her on a couple of occasions when his temper got the better of him, but he'd never struck her. "Did your ma ever have bruises on her face?" she whispered when the question crossed her mind. She braced herself for her stepson's answer.

"Sometimes…when Pa…got angry..." Edward spoke around his mouthful of cookie. He swallowed and met her eyes. "I just don't want you to die like Ma did."

Ellie felt the blood drain out of her face. She reached for Edward and dragged him onto her lap. "I'm not going to die. Your ma died of fever." At least, that was the story Jimmy George told her.

"Ma's face was bleedin', and she was hurtin' somethin' awful. Pa didn't see me watchin' him. He hurt her pretty bad, but I was too scared to help Ma. I didn't stop Pa from hurtin' her." Edward's eyes filled and then he burst into tears.

"Sweetheart, you didn't do anything wrong. You're just a little boy. If your pa was angry you did the right thing. Whenever your pa is angry, you hide somewhere safe. You hear me? You hide where he won't find you." Ellie dried her son's tears with the corner of her apron. "Promise me."

"Okay, Mama," sniffled Edward. "I promise."

"Now, no more talk of me dying. I'm as strong and healthy as an ox." Ellie hugged him while fighting her emotions—it was the first time he'd called her Mama—and then she waved him back to his own chair. "Now, finish your milk."

A jumble of conflicting thoughts raced through Ellie's mind. Did Jimmy George beat his first wife? Did he contribute to her death? Or was she letting her imagination run amok on the say so of a child?

Jimmy George was a deputy and now a sheriff, sworn to protect people. Why would a lawman harm his own wife? The whole idea was totally absurd.

Saturday, May 24, 1890

"Good afternoon, Mrs. Waverly." Ellie and Edward entered the Spirit Creek General Store as the little bell above the door tinkled and announced their arrival.

Ronald and Elizabeth Waverly operated the store and occupied the living quarters in back. The store was crammed from floor to ceiling with a wide variety of goods. Shelves sagged with an assortment of clothing for men, women and children, and a good supply of footwear could be found. Staples like flour, sugar, coffee, and canned goods were always available. Gentlemen conversed over the checkerboard set up beside the pickle barrels, and womenfolk examined various bolts of cloth while exchanging the latest gossip.

Ellie had loved the place since her first visit years ago. Every time she entered the establishment, she found another treasure hidden in a corner, an unexpected trinket that she wanted so badly to buy but could never afford. Occasionally in the past, Elizabeth would set something aside until she could pay for it from her hard-earned teaching wages. Those days were behind her now. Thanks to Franklin's foresight and generosity, she could purchase anything in the store that she fancied. She could buy the business if she'd been of a mind to.

"Good afternoon, Mrs. Barkley," replied Elizabeth Waverly, wiping her hands on a towel. "And who is this handsome gentleman accompanying you?"

"I'm not a gentleman, I'm a boy." Edward peeked up at his new ma.

"And a very good boy he is. Edward deserves a few pieces of candy, if you know where we could find some," teased Ellie.

"The candy jars were topped up this morning. Go fetch what you'd like, Edward, while your ma and I enjoy a chinwag," encouraged Elizabeth, shooing the child toward the candy display beside the main counter.

"Thank you for being so kind to him." Ellie sighed. "He's experienced more trouble in his short life than most adults: losing his ma, moving to a strange town, acquiring a total stranger as his new mother."

She decided against divulging her conversation with Edward concerning his birth mother. Mrs. Waverly would believe Ellie had lost her mind if she suggested their new sheriff might have contributed to his wife's death. But Ellie suspected Edward wasn't a child who fabricated stories. She intended to bide her time while keeping Edward safe and staying alert to her new husband's penchant for sudden fits of temper.

"I haven't a doubt in the world that you're the best thing that ever happened to the boy. Before you married his father, Edward spent a lot of time alone in June Davidson's care at her hotel while his pa was working or spending the night in the saloon. Occasionally, his father even shuffled him off to me." Elizabeth pursed her lips. "I'll never understand folks treating a child so poorly."

Ellie patted the storekeeper's hand. Elizabeth had never conceived a child, and Ellie suspected it bothered her more than other folks seeing a child neglected or abused. "Well, for better or for worse, Edward is stuck with me now…strict rules and all."

Ellie collected the dry goods she required while Elizabeth gathered up her list of staples. "Put these on my account, please," instructed Ellie.

Having moved into Franklin's rented house, she prayed Mr. Rutherford wouldn't believe she'd become a spendthrift since acquiring her inheritance. She'd spent a tidy sum outfitting the previous bachelor's home with necessities as well as clothing for her new son and herself. Jimmy George was too self-involved to even notice.

Just then, the bell tinkled above the front door and all heads turned. Ellie stiffened when Robert Rutherford entered the store. He spotted her immediately and he strode toward her.

"Ellie, how are you today?" He extended the greeting, a broad grin creasing his face.

"I'm fine, thank you for asking." Her heartbeat quickened at hearing his voice.

"Wonderful. I happy to hear it." Robert's smile hadn't diminished. "If I'm permitted to say so, you're looking lovely as always today."

Ellie felt herself redden and she refused to meet his hypnotizing eyes. Was he just being friendly or was he flirting with her? "Thank you," she replied, simply. She shouldn't encourage him.

"Are you two looking forward to the big party?" inquired Elizabeth, busily tallying Ellie's order.

"I most certainly am," replied Robert.

"What big party would that be?" asked Ellie.

Elizabeth paused in her ciphering and met Ellie's eyes. "Luke and Maggie Carlyle's anniversary party, of course. They were married a year ago next Saturday."

Robert added, "There's a huge affair planned at the Spirit Creek Hotel, and the entire community's invited."

"It should be quite the shindig," summarized Elizabeth.

"I'm surprised your new husband hasn't mentioned it," commented Robert.

Considering his previously playful conversation, the tone of his remark suggested an accusation was intended. "I suspect it just slipped his mind," speculated Ellie, covering her surprise. Most likely, her husband planned to attend the event alone and leave her at home with his son.

Well, she would just see about that.

May 31, 1890

"Stop fidgeting, Edward." Ellie combed her stepson's sun-bleached rooster tail into submission while the lily-of-the-valley scent from her soap wafted into her nostrils from his shiny locks.

This morning, after Jimmy George rushed off to the jailhouse, Ellie and Edward took turns bathing in preparation for their outing. Edward insisted on washing himself and hopped in and out of the tin bathtub within ten minutes. After he'd dressed, Ellie shooed him outside to play while she savored a relaxing thirty-minute soak.

"My shirt is scratchy," complained Edward.

"I starched your new shirt, so you'd look nice for the party at the hotel. You'll be the handsomest lad there." Ellie grimaced, inhaling sharply and forcing a smile through her clenched teeth. Since before dawn, she'd been experiencing mild cramping, but thankfully, no spotting. Just nerves, she told herself. The anniversary party could prove to be the social event of the year, and she refused to miss it. Besides, this would be her first public appearance as Mrs. Jimmy George Barkley. She smiled, knowing that, of everyone at the party, her husband would be the most-surprised person to see her in attendance.

Edward peeked up at his new stepmother. "Are you okay, Mama?"

"Yes, sweetheart, I'm fine." Ellie smiled at her son, her curiosity finally getting the best of her. "Edward, you called your mother Ma. Why do you call me Mama?"

"My friend Sam calls his mother, Mama. I guess…I just…" Edward took a step back. "Am I in trouble?"

"Heavens, no! I like the name Mama very much." Ellie smiled through another pang. Sam was Maggie's son, and Luke was raising him as his own. Maggie was secretly making arrangements through Robert Rutherford to legally change Sam's name to Carlyle, to surprise Luke.

"You can call me Mama as often as you want." Ellie tweaked his nose.

"Thank you, Mama." Edward kissed her cheek.

"Is Pa coming to the party with us?" Edward stuffed something into one new trouser pocket, and Ellie hoped it wasn't a frog or some such thing. You never knew with little boys.

"As sheriff, your father went ahead to ensure things are in order and no drunken louts from the saloon wander into the festivities," explained Ellie truthfully.

At least, truthful in part. Her new husband certainly didn't expect they'd be attending also. She had remained in her calico housedress until Jimmy George charged out of the house an hour ago. She couldn't wait to see the expression on his face when she and Edward strolled into the party room, dressed in their new store-bought finery. If he even noticed. He hadn't mentioned any of the improvements she'd made to their home. He seemed totally oblivious to everything but his own amusements.

She'd outfitted Edward from head to toe in new trousers and waistcoat, a white shirt, and black leather boots. She purchased a lovely loose-fitting cerulean silk gown with a dainty hat to match and new black leather button-up boots for herself. She wrapped a white lacy shawl around her shoulders and studied herself in her new cheval mirror. Her middle would soon expand enough that her secret would be out. She'd probably never wear the dress again for months. But for tonight, she looked marvelous, and Edward was equally handsome in his new duds.

"Can I bring Captain?" Edward looked up at her, hopefully.

"Absolutely not! That hound stays put in the back yard." Ellie wagged her finger, and her son's forlorn expression tugged at her heartstrings. "After the party, ask Mrs. Davidson for a soup bone from the kitchen for Captain."

"Okay, Mama!" Edward threw his arms around her middle.

Ellie smiled as they wandered down the narrow hallway toward the front door. She'd quickly become accustomed to her son's more affectionate nature. Perhaps she was excelling as a stepmother better than her earlier self-evaluation had indicated.

The cramping seemed to have passed, and she breathed deeply and attempted to relax. With a party to attend, she didn't have time for silly, anxiety-induced cramps.

"Let's go, Edward, before my nerves get the better of me. We're not missing a minute of this party. Besides, I can't wait to show everyone my handsome new son."

"That's me!" Edward giggled and skipped out the front door.

The party noise assailed her ears the second she stepped through the hotel dining room's main entrance. Everyone was dressed in their Sunday best. The ladies chatted together in small groups while the gentlemen smoked cigars and argued cattle prices. Children raced between the adults in a game of chase.

"There's Sam, Mama. Can I go play with him?" Edward peeked up at her expectantly.

Maggie's five-year-old son waved to them from across the room. "Yes, go and play and make some new friends," encouraged Ellie, waving to her son's friend.

Edward disappeared, leaving her standing alone.

"Good evening, Mrs. Barkley." The greeting sent her heartbeat racing. Pasting a smile on her face, she turned around.

"Mr. Rutherford," acknowledged Ellie, extending her gloved hand. "It's a pleasure to see you again so soon," she lied through her teeth. Who would have guessed that a talent perfected in her misspent youth would come in so handy at her age? In truth, she dreaded their encounters, especially considering her unaccountable attraction to the man!

Robert shook her hand, sending an electrical charge through her entire body. "I wouldn't miss such a special occasion."

Ellie drowned in his eyes for a second before she found her voice. "Neither would I."

"You most certainly surprised everyone in town with your recent marriage."

Ellie heard the disapproval in his voice, and she couldn't blame him. He probably considered her eligible for commitment to an insane asylum. There were days when she'd go willingly. "Sometimes, we even surprise ourselves," she whispered her reply.

His odd expression encouraged further explanation. When she offered none, his disappointment appeared evident.

Having depleted the topic of her marriage, Ellie gazed around the room and contemplated a suitable topic of conversation with which to fill the void. Her eyes tripped over Jimmy George, glowering at her from across the room. Her new husband stood leaning against the bar, and he saluted her with his crystal glass before tipping back its contents.

"There's my husband." Ellie patted Robert's arm. "Please excuse me."

Jimmy George waved her over, not appearing happy at all to see her. Ellie strolled across the room, stopping a couple of times to greet friends. Finally, she stood at his elbow.

"What in hell are you doing here?" whispered Jimmy George through clenched teeth. While attempting to suppress his simmering rage, a portion of his refilled drink spilled over the rim of the glass and landed on his shiny new black boots.

Ellie suppressed the urge to laugh. "It's lovely to see you, too, dear husband," she greeted him, in a subdued voice.

"I asked you what you're doing here." Jimmy George grabbed her arm and squeezed hard.

Ellie yanked her arm free. "It's my understanding that the entire community is invited to this social affair. Without a doubt, Edward and I qualify as citizens in good standing, and thus, we're here to enjoy ourselves." With a swish of her skirts and head held high, Ellie Barkley disappeared into the crowd before her husband could voice a reply.

CHAPTER 7

"Are you not feeling well, Ellie?" inquired Maggie Carlyle, concern evident in her voice.

Ellie had been leaning against the wall nearest the hotel's kitchen, hoping no one would discover her hiding place. She met Maggie's eyes and smiled. "I've had better days," she admitted, reluctantly.

"What's the matter?"

"Cramping," whispered Ellie, fighting the pain through clenched teeth. Since her arrival, she'd partaken of the sumptuous meal and enjoyed the company of everyone in attendance. Well, almost everyone. She'd ignored Jimmy George the entire evening, hoping everyone would just believe her husband was preoccupied with keeping the peace.

"Cramping? Oh, my. I don't like the sound of that."

"The pain's becoming increasingly difficult to tolerate," whispered Ellie. For the past half hour, severe cramps had dampened her enjoyment.

"I like the sound of that even less. I'm taking you home immediately," stated Maggie, grabbing her friend by the arm and almost dragging her toward the banquet room's main door.

"No, I can't leave Edward alone," protested Ellie. "He's playing with Sam somewhere."

"He'll be fine. On our way out, we'll ask Luke to watch over him." Maggie spotted her husband across the room and beckoned him with a wave of her hand. Within seconds he appeared at her side.

"Is something wrong? Is it one of the children?" Luke moved his hand to her elbow.

"No, the children are fine. Elizabeth is shamelessly spoiling Willie and the girls are playing with their friends. I'm taking Ellie home; she's under the weather. Please mind Edward and bring him home for us. Ellie won't be returning."

"I'll keep an eye out for Edward. He's playing with Sam and Patti.

Take our carriage, sweetheart. Shall I check on you in a few minutes?" Luke kissed his wife on the cheek.

"If I'm not back in a half hour, please do," suggested Maggie.

"I can walk home alone. There's no need…" began Ellie.

"Hush." Maggie swatted her friend's arm, and then pecked her husband's cheek.

"I hope you're feeling better soon, Ellie."

"Thank you, Luke. It's probably nothing." Ellie rushed out of the door with Maggie on her heels.

Five minutes later, the ladies arrived at the small house Maggie once shared with her first husband. Luke had bought the house, after the banker foreclosed on it forcing her friend into dire poverty and, at the time, necessitating a marriage of convenience. Someday, Sam would own the home, a legacy from his father.

"Such memories," whispered Maggie upon entering through the front door.

In extreme pain, Ellie stumbled directly to the bedroom she shared with her new husband and began removing her new gown and petticoats.

"Has the cramping lessened?"

"I believe it's becoming worse."

"Goodness gracious!" Maggie gaped at her friend's legs.

Ellie bent forward and gasped. Both of her legs were heavily streaked with blood. "I wasn't even spotting when I left for the party," she whispered.

"*This* is not spotting." Maggie helped Ellie onto the bed. "Get off your feet now."

There was a loud knock on the front door. "Ladies, is everything okay?" called Luke.

"Fetch Doc Benjamin immediately!" screamed Maggie from the bedroom.

* * *

Luke Carlyle occupied a chair at the Barkley's kitchen table, working on his third cup of coffee. He'd gotten Edward to bed an hour ago, and he'd sent his own children back to the ranch with the recently-married Mike and Agnes Armstrong.

Five minutes ago, Spirit Creek's newly-hired sheriff had staggered into the kitchen, obviously having consumed a generous amount of the complimentary spirits at the party. Jimmy George Barkley glowered at Luke, seated in the chair across from him.

"She lost the baby, Jimmy George," whispered Maggie, standing behind Luke with her hands resting on his shoulders. "Doc Benjamin is with Ellie now."

"Lost it?" asked Jimmy George, his brain obviously fuzzy from the liquor.

Luke entered the conversation. "Ellie suffered a miscarriage," he clarified.

"Are you sure?" Jimmy George blinked and met Maggie's eyes.

"Positive. Ellie will be heartbroken. If this had happened to me when I took that spell after Doc Fitzgerald's burial…" Maggie had experienced several tearful days of uncertainty, but the bleeding finally abated and her baby was saved.

"Thankfully, we have Willie." Luke rose from his chair and engulfed his wife in his arms. "Ellie wasn't as fortunate, but there'll be other children."

"But it was…" Maggie began, and then her eyes flew to Jimmy George.

"Go ahead. Say it. It was Franklin's baby she wanted." Jimmy George spat the words.

"She'll want your children, too, someday," said Maggie.

Jimmy George glared at her and then stumbled out of the house, slamming the door closed.

* * *

"Was that Jimmy George's voice I heard?" Ellie held her breath, waiting for Maggie's answer. If she was expected to face her abusive husband any time soon, she'd never survive it.

"Yes," replied Maggie.

Ellie sucked air into her lungs. She'd lost the baby, Doc said. She couldn't believe it, wouldn't believe it. Franklin's child was the only important thing she had left of him. She would gladly have given back all the money he'd bequeathed her, if she could have kept his baby.

Why had Doc failed to prevent the miscarriage? Was this God's final punishment?

There must be a reason why her life was being sabotaged at every turn. Reverend Gerald preached about a loving God, but clearly He didn't love Ellie Barkley. Doc had no reason to lie to her.

"My baby is gone," Ellie finally admitted the truth, voiced it aloud. "Up in heaven with Franklin, his or her father."

And then she burst into tears.

"Jimmy George was here for a few minutes. When we told him what happened, he just stormed out of the house." Maggie tucked the covers around her friend.

Ellie couldn't think about Jimmy George's short-fused temper right now. No doubt he was angry with her again. She sniffled, attempting to stifle her tears but failing miserably. Accepting she'd lost the baby hurt too much. For several minutes, she fought bravely and then succumbed to her grief. Sobbing loudly and pounding the bed covers, she wailed, "Why, Maggie? Why?"

"There are never any answers at a time like this. Just cry out all the hurting," Maggie counselled, wrapping her arms around her friend. "Today is just a hiccup in time. Things will get better. There will be other babies."

Ellie couldn't reply. Losing Franklin's child tore a hole in her heart that she doubted would ever totally mend. In the blink of an eye, she'd lost what seemed like her entire reason for living. She sobbed uncontrollably for almost two hours, held tightly in her friend's arms. Finally, Ellie fell back against the pillows, totally exhausted.

"Luke left a few minutes ago, but I'm staying with you tonight. For now, I'll brew you a cup of tea." Maggie slipped out of the room and closed the door behind her.

Ellie sighed, wishing the bed would swallow her whole. Take her to a place where there was no death, no grief, and no hurt. How would she ever survive this? First Franklin and now their baby.

When Maggie returned with the cup of tea, Captain slipped through the open doorway and jumped onto the bed. He laid his head on Ellie's leg and his sad brown eyes met hers. Instead of scolding Captain as she normally would, Ellie reached over and patted the dog's head. Evidently, even the dog sensed her loss and demonstrated more understanding than she suspected would be forthcoming from her miserable husband.

What concerned her most was Jimmy George's reaction.

Had he realized he'd married her for nothing?

She recalled her conversation with Edward. *I just don't want you to die like my ma did.* What if the child was telling the truth?

Monday, June 9, 1890

Ellie clasped her heavy woolen shawl tighter around her shoulders and staggered down the hallway toward the kitchen to brew a pot of tea. Over a week had passed, and she finally felt strong enough to venture out of bed.

After Maggie's time at Ellie's side, she'd spread the word that Ellie Barkley had taken ill at the party, and she'd summoned Doc fearing it was her friend's appendix. But she'd assured everyone that Ellie suffered from a mild case of influenza and would soon be on her feet again. Bless Maggie's heart. No one would ever know her secret, destroyed by God and a little white lie.

Jimmy George complained about the ladies who dropped by throughout the past week to inquire how Ellie was holding up. Being neighborly and knowing she wouldn't feel up to cooking or baking, they'd shoved offerings of food through the open doorway, refusing to enter the house for fear of catching her influenza.

"You fooled all of them old biddies, didn't you?" he'd sneered.

As she entered the kitchen, Ellie was overcome by another bout of tears.

"Quit sniffling over losing the damn kid." Jimmy George's face reddened with anger and he pounded the kitchen table with his clenched fist, sending dirty plates and cups dancing across the surface. Fortunately, none crashed to the floor.

Ellie didn't recognize the man sitting in her kitchen. The usually impeccably-dressed sheriff of Spirit Creek wore wrinkled, dirty clothes, and it appeared he hadn't bathed or shaven in days. She could smell the liquor on his breath clear across the room. She wondered if Jimmy George had even been to the jailhouse in ages. Something was definitely wrong, and it was more than her losing Franklin's baby.

"If I hear one more word about how badly you feel, losing Smith's brat, I won't be responsible for my actions," he warned, seriously threatening her with his tone alone.

"I'm sorry, Jimmy George. It's just…it hurts so much." Ellie removed a lacy white handkerchief from the pocket of her calico dress. Her husband had punched her in the face twice yesterday when she refused to get out of bed, and even drying her tears pained her. She placed a shaking hand on her flat middle, now void of the growing life that had meant everything to her.

Foolishly, she'd hoped in time her husband would feel something for her and the baby. But he'd never shown her one iota of affection, and he'd never spoken a kind word for Edward, his own son. She doubted he had a soul. Marrying this monster was the worst mistake she'd made in her entire life.

"Married you for nothing! My brains must have been as addled as old Third's when I agreed to marry you." Jimmy George glared at her, fisting his hands. Ellie shrunk back against the far wall, remembering the pain of his fist striking her face. "Now I'm harnessed to a frumpy schoolteacher for the rest of my days; this marriage yoke around my neck feels like a damn noose."

"We'll…we'll get a divorce," suggested Ellie, grasping for a solution. She couldn't tolerate another moment of this. If he punched her again, she would surely shatter like a china doll. Even as scandalous as a divorce would be, it was certainly preferable to her husband's abuse.

"You want to scandalize the old ladies by getting a divorce?" Jimmy George sneered. "A divorce would probably cost a fortune. All a woman like you is good for is spending a man's money."

Ellie almost laughed in his face but caught herself. Spending *his* money? He hadn't given her enough funds for one person to live on, never mind a family of three. He never questioned how she paid the rent, clothed herself and Edward, put food on the table. And he never came home for meals, perhaps eating at the hotel before heading to the saloon. If it hadn't been for Franklin's money, she and Edward would have starved to death by now.

"I'm sorry," she whispered. What more could she say? What more could she do?

"You're going to be sorry all right," muttered Jimmy George, charging out the back door.

Ellie flopped onto a chair, dropped her head on her arms, and wept. Why didn't he understand? He'd stood at the altar willingly enough, agreed to their marital arrangement. She couldn't help losing the baby; she hadn't done it on purpose. And she was a wonderful, loving stepmother to Edward. Of that she was certain. None of it had ever been enough.

Ten minutes later, Ellie regained control of herself and a generous serving of guilt threatened to choke her. Every time she thought of Edward, she vowed to make the marriage work for her new stepson's sake. Fully prepared to offer yet another apology, she crossed the kitchen floor and soundlessly cracked open the back door.

Jimmy George sat perched on a stump half way across the back yard with his back to her. He was intent on stuffing something into a large saddlebag.

"Just because Edward's fond of her, I ain't smitten at all," complained Jimmy George, talking aloud to himself. "All the damn woman does is whine about what a wonderful man Franklin was. Bawls her head off over losing his brat. As if I care one whit about her or the damn kid."

Ellie sucked in her breath. As much as she wanted to, she couldn't turn away, couldn't close the door and put a stop to his hurtful words. For some reason, she needed to hear it all.

"Says she's so sorry." Jimmy George's high-pitched laughter sounded insane to her ears. "She's going to be sorry all right. Got rid of one wife. No reason why I can't get rid of another. Doing it shouldn't be a problem at all, if I think on it long enough."

Ellie's blood ran cold. She silently eased the back door shut, stumbled across the room, and collapsed onto a chair. Had she heard him correctly? Oh, Edward, were you telling the truth? What a fool she'd been! She took a deep breath, forcing herself to think rationally.

Was this mean-spirited Jimmy George truly the man she'd married?

The man she'd believed so kind-hearted, generous, and selfless in his initial actions toward her? True, Jimmy George had a temper, and he'd slapped her whenever she'd done something to annoy him. He'd even punched her in the face on a few occasions. At the time, she'd believed it was her fault.

But truly, had she deserved it?

In Jimmy George's opinion, she wasn't much of a homemaker. Was his first wife an exceptional homemaker and mother? Ellie had never been married before; she hadn't a clue what was considered a good wife or not. But she'd done her best.

Was her husband truly planning to kill her? Was her life in danger?

She needed to get a grip on herself. They'd been thrust into this marriage with no time to get to know each other, no time to learn each other's habits, likes and dislikes. No time to establish their roles within the marriage. They disagreed constantly. Did they just require more time to settle into married life? Doubtful.

She'd heard Jimmy George's threats with her own ears, but if she shared her suspicions with anyone, would they believe her? Or would she be the laughing stock of Spirit Creek?

Jimmy George suddenly charged into the kitchen, and her heart almost stopped.

"I'm leaving for Miles City," he announced, swinging his saddlebag over his shoulder.

"Whatever for?" she asked, and then instinctively her whole body stiffened. Would her curiosity result in more abuse?

"None of your damn business." Jimmy George clomped through the house in his boots, leaving a dirty trail behind him. He grabbed his gun belt and Stetson off the peg and then opened the front door, sending it crashing back against the wall.

She cautiously followed him outside, stood wringing her hands on the front step.

"I'll be back in three or four days," stated Jimmy George.

"We'll see you when you get home." Ellie slipped back into the house, closed the door, and heaved a sigh of relief. Had Jimmy George detected any insincerity in her send-off?

Insincerity?

She felt giddy with happiness.

She'd never properly mourned her lost baby. Jimmy George hadn't permitted it. Every time he'd discovered her crying he'd shout at her. *Stop that infernal sniffling. Don't you have work to do, woman*? Finally, she could grieve in peace.

As she watched from the hallway window, Jimmy George rode down the street heading north. She smiled, happy to be rid of him for a couple of days. She could grieve both Franklin and his baby now. She touched her swollen face. And she would formulate a plan. There must be some way to escape from this marriage.

CHAPTER 8

Every night after Robert Rutherford finished his supper at the hotel, he'd pay his bill and spend a few moments chatting with June Davidson, the establishment's owner. Excusing himself to partake of an evening walk around town, he'd exit the hotel with a wave and a promise to patronize the dining room again tomorrow.

While strolling up one street and down the other, he greeted folks and claimed to enjoy the fresh air, so pleasant compared to living in a crowded city like Boston. Everyone in Spirit Creek believed him. And why would they doubt the sincerity of such an upstanding citizen?

When dusk's last vestiges of light retired for the day and the town became cloaked in darkness, Robert silently stood sentinel beside a vacant house, observing Ellie and Jimmy George's home from across the street. This new nightly habit felt deranged, but he couldn't stop himself. He had to know the woman he loved was all right.

He'd heard she'd succumbed to a bout of influenza during the recent Carlyle anniversary party. She'd looked a little peaked that night, now that he thought about it. Funny though, he hadn't heard of anyone else contracting influenza.

He'd casually asked Doc about his recent caseload at church on Sunday, and Doc admitted things at the clinic had been fairly quiet of late. Children's scrapes and scratches during outdoor play, and a couple of births, he'd said. In fact, Doc was enjoying the respite from being so busy during the winter months when folks were more prone to ailments.

Word of Ellie's recent illness didn't make sense. Usually where there was one case of influenza, several followed as if marching to the same drummer. But what reason would there be for her to lie about it?

Sunday night, Robert left for home, deserting his sentinel post shortly after midnight. He needed at least some sleep to work the next day. He'd stumbled home in the dead of night and flopped into bed, cursing his lot in life. Again, he'd lost the woman he loved to another man.

On Monday for some reason, the idea of taking a walk during his lunch hour niggled his mind. Fifteen minutes later, he'd found himself hiding alongside the empty house. Suddenly, Jimmy George Barkley stormed out the house, resembling some drunken derelict Robert might have discovered living on the back streets of Boston. For a brief moment, his ne'er-do-well twin brother came to mind. Ellie followed her husband out and stood staring at him from just outside the front door.

She must have been ailing with influenza; he barely recognized her. She'd dropped a substantial amount of weight, and even from this distance he could tell her face was swollen. Robert stood dumbfounded, fury building in him. Had that bastard hit her in the face? He couldn't be certain without his spy glass, forgotten at home atop his desk. What on earth had possessed Ellie to marry that man?

"I'll be back in three or four days," stated Jimmy George.

Without a hint of emotion, Ellie simply said, "We'll see you when you get home." And then she slipped back into the house as her husband rode away.

More confused than ever, Robert returned to his office. He couldn't keep his mind on work the remainder of the day.

After supper at the hotel, Robert returned home. He'd heard the bastard say he'd be away for several days. With Barkley out of town, Robert hadn't a reason to spy on Ellie. She'd be safe in her husband's absence. Besides, he knew now that keeping watch from a distance hadn't kept Ellie from harm anyway. There must be something more he could do.

Alone with a glass of whiskey, he fought the urge to weep for his lost opportunity to be with the woman he loved. How had she slipped through his hands again? If Ellie had wanted a damn husband that badly, why hadn't she come to him? Her legal and financial advisor? He would have wed her in a heartbeat. And he'd certainly never lay a hand on her. Mind you, she had no way of knowing any of this. Fool that he was, he'd neglected to divulge his true feelings for her.

For the hundredth time he asked himself, why had Ellie married that poor excuse for a man?

Robert speculated that somehow Jimmy George had learned about the money Ellie inherited. That would explain why the reprehensible fellow whisked her off to a preacher so soon. She'd appeared beside herself with grief during the reading of Smith's will in his office. Barkley had taken advantage of her fragile state and swooped in. But if that was the case, why hadn't he spent any of Ellie's money? He'd paid the account on her behalf at the general store where a great number of household items were purchased, but nothing hinting at extravagance. None of this made sense.

Robert paced the room, his anger growing with every footfall. The fact that Barkley had never shown up at the bank demanding to withdraw any funds from Ellie's substantial accounts remained a mystery. Perhaps Robert was mistaken and Barkley hadn't known. Robert felt back at square one.

Even more perplexing, if Barkley had been abusive, why was Ellie still with him?

Robert had handled wife-beating cases in Boston, strictly on the low-down of course. Much too scandalous if the gossips got wind of such things. He couldn't understand such behavior in a man then, and he couldn't understand it now. A woman was such a precious gift in a man's life, she should be cherished and spoiled and loved through eternity.

Robert stared at his white-knuckled grasp on the whiskey glass. How dare the bastard abuse the woman he loved. He hurled the crystal at the brick fireplace and watched it shatter into a hundred pieces. Just like his heart had shattered when he realized he'd lost Ellie again.

Robert could kill that Barkley fellow with his bare hands!

* * *

Warner Jenkins couldn't recall the last time someone had addressed him as Warner. Not since growing up on the family farm in California where he'd broken every one of his ma's rules. Of course, every time he'd been caught, he'd done his penance—everything from peeling potatoes to mucking out horse stalls—and every time he'd promised his ma he'd do better. Ten years ago, shortly after he turned sixteen, he'd struck out on his own. He and his pa had never seen eye to eye on anything anyway, and his ma had eight other mouths to feed. The way he saw it, he'd done his family a favor.

He'd first sought employment on a neighbor's ranch. He got along with the other cowhands, but lacking in stature, he soon acquired his nickname. Shorty Jenkins worked hard, and he towed the line where the law was concerned. True, the occasional Saturday night of drinking and fisticuffs earned him accommodations as the guest of the local sheriff. But come Sunday morning, the sheriff would send him on his way with a hangover and a warning, *don't want to see your hide crossing my threshold again, son.*

Shorty dismounted and tied the stolen pinto to a nearby tree branch. Good horse, but as stubborn as Shorty himself. His partner rode up and dismounted beside him. Shorty grabbed the bottle of whiskey he'd found in the saddlebag and crept toward the edge to get a closer look from atop the butte. This waiting was killing him. He continued to ponder his past.

In no time wanderlust had struck, and he headed out for greener pastures. He found another job as a cowhand, but eventually boredom set in. Shorty packed up, hired on at a different place, made new acquaintances, and after a spell he moved on again. For several years, the pattern continued.

Shorty whipped his battered Stetson off his head, wiped his sweaty brow with a shirt sleeve, and slapped the hat back on his head. His partner shimmied up alongside him, joining in the waiting.

"Hurry the hell up already," he cursed, taking a long drink of the rotgut whiskey. Where had the man who owned the horse bought this stuff? It tasted like kerosene.

"Ya got that right," the man beside him replied.

Shorty couldn't recall when he'd signed on to rob that first bank. Probably on a Saturday night drinking spree, falling down drunk, and it sounded like a good idea at the time. In hindsight, bank robbing and train robbing were the stupidest decisions he'd ever made. Oh, he'd enjoyed the adrenaline rush during the actual bank robbing, and nothing got a fellow's heart racing like robbing a train. The stupid part involved getting caught and going to prison.

"See any sign of the bastard yet?" he inquired, sprawled on his belly overlooking a lush valley. Montana had its own beauty about it, but he preferred California. Deciding it best to avoid home, he intended to head out for Texas next.

"I reckon maybe he never left at first light like we was figurin' he would," answered Billy Bob Newberry, lying alongside Shorty. "Pass that bottle over."

Shorty complied.

Billy Bob had told him he'd run away from an orphanage at age thirteen. With the fellow's substantial size, Shorty could see how he'd passed for eighteen and landed himself that first job. A couple days after Shorty met the man he could understand why his new buddy had never succeeded at honest work, never kept a job for long. The fellow possessed a dandy of a temper which he claimed earned him his final pay and an escort off every ranch where he'd been employed. Finally, old Billy Bob had just given up.

"Well, he sure enough better hurry it up," complained Shorty. "Looks like rain's on the way, and I ain't fixin' on gettin' soaked."

Like himself, Billy Bob learned that a life of crime paid better than honest work. Of course, Billy Bob enjoyed being the boss, but Shorty was more of a just-get-along kinda fellow. Both of them loved the thrill of robbing a bank or a train, and they'd been self-employed on the other side of the law for several years together. Until they got caught.

"That sneaky, cheatin' piece of garbage had better not be considerin' a double cross. Turnin' us back over to the law." His accomplice spat chewing tobacco juice out of the side of his mouth, totally missing the fly he was aiming at. He cackled, "Can ya believe the fool got himself hired on as a deputy? Instead of Theodore James, he's callin' himself Jimmy George Barkley now."

"Wonder which, if either one of them, is his real name?"

"Don't rightly know, and could care less either way. But the man has himself a set of balls, I'll give him that." Billy Bob handed him the bottle.

"Sorta like puttin' the rooster in charge of the henhouse," added Shorty, giggling like a drunken whore. He took another swig of whiskey and passed the bottle again.

"Well, if he plans to double cross us or shows up without our money, he'll be taking his morning coffee with cream, sugar, and Satan!" His partner tipped the bottle back and then belched loudly.

"Ya ain't gettin' no argument here."

"I'm sick of sayin' the feller's name. Just want my share of the loot and then I'm headin' out for Mexico." Billy Bob passed the bottle to him. "I curse the day we met up with the no-good bastard. Been nothing but capital T trouble for us. *Robbing trains, that's where you'll find gold and cash,* he said. *Mining payrolls, railway payrolls, we'll be rolling in money*, he said. And like a couple damn fools, we believed him."

"And how did the bastard convince us to keep his name out of it so he could hide the spoils, while we go to prison?" Shorty shook his head. "It plumb boggles yer mind."

"Makin' us look like damn idiots is what he done," spat Billy Bob, glancing over at his cohort. "Where do you suppose he hid the loot all this time?"

"I don't double damn care, but he better have it with him today," he cursed. His eyes misted and he blinked furiously. "James or Barkley or whoever he is, said he'd send Ma some of my share. I wonder if she ever saw one dollar of that money."

"We sure as hell didn't see a penny of it yet." Billy Bob tossed aside the empty whiskey bottle.

"What are we going to do about that?" asked Shorty.

"Quiet," whispered Billy Bob. "Listen. There's a rider approaching. And he'd better be Jimmy George Barkley or Theodore James or whatever the hell his name is."

They shuffled backward from the edge of the butte the minute they recognized the rider. Safely out of range of detection, they stood and headed back to the stolen horses tied to a nearby cottonwood. The bedrolls were secured behind their saddles and the camping gear was stowed in their saddlebags. Both men mounted up and headed into the valley.

They rode in silence. No sense in warning the fellow. Billy Bob reined in his mount and Shorty stopped alongside him, hidden by a cluster of bushes. A few minutes later, Jimmy George Barkley rode within a few feet of their hiding place. The man was muttering to himself about his spineless wife, bawling all day long. Rattling his nerves.

Shorty swore under his breath. So old Jimmy George had gotten himself hitched while they were in prison as well. Damn him to hell anyway. Getting himself regular female attention, hot meals, clean socks, while Shorty and Billy Bob were rotting in a damn jail cell. Shorty hadn't gotten laid in months until they escaped prison a few weeks back. He hated Barkley more every minute.

Shorty rode out from behind the bush. "Well, how-do, Mr. Lawman. Imagine seeing you here?" he cackled.

Jimmy George reined in his horse, gaping. "Why, Shorty! Long time, no see."

Billy Bob rode into view. "Guess ya got our telegram. How ya been?" he asked, sarcasm evident.

"Well, boys, I've kept my nose clean and stashed our money in a nice safe place," claimed the would-be sheriff, smiling broadly.

"Then let's divvy it up," suggested Billy Bob.

Shorty chuckled. "Them plump saddlebags of yours seem stuffed pretty full. You got our money in there?"

"For the good of his health," observed Billy Bob. "He'd better have."

CHAPTER 9

Monday, June 16, 1890

"Good morning, Ellie," called Maggie Carlyle, crossing the back yard of the house she used to inhabit.

Ellie turned toward her visitor and cringed as she watched Maggie lift her skirts above her ankles to keep from soiling the hem. Maggie would notice the obvious neglect. Even in mid-June, the grass remained quite sparse compared to when Maggie lived here, recalled Ellie. She hadn't even planted flowers in the flowerboxes out front. Until a week ago, every waking moment since moving in had been spent cleaning the house, doing the laundry, picking up after her men, baking and cooking meals. She could only do what she could do, and Jimmy George hadn't been any help.

After the miscarriage, she hadn't felt up to doing much of anything, and since her husband left a week ago, she'd spent most days mourning her losses. She'd cooked for Edward, eating very little herself. And she dreaded her husband's return, fearing the abuse would resume the minute he walked back into the house.

She'd considered taking Edward and heading out for parts unknown to escape Jimmy George. But she hadn't the energy, extremely weak from having lost the baby so recently. And she hadn't come up with an alternate plan either. But one thing was certain, she wouldn't tolerate the abuse again.

"Good morning, Maggie." She tugged her sunbonnet lower and continued hanging laundry on the clothesline. Even a week later, the bruises hadn't faded much, although the swelling had gone down.

Ellie's heartbeat raced. The last thing she wanted was company, but Maggie was her best friend and she couldn't refuse to talk to her. Hopefully, she only intended to chat for a few minutes and be on her way.

"We missed you at church again yesterday. Has Jimmy George

returned from Miles City?" She advanced at a good clip.

"No, he hasn't."

Maggie halted at Ellie's side. "Have you heard from him? Received a telegraph?"

"No, and I don't imagine I will," she sighed, hanging a towel on the line. "He said he'd be away for four days. It's been seven now. I suppose he's been delayed with his business, whatever it was." Ellie bent over and grabbed a pair of Edward's trousers out of the laundry basket at her feet.

"My goodness, you're a busy beaver today."

As Ellie rose to her full height, Maggie grabbed Ellie's sunbonnet and tugged it back off her face. "That's better. Now I can see your eyes."

Ellie was too stunned to move.

Maggie gasped. "What happened?"

"Clumsy me." Ellie attempted a smile. "I tumbled down the back stairs over there. But I'll be fine. Nothing to be concerned about."

"Back stairs, my foot! Did Jimmy George do that to you before he left?"

"He wouldn't…it was just…" stammered Ellie. Her hands continued shaking, but somehow she managed to peg the trousers onto the clothesline. She glanced at her friend whose expression confirmed that she wasn't buying a word of it. "Just let it be, please."

Maggie frowned.

Ellie finished hanging the laundry on the clothesline. "Will you come in for a cup of tea?" she asked, feeling her face redden with embarrassment.

"I'd love a cup of tea," said Maggie, graciously accepting the invitation.

Ellie reluctantly removed her sunbonnet when they entered the house, and she sensed Maggie's eyes drilling into her while she filled the kettle and set it on the woodstove. Maggie sat in silence at the kitchen table while Ellie set out teacups, sugar and cream.

"The weather has been so lovely, the children enjoyed a picnic with the Morgan children yesterday," Maggie chatted animatedly.

Ellie carried the teapot to the table and lowered herself onto a chair. She considered confiding her suspicions that her husband had killed his first wife and he intended to kill her, too. Would Maggie believe the whole idea total foolishness?

"I'm sorry. I will not hold my tongue. I cannot believe Jimmy George could do such…" Maggie was interrupted in mid-sentence by a loud knock on the front door.

Ellie leapt out of her chair, grabbed the sunbonnet she'd tossed on the corner of the kitchen worktable, and fled down the hallway. She pulled the hat low on her face and quickly tied it beneath her chin before yanking the door open.

"Good morning, I was just heading out. May I help you with something?" Ellie stood, wringing her hands. Deputy Ernest Jones stood before her, his tin star pinned to his chest. The local lawman, now in charge with Jimmy George out of town, dragged his hat off his head and cleared his throat.

"Ma'am, would you permit me to step inside for a minute? I have a few questions for you."

"Heavens, where are my manners," responded Ellie, nervously. She stepped back out of the way. "Please do come in."

"Pretty home you have here, Mrs. Barkley," expressed Ernest as he stepped inside.

Ellie immediately realized her mistake. She should have left the fellow standing at the door while she answered his questions. She mentally kicked herself for her carelessness. What plausible reason could she offer for wearing her sunbonnet in the house? But if she removed it as reason dictated, the deputy would surely notice the bruises on her face.

Hang the consequences, she decided. Ellie removed her bonnet, set it down on the hallway table, and led her former student into the parlor.

"Please take a seat, Ernest," said Ellie, indicating the rocking chair while she lowered herself onto the sofa. Holding her head high, she met his eyes. "You mentioned some questions. Nothing too difficult I hope."

Maggie wandered into the parlor from the kitchen and the deputy leapt to his feet.

"Ernest has a few questions for me," explained Ellie, forcing herself to smile.

"Good morning, ma'am." The deputy nodded to Maggie, clasping his Stetson tightly.

If he'd noticed the cuts and bruises on Ellie's face—how could he not?—he withheld any mention of them. He took his seat again while Maggie settled beside Ellie.

"Have you heard from my husband? Is he in some sort of trouble?" Ellie held her breath. Nothing about Jimmy George Barkley would surprise her anymore. During the past couple of days, she'd been thinking about her husband. Any man who'd threaten to get rid of his wife, even in jest, was suspect in her books. And she wasn't the least bit certain his words had been in jest.

"Ma'am, I haven't heard a peep," he admitted and shrugged his shoulders. "I was going to ask if you'd been in contact with him. Word from someone returning from Miles City? A telegraph? Anything?"

"Nothing?" Ellie's brain couldn't quite grasp the concept. "I would have thought he'd inform you if he'd been delayed. I certainly haven't heard from him."

"He told me he'd be in Miles City for three or four days. To just hold the fort and he'd see me when he returned. I expected him back last Thursday at the latest. Haven't seen hide nor hair of him." The deputy leaned forward in the rocker. "I don't mind admitting, I'm getting a little concerned."

"I can hardly believe it. Are you certain he hasn't been in contact with anyone? What about Mayor Barker?" asked Maggie.

"No. Hasn't heard a word either."

"That's strange. You'd imagine he'd be in contact with his boss at the very least if he was going to be delayed indefinitely. What could have prevented his return?" Ellie attempted to muster up a concerned expression. Wasn't going to happen. She didn't rightly care if her husband ever showed his face in town again. At least she wasn't smiling like the cat that got the cream. Dozens of butterflies were dancing a joyful jig in her stomach, however.

"Barkley worked for several months in Miles City. I'll send Sheriff Sanders a telegram and inquire about Jimmy George." Ernest leapt off the rocker. "I assumed Jimmy George was heading to Miles City on business. It would make sense that he'd meet up with Sanders if that was the case."

"Jimmy George gave me the same impression. He made it clear the reason he was going to Miles City was none of my business, so I assumed it involved his work. He was always very tight-lipped about it."

"Ma'am, it's nothing personal. Just a requirement of the job. We can't discuss what happens in our line of work."

"That makes sense," agreed Ellie. "Mr. Rutherford's law work is the same. I imagine even Janie can't divulge anything she learns while on the job." Ellie suspected Janie was privy to her inheritance, but she'd never mentioned that fact to anyone. Such a thing would surely have gotten back to Ellie herself.

"Well, I'll let you return to whatever I interrupted. You'd mentioned heading out somewhere." Ernest twisted his hat in his hands.

"That was just a ruse…" Ellie touched her hand to her face and rose to her feet. Maggie followed.

Ernest appeared to be struggling with his conscience, deciding if he should say something or not.

Maggie smiled at him. "I think she should leave this house and divorce him, and I'll try to convince her to do just that."

Ellie gasped.

Ernest's jaw dropped.

"I suspect there's more to Jimmy George than we could ever imagine," speculated Maggie.

"Considering the secrecy surrounding his trip to Miles City… Do you suppose my husband was involved in something…illegal?" whispered

Ellie.

"Ma'am, I'm plumb stumped by this whole thing. But there's a reason for his delay. I've just got to set my mind on figuring it out." The deputy slapped his Stetson on his head and opened the front door. "Guess I'm in charge a while longer."

Ellie and Maggie led the way outside.

"Please let me know if you learn anything," requested Ellie.

"Will do." The deputy tugged on his brim, strode down the front steps, and mounted his horse. "I'll talk to you soon, ladies."

"Ernest, inform the mayor of the situation and request permission to deputize someone to help you keep the peace until this matter is resolved," suggested Maggie.

"I'll do that, ma'am. Gets a mite rowdy some Saturday nights." Ernest smiled and rode away.

Maggie and Ellie linked arms and stepped back inside, closing the door behind them. For several minutes, the women stood together in the silent entryway. Finally, Maggie whispered, "Well, at least for now I won't worry about any more bruises on your face."

Ellie met her eyes, struggled to maintain her composure but lost the battle. Smiling, she asked, "Is it a sin to feel such happiness that that despicable man is missing?"

"Truly sinful, Ellie," answered Maggie, smiling broadly.

"Perhaps we should ask for forgiveness." Ellie clasped her hands together.

"Perhaps we should just drink our tea before it gets any cooler." Maggie tugged on her friend's arm, heading toward the kitchen.

"A much better idea," agreed Ellie, following along. "But what do you suppose happened to him?"

* * *

At six o'clock the back door flew open, and Edward charged into the kitchen. "Am I late?" he gasped, winded from running home for supper.

"Right on time, sweetheart," answered Ellie.

"Robbie Wakeman showed me his set of toy soldiers he got for his last birthday. And then we started playing war, and I forgot about my chores, and…"

"It's all right, Edward. Wash up for supper. You can finish your chores while I wash the dishes." Ellie ruffled his hair.

Edward scrubbed his face and hands at the sink, toweled himself dry, and flopped onto a kitchen chair. "What's for supper, Mama?"

"Leftover stew from last night." Ellie sat on the chair opposite her son, and then leaned forward with her elbows on the table. "Before we eat, there's something I have to tell you."

"Is Pa back?" whispered Edward, his head swiveling on his shoulders. Did he expect a backhand or having his ears cuffed in greeting from his father?

Ellie had been dreading this all afternoon. She knew Edward would have questions, but he needed to be told. Having given her own imagination free rein, she'd conjured up the most horrendous scenarios in her mind. Where Jimmy George Barkley was concerned, anything could have happened. And he probably deserved it. As uncharitable as the thought was, that's how she felt.

"When your pa left here a few days ago, he headed for Miles City. He should have been home last Thursday, but nobody has heard from him since." Ellie opened her arms.

Edward threw himself into her embrace, clinging to her for several minutes, resting his cheek on her shoulder. Finally, he raised his head and met her eyes. "What happened to him, Mama?"

"I don't know, sweetheart. There's no shame in a boy crying for his missing pa."

"I cried when Ma died," confessed Edward, shifting from one foot to the other. "I cried a lot, and Pa said only sissy boys cry."

"Your pa was wrong, Edward. Very, very wrong." Ellie clasped his thin shoulders in her hands. "A little boy is entitled to cry if his ma dies. And if his pa goes missing, too."

"Pa was a bad man. He hurt Ma, and then he hurt you. I ain't crying." Edward straightened, stood tall. "And I ain't sorry he's gone. He was a terrible pa, not like Mr. Carlyle or Mr. Wakeman are good to their boys. I don't care if he ever comes home."

Ellie's heart almost broke, hearing her son's words. "Edward, your pa did the best he could, but his temper got the better of him sometimes. I'm sure he loves us in his own way. He's never laid a hand on you, Edward. He loves you, you're special to him."

"Pa don't love nobody," whispered Edward, shaking his head emphatically.

Ellie wouldn't argue with him. Her son hadn't believed a word of her attempt to justify Jimmy George's actions. Edward knew firsthand what his pa was capable of.

They both did.

"Sweetheart, I don't want you to worry about this. You're safe with me, and I'll be the best mother any little boy could wish for." Ellie hugged him to her bosom and kissed his cheek. "You may have become my son only because I married your pa, but believe me, I love you more than you'll ever know."

Edward smiled.

"Until your pa returns, we'll just be a family of two, you hear me?"

"I guess so," whispered Edward as he hugged her neck.

Ellie ached for her son because of the painful childhood he'd endured. No little boy should witness his ma's killing, if that had actually been the case. No little boy should find himself left at the mercy of a virtual stranger. But Ellie adored Edward—in truth, it frightened her how much she loved him—and she would protect him with the conviction of a mother bear with a cub until his father returned.

God had taken one child from her, the baby she'd conceived with Franklin. A child conceived in sin. Had God forgiven her? She prayed He would allow her to keep Edward, even if it was months before Jimmy George returned, or they learned something of his whereabouts.

CHAPTER 10

The next afternoon Ellie occupied her time with ironing yesterday's laundry while a pot of hearty soup simmered on the stove for their supper. If not frequently distracted by troubled thoughts about her missing husband, her life would have seemed almost normal.

Ellie hummed a tune she often sang with her school children. Classes were finished for summer and Edward spent most days outside playing with his friend, Robbie Wakeman. Captain stuck to him like a burr, and when her son wasn't at home, Ellie never worried about him. Well, not too much.

She folded the tablecloth she'd just ironed and considered resting with a glass of cold lemonade she'd made this morning when someone knocked on her front door.

Ellie whipped off her apron, patted her hair and strode down the hallway. She swung open the front door to discover Walter Barkley and his wife, Belle, standing there. Belle cradled their baby girl wrapped in a lacy white blanket in her arms.

"Good…good afternoon," she stammered.

"Same to you," said Walter, sounding somewhat chipper.

"Have you ever witnessed such a glorious summer day, Mrs. Barkley?" asked Belle and then she laughed. "There's an overabundance of Mrs. Barkleys in this town."

"Please call me Ellie," she offered, chuckling nervously.

"Then you must call me Belle."

"Don't even think of calling me Mr. Barkley, Ellie. I still answer mostly to Third."

"Hello, Third. Come in please," said Ellie, smiling. "Let me take your hats."

"Hold Matilda for a moment please, Ellie, while I remove my shawl and hat." Belle shoved the baby into her arms.

Ellie's eyes welled as time screeched to a halt. This should have been me, she thought, holding a baby in my arms. Why would God bestow such a precious gift on a former saloon whore but deny me equal pleasure and joy? The uncharitable thought seemed unfair, but she couldn't help it.

Third finished hanging up hats and shawls, and everyone wandered into the parlor. Ellie cautiously opened the top corner of the blanket. A pair of the brightest blue eyes she'd ever seen peered back at her. Ellie tried to remember when Maggie told her Agnes Armstrong delivered the little girl, must be four months ago now. The little sweetheart cooed and wiggled her arms. Before Ellie could pass her back to her mother, the baby's face crinkled and she set about howling like a banshee.

"Precious, whatever is the matter?" Belle scooped the baby out of Ellie's arms and settled her over one of her shoulders. "You can never tell if it's a burp or a changing or what is bothering her. Being mother to an infant is mostly a guessing game," teased Belle, patting the infant on the back.

"And you love every minute of it, Belle," laughed Third, kissing his wife's cheek.

An instant flash of jealousy swept over Ellie, seeing Third and Belle so happy, so comfortable with each other and little Matilda. "Please take a seat," she gestured at her visitors.

Belle settled herself on one end of the sofa and Ellie sat on the other.

Turning toward Ellie, Third inquired, "How are you doing?" Third shuffled toward the rocking chair. "I don't imagine there'll be a pay envelope coming your way now that my son has gone astray. Is there anything you need?"

"Nothing at all, Third," she answered, and then it dawned on her that Third wasn't apprised of the fortune she'd inherited from Franklin. No doubt he was extremely concerned as to how she intended to provide for herself and his grandson. "Mr. Smith left me enough money to manage on when he passed, even though we hadn't married yet. Don't worry, Edward and I will be fine."

"That's good. Puts my mind to rest." Third leaned closer, intently examining Ellie's face. "Did my son do that?"

Ellie's hand flew to her cheek where the partially-faded bruises gradually turning from purple to yellow evidenced her husband's abuse. She'd totally forgotten about them when she rushed to answer the knock at the door.

"Yes, I'm afraid he did. Jimmy George didn't have much of anything nice to say about me," admitted Ellie, feeling her face redden. "I disappointed him as a cook and as a homemaker. I starched his shirts when I shouldn't have. I'd burst into tears whenever I thought of…losing my fiancé. He couldn't tolerate my crying most of all."

"Well, I'd like to apologize on my son's behalf. He had no call for hitting a woman. I don't imagine you're of a mind to forgive him and I can't say that I blame you." Third sighed heavily. "I suppose I should blame myself for his behavior. Disappearing like I did when he was only ten years old. He grew up without a father's influence, although he claims a preacher and his wife raised him. Doubt that's anywhere near the truth, considering…"

Ellie stared at her hands resting in her lap. She couldn't think of a suitable response to Third's self-criticism. Especially being that she agreed with him to a degree. Whoever raised Jimmy George did a terrible job of it!

"Well, I can assure you he never hit his son." Ellie wanted to offer Third some comfort. She wouldn't mention her suspicions that her husband might well have killed his first wife. "Edward is my only concern. Even if Jimmy George returns, I'll never let him hurt my son."

Suddenly, Ellie recalled the refreshments she'd prepared in the kitchen. "Heavens, where are my manners? Does anyone care for a glass of cold lemonade?"

"I do, I do," answered Edward, charging into the parlor, Captain bounding along on his heels.

"Then why don't we go fetch it together, young man," suggested Third, rising from his chair.

"There are two full jars down in the root cellar. You show him, Edward. And remember to wash your hands, young man," instructed Ellie.

Third glanced at Ellie and then wrapped his arm around Edward's shoulder. "We'll let the womenfolk get better acquainted while you tell me about yourself, grandson."

Edward stared up at the older man, wide-eyed. "*I'm* your grandson?"

"You surely are," answered Third, his eyes misting. "Your pa never encouraged our meeting, but I'm delighted to finally come visit you, young feller."

"Mama! I've got a grandpa!" Edward startled the baby, and Matilda started crying.

"He's a very nice man, Edward. Go visit with your grandpa." Ellie had to raise her voice to be heard above Matilda.

"Grandpa, does that baby get to hollerin' like that a lot?" Edward frowned, accompanying Third out of the parlor, heading toward the kitchen.

"Her name's Matilda, son. I believe she's destined for a career as an opera singer." Third tousled his grandson's hair while he followed him out of the room.

Ellie's heart melted at the sight of the two of them together. Why would Jimmy George not encourage a relationship between his son and the boy's grandfather? Her husband was a total mystery to her. Being raised an orphan, she'd have given her eye teeth for a grandparent at Edward's age!

Belle tossed the white blanket over her shoulder and nursed her daughter. "Well, the two of them are hitting it off, aren't they?"

Ellie was momentarily shocked. Should she show Belle to one of the bedrooms? Her visitor appeared quite content right where she was, without a hint of embarrassment. Ellie decided to leave the matter be.

"I'm happy Edward will know his grandfather," sighed Ellie. "I was raised in an orphanage, haven't any kin at all."

"Third is such a nice man, certainly rescued me." Belle blanched. "I know you thought Jimmy George was coming to your rescue, too. I'm so sorry things turned out so badly."

"I don't…" Ellie's face warmed. How did she know?

Belle leaned forward and whispered. "Maggie told me about you being with child, and about you losing the baby the night of their party, and then about Jimmy George's abuse. Maggie and I tell each other *everything*. But I'll go to my grave with your secrets, Ellie. I swear I will. I'll never breathe a word of it, I promise, not even to Third."

Ellie experienced a brief moment of jealousy. She'd never shared a close friendship with any woman except Maggie, and now Belle and Maggie obviously had forged a similar closeness.

"Maggie speaks highly of you. I hope we become friends, too." Ellie didn't add, since my son will probably be living with you. Third hadn't specified the purpose of the unexpected visit but she had her suspicions.

Ellie felt comforted, seeing Belle with little Matilda. Obviously, Belle was an excellent mother. Edward would be in good hands, in a loving home with two wonderful parents—she didn't believe for a second that Third was anything like Jimmy George—and her son would thrive while living on the ranch. Ellie smiled, wondering if Third would consider adopting her, too. If Jimmy George did show up some time down the road, she prayed Third would insist that the boy stayed on the ranch. Ellie would know he was safe, and if she took Maggie's advice, Ellie might even be divorced from the monster if the man stayed missing.

"Of course we'll be friends. And you're right. Maggie is an exceptionally caring soul. She's accepted me as a friend, welcomed me into the Diamond C family." Belle laid a sleepy Matilda down beside her. With the nursing complete, Belle adjusted her clothing and buttoned her dress.

"Here's the lemonade, ladies," whispered Third, carrying a large tray of glasses at an odd angle. Ellie leapt out of her chair to assist him.

"Grandpa let me pour the lemonade, Mama," whispered Edward, following closely behind and following his grandpa's example and whispering so as not to disturb the sleeping baby.

"Got most of it into the glasses, too," added Third, beaming proudly.

Everyone enjoyed the cool drink in silence. After a few minutes, Third cleared his throat.

"Ellie, I figure you know the reason why we're here," he began in a soft voice. Third leaned over and tousled his grandson's hair.

Ellie swallowed, hard.

Edward sat cross-legged on the floor beside Third's chair. His dog flopped down beside him. While her son sipped his lemonade, he reached over and threw his arm over Captain's back. Ellie's eyes misted, knowing Edward was blissfully unaware of the turmoil surrounding his future. Today's decisions would influence the rest of his life. But Ellie would accept the best decision for Edward. Even if that meant she would lose him forever.

"I don't expect you to consider me Edward's family…" began Ellie.

Third silenced her with a wave of his hand. "Let me finish. Since we've both recently entered the boy's life—he just discovered I'm his grandpa a few minutes ago and he's only been here with you for a short time—we'd best ask Edward who he wants to live with. At least until his pa returns."

Ellie hadn't expected this turn of events. Was there still hope? Would Edward choose her, having lived under the same roof with his new mother? Or his grandfather who was no better than a stranger?

"Edward, climb up on my lap, son," Third patted his knee.

Edward scampered onto his grandpa's lap and peeked up at him. "Am I in trouble?" he whispered.

"Heaven's no, boy. You're no more in trouble than I'm a bullfrog." Third and Edward shared a laugh.

Ellie and Belle chuckled, and Ellie felt herself relax a little.

"Since your pa's gone missing, the lawyer feller in town insisted we decide where you should live. But I believe it should be your decision, Edward. Where would you be most happy?" Third patted down his grandson's rooster tail. "Now I reckon you've got yourself two choices. The first option is move in with Belle and me in our little house at the Diamond C Ranch where I work. There are horses to ride, and your friend Sam to play with every day."

"That sounds like fun." Edward tilted his head.

"Option number two, you remain here with your new ma. She's been wonderful, a perfect mother. Now there's no time for thinking on this. We gotta inform that lawyer feller what's been decided. Take a minute, and then tell me your decision."

From the corner of her eye, Ellie noticed Matilda squirming in her blanket and beginning to fuss. Belle scooped up the baby and rocked her back to sleep. All eyes focused on Edward. Ellie could visualize the cogs turning in his small head as he contemplated his choices.

Ellie prayed Edward would choose her, but she couldn't compete with a proper family, and a ranch filled with horses and Sam. She just hoped Captain would be allowed to accompany her son to his new home. She would pack up Edward's clothes and toys and the dog's old blanket and dishes for his food and water.

She'd loved being a mother, even a stepmother, for the brief time she'd lived with the child. And the affectionate and lovable little boy was increasingly well-behaved since order had returned to his life again. Edward's presence in her life had softened the pain of losing her baby, and she would miss the charming child more than words could say.

"Grandpa," said Edward, meeting the older man's eyes.

"Yes, son."

Edward placed his chubby hands on his grandpa's ruddy weathered cheeks. "I decided," he whispered, nodding his head.

"Well, I'm in favor of whatever you decide. You're more than welcome at the ranch. But if you choose to live in town with your new ma, you can still visit the ranch and learn to ride horses and play with Sam."

"I never had much of a family before. Pa was away most of the time, and when he finally came home, he just argued with Ma and yelled at me until he left again." Edward wasn't smiling when he peeked over at his stepmother.

This was it, thought Ellie. Edward will choose to live at the ranch with Third and Belle and Matilda. He'll choose a whole houseful of folks, a family. With no way to compete with that and resigned to the inevitable, Ellie clambered out of the chair and headed toward her son's bedroom at the end of the hallway, intent on packing his belongings.

"I hope you aren't mad at me, Grandpa, but I'd like to stay here with Mama."

Ellie whipped around and gaped at her son.

Edward rubbed his nose. "Mama will be all alone if I take Captain and we go live on the ranch. She's a real good mother, Grandpa. I love her a lot. All the time, not just when she bakes cookies. So, I'm going to stay right here."

Ellie raced across the room and scooped her son up in her arms. "Thank you, thank you, thank you for choosing me, Edward. I couldn't love you more if you were my own son. I promise to love you forever, and I'll take wonderful care of you."

"Hotcakes!" Third slapped his knee. "I was hoping you'd choose your ma."

"You've made a wise choice, for a little boy," added Belle, smiling. "Our house is on the small side, but we surely would have welcomed you anyway. But I can tell that your ma loves you a lot."

"You're both welcome at the ranch anytime." Third ruffled his grandson's hair. "And we'll drop by and say hello whenever we're in town."

"Thank you, Third. You folks will always be welcome here, too." Ellie swiped at the tears pouring down her cheeks.

"Mama, why are you crying?" asked Edward, knitting his brow. "Aren't you happy?"

"I am, sweetheart. I couldn't be happier." She squeezed him tightly.

Third smiled. "Edward, it's a female thing. Don't try figuring it out. I'm pushing sixty and I still don't understand that crying because we're happy stuff."

Fifteen minutes later, Ellie and Edward waved from the top step until Third's buggy disappeared from sight. They wandered back inside.

"Help me tidy up, Edward," said Ellie, collecting the empty glasses.

Edward placed the glasses on the kitchen table and opened the back door for Captain to go outside.

"Sweetheart, why did you choose me?" asked Ellie, unreasonably curious why Edward would do such a thing, but grateful beyond words. "You could have lived on a big ranch, and rode horses, and played with Sam every day. Why would you give all that up?"

"I didn't want you to be lonely." Edward sighed. "I know Pa is gone for now, but what if he comes back and hurts you. Mr. Waverly at the general store said I was the man of the house until Pa returns. And I guess that means I got to stay here with you."

"Edward, you're not responsible for me." Ellie hugged her son. "It's not too late for you to change your mind. If you'd rather live at the ranch with your grandpa…"

"No!" Edward's eyes widened. "Don't make me go live with that baby. Grandpa and Belle seem pretty fond of her, but she's too loud."

Ellie threw back her head and laughed. So, Edward wasn't fond of babies. Maybe just the two of them were meant to be together after all.

"I want to stay here with you, Mama. Captain will bark if anybody comes around, and I'll be the man of the house. You're a real good cook, and you clean stuff and look after me." His eyes implored her to agree with him.

"Edward, the two of us will just settle in and become our own family." Ellie decided, for now, she'd concentrate all of her love and attention on Edward. If Jimmy George suddenly dropped back into their lives she'd deal with him then. Meantime, she'd block him from her mind.

"You're the bestest mama in the whole world, and I don't need no mean pa." Edward hugged her neck, and then skipped outside, Captain waiting for him on the top step.

Her son's kind words would go a long way toward completely

healing her heart. Ellie missed Franklin and the baby she'd lost a little less every day, although she'd love them forever. Edward gave her life purpose, and she looked forward to making a home for them. The past couple weeks when it had just been the two of them had been heaven.

"I'm going to be truly happy," she vowed. Mr. Rutherford would handle all her financial matters and arrange a divorce.

But there remained one sore spot in her life. She'd been lying awake until the wee hours of the morning, plagued by her fears. Every day she completed her household chores, constantly on pins and needles. Worrying. Would today be the day Jimmy George walked through the door? First thing every morning and last thing every night and a hundred times in between, she asked herself, would the lawmen ever discover the whereabouts of Jimmy George Barkley?

CHAPTER 11

Monday, June 23, 1890

"I'm so happy you dropped by this morning, Maggie. I've really been at loose ends," confessed Ellie, pouring tea into china cups at her kitchen table. Jimmy George remained missing, but Edward and she had settled into some semblance of routine. She loved having her son home every day during the summer. Better still, she loved days when her friend arrived for a visit. For a short time, at least, she wasn't constantly wary, watching the door.

"Have you heard anything from Deputy Jones or Sheriff Sanders?" asked Maggie, leaning forward in her chair.

"Not a word."

"Don't you want this whole business behind you?" Maggie reached for her friend's hand.

"Of course I do!"

"You should arrange for a divorce, and Mr. Rutherford would handle everything for you. At least, please promise me you'll meet with him and discuss the matter. If it's money holding you back, Luke and I will gladly pay the cost."

"I need to confide in you about something." Ellie met her friend's eyes. "Franklin left me financially set for life. I'm talking a fortune."

Maggie's mouth dropped open. Ellie had never seen her friend speechless before.

"Apparently, his deceased parents were quite wealthy. Anyway, I'd like nothing more than to dedicate my life to Edward's upbringing right here in Spirit Creek." Ellie paused to sip her tea. "I've toyed with the idea of a divorce. But what if the law rules in Third's favor? What if I'm forced to hand Edward over to his grandfather, a blood relation? What if the courts decide I no longer have a claim to my husband's son? I'm more frightened of losing Edward than I ever was of facing Jimmy George's fisted hand."

"Third realized you're the best option for that boy." Maggie touched Ellie's arm. "I doubt a divorce would change his opinion. And he'll totally understand the necessity."

Ellie smiled at her. "Yes. Third even apologized for the poor excuse of a man his son had become. And I'm so thankful he allowed Edward to remain with me. But after the divorce, if he threatened to take Edward, I'd leave town with the boy."

"No! I would miss you too much. And running away wouldn't be the answer," insisted Maggie.

"It appears to be working for Jimmy George!" Ellie immediately regretted her words. "I'm sorry, that wasn't called for."

"Your nerves are frazzled, you're still in mourning. I understand."

"Edward has become my reason for living. I can't believe how far he's come when I recall the antics on his first day at school. I could have throttled him when I discovered that frog hidden in my desk. I've never come closer to heart failure." Ellie could laugh now at the memory.

"You're the reason he's a changed child. He needed a mother like you," replied Maggie.

Ellie smiled. "If someone had told me that unruly little boy would become the most important person in my life someday, I'd never have believed it."

Maggie straightened in her chair and sipped her tea. "So you'll drop by the law office and discuss all this with Mr. Rutherford?"

Ellie grimaced.

"Please promise," urged Maggie.

"All right. I'll meet with Robert and discuss my options. But I'm not promising anything. If a divorce will jeopardize my relationship with Edward in any way, I won't go through with it. I couldn't," vowed Ellie.

"Fair enough." Maggie finished her tea. "No time like the present. Go change your dress. I'll go with you."

Ellie opened her mouth to protest but realized it was pointless. "Don't worry. I'll go alone, but thank you for offering." She headed toward her bedroom.

"If you need someone to talk to later, I'll be in town all afternoon. You'll find me at the church, helping plan the summer picnic."

"Thank you, but I'll be fine," she called. As she tugged her housedress over her head and tossed the garment on a high-backed chair, she heard the front door close behind her friend.

* * *

"I cannot believe I'm doing this." Head held high, Ellie walked with purpose toward Mr. Rutherford's office. She wore a stylish blue silk dress, the same color as her eyes, with a pretty matching hat and her new fancy boots. The outfit had cost a fortune but Elizabeth Waverly talked her into it. Ellie certainly could afford it and with all that she'd been through these past few months, she considered herself more than deserving.

One of her problems was demonstrating sufficient distress over her missing husband. Of course, contemplating a divorce might excuse her lack of concern. Although a hateful man, Jimmy George had rescued her when her reputation needed saving. She'd paid dearly for the foolish decision to marry a stranger to save her reputation. But in spite of the pain and suffering she'd endured, she had no regrets. Edward had walked into her life.

Which led to problem number two. She truly hoped the law would award her sole custody to raise Edward despite the fact they shared no blood ties, if a divorce was granted. She could prove herself financially capable of raising the boy. Emotionally, she couldn't love him more if he were her own flesh and blood.

But was all that enough?

"Mrs. Barkley, where are you off to in such a rush?" asked a young female voice. Ellie's head jerked up, and she found herself eye to eye with Sadie Peterman.

Banker Peterman's only daughter, a spoiled brat and graduate of a prestigious finishing school back East, had set her sights on landing a suitable husband. Since a badger possessed a more agreeable personality, so far her objective had proven rather difficult.

"Good morning, Miss Peterman," said Ellie, ignoring the posed question, her destination none of the snooty girl's business.

"You are still Mrs. Barkley, are you not? My heavens, you go through fiancés and husbands so quickly, it's a pure challenge keeping track of them all." Miss Peterman smiled sweetly.

"My husband is missing, but he is still my husband." Ellie couldn't believe the hurtful words that spewed from Sadie's lips. Refusing to dignify the mean-spirited girl's comment with further response, she attempted to walk around her.

Sadie grasped her arm.

"I have important business to attend to at the law office," spat Ellie, yanking her arm free. "Please allow me to pass."

"Do give my best to Mr. Rutherford. Such a fine gentleman and a very good friend of the family. Comes to supper twice a week depending on his work."

Ellie experienced a brief flash of jealousy, but it quickly passed. She blushed, feeling like a fool. Why should she care where Mr. Rutherford took his meals?

Sadie Peterman leaned closer. "Papa's given Robert permission to court me. Robert and I are quite well-suited, of course. Why, I cannot think of a better match for either of us in this unpleasant little town." Sadie brightened. "Perhaps I should convince Robert to return home to Boston once we're married."

Ellie gaped. Surely someone had warned Robert about the banker's scheming daughter. Sadie set her sights on new husband material every other month. Or as soon as the target in question wised up to her plans and dumped her on her conniving little bustle. Why on earth would a kind, thoughtful gentleman like Robert Rutherford be courting the likes of Sadie Peterman? Well, it was none of her business.

"Good luck with that," muttered Ellie, as she brushed past Sadie.

"Thank you for your kind wishes, Mrs. Barkley."

Sadie had failed to detect the sarcasm in Ellie's voice. Poor Mr. Rutherford has no idea what he'd gotten himself into, she thought.

* * *

"I do hope you haven't been kept waiting, Mrs. Barkley." Mr. Rutherford rushed into his office carrying several files under his arm, which he deposited on his desk. He enthusiastically shook hands with Ellie, holding them in his for an embarrassing length of time.

"I've…only…just arrived," stammered Ellie, fearing her arm would be dislocated from its socket with his zealous handshake. He'd asked that she call him Robert, but considering their business ties, she mostly considered him Mr. Rutherford.

When the flustered gentleman apparently realized he hadn't removed his hat, he released her hand and placed his bowler on the top peg of the coat tree. He retraced his steps to his desk and seated himself. He stared at her with such intensity she felt herself blush clear to her hairline. One glimpse of those eyes and all intelligent thought escaped her brain.

"Wonderful." He searched his desktop for something.

"I apologize for dropping by without arranging a…" she began.

He beamed. "You're welcome to pop in any time. No need for an appointment."

Ellie studied him for a moment. He wasn't as handsome as Franklin by any stretch of the imagination, but he more than made up for his minor physical shortcomings with his gentle nature and kind heart. Sadie Peterman hooked a prize catch, but only time would tell if she could land him.

"May I offer you some tea or a cold drink?" Mr. Rutherford wiped his hands on his trousers and took a deep breath.

Ellie reached for the cup and saucer she'd set on the corner of his desk. "I have a cup of tea, thank you. Miss Jones has seen to my every need." Ellie sipped her tea and silently questioned his discomfort. The poor man appeared as flustered as a school boy. Whatever would cause him to be so nervous around her?

"Is there anything I can get for you, Mr. Rutherford?" inquired Janie Jones, standing in the doorway.

"Nothing for me, thank you."

Miss Jones slid the pocket doors closed.

"May we get started, please? I've left *my son* with Elizabeth Waverly, and I assured her I wouldn't be long." Ellie hoped that her emphasis on the words would stick in the lawyer's mind.

Since her husband's disappearance, she'd caught herself shamelessly beaming with happiness on several occasions. No more arguing, no more abuse, no more living in fear. At least, none of it as long as Jimmy George stayed away until a divorce could be arranged. But Mr. Rutherford would be purely scandalized if he suspected how happy she was. More importantly, she must impress upon him the importance of keeping her son. If she lost Edward, she couldn't go on.

* * *

Robert smiled at Ellie, leaned forward and rested his arms on his desk. "How can I be of service?"

Ellie straightened in the chair and took a deep breath. "As you've heard no doubt, my husband went missing on the 9th of June. No one has heard a word from him, nor has he been spotted anywhere. It appears he's fallen off the earth."

"Actually I've been in contact with a lawman in Miles City regarding Jimmy George Barkley."

Ellie gasped. "You have?"

Robert didn't mention that he'd kept his eyes on the local sheriff since the day Ellie had suddenly wed the fellow. Apparently, he'd never learned of her substantial wealth. The only withdrawals at the bank since their marriage were his own, in the capacity of her financial manager, to settle her accounts at the general store. And Robert was duly impressed with her penchant for frugal spending; Ellie was definitely not wasteful or impulsive.

"Did Sheriff Sanders contact you?" ventured Ellie. "I've heard Luke Carlyle mention his name on a couple of occasions."

"Actually, yes. Sheriff Sanders and two other fellows have provided proof that there is more to Mr. Barkley than meets the eye. About a month before his disappearance, two bank robbers reportedly escaped prison in

California, and the authorities suspect they've been headed our way." Robert observed Ellie; her face paled with each new disclosure. "Mrs. Barkley, do you require a minute to composure yourself?"

"No, please continue." Ellie waved off his concern and met his eyes.

"No one reported seeing these bank robbers in Miles City, but that doesn't mean they weren't somewhere nearby."

"How does this relate to Jimmy George?" inquired Ellie.

"Sheriff Sanders contacted the local banks to see if your husband had withdrawn funds shortly before or immediately following his disappearance. The bank managers reported that he hadn't. But the Miles City manager informed the sheriff that your husband holds substantial funds on deposit in bank accounts in Spirit Creek, in Miles City, and in San Francisco. Sanders checked and none of these monies have been touched." Robert watched for her reaction. If he owned a ranch, he wouldn't hesitate to wager it, betting that Ellie had no idea of the money's existence.

"I'm absolutely floored by this. My husband worked as a deputy and then as a sheriff for only a few weeks. Jimmy George told me he was raised alone by his mother, and then by an impoverished preacher and his wife. How did he acquire so much money?"

"An excellent question, Mrs. Barkley." Robert smiled, his suspicions confirmed. Ellie was completely unaware of her husband's past doings. "Several lawmen asked themselves the same question. And they initiated an inquiry into Mr. Barkley's past."

"Oh, my." Ellie set her teacup on the corner of his desk.

"Are you certain you want to hear more?" asked Robert.

Ellie steeled herself; Robert witnessed the change in her. "Mr. Barkley wasn't the man I believed him to be when I married him. He turned mean-spirited and…and…"

"Abusive," finished Robert. The second he uttered the word, he could see the pain in her eyes. "Mr. Barkley's behavior in no way reflects upon you, Mrs. Barkley. You were obviously no match for his size and strength. But you should have reported the man to Mayor Barker. Randy hired Jimmy George, and I would hope he'd have incarcerated Barkley for what he'd done to you."

"I was so ashamed…" Ellie fought to control her feelings. "I consider this marriage an unfortunate spell of temporary insanity. In fact, I arrived here intending to enquire about a divorce."

Robert reared back in his chair. Goodness, he hadn't expected that to be the reason for her sudden appearance in his office. His heart sang, however. If she acquired a divorce, he'd start courting her immediately. He wouldn't allow her to slip through his fingers again!

He calmed his beating heart. Divorces took time. Sometimes as long as a year to complete. If nothing else, he could be a very patient man.

"Why abuse against women is tolerated by society..." Robert shook his head.

"It will certainly never be tolerated again by me. I've had my fill of men!" insisted Ellie.

Robert's heart almost stopped with the force of her statement. How would he ever win her for himself if she'd sworn off men? Could he convince her to make him the exception once she divorced? Would she someday reciprocate the attraction he felt for her?

He'd never known a stronger woman. Ellie fought admirably to overcome the recent adversity in her life: losing her fiancé, suffering her husband's abuse, dealing with his disappearance, being left to raise another woman's child. Knowing Ellie's caring nature, she'd welcomed the latter, most likely.

But, she was financially set for life. Robert grimaced with the realization that Ellie Barkley didn't *need* him, or any man. Somehow he must convince her that she *wanted* him.

"Where was I?" Robert pretended to search for his place in the document on his desk, stalling for time to regain control of himself. "Ah, yes, we were discussing how Mr. Barkley acquired his small fortune."

"Please continue." Ellie slid forward in her chair.

"About a year ago, a string of bank robberies and train robberies occurred around the San Francisco area and several points north. The two prison escapees were the only culprits caught and proven guilty. The authorities suspected Jimmy George Barkley, known then as Theodore James, was involved with these other two fellows, but there was no evidence to hold him nor would the other two testify against him. Once released, he simply disappeared. None of the cash or other stolen goods were ever recovered."

"That would explain where Jimmy George got the money!"

"Not conclusively, Ellie. I didn't inquire if your name had been added to these accounts. But if that's the case, I would consider it prudent if you didn't spend any of those funds." Robert crossed his arms and leaned back in the chair.

"I couldn't touch a penny! You and I both know that money was ill-gotten." Ellie waved off the notion. "And I certainly have no need of it."

"The robbery investigation has been reopened in light of the authorities' discoveries: Mr. Barkley's identity, his bank accounts, and his subsequent disappearance," he explained.

Robert beamed with pride at the woman seated before him, the woman he loved so dearly. Honesty and integrity oozed from every pore in her body. His client meant it when she vowed to never touch that money, and he couldn't be more pleased. If he searched the earth for eternity, he'd never find himself a more perfect wife.

"Do you believe he's guilty?" asked Ellie, twisting her handkerchief in her hands.

"I have my theories." Robert met her eyes. "And the Miles City lawmen have similar ideas."

"Tell me, please," pleaded Ellie.

"I don't think…" he began.

"I promise. I'll never breathe a word of it," she whispered.

CHAPTER 12

Robert searched Ellie's eyes that spoke volumes: the pain, the suffering, the loss of faith in mankind. She was grasping for a small thread of understanding, but if anyone learned that he'd divulged details of an ongoing investigation, he'd be ruined. He couldn't deny her, even if it meant he might never practice law again. But she had sworn to never breathe a word of it.

He believed her.

He trusted her.

He loved her with every fiber of his being.

"You didn't hear this from me," whispered Robert. "I could lose everything."

"Hear what?" she asked innocently and winked at him.

Robert laughed, feeling himself blush at her boldness. He could see himself sitting across from her at the breakfast table every morning. Teasing her about her upcoming day. Loving her into the wee hours every night. Relishing every moment of their lives together.

"The lawmen believe Jimmy George kept all the money from the robberies for himself, which explains the bank accounts. After your husband's partners escaped from prison, the lawmen believe the three of them—the two robbers and Jimmy George—arranged to meet outside Miles City and divide the spoils."

Ellie's eyes lit up. "I saw Jimmy George stuffing something into a large saddlebag just before he rode out."

"Did you see what it was? Could it have been large sums of money?"

"I didn't see, no. It could have been anything," admitted Ellie.

Robert leaned closer. "One theory held by the lawmen…they believe your husband showed up empty-handed, intending to kill the other two robbers."

Ellie gulped and whispered, "Kill them?"

"Judging by his violent nature, even toward women, anything is possible," speculated Robert. The thought of the woman he loved being married to this terrible person sent a shiver of dread up his spine. What if the bastard returned? What if there was no one but Ellie at home? What if he…?

"Or he high-tailed it back to California with them, and they intend to withdraw the money later."

Ellie's words drew him out of his dark thoughts. "Or the escaped bank robbers suspected something was amiss and killed your husband instead." Robert voiced his wishful thinking aloud.

Ellie paled and her hand flew to her mouth.

Robert immediately regretted his bluntness.

She speculated, "These men sound like desperate outlaws. I can't believe Jimmy George fooled me so completely."

Robert chuckled. "Fooled you? Sheriff Sanders hired Jimmy George to work as a deputy. How do you think he feels?"

Ellie smiled and then sobered. "The poor fellow is probably doubting his instincts, having been deceived by such a despicable person."

"You don't know the half of it." Robert grimaced. Damn, he never intended to tell her about the first wife. How could he be so careless?

"Please tell me."

Robert met her eyes and his resolve evaporated. Ellie completely held his heart hostage, although she wasn't aware of her powers over him. There was nothing he could refuse her. "Again, you did *not* hear this from me."

"Hear what?" she repeated, her expression as innocent as before.

"There were questions surrounding his first wife's death," began Robert. "Her body was covered in bruises and her jaw was broken. The doctor's report stated that the first Mrs. Barkley had taken a bad fall off her horse an hour before she'd died. The doctor ruled that she'd died of a high fever."

"But folks questioned it?"

"None of Mrs. Barkley's friends recalled her ever riding a horse; she was terrified of them. I suspect the doctor was paid off by Mr. Barkley's substantial cache of ill-gotten gains," he whispered. "Of course, there's no way to prove any of this. The Miles City doctor passed away recently from consumption."

"That's unfortunate."

"I doubt even Jimmy George could arrange for someone to die of consumption. The lawmen believe the doctor died as a natural result of the disease. No suspicion surrounded his passing."

* * *

"Makes sense," agreed Ellie. "But there's a more pressing matter that concerns me. Another reason I'm here besides wanting a divorce. What about my son? Will the law allow me to keep Edward?" Ellie held her breath while she waited to hear what the lawyer had to say.

"Right, the divorce. And you want to retain custody of Edward."

Ellie nodded. "I met recently with Edward's grandfather, Walter Barkley. He's known as Third and he's Edward's only living blood relative, other than his dad. Third agreed that Edward should remain with me, and we've agreed to visit each other as often as possible. The meeting and settling of the arrangement was quite cordial."

Robert smiled. "Glad to hear it. Edward couldn't ask for a better mother."

"Thank…you," stammered Ellie, a little startled. How would Mr. Rutherford know what kind of mother she was? Was he investigating her, as well as her husband? Suddenly, her brave façade escaped her and she rose from her chair. She couldn't do it. Not right now, at least. "I'd best be fetching my son from the general store. He'll eat Elizabeth out of candy if I don't get him home soon."

"If I could make a suggestion?"

"All right," said Ellie.

"Before pursuing a divorce, you should legally adopt Edward. He's your husband's son and despite the fact the man is missing, I don't foresee a judge denying your right to the boy."

"Goodness sakes! What a wonderful idea. And so simple." Ellie beamed. "If he's my son, all well and legal, even if I divorce his father I'm not divorcing Edward. He could remain mine."

"Exactly. I'll draw up the papers and put the adoption in motion," stated Robert. "Now, it's quite difficult for a woman to obtain a divorce, but there is a reform movement beginning. And the longer your husband remains missing the better for you. Jimmy George's disappearance strengthens a case for divorce based on the grounds of desertion. Meantime, I'll keep you posted on the investigation. I'll suggest to the authorities that the funds remain frozen in Mr. Barkley's bank accounts until someone finds him or…his body."

Ellie's breath caught but she quickly recovered. "Thank you so much for your help. As you can imagine, I want this whole business behind me as soon as possible." Ellie offered him her hand. Perhaps by the time the adoption was finalized, they would have received news of her husband's whereabouts. And if he had been killed, she would be spared the bother of initiating a divorce. She'd become a widow, a much more respectable title than divorcee. But if that wasn't the case, she resolved to pursue the divorce. She would rid herself of Jimmy George Barkley, one way or the other.

Robert met her eyes. "Do you believe your husband capable of murdering his first wife? Of murdering his partners?"

Ellie almost related Edward's story about witnessing his pa hurting his mother, but she was reluctant to draw the child into the whole sordid business. Unless forced to give testimony in a court of law, she'd keep silent on the matter. But even for her son, she could never lie to a judge.

"I would think…" she began. And then she simply pointed to her cheek where the telltale signs of her own faded bruises were still slightly evident.

Mr. Rutherford closed the door behind her. She'd told him everything he needed to know.

Wednesday, June 25, 1890

"Edward, look at the grouping of rocks layered atop that butte." Ellie pointed from her seat on the hard wooden bench. She'd rented a buggy and horse from Mr. Wallace at the livery. July would be upon them in less than a week and the weather grew hotter with each passing day. Edward visited the ranch with his grandpa a couple of times since she made the arrangement with Third, but this was Ellie's first time.

No doubt hoping for a better view, her son stood up. "It's pretty, Mama."

Ellie grabbed his arm to steady him and squinted in the bright sunshine. "I believe an enterprising giant meticulously set each rock in place."

Edward laughed and plopped back down on the seat. "Pa told me there's no such thing as giants."

"Use your imagination, Edward." Ellie tweaked his nose. "We'll be at the Diamond C in a few minutes. I bet you can't wait to see Sam and ride the ponies."

"Grandpa's going to ride with us way out on the range, and I bet Uncle Ned will come, too."

"Uncle Ned?"

"He's an old man like Grandpa," explained Edward. "Uncle Ned is Grandpa's boss, but Grandpa really likes him."

"Oh, you mean Ned Armstrong, the ranch foreman." Ellie smiled. "Why do you call him Uncle Ned?"

"Sam calls him Uncle Ned, and he said I could call him Uncle Ned, too." Edward reached down and patted Captain's head.

Catching a quick movement out of the corner of her eye, Ellie brushed Edward's arm and then pointed. An antelope bounded gracefully across the open prairie. A second later, another joined the first. In a flash, their white-tailed posteriors disappeared from sight.

"Did you see that?" Ellie whispered in amazement.

"That was an antelope, Mama. Grandpa showed me a whole bunch of animals when I went riding with him and Sam. Sam calls them 'critters'." Edward giggled.

The rangeland provided a whole new world of lessons and adventures for Edward. Ellie could easily count on the fingers of one hand how many times she'd traveled to Miles City or beyond during the time she'd lived in Montana. Every trip to the Diamond C had become an adventure for her son and she couldn't be happier for him.

The buggy approached the tall timbers and crossbar displaying the sign announcing their arrival at the Diamond C Ranch. Ellie drove the rig onward toward the buildings seen in the distance while recalling her recent meeting with Robert at his office. He'd informed her that Jimmy George's disappearance hadn't been solved, and there'd been no sign of the bank robbers either. The future seemed so uncertain until her husband's whereabouts was solved, and she just wanted the whole matter settled. She lived in a constant state of alertness, jumping at every little sound in the house, day and night. She hoped Jimmy George never returned. Could she be that lucky?

Robert assured her that by leaving the money untouched, there was no way she could be implicated in any of Mr. Barkley's scandalous ill-doings. He'd checked and Jimmy George Barkley was the only name on all of the accounts. As a last resort, she had the option of packing up and leaving town, starting fresh for Edward's sake, where no one knew about her past. If Jimmy George could disappear, then why not her and Edward?

Regardless, Edward's adoption was moving forward, something positive for herself and her son. Taking action and working toward a solution felt wonderful. But today, she intended to enjoy every minute of freedom from worry on this beautiful ranch!

"Good morning, Ellie. Howdy, Edward!" Third greeted them as the buggy approached the horse barn.

Ellie reined in the energetic mare and halted the buggy alongside Third. "Hello! We made it."

"Hi, Grandpa," shouted Edward, leaping off the seat into his grandfather's arms.

Third set the boy on the ground and helped Ellie down from the buggy. "Go on up to the cabin, and I'll tend to the rig, Ellie. Belle's been waiting all morning for you."

"Thank you, Third. Edward, you mind your grandfather, you hear?" warned Ellie.

"Yes, ma'am." Edward beamed up at his grandpa.

"Sam's waiting with Mike and Ned in the horse barn. Let's go!" Third led the horse and lumbered toward the big red barn with Edward trotting along beside him.

"Ellie!" called Belle, waving a dish towel above her head. "Maggie just arrived for tea with us."

An hour later, Ellie couldn't remember the last time she'd enjoyed herself so much. Her sides actually pained from laughing while Maggie and Belle teased each other, chuckled at their children's antics, and compared notes on their husbands. They'd shared everything with Ellie. If she hadn't known them, she would never have guessed one was a refined lady from Philadelphia and the other an illiterate, former soiled dove employed at The Joker's Wild Saloon.

She loved them both dearly.

"Ladies, you've lifted my spirits more than anything in weeks. And to think I actually contemplated leaving town."

"What?" exclaimed Belle.

Maggie choked on a mouthful of tea and spluttered, "You're not serious."

"With all the kafuffle surrounding Jimmy George's disappearance and his questionable past, I'm certain Ellie Barkley is the main target for the gossips these days. Those horrid women and their vile tongues will guarantee my reputation is ruined, no matter how innocent I am of any wrongdoing."

"Nonsense, I haven't heard one ill word spoken about you. In fact, I've heard nothing but sympathy for your situation and flattering praise of your aptitude as a stepmother. Everyone is so proud of you for raising Edward so well," said Maggie.

"He's my son," said Ellie. "Of course, I'm teaching him manners."

Maggie patted her hand. "If the gossips are talking, Ellie, no one will believe a word of it. Few people in the community take them seriously. Don't allow a half dozen spiteful old women with too much time on their hands to threaten your happiness with that little boy."

"But my life rivals the plot of one of those trashy dime novels. I would be gossiping about me, too. I have considered leaving Spirit Creek and starting fresh somewhere far away."

"Ellie Barkley, sometimes I am so jealous of you…I…I could chew nails!" uttered Belle.

"Jealous of me? Are you serious?" Ellie gaped, slowly shaking her head. "I'm a foundling, raised in a Boston orphanage. When the nuns tossed me out and insisted I train as a teacher, I slaved from dawn to dusk to pay my way and excel at my classes. I taught school in Spirit Creek for years believing myself an old maid. Franklin got me with child and then managed to get himself killed. My impromptu marriage has been a total disaster. My missing husband lived under a false identity and robbed banks. I'm definitely someone to be jealous of."

"Really?" Belle stood with her hands on her hips. "For years my mother insisted she worked as a saloon singer. By age ten, I realized the woman couldn't carry a tune in a bucket. I soon discovered exactly what my mother did at that saloon. I never attended school a day in my life. The townsfolk wouldn't have the saloon whore's child in the same schoolhouse as their children. I can't read or write a word to this day. The bartender was my best friend since there were never other children around to play with. By age thirteen, I'd followed my mother's footsteps into her chosen career." Belle sucked in a deep breath while she appeared to be collecting her thoughts or harnessing her emotions or both. Finally, she continued, "Had I been an orphan, I'd have had children to play with, I'd have learned to read and write, and I'd have learned Bible stories instead of how to cheat at poker! Yes, I'm damn jealous of you."

Belle started to cry.

"Oh, Belle, forgive me. I had no idea how difficult your life has been." Ellie slipped her handkerchief into Belle's hand.

"Thank you," she blubbered.

"Every time I watch you nursing Matilda, I'm so envious of you. I was devastated when I lost my baby. You're so happily married to Third, but I've ended up with Jimmy George. I've never been so frightened of anyone in my life."

Ellie burst into tears.

Maggie stood dumbstruck while Belle and Ellie cried on each other's shoulders. For good measure, Matilda started bawling, having heard her mother crying.

"For Pete's sake. Enough!" Maggie scooped Willie up in her arms for fear he'd join in. "We're supposed to be enjoying a cup of tea together on a pleasant summer morning."

"I'll stop crying if Ellie forgets this crazy notion of leaving Spirit Creek," offered Belle, sniffling loudly.

"I promise I'll stay here." Ellie sighed and wiped her wet cheeks with her handkerchief.

"Well, good." Belle straightened her back and dried her eyes on Matilda's lacy blanket. "If you hustled Edward away, it would just kill Third. He's grown so fond of his grandson. Guess that makes me Edward's grandmother, and as such, you'll leave town over my dead body."

Maggie choked on a mouthful of tea and patted her chest. "As Edward's grandmother? Belle, you celebrated your nineteenth birthday last week."

Ellie's serious façade crumbled and a wide grin creased her face.

"Well now, I certainly can't go against the wishes of Edward's old gray-haired granny."

All three women burst into laughter.

At three o'clock, Third had hitched the mare to the buggy and parked the rig outside his cabin. Everyone shouted their goodbyes as she and Edward climbed aboard. Ellie flicked the reins and the buggy rumbled down the driveway.

"Come for Sunday dinner after church." Maggie extended the invitation, and Ellie waved and nodded to indicate she'd heard.

"Thank you. We'll see you at noon," she called over her shoulder just before the buggy entered the cottonwood-lined driveway and disappeared from Maggie's sight. Ellie glanced at her son who appeared too tired to sit upright. "Did you have fun, Edward?"

"It was the mostest fun ever." Edward yawned and curled up on the buggy's seat, using his mother's lap for a pillow. A second later, he poked his head up. "Mama, why don't roosters lay eggs?"

Ellie felt her face turning several shades of red. At age six, Edward was asking questions relating to the birds and the bees? She contemplated her answer for a second. "Ask your Uncle Ned. I imagine he'd know."

"I did ask him. He told me roosters are boys, Mama," said Edward. He laid his head on her lap again and closed his eyes.

The little devil had fooled her with his question, and he appeared satisfied with the simple explanation. But some day Edward would require the birds-and-the-bees talk, a subject best discussed between a boy and a man. Would Edward be blessed with a new father when the time came? She considered the possibility encouraging and terrifying in equal measure.

CHAPTER 13

Sunday, August 3, 1890

Ellie skipped the morning service at The Spirit Creek Church, avoiding the gossips and their probing questions. She resolved to do so until the mystery surrounding her husband's disappearance was solved, for Edward's sake as well as her own. Remembering Maggie's invitation, Ellie rented a conveyance from Kenneth Wallace at the livery, to partake of the noon meal with Edward and the Carlyle family.

The high-noon sun beat down on their heads. Ellie sat tall, confidently driving the rig, with Edward seated beside her and Captain at his feet. She couldn't put a name to it, but the weather felt strange. Stifling heat and a ruthlessly-strong wind blowing hot, the air almost crackling around them. Thankfully, in this wind, she'd chosen a sunbonnet tied beneath her chin for the trip and not a Sunday-going-to-church hat. The poor thing would have been ripped from her head and blown half way to Miles City by now.

The buggy rumbled past a narrow creek snaking its way through the sage-covered rangeland. On the surface, the creek appeared calm and innocent, but creeks ran deep and dangerous in many places. Even with her limited knowledge of ranching, Ellie understood that a good source of water represented the lifeblood of every free-range operation. The Carlyles were fortunate that this tributary of the Powder River meandered throughout the entire ranch.

Ellie's sweaty hands slipped on the supple leather reins and she tightened her grip. When the buggy passed under the mammoth wooden Diamond C Ranch sign, Edward wiggled beside her and Captain stood, his tail wagging.

"We're almost there, Edward. I think Captain enjoys a visit with Sam's dog as much as we enjoy spending time with our friends," observed

Ellie.

"Captain races Rags around the yard, and he chases the cats in the barn, too." Edward patted his dog's head.

Several minutes later, the buggy arrived in front of the main house.

"Good day, folks," called Luke, crossing the yard in a loose-limbed gait.

"Good afternoon. Isn't it a glorious day?" Ellie climbed down from the bench seat and handed Luke the reins, before she shook out her skirts and adjusted her sunbonnet. The sun's rays felt wonderful, but with her complexion, she could almost feel a new crop of freckles popping out.

Luke gazed up at the sky. "Certainly, hot and windy. We've been a bit concerned actually. The ranch hands reported hearing distant thunder and that means a dry lightning storm is possible. I've got some of the ranch hands on alert. Dry lightning could mean a strike that causes a grassfire, potentially devastating out on the range."

"That doesn't sound good." Ellie gazed up at the sky.

Luke nodded. "It never is. Let's hope for the best."

"Hello there, young fella," greeted Third, stepping up to the buggy. Edward leapt into his grandpa's arms, and Captain jumped to the ground.

"Hi, Grandpa." Edward beamed.

"Mike will tend to the horse for you, Ellie," said Luke, handing the reins to his assistant foreman. "Come into the house."

"Afternoon, ma'am," said Mike Armstrong, smiling and touching the brim of his hat.

"Good afternoon, Mike." Ellie smiled at her former student. For several months last year, an illiterate Mike visited Ellie for evening reading and ciphering lessons, in hopes of winning the heart of Maggie's mother's helper. It had worked; Mike and Agnes Jones were married now.

"I've been keeping up with the reading, Mrs. Barkley."

"Someday you'll be reading bedtime stories to your children."

"Yes, ma'am," replied Mike, blushing. "I suppose I will at that."

Ellie wondered if perhaps there was a child on the way already. The couple were married in early June. The young man hopped aboard the buggy and drove it toward the horse barn.

"Ellie, welcome!" Maggie waved from the veranda. "We've invited Third and his family to join us for dinner, too."

"I'm delighted to hear it. It's always a pleasure spending time with all of you." Ellie strode toward the house, feeling blessed that for the first time in her life she felt like a member of a family. She couldn't be happier and Edward thrived because of it.

Maggie's baby son, Willie, and Belle's infant daughter, Matilda, slept in separate baskets on the veranda, and Sam and Edward played in the yard under Sam's eight-year-old stepsister's watchful eye. Soon, Patti had organized a game of hide and seek. Eyes closed, she started counting while the two boys dashed around the corner of the house in search of good hiding places.

Once the hellos were exchanged, Luke and Third settled into side-by-side wicker chairs on the veranda to watch over the babies while the womenfolk headed inside.

"It's such a treat having a day of rest," sighed Maggie, leading her friend toward the kitchen. "Agnes and I preserved vegetables and picked berries and made jams and jellies and pies every day this week."

"Goodness, you have been busy. And in this heat? No wonder you need a rest." Ellie settled on a chair at the enormous kitchen table.

"If I never see another berry…" complained Maggie, good-naturedly.

"I've been busy, too. Our new schoolteacher, Ivy Paterson, arrived in town last week, and Ronald asked for my assistance in readying the classroom for fall classes." Ellie held up her hands, red and cracked. Ronald probably thought he was doing her a favor, providing an opportunity to earn a few extra dollars. "I've been scrubbing walls, polishing floors, washing windows, and loving every minute of it. Performing purposeful work is an absolute pleasure."

Maggie passed Ellie a jar of petroleum jelly. "This is ideal for a ranch woman's hands."

"I've been using it. I remember you singing its praises." Ellie opened the jar and scooped out a gob.

"I talked with Miss Paterson briefly after church today. She hails from San Francisco. I never mentioned that I'd grown up there, too. She certainly wouldn't have crossed paths with the likes of me. Such a lovely young lady," added Belle.

"She'll catch the eye of some rancher, forcing the School Committee to seek out her replacement in no time," predicted Ellie.

"Ronald is quite annoyed that the town sheriffs keep marrying the schoolteachers. I pray no one introduces Ivy to Ernest Jones." Maggie laughed while stirring a pot of soup atop the woodstove.

"Captain disappeared for a spell this morning, and I missed church while searching for him with Edward. At least, that's the excuse I gave him. I intend to avoid the gossips for his sake." Ellie applied more of the product to her hands. "Was the scandalous adventures of Mrs. Ellie Barkley still the latest topic for the gossips?"

"Actually, you are." Maggie settled back onto her chair. "But not for the reason you think. Nothing about Mr. Barkley's disappearance was mentioned. In fact, rumor has it that Mr. Rutherford, Spirit Creek's most eligible bachelor, is quite smitten with you."

Ellie gasped. "You're pulling my leg. I'm still married."

"Not a word of a lie." Maggie smiled, raising her hand as if swearing an oath. "I've observed Robert during Sunday services when he's devouring you with his eyes. And you've been seen entering the law office on several occasions."

"That was for business purposes only. Besides…" began Ellie. Before she could relate her encounter with Sadie Peterman, she was interrupted by a commotion at the front door.

"I believe our other guest just arrived." Maggie removed her apron and headed out of the kitchen.

"What other guest?" asked Ellie, frowning.

"Maggie mentioned that Luke invited Robert to dinner." Belle smiled, wickedly, and drawled, "Now, isn't that a coincidence."

"Coincidence, my foot," muttered Ellie, her cheeks warming.

Had Robert heard the gossip, linking him with a married woman? If so, he must be purely mortified. She could only hope he possessed the good sense and proper manners to ignore any gossip circulating about them, since they both knew there was absolutely no truth to it. Their relationship was strictly business, nothing more. Ellie experienced a brief moment of sadness that what she shared with him wasn't more. Certainly, she felt an attraction to him.

Ellie braced herself and joined the others in the parlor. Third and Luke had carried the babies' baskets inside, and Belle and Maggie tended to their needs. Luke distributed glasses of cold lemonade to his guests.

Soon, Sunday dinner evolved into a happy, boisterous affair. Ellie suspected the hostess had intentionally seated her beside Robert, although Ellie could never prove it, of course.

"Please pass the potatoes?" Maggie extended her hand.

Ellie and Robert reached for the potato bowl at the same time, their hands touching. Ellie's cheeks flamed while an electrical charge raced up her arm. She pulled her hand back as if scalded.

"Sorry," mumbled Robert, gazing into her eyes as he passed the bowl to the hostess.

He didn't appear one iota contrite. In fact, if Ellie didn't know better she'd swear he'd orchestrated the collision on purpose.

Maggie smiled sweetly, pleased with herself no doubt, knowing she'd caused the interaction between them. "Thank you, Robert," she purred.

Luke engaged Robert in conversation about land prices in the area. A lengthy discussion on possible reasons for recent unexplained price increases occupied them for several minutes. Ellie relaxed momentarily.

Sam and Edward started giggling and both boys were quickly reprimanded by their mothers. While keeping an eye out for further shenanigans from her son, Ellie tuned one ear to the gentlemen's conversation.

Robert presented his theories and argued his points admirably, causing Ellie to question whether Spirit Creek's most eligible bachelor was the man for her, should she manage to obtain a divorce. She suspected the lawyer's intelligence exceeded her own, although most conversations with him had been positively boring. Never in her wildest dreams would she consider them compatible. Had the gossips detected a suitability between herself and the worldly, learned man? Even so, she'd be heartbroken if something developed between them and then he tired of her company.

Robert lacked a buoyant personality, but after Jimmy George Barkley, even-tempered, kind-hearted, sensible-minded Robert would be a pleasant change. She scolded herself for even considering a relationship with another man. She was still a married woman until she learned what had become of her husband. Or she managed to divorce the skunk. And hadn't she sworn off men altogether? What had happened to her resolve?

Suddenly, she wondered why Sadie Peterman hadn't accompanied Robert today. And why hadn't the local gossips been discussing the pair of them? Was it possible Sadie had lied about Robert courting her? Ellie risked sneaking a peek at Robert and discovered him staring at her. He smiled. Proper manners dictated some form of acknowledgment, but while she searched her mind for something suitable to say to the other dinner guest, Maggie saved her.

"Ellie, would you mind helping me serve the pie?" Maggie rose and began collecting plates.

"I don't mind at all," replied Ellie, relishing the excuse to distance herself from Robert's mesmerizing eyes for a few minutes. She simply reached for his empty plate, and then headed for the momentary sanctuary in the kitchen.

* * *

During dinner, Robert noticed Ellie's thoughts appeared to drift miles away. She'd only spoken a few words to him all afternoon, perhaps purposefully avoiding him. Had she heard that the local gossips were whispering about them? He felt himself redden. Was she equally embarrassed about the whole business? He'd believed he'd cleverly hidden his love for her from everyone. Apparently, he'd failed.

When Ellie hadn't attended church this morning, he'd experienced a moment of panic. Was she ill? Had something happened to her or the boy? Had she left town without a word? Elizabeth Waverly mentioned something about a lost dog and had eased his mind.

Robert had closely watched Ellie while sipping lemonade in the parlor and later during the meal. She'd conversed and laughed with Maggie and Belle, picked up the babies and bounced them on her lap, smiled and cooed at them. But despite her cheery façade, she couldn't hide the sadness he saw in her eyes. One minute he would catch her staring daggers at him, and the next minute she would appear on the verge of tears. And then a minute later she was laughing at someone's joke. The woman completely puzzled him.

Robert popped the last forkful of berry pie into his mouth. He hadn't enjoyed a meal so much in ages. Definitely must be the company. He swiped his napkin across his lips, set the cloth on his plate, and leaned back in his chair.

At this very moment Ellie cuddled little Matilda in her arms and kissed the golden tuft of hair atop her small head. Robert blushed with the realization that he yearned to conceive a baby with her someday. Edward was a delightful boy, but he wanted a child of his own. Boy or girl, no preference, as long as Ellie was the child's mother. He needed to start the paperwork for her divorce as soon as possible.

He'd almost burst into flames when he and Ellie's hands touched over the table. What would happen if he ever kissed her? Touched her skin? Wrapped his arms around her? Made love with her? The possibilities boggled the mind.

"Robert, can I interest you in a cigar out on the veranda?" asked Luke, pushing his chair away from the table.

"You certainly can, and thank you again for the invitation to dinner." Robert rose from his chair. He didn't add that he couldn't have withstood another invitation to the Peterman house. Enduring even one more meal with Sadie and her family would have killed him.

"You're always welcome at our table, Robert."

* * *

Ned stood, gazing out the open cookhouse doorway, sipping a cup of coffee brewed strong enough to peel the paint off a barn. The wind howled like a forlorn coyote calling to his kin while ominous, onyx-colored clouds marched across the sky.

"A storm's on the way but we need the moisture, Mike. Mind ya, rain would bounce off this hard-packed earth like corn kernels poppin' in a hot pan."

Shards of lightning severed the sky and thunder rattled the cookhouse windows. Mike stepped up beside his pa, and Ned leaned back against the doorjamb.

"Few things I fear more than a damned grassfire," observed Ned.

"Bet you've seen a few fires started from a lightning strike on a day like today. Lightning, no rain," observed Mike.

"That I have, son. The fellas are watchin' for signs of a strike." Ned tossed his empty cup into a tub of soapy dishwater. "If'n they see somethin' we'll git on 'er right away."

The ranch hands finished their noon meal and headed to the bunkhouse. Ned and Mike joined them. A group of men settled in for a game of poker at the rickety wooden table, and one fellow whittled in the far corner. Scotty lay sideways on his bunk and buried his nose in one of those western dime novels no one ever admitted to reading.

"Scotty, I thought you couldn't read?" accused Ned.

The young fellow glanced over. "I can read some. I just don't go around braggin' on it." Scotty returned to his story.

"Got a bad feeling about this storm." Mike drew up a chair beside his pa and joined the poker game.

"Lightnin' storm's the one thing I hate about livin' on the open range." Ned shuffled the well-worn deck of cards. "Can't tolerate havin' no control over nature."

Mike cut the deck, and Ned dealt the cards. The room quieted for a minute, while everyone contemplated their hand. The cowhands' calm exteriors didn't fool Ned. The room pulsed with energy; every man braced for action should their worst fears become reality.

"We've been lucky so far." Ned looked up from his poker hand. "Only had that one small fire out by Wilber Simpson's place in early May."

No sooner had Ned spoken but the bunkhouse door flew open. One of the hands on fire watch yelled, "Have us a lightnin' strike by my reckonin' way over in the direction of the graveyard, Ned. There's a lot of smoke. We oughta be gettin' out there."

"Let's go, men!" shouted Ned. "Could have us some trouble here."

A flurry of cards landed in a heap on the rickety table, and the ranch hands leapt out of their chairs.

"Blast it! Best hand I've had in ages," complained Mike, tossing his flush onto the table. He quickly rose, almost tipping his ladder-back chair onto the rough-hewn wood floor.

"Shake a leg, fellas. Hitch up them horses and git the water wagon on the way. Double check none of that gear gits left behind," called Ned, shaking his head. "I've seen more of these dang fires than I care to remember."

"We'll get her under control, Ned," promised one of the hands.

Barely avoiding a collision with each other, the ranch hands grabbed their hats and headed out the door.

"I hope so, dammit," muttered Ned, grabbing his Stetson off a rusted peg.

Mike called, "I'll race up to the main house and let Luke know what's going on. For sure, the neighbors will come lend a hand with this and we'll need food and lots of it."

"Come on, fellas, let's git this done!" Ned slapped his hat on his head.

Mike lit out for the main house.

* * *

"What's wrong?" Maggie leapt off the sofa as Luke stormed into the parlor with Robert on his heels.

"There's been a lightning strike out west, near the graveyard. Don't know how bad it is." Luke dragged his hands through his hair. "Ned's sending the water wagon out. Hopefully, we'll soon have everything under control."

Maggie had heard about rangeland wildfires but never experienced one on the Diamond C before. She searched her husband's eyes. Was the fire worse than he was letting on?

"Wish I could tell you it's nothing." Luke grimaced.

It annoyed Maggie how easily he could read her thoughts.

"It's the wind that concerns me," her husband continued. "You'd better get Morning Star and Agnes preparing sandwiches and tea. The neighbors are bound to see the smoke and show up to help."

Ellie and Belle exchanged glances and leapt to their feet.

"We'll help, too," offered Ellie.

"Me, too," chimed in Robert.

As they moved out to the hallway, the unmistakable slam of the back door was heard.

"Maggie, where are you?" questioned a familiar voice.

"We're in here, Morning Star," answered Luke.

Ned's wife, a Cheyenne Native American, swept into the hallway. "Mike ask me make food."

"Thank you for coming to help, Morning Star." Maggie hugged herself, wrapping her arms around her middle, but she still shivered slightly.

"You go now, Mr. Carlyle." Morning Star shooed him toward the door. "We make plenty food for men."

Maggie met her husband's eyes.

Luke wrapped her in his arms. "Don't worry, sweetheart. Everything will be fine. Keep the children close to the house."

"Please be careful." Maggie kissed him quickly and whispered, "I love you."

"Find me some suitable clothes," stated Robert, unbuttoning his waistcoat. "I'm going with you."

Luke glanced at his own Sunday duds. "Come on upstairs with me, Robert. We're about the same size. We need to change quickly." The men raced up the curved staircase.

The ladies followed Morning Star into the kitchen where Agnes had already started slicing bread for sandwiches. Maggie prayed things would go well at the graveyard.

CHAPTER 14

A wall of flames advanced with the precision of a well-rehearsed military charge, aided by the strong wind. Black smoke rolled across Luke's land, inhibiting the fire fighters' visibility and choking everyone with its toxic composition.

Thunder, Luke's magnificent Morgan stallion, sensed his master's urgency. His ears lay flat against his head and his nostrils flared. The horse raced across the range, the sound of his pounding hooves lost in the howling wind. Robert rode alongside on his gelding, purchased from Robert Morgan shortly after he settled in Spirit Creek.

Arriving at the scene of the lightning strike, Luke immediately realized the situation was far from under control. Due to the day's heat, his sweat-soaked clothing clung to him like a cumbersome second skin. His mouth tasted of dust and soot, and his nose and throat stung. The dust and smoke set his eyes to tearing, forcing him to blink almost constantly to clear his vision.

"Cover up, Robert," shouted Luke to be heard over the wind as he wrapped a tattered bandana around his face, leaving only his eyes visible.

Robert copied him.

"Ned, I'd hoped you'd have the fire out by now," said Luke as he and Robert approached the foreman, surveying the destruction.

"We was losin' the damn battle afore we got here. The lightnin' hit one of 'em old drier-than-dust gravemarkers and ate up the whole lot of 'em in flames. Then it spread to the tall grass and there was no stoppin' the fire from spreadin'. And that damned wind is howlin' like a banshee."

"Much damage to the graveyard?" Luke couldn't distinguish anything but flames and a cloud of acrid smoke. Was this a glimpse of Hell? He vowed to remain a Christian gentleman until the day he died, fearful of facing this misery for eternity.

"It's pretty bad: markers gone, flowers kilt, trees charred, fence burnt." Ned's voice caught.

"I've never seen anything like this," observed Robert, shaking his head.

"Let's get this under control. If the fire reaches the valley, every building on the Diamond C could be lost." Luke slapped Robert on the back, and then all three men headed toward the water wagons.

Ned hobbled along, doggedly keeping abreast of the younger men. "Neighbors…arrived with water wagons…and ranch hands. With a bit of luck…we'll stop…this damned thing," stammered Ned, puffing, barely able to run and talk at the same time.

"I'm not risking my home and family solely on a bit of luck. Do whatever it takes, Ned." Luke's stomach churned; he fought to keep his anxiety in check. His pulse raced and his hands vibrated with the momentary adrenaline rush. Luke hated showing his emotions, pure sign of weakness. But the situation had him damned worried. No telling the damage this grassfire might do.

"Don't worry yerself sick, Sonny Boy. We'll git her out."

Luke grimaced behind his bandana; the old fellow knew him too well. His hands felt cold and clammy inside his gloves. "I hope you're right."

"I second that," said Robert.

Ned looked skyward. "Wish the hell it would start raining."

The flames dipped and rose in a shimmering dance while Luke slapped at the fire with his sodden gunnysack. The heat from the grassfire's flames licked at his body like a fiery tongue, and acrid smoke continued to burn his throat and blind his vision. The strip of blackened prairie landscape grew wider by the hour. Thankfully, all of his livestock were miles away from here.

Luke recalled how recently he'd admired the range's beauty with Maggie during their tour of the ranch. As long as he drew breath, this fire wouldn't win, he silently vowed.

Robert worked in a steady rhythm beside Luke, dousing the flames with another wet gunnysack. "Luke, this could easily spread to your house."

"That's got me worried, Robert," admitted Luke, impressed with the city-bred fellow who was proving he wasn't afraid of a bit of hard, dirty work.

Heat from the wind that was blowing hot as the Devil's breath, penetrated Luke's clothing. Sweat beaded on his forehead and ran into his eyes. More sweat trickled down his back while a cold chill raced up his spine. The fire was heading directly for the valley. And his ranch.

"Three more water wagons just arrived. If we contain this main blaze, have we got a fighting chance?" asked Robert.

"I hope so." Luke welcomed the newcomers and set them to work, praying everyone's coordinated efforts would slow the fire's progress before all was lost. He backtracked and tossed his smoldering sack onto the Diamond C's water wagon.

"Here ya go, Luke," yelled Third, handing the boss a freshly-saturated replacement.

"What the hell are you doing out here?" Luke was shocked that the old fellow had come along. Third must have slipped out of the house when Luke and Robert went upstairs to change. It appeared Ned and Third were holding their own with the much younger ranch hands though.

Robert tossed his sack alongside Luke's.

"Now, this is my home, too, and I ain't too old to help you save it." Third grabbed the dry sacks Luke and Robert dropped off and plunged them into the water.

"Hell of a thing, sir."

Luke turned and recognized Mike's black piercing eyes in spite of the bandana that covered most of his face. "Ride back to the main house, son, and assure the women things are looking as good as can be expected. Don't mention the damage to the graveyard. Just let them know we'll need all the food they can put together."

"Righto, sir." Mike passed his sack to another fellow.

Robert Rutherford stepped forward, shaking his head. "Let me go, Luke. Mike's more useful to you out here. He knows what he's doing. I can find my way back."

Luke shook the man's hand. He respected a fellow who recognized his limitations. "Not a word about the seriousness of the situation, Robert. I don't want the women fretting."

"I'll say everybody's fine and ask that they get the food ready." Robert untied his skittish gelding from the water wagon, tightened the cinch and climbed into the saddle. With a quick wave, he headed off at a gallop in the direction of the ranch.

Luke returned his attention to fighting the fire which continued to deposit a trail of death in its wake. Charred reminders of wildlife that had been so alive and vibrant only hours before littered the range. Luke loved all creatures and the sight sickened him.

"Should we fetch the women and children, Luke? Get them away from the ranch?" asked Robert Morgan, who appeared at Luke's side.

Luke trusted his neighbor and life-long friend like the brother he never had. Their eyes met and further words were not necessary.

* * *

Maggie paced the front veranda, wringing her hands and watching a black cloud of smoke waft across the horizon. What was happening out there on the range? There'd been no news of the fire, no word from the men, and no report on the extent of the damage. Was anyone hurt?

More importantly, was Luke safe?

"The men will be fine, Maggie."

Maggie startled when Ellie spoke. She turned and met her friend's eyes. "I hope you're right."

"Don't worry. The men will have the fire out in no time."

"I wish I had your confidence. I'm certain every one of them is as busy as a hound with a dozen pups, fighting the fire and all." Maggie smiled weakly.

"Someone will ride into the valley any minute, warning us the men are hungry as bears in spring and they're on the way here." Ellie grasped Maggie's arm, halted her pacing. "We've prepared enough food to feed a small army. We're ready for them."

Maggie felt totally helpless. She silently prayed for everyone's safe return, especially Luke. "We'll hear something any minute now, won't we?"

"They'll report the fire is out, and they'll be tired and hungry. Just needing something to eat before heading home." Ellie patted her friend's arm.

"I hope you're right. I can't help worrying about Luke. He'll stop at nothing to save his ranch, our home." Maggie twisted her handkerchief in her fingers. "He won't hesitate for a second to put himself in the path of danger if he believes it's necessary."

"Ned will stop Luke from doing anything stupid. Robert's level-headed, and he's with him, too. Luke will be fine." Ellie's hands were shaking.

Maggie met her eyes. "You're worried about Robert, too, aren't you? Admit it."

"Of course, I'm worried about Robert. And Luke and Third and Ned. All of them." Ellie reached up and patted her hair. "It's not the same. I'm not in a relationship with Robert. But we're certainly…acquaintances. You might even consider us friends."

"But you'd like the friendship to become more?" Maggie's eyebrows rose.

Ellie conceded, "Perhaps. One day. Once my life returns to some semblance of normal. Once Edward's adoption is complete. Once I acquire a divorce."

"Will your heart wait that long? I believe you care more for the man than you're willing to even admit to yourself."

Ellie opened her mouth.

"Don't as much as attempt to deny it. I've noticed the way you sneak a peek at him when you think he's not looking. And he stares at you with his heart on his sleeve when you're not aware of it, too." Maggie chuckled. "The two of you couldn't be better suited. Get your lives sorted out and then plan a future together."

"But I think…"

"Don't fret. I know you're not ready to plan a future with anyone until this mess surrounding Jimmy George's disappearance is resolved." Maggie smiled and touched Ellie's arm. "I pray that happens soon. I recall how I felt when William was killed, and the banker foreclosed on my home, and my entire life was a jumble. I wouldn't wish that feeling of helplessness and indecision on anyone."

"Helplessness. What a perfect description."

"Everything will work out. Things happen for a reason. Well, go tell Morning Star there's no sign of anyone yet." Maggie's worry-filled thoughts returned, swirling about in her mind like butter in a churn.

"All right, Maggie." Ellie dragged a wicker chair over. "Sit and watch for the men. Shout the minute you spy someone coming."

"Thank you, I will." She sat on the edge of the chair, and Ellie headed toward the cookhouse.

Maggie twiddled her thumbs in her lap. Just as she was about to cross the yard, storm into the horse barn, saddle up and head out to satisfy herself that everyone was all right, she spotted a rider coming hell bent for leather through the valley.

Oh, Lord. Was someone hurt? Was the rider stopping at the main house before heading to town for the doctor?

"Ellie! Someone's coming!" she called, holding her breath and praying even harder.

Ellie whipped around; she hadn't quite reached the cookhouse. She raced back to Maggie's side. "Who is it?"

Maggie squinted as the rider closed the distance between them. "I think that's Mr. Rutherford's horse."

* * *

Robert's gelding galloped at full speed across the range. Flames roared from behind and smoke converged from every direction, choking him, blinding him. He wiped his eyes with his sleeve. Somehow he'd lost the bandana Luke had loaned him.

He rode onward toward the ranch. Smoke burned his eyes, causing constant tearing and he blinked, attempting to clear his vision. Dark shadows from the smoke loomed in front of him, and then receded, disappearing like an apparition. Had they existed only in his imagination? He'd never been so intimidated by nature, frightened beyond belief.

Soon he'd outrun the flames and smoke, and he inhaled deeply, swiping the soot and dirt from his face and eyes. Fifteen minutes later, he crested the valley and saw the Diamond C Ranch buildings below. He'd never witnessed a more beautiful sight. He could understand Luke's love of this land, a legacy for future generations. Suddenly, Robert realized he wanted the same for himself. Some day he'd buy his own property, hopefully, a home to share with Ellie.

But those damned flames weren't that far behind him. Instead of giving Luke's wife a report, maybe he should insist the women and children leave the ranch. He could pack everyone into a wagon and head for town. Luke would want his kinfolk and friends safe. Maggie would argue, no doubt. Probably Morning Star and Belle were worrying about their husbands and would give him trouble, too. Ellie might be the only voice of reason, if he was lucky. He'd be firm, insist every one of them leave.

Horse and rider finally reached the safety of the Diamond C, galloping into the barnyard. At least, the ranch was a safe haven for the moment. Having looked those devil flames in the eye, Robert knew the situation would change soon enough. The fire was headed directly for the ranch. The moment it crested the valley, all would be as good as gone. How would Luke survive losing the beautiful home his father had built?

More importantly, how would the man survive losing the family he loved? In an instant Robert realized he couldn't allow that to happen. He leapt off his mount as Maggie and Ellie raced toward him, holding their skirts aloft to make better time.

"Where's Luke? Is he safe?" Maggie shouted above the roaring wind.

Robert glanced at Ellie, standing beside her friend, wringing her hands.

"He's fighting the fire, but he sent me to assure you that no one is injured. But we must evacuate the ranch, now."

Maggie gasped and her hand flew to her mouth.

"Now don't argue. I'd like to say it's just a precaution, but…"

"No!" exclaimed Maggie, denial evident on her face. "There must be something we can do. We'll form a bucket brigade and water down the buildings…"

"No, Maggie. Everyone needs to leave now," insisted Robert, trying his best to rein in his annoyance. If the woman didn't soon see reason, he would resort to explaining exactly how dire the situation had become, whether or not he frightened her half to death.

"Couldn't we wait just a little longer? Maybe if we…" continued Maggie.

"Absolutely not! There's no time to waste. The flames will crest that valley in a matter of minutes and soon after, all will be lost. I don't want anyone in the fire's path."

Maggie and Ellie gasped, the realization of how serious the

situation had become evident on their faces.

"I'll rig up a wagon while you ladies gather up the other women and all the children. Grab a couple of mementos that are most important to you and leave everything else." Robert grasped his hostess by the arms, shaking her gently. "Don't argue. We need to…"

Just then a crack of thunder that would wake the dead crashed overhead. Robert, Ellie and Maggie jumped a foot.

"Heavens above!" exclaimed Maggie.

Robert's mouth dropped open.

Almost immediately, the sky opened and it started to sprinkle rain. Over yonder by the bunkhouse, the ladies scrambled to collect the bowls and platters of food off the tables and stash everything in the bunkhouse. The older children lugged the baskets with the babies inside as well.

In no time, the rain turned into a downpour, and Robert closed his mouth for fear of drowning in the deluge. "Holy cow."

"Indeed," cried Ellie, laughing. "Someone up there listened finally, turned the water on."

Maggie smiled broadly. "It's raining! It's raining!"

"Indeed it is." Robert grinned. "I guess I won't be rigging up that wagon after all. Run for cover in the bunkhouse, ladies. I'll settle my horse in the barn and then I'll join you."

"Oh, my goodness." Maggie headed for cover from the storm.

"I'll go with you, Robert," said Ellie, wiping rain from her eyes.

Together, they led the nervous animal, skittish since the thunder crash, toward the closest barn.

Robert gazed toward the valley's crest. "I wonder, what's happening out there?"

CHAPTER 15

"Robert Morgan, I won't panic the women and children without reason! But I can't delay things until it's too late either." Luke was heartsick, knowing the fruits of two generation's labor were at risk. Would all that his father and Luke himself had created be destroyed by the out-of-control grassfire?

An instant later, he reminded himself a man could build another home, raise another barn, buy more stock, and plant another garden. But if something should happen to his family? Luke couldn't fathom such a thing. Losing the woman he loved, again, and losing his children would kill him.

"It's your decision, Luke. Whatever you think is best." Robert wiped his sooty forehead with his shirt sleeve, leaving a lighter streak of grime across his blackened face. "Who was that fellow, working with you so fervently?"

"Robert Rutherford."

"The lawyer? Are you serious?"

"Yep. Happened to be out at the ranch when we got word of the lightning strike. Insisted on coming out here to help. Damn hard worker. I'm mighty impressed with him to tell you the truth." Luke suspected both Roberts would be his lifelong friends. Especially if Rutherford pursed a relationship with Ellie in the future. "We'll wait a few more minutes and then decide what to do about the womenfolk."

Robert nodded and headed back to work.

Luke gazed around at the devastating sight before him. His neighbors and their ranch hands worked the two dozen fire rigs like a united fighting force soldiering onward in a valiant attempt to conquer the blaze.

"It's useless," he whispered as he headed toward the Diamond C's wagon. He stumbled and almost lost his footing, with the realization probably everything on his ranch would be destroyed. But not his family.

Never his family.

Ned appeared at his elbow. "Damn it, Sonny Boy. We're in trouble here. That wind is ablowin' even stronger. Ain't gonna be long afore the fire crests the valley."

"I have to evacuate the women and children, Ned." Luke ducked his head. Admitting defeat wounded his pride, but with the possibility of losing Maggie and their children, common sense won out over his ego.

Luke almost jumped out of his boots when the ear-splitting crack of thunder nearly deafened him. And then the heavens opened. Ned raised his arms to the sky and danced a little jig. Within a minute their clothes were soaked.

A tall fellow grabbed Luke around the middle from behind and swung him in a circle like a crazy man. Luke couldn't identify the man due to the bandana covering his face. "It's pouring rain, Luke. That will put out the fire sure as anything." The man set Luke back on his feet.

"You got that right, Cody," agreed Luke, recognizing Cody Maxwell's voice. Cody and some of the ranch hands from the Circle M were among the first to arrive. He doubted his pa, Buddy Maxwell, would have made the trip. He'd heard Buddy had been ailing lately.

Beaming beneath his bandana, Luke remembered how close he'd come to losing everything his pa had worked so hard to build. Luke would have rescued his family, but the house, the barns, all else would have been a pile of burnt rubble.

Wilber Simpson grabbed Luke by the shoulders and almost smothered him in an enthusiastic bear hug.

"Careful, Wilber, my ribs are cracking," teased Luke, grinning. He'd never appreciated a hug more in his entire life. When Wilber released him, Ned slapped his back from behind, knocking him off balance. The old fellow was stronger than Luke gave him credit for.

"I near can't believe it!" exclaimed Ned. "We're seein' us a miracle here. Our womenfolk must have been doin' a mess aprayin'."

Luke embraced Ned in a bear hug, similar to the one he'd just received. Damn it felt good!

"Look at them dern fools." Ned sounded disgusted but grinned broadly.

Luke glanced about. "Taken leave of their senses," agreed Luke, as he watched the firefighters whooping it up and dancing in the rain. "But all for a good cause."

Luke stopped beside the Diamond C's water wagon, and Ned almost collided with him. "Good job, fellows. I appreciate your help more than I can say. Now let's head over to the house and eat. I'm starved!" Luke had left his pocket watch at the house, but he'd guess it was probably past seven. Regardless, the women would be waiting for them.

By seven-thirty, the rain had snuffed out the fire and reduced itself to a light mist. Cody Maxwell organized a few younger men to stay behind with him and watch for hot spots when the rained stopped. The rest of Luke's neighbors headed for his house for a well-deserved meal. Mike volunteered to bring out some food for the men left behind.

Luke reined in Thunder at the main corral, and he gazed around the yard. Several tables were set up outside the cookhouse, ready for their arrival. Morning Star and Agnes stuck their heads out of the door. "They're coming," cried Agnes, and the women materialized with towels to wipe down the tables, followed by tablecloths and platters heaped with food.

Luke dismounted and handed the reins to one of his men. He patted Thunder, removed his Stetson, shook the rain from it, and then set it back on his head. A female voice he would recognize anywhere screamed his name. Maggie flew across the yard, holding her skirts aloft as she headed for Luke on the run. He raced to meet her. "Slow down woman, you'll trip and ruin that pretty dress, petticoats on display for God and half the male population of Spirit Creek to see," he teased.

"You're safe. Oh, you're safe, Luke." Maggie threw her arms around his neck.

Grinning like a schoolboy, he lifted his wife off her feet in a tight embrace. Forgetting himself, he kissed her full on the mouth. From the direction of the cookhouse, a cacophony of hoots and whistles drifted to his ears. He might be the target of a good ribbing at the moment, but damned if it wasn't worth it.

Luke set Maggie down, and for several seconds they just stared into each other's eyes.

"It's over, sweetheart. The fire's out." Luke kissed her again, unable to contain his happiness. "For a time, I thought we would lose everything. But your prayers did the trick."

"I prayed so hard, I was afraid I'd hurt something," teased Maggie, laughing despite the tears streaming down her cheeks. "Everything is saved: the house, the barns, the entire ranch."

* * *

Ellie observed Robert while he unsaddled his horse and tended to him. Robert's face was covered in soot to the point he was unrecognizable when he first rode into the barnyard. She'd never seen him looking so dishevelled: clothes caked in mud, hair plastered to his head, face streaked with mud. Despite his appearance, he'd never looked better to her. The thought shocked her. Did her feelings for Robert run deeper than mere friendship? Soon, Robert completed his task and led his horse into a vacant stall.

Minutes later, hidden from view just inside the horse barn's doorway, Robert and Ellie observed the touching reunion playing out before them.

"Luke will squeeze the stuffing out of his wife if he's not careful," whispered Robert, as he stepped behind Ellie and wrapped his arms around her.

Ellie's body stiffened for a moment before she relaxed and savored his warmth. With his mouth a mere inch from her ear, his breath tickled the back of her neck. A shiver raced through her body. She should wiggle out of his embrace, being so intimate with a man who wasn't her husband seemed wrong. But at the same time, it felt so wonderful. Just another minute, and then she'd move away.

"Look. Ned and Morning Star exchanged a kiss." Ellie smiled when Morning Star smacked her husband's arm afterward. "I'm not certain she's comfortable with public displays of affection."

Robert pointed and Ellie gazed across the yard.

She burst out laughing. "Do you suppose Mike and Agnes will be coming up for air any time soon?"

"It's obvious the honeymoon isn't over yet," observed Ellie.

"Do you know what we're looking at?"

Robert shook his head.

"Real relationships, with the forever kind of love." Ellie sighed. "What I wouldn't give to be blessed with that some day?"

Robert patted her arms and turned her around to face him. "Anything's possible. If you want it badly enough. Or you could just make it happen."

"Seems out of my reach, too much to expect." Ellie blinked back the tears that burned behind her eyes. She'd recovered from the shock of Franklin's death. But could she trust her own judgment, considering she'd fallen for Jimmy George's offer, oblivious to his true abusive, hateful nature?

Robert met her eyes. "Commitment from a man, unconditional love, family and children. None of that is too much to ask for. Once a man finds the woman he wants to wake up beside every day for the rest of his life, the woman he wants to bear his children, anything is possible." Robert gazed across the yard. "Belle's going to curl that old fellow's toes so badly, Third will never straighten them out again."

Ellie smiled as she gazed at the couple locked in a passionate embrace. A second later, they broke the kiss and stared into each other's eyes, both talking at once. Ellie couldn't hear what was being said from this distance, but tears streamed down Belle's cheeks. Despite their forty year age difference, any fool could see they loved each other dearly.

"I couldn't believe how well those men performed together, Ellie.

Wealthy ranchers toiled alongside ranch hands who haven't two nickels to rub together. Covered in dirt and soot, the men were indistinguishable as they worked toward a common goal. I admit, I couldn't have been more surprised. But I was equally impressed."

"*You* were impressed?" Ellie laughed. "I spent the day in the kitchen with a native woman, a retired soiled dove, and a former Philadelphia debutante!"

"Country folk are special." Robert ran his hand up Ellie's back.

His touch burned through her soaked dress. She looked down and gasped, the outline of her figure quite evident with the wet garment plastered to her body. She wrapped her arms across her chest to cover her unseemly display of raised nipples, hoping for some semblance of modesty.

"Here, this will help." Robert tugged off his vest, shook out the rain, and wrapped it around her shoulders.

"I'd better change before I catch my death," whispered Ellie, touched by his thoughtfulness.

Robert chuckled. "It's still eighty degrees in the shade. I doubt you'll catch pneumonia, sweetheart."

"I suppose not." Ellie felt herself blush to her hairline at the unexpected endearment.

For a moment, they stared into each other's eyes.

"I'm glad you're back safe, too," she whispered, the body heat generated from him standing so near was drying her dress. She'd never experienced such a strong response to a man's touch before, drawn to him like a magnet to metal.

"Thank you. It means a lot that you care." Robert placed his hands on her shoulders.

Ellie tipped her head back and gazed into his hazel eyes holding her spellbound. He looked so exhausted, she thought, but she'd been so pleased when he'd willingly risked his own safety and promptly volunteered to help Luke and the others.

Robert wrapped her in a tight embrace, drawing her body close against his. She immediately felt the evidence of his attraction to her. Before she realized his intention, Robert pressed his mouth to hers. She rose on her toes, closed her eyes and kissed him back, savoring the warmth of his lips on hers. Sparks snapped between them and she almost fainted from the pleasure of being in his arms, being kissed so passionately.

Finally, Robert broke the kiss. Ellie opened her eyes to discover him smiling. "If I'd known it would be that wonderful, I would have started a grassfire myself, weeks ago."

"Don't even joke about such a thing!" she scolded him.

"I'm sorry." Robert lifted her off her feet. "I could get used to coming home to you every evening. Perhaps I should initiate your divorce paperwork tomorrow."

For a moment, Ellie stood stunned. *Home to you every evening?* Were the gossips correct? Did Robert covet her for his own? Did he intend to pursue her until she agreed to marriage? Hoped she'd bear his children? Was he in love with her?

The idea appealed to her.

"Please set the divorce in motion," she whispered. Once she rid herself of Jimmy George, she would be free to pursue a relationship with Robert and discover if they were well-suited. Was it possible they were destined to share a lifetime together?

Regardless, she'd learned her lesson; there would be no funny business or a baby started until the 'I do's' were said. She wouldn't put herself through such an ordeal again. She wouldn't allow him liberties beyond a few kisses until they were wed. If they were wed. Was it possible she only imagined his intentions?

"Our hideout is about to be revealed," he whispered in Ellie's ear, just as Luke arrived outside the barn, leading Thunder.

"I can't tell you how happy I am that this all turned out well for you," stated Robert, stepping aside so Luke could enter with his stallion.

"Thank you, Robert. I appreciate your help today. You're a hard worker and not afraid to get a little dirty. I must say, I've earned a new respect for you." Luke removed the horse's saddle and blanket.

"That means a lot. Thank you. I can see why you love ranching so much, Luke. Wide open spaces, good men working for you, lifelong friends and neighbors who'll drop everything to come give you a hand in a time of need." Robert reached for a brush to groom the horse. "Don't know as you'd find as many selfless folks in a big city."

"It's just the way of the West, Robert. Back when my father and others first settled here, folks knew their survival depended on everyone pitching in to help each other." Luke measured a ration of oats for his prized mount.

"I certainly saw it today." Robert patted Thunder. He completed the grooming and tossed the brush back in the tack box.

"I dare say you're one of us now, Robert. A man of the West, despite the fact you're a lawyer," teased Luke, leading Thunder into a stall.

Robert chuckled. "Spirit Creek needs a lawyer to keep all you western folks on the straight and narrow."

Luke tossed his head back and laughed. "No doubt, you're right. Let's get a plate of grub and eat with our women folk."

Robert's mouth fell open. "I don't have women folk."

"Yet," replied Luke with a wink for Ellie.

Ellie dipped her head, feeling herself blushing again. Would she be his wife some day? She had to admit the idea was growing on her, more and more by the hour.

* * *

After a meal of thickly-sliced beef sandwiches with cheese and pickles was consumed, gallons of coffee and tea disappeared in minutes, along with every piece of cake and slice of pie the ladies set out. Then the men tipped back their chairs and the pipes and cigars were lit.

"Speech, speech," yelled someone from the closest table.

Luke stood, gently pulling Maggie to her feet and clasping her hand in his. "We haven't the words to express our appreciation for your tireless efforts today. Where would any of us be without our faithful neighbors and trusted ranch hands helping out on a day like today? A mere 'thank you' doesn't seem sufficient to my way of thinking." Luke met his wife's eyes. "You men have helped save our ranch. And you've saved the annual Carlyle community picnic, to be held right here on the Diamond C Ranch on August 30. I expect to see everyone one of you back here for that."

"Hear, hear," shouted a fellow near the back.

Raucous applause, foot-stomping, cheering and whistling followed.

Soon, one by one the men extended their goodbyes and headed home. Everyone appeared dead tired, but every man took pride in knowing he'd contributed to the happy ending. Bone-weary but exhilarated, the women cleaned up and washed the dishes while four ranch hands stayed behind to haul the tables and chairs back inside the cookhouse.

With the cleanup complete, Luke brought a couple of bottles of whiskey into the bunkhouse, accompanied by Robert. Somehow a toast seemed a fitting end to the day's success. The old hands joked about past community picnics and the young men issued challenges among themselves in the horseshoe matches, shooting contests, and foot races. Robert, the town dweller, had been accepted by the other men, and someone challenged him to enter the horse race with his impressive Morgan gelding. Luke explained the day's events to Robert who'd never attended before, despite the fact he'd lived in Spirit Creek for a few years now. Everyone was looking forward to the special day, and Robert accepted the invitation to participate.

At nightfall, Luke and Robert washed up with the ranch hands, a rowdy affair involving a dunking in a horse trough followed by several basins of hot water. Ned and Third said their goodnights and headed home to their wives. Dressed in clean clothes again, Luke and Robert left the tack room and headed up to the main house.

* * *

After chatting for a few minutes with Maggie and Ellie, the men retired to Luke's study. Robert's gaze moved to the painted bookshelves that lined three walls and strained under the weight of hundreds of books. A small fireplace stood in the corner of the fourth wall. A huge mahogany desk and leather upholstered chair monopolized the floor space. Two ladder-backed chairs flanked a small round table to the left of the desk, and an assortment of spirits and crystal glasses rested atop another small table in the far corner.

Luke poured two glasses of brandy, handed one to Robert, and then seated himself behind his desk. Robert sat opposite Luke on one of the ladder-backed chairs. Each man took a sip of his drink.

"May I ask you a question concerning Ellie?" Robert ventured, hoping Luke wouldn't consider him no better than the local gossips. Ellie and Maggie were the best of friends, and perhaps Maggie and Luke had discussed his friendship with Ellie.

"Do you have something on your mind?" Luke set his drink on the desk, leaned back in his chair, and crossed his arms.

Robert shifted in his chair and cleared his throat. Why was he sweating like a schoolboy hauled up in front of the headmaster? "I'm certain you've heard the gossip about Ellie and me."

"Unless you inhabit a cave, you can't help but hear the latest gossip."

"Well, I can't deny that I'd like nothing better than Ellie's permission to court her. But we need to see if that scoundrel Barkley returns home. Or, get the paperwork started on a divorce. I assume Maggie has mentioned that." Robert's foot tapped on the plank floor; he couldn't hide his nervousness. And perhaps he'd let slip a client's plans.

"Yes, she mentioned her plans. She's so afraid Barkley will return, I imagine she's made up her mind about the divorce," stated Luke, leaning forward in his chair.

Robert experienced a moment of euphoria. He hadn't given Ellie enough credit. Of course she was too sensible to waste another moment of her time on the likes of Barkley. But he'd wager, until he returned from fighting the fire tonight, she hadn't spent much time thinking about him. Or had she? His heart flipped over in his chest at the possibility she shared his feelings. The passionate kiss they'd exchanged while secreted away from prying eyes certainly indicated she was developing strong feelings for him. Could they have a future together?

"Even if she divorces Barkley, I suspect she's still mourning her fiancé who died during the capture of the gang of rustlers." Luke sighed, shook his head. "Smith was a good lawman and a dear friend. I miss him, too."

Robert's mood plummeted. It had never occurred to him that Ellie would be mourning Smith still, especially since she remarried so soon after the fellow's death. And he'd never understood her reasoning behind such an impulsive move. She didn't strike him as the type of woman who constantly required a man at her side, unable to stand on her own two feet for even a minute." Robert set his glass on the corner of the desk. "Ellie was certainly financially capable of supporting herself after Smith's death, so I have no idea why she married Barkley in the first place."

"Ellie had her reasons, but you'll have to question her about that yourself." Luke stubbed out his cigar and rose to his feet.

Robert recognized the unspoken signal that the conversation had ended. He had hoped Luke would satisfy his curiosity, but he still had no idea what prompted Ellie's hasty decision. After Smith's death, she'd barely taken a deep breath before marrying Barkley. And why would Ellie still be mourning Smith? Instead of receiving answers, he had even more questions concerning the whole mystery. And why was Luke being so secretive? Obviously, he was apprised of the reason. Well, he'd simply take Luke's advice and ask Ellie.

"I'd better be leaving for town. It's almost dark." Robert downed the rest of his drink, set his glass on Luke's desk, and rose to leave. At the door, he turned and paused for a minute.

"Was there something else you wanted to discuss?" asked Luke.

"No. You've been very helpful. Thank you." Robert smiled. When they were in the barn, Ellie had given him permission to initiate divorce proceedings. At least Luke had confirmed that Ellie was eager to divorce Barkley, scandal be damned. "I'll tie my horse behind Ellie's rig and drive her and Edward back to town. Wouldn't feel right sending the pair of them off alone in the dark."

"I'm certain she'll appreciate your thoughtfulness, Robert."

The men shook hands and headed out of the house.

* * *

"Don't be a stranger, Ellie," said Maggie, hugging her friend tightly. "I'm coming to town mid-week and I'll drop by for tea. Perhaps I'll bring Belle with me."

"That would be lovely and bring the babies, too." Ellie smiled, recalling her enjoyment, playing with Willie and Matilda today. Her heart was healing; her loss was less painful. She climbed into the buggy that Third had brought round for her, lamp lit to guide the way. She settled her skirts. It had been a long, exhausting, and emotional day, and she couldn't wait to return to town. Third kissed his grandson's cheek and then lifted him into the buggy.

"Ellie, hold up a minute," called Luke. "It will soon be pitch black out there. Robert is tying his horse to the rig and driving you and Edward back to town."

"That won't be necessary. I have lamplight to see the way. Edward and I will be fine." Ellie smiled, but her heart pounded like an Indian war drum. She shouldn't be traveling with Robert, considering her new-found attraction to the man. How could she avoid Robert's kind offer short of slapping the reins across the mare's back and high-tailing it off the ranch?

"Nonsense, I'll only be a minute." Robert lit out for the barn to fetch his mount.

"Whose idea was this?" grumbled Ellie, glaring at Luke while her face warmed.

Luke grinned and slipped an arm around his wife's middle. "Good night, Ellie. Safe trip home now."

"Safe trip, my foot," she muttered, feeling her face flaming. She couldn't remove from her mind the memory of that bone-melting kiss she shared with Robert in the barn. What he must think of her! A married woman acting so brazenly. Why had she done such an outlandish thing?

Peeking in back, she discovered Edward was already sound asleep, one arm wrapped around Captain. Even the dog was asleep. How would she survive a twenty-five minute buggy ride with Robert at her side?

CHAPTER 16

Ellie reasoned that Robert had insisted he accompany her home due to his penchant for thoughtfulness. His willingness to help out with the grassfire proved the point. But a dozen questions begged for the asking, and he alone could answer them. The buggy rumbled toward town, and although they'd only just travelled beyond the Diamond C Ranch sign, she couldn't contain her curiosity a minute longer.

"Why didn't Sadie Peterman accompany you today?" she blurted into the darkness.

"Why would I take Sadie Peterman anywhere?" Robert's response exploded from him.

Ellie's jaw dropped and her gloved hand flew to her mouth. Feeling herself blushing, she twisted in her seat to check on Edward. Her son, exhausted from a fun-filled day at the ranch, slept through her companion's outburst. Captain leapt to his feet and growled deep in his throat, prepared to defend her from the angry-sounding man.

"It's okay, boy." Ellie patted the dog's head, and Captain settled down beside Edward. Captain eyed Robert's back for several seconds before closing his eyes and sleeping again.

Ellie twisted forward on the bench seat and met Robert's anger-filled eyes discernible in the shadowy moonlight.

"Because…you're…courting her," she stammered.

"Courting her? Are you daft, woman? I'm not insane!" Robert's face reddened to the point of apoplexy. And then he added, "I apologize for that display of bad manners. Please forgive me."

"I hadn't anticipated inciting such a volatile reaction. I apologize for upsetting you." Ellie twisted her handkerchief in her hands. She gritted her teeth. For a second, she regretted bringing up the subject, but she'd wallowed in too deep to stop now. She just hoped Robert didn't consider her one of Spirit Creek's deplorable gossips. "I'm not making this up. Sadie

Peterman informed me in no uncertain terms that her father granted permission for you to court her." Ellie sat a little taller and glared at her seat mate, daring him to deny her allegations. Her heartbeat slowed to normal, but her face felt warm.

"From the moment I relocated here and transferred my funds to Peterman's bank, he has encouraged his daughter's flirtations. She has invited me to supper so often I've lost count. Mrs. Peterman employs an exceptional cook, but I doubt very much if Sadie could boil water."

Ellie attempted to stifle a snicker, but failed.

"For weeks Peterman has encouraged me to share their family pew on Sundays, but I've always graciously declined. Now, Sadie has taken to hovering in the church doorway until a second before Reverend Gerald begins his service. As soon as everyone stands for the opening hymn, Sadie dashes inside and sidles into the pew beside me."

"I've noticed that you sit with her every week."

"Not my doing, I assure you. I'm certain Miss Sadie Peterman is more interested in my bank balance and my position in the community than she is in me," said Robert, patting her hand in the darkness.

Ellie jumped a foot.

"I'm sorry if I startled you."

"I'm still a little jittery… after Jimmy George…" Ellie grimaced but hoped he wouldn't notice in the dim moonlight.

"Understandably, you're a little skittish still."

"You're a kind-hearted fellow," she whispered in the dark. Ellie had detected a great deal of sympathy and caring in his voice. Could he genuinely care for her? If that kiss they shared in the barn was any indication…

They rode in companionable silence for several minutes, and then Robert startled her again when he spoke. "Apparently, Ellie, half the citizens of Spirit Creek believe I've developed strong feelings for you."

"So…you've heard the gossip…about us," she stammered.

"Perhaps Sadie heard the rumors. Likely as not, she hoped to convince you I'd transferred my affections her way," speculated Robert.

"Anything is possible with Sadie." Ellie caught the word 'transferred' and her heart leapt unexpectedly. How long had she already held his affections, if transferring would have been required? Was she missing something here? How long had he considered her more than just a client or friend?

"I'm fully aware of Sadie's shortcomings. While partaking of a whiskey in Darby O'Dell's establishment two days after I arrived in town, several fellows warned me about the town's husband-hunting vixen."

Robert sounded annoyed.

"And you've heeded their warning?" she ventured.

"After Luke Carlyle introduced me to Miss Ellie Thomas following a church service one Sunday, I was smitten and have been ever since. Engaged or not, married or not, you're the only woman for me," admitted Robert, meeting her eyes.

Ellie sat, speechless.

* * *

Now he'd done it! Robert silently declared himself a first-rate fool for confessing his deepest feelings for Ellie. She'd consider him deranged, possibly dangerously so, after such an inappropriate admission.

"I shouldn't have blurted that out, Ellie. Please forgive me." Robert awaited the tongue lashing he certainly deserved. For a moment, he considered the possibility she'd secreted away a small pistol in her handbag. If she whipped out a gun, he just might shoot himself with it and save her the grief. He braced himself for her reaction.

Ellie remained silent, her hands clasped together in her lap.

"Are you all right, Ellie?" he asked, softly.

"Actually, I'm contemplating how best to respond," she spoke without looking his way. "Should I be shocked, or flattered, or pleased, or…"

"Frightened, or horrified…," added Robert.

"No, never frightened. After enduring my husband's abuse…I could never be afraid of a wonderful man like you, Robert."

She smiled; he heard it in her voice At least, she didn't consider him a candidate for commitment. "Ellie, I'm prepared to bide my time while you grieve your young fiancé who died so tragically. Luke told me you loved him very much." Robert grimaced.

Now why had he shared the fact that he'd spoken to Luke? Would Ellie believe he'd questioned Luke at length about every aspect of her life? Frankly, it wasn't any of his business. A gentleman could offer condolences, voice concern for a woman's well-being. But a normal fellow didn't grill another man for intimate details concerning a lady's personal life.

Robert glanced over at Ellie.

"I'd given up on marriage and children of my own. I'd declared myself a spinster, destined to teach other folks' children for the rest of my days. Then Franklin arrived in town." Ellie sighed and she whispered, "He showed an interest in me and I believed Franklin Smith was the love of my life. I miss him, but the pain has lessened each day."

In truth, after sharing that mind-numbing kiss with Robert, she wasn't all together certain about her feelings for Franklin. Perhaps he'd become a pleasant habit, a comfortable companion. She'd certainly never experienced a lightning-bolt response to his kisses like she had with Robert today. She'd felt certain Franklin was the man for her. Could she have been wrong?

Was Robert her destiny?

"I'd never found a woman that I knew was meant for me until you crossed my path." Robert contemplated his next question for a second, and then decided to jump in with both feet. "Would you ever consider marrying again, Ellie?"

"Even if starving, I would never put myself or my son in such a precarious position again. I would never marry a man I didn't love just to provide a father for Edward. I've learned my lesson with Jimmy George," she stated firmly.

Judging by her answer, Robert realized that monster Barkley had hurt her as much emotionally as physically. No woman should be subjected to such abuse. Robert didn't consider himself a person capable of violence, but he hoped Jimmy George Barkley was dead. If not, he could strangle him with his bare hands.

Robert felt his face pale. "I'm nothing like Jimmy George Barkley!"

"I know."

"I want nothing but the best for you."

"I know."

"I wasn't proposing we marry this minute." Robert sighed and lowered his voice almost to a whisper. "I'm willing to wait until you're ready for courting. I'm just hoping someday…" he left his fondest wish hanging in the air.

She remained silent and looked away.

Let it be, he decided. He'd made enough of a fool of himself. Ellie didn't reciprocate his feelings and perhaps she never would. That sharp noise he heard was his heart breaking.

* * *

Ellie was surprised at her strong opposition to Robert's innocent question. He slumped on the bench seat beside her. Was he angry? Had she hurt his feelings? Should she apologize? Perhaps it would be best to just leave it alone.

She revisited his question in her mind. *Would you ever consider marrying again?* She couldn't deny the fact Edward would benefit from a decent father, a kind and dependable man to guide him as he grew and matured into manhood. Robert would be an ideal candidate; she liked him, admired his work ethic, and appreciated his friendship. Would her attraction to him deepen to love over time?

"It wasn't my intention to hurt you, Robert. I'm just confused. I'm grieving more than you know, and I'm waiting to hear if Jimmy George has been located. I've become the sole parent of a wonderful little boy, whom I love very much. My life is a roiling sea of uncertainty right now. I can't think beyond tomorrow, never mind consider the future." Ellie reached out and touched his arm. "I'm sorry. Maybe when my divorce is granted…"

"I understand, Ellie." Robert covered her hand with his and she didn't pull away. "I've patiently stood by for months now, watching you plan a wedding with one man, and then marry another one. Quite frankly, I've been quite confused about the whole business myself."

"You don't know the whole story, Robert."

The buggy pulled up in front of her small house.

"I'll return the rig to the livery for you." Robert helped Ellie down, scooped Edward up in his arms, and gently laid the child's head on his shoulder. Captain stretched and then leapt to the ground.

As Ellie led the way into the house, shadows crossed the pathway and the moon peeked out from the clouds overhead. An owl screeched from a low-hanging branch of a cottonwood, startling Ellie, and she tripped on the top step. Robert quickly reached out to steady her. She opened the front door, lit a lamp, and guided Robert toward the parlor. He almost tripped over Captain racing inside around his feet. The dog's eyes never left Robert as he carried Edward.

Robert settled Edward on the sofa, and then lovingly brushed the child's cheek with his hand. Ellie's breath caught, witnessing the affectionate gesture. Robert and Ellie retraced their steps to her doorway. For a minute, they stared at each other and Ellie feared he would kiss her, equally afraid he wouldn't.

"I talked to Luke after dinner."

"I know," whispered Ellie.

"I asked him why a seemingly sane woman would marry so soon after her betrothed died. He insisted I ask you about it." Robert met her eyes in the flickering lamp light.

"Personal reasons, Robert." After their conversation on the way home, she felt closer to him than ever before, but she couldn't reveal the secret she'd paid so dearly to keep.

Admitting the sin of conceiving a child out of wedlock would be too humiliating. Robert might understand why she'd married a total stranger, but most certainly, his opinion of her would be altered forever. As an honorable man with impeccable morals, Robert would lose all respect for her. She valued his friendship, and she couldn't risk jeopardizing his help with her finances. Perhaps she should forget about any hopes of there being more between them.

"Luke insisted you had your reasons, but he wouldn't clarify what he meant by that." Robert reached for her hand and raised it to his lips. Smiling, he placed a gentle kiss on each finger.

"Robert," she whispered, her head spinning with unexpected desire for him. She searched his eyes, witnessed his efforts to quell his own passion.

"Before I leave, I demand an answer. Why on earth did you marry Jimmy George Barkley?" Robert released her hand and stared at her intensely.

Ellie gasped at the intensity of his question, the impatience she saw in his eyes. With a strength she didn't know she possessed, she shoved him through the threshold and slammed the door in his face. Shocked by what she'd done, she collapsed on the floor and succumbed to a bout of tears.

CHAPTER 17

Tuesday, August 12, 1890

Shorty leaned forward in the saddle, stretching his back. Patience was about his least favorite thing, and he'd been waiting, hidden out of sight behind this thicket, for almost an hour. Shorty swatted at the flies buzzing around his head. Dang it all anyway. Weren't nobody traveling into Miles City today?

Hell, how on earth had Billy Bob talked him into this hair-brained idea? Knock a traveler out cold, rob him of his clothes, and leave him hidden in the bushes. That seemed the easy part. Sneak into Spirit Creek and learn something about Jimmy George's woman without raising any suspicions about himself. Ha!

Shorty would have preferred to just ride into town, sidle up to some fool in a saloon and start jawing with him. Oh, no. Billy Bob wasn't having any of that. Can't let anyone see him for fear some lawman recognizes Shorty Jenkins from a Wanted poster. He pushed his hat back on his head as he swiped his sweaty brow with his shirt sleeve. He settled his hat back on straight. If Billy Bob was here, Shorty would give him a piece of his mind!

The sound of a horse's hooves pounding the parched ground drew Shorty's attention and he peeked from behind the thicket. A lone rider was approaching. The well-dressed fellow looked about Shorty's size. Before he could second guess his decision, Shorty kicked his horse in the sides and leapt into view. The rider pulled up on his mount's reins hoping to avoid a collision.

"What the hell…"

Shorty swung the heavy tree branch and connected with the man, knocking him out of the saddle. Quick as you please, Shorty dropped the branch, leapt off his horse, and tackled the fellow. A few well-placed fists had the traveler sleeping soundly.

Five minutes later, the man had been relieved of his trousers, shirt, waistcoat and boots. Down to his long johns, he slept behind the bushes. Meanwhile, Shorty was dressed to the nines in the finest duds he'd ever seen. Dang he wished he had a mirror so he could see himself, looking a fine specimen of a man. He slapped the fellow's bowler on his head.

"Well, that went real good." Shorty laughed and flapped his arms until the fellow's horse ran off. Shorty returned to his own mount and leapt into the saddle. "Bet you don't recognize me, Rex," he observed, patting the animal's neck. "I'm…oh, hell. I forgot the name Billy Bob said to call myself."

Shorty reined his horse toward Spirit Creek.

"Jamison. No, Johnson. No, Jackson." Shorty muttered possible monikers aloud. He'd better high-tail it into town and find out what he wanted to know before that fellow came to and made his way to either the Spirit Creek or Miles City sheriff's office. Provided, of course, his horse returned.

Around five o'clock, Shorty rode into Spirit Creek, sitting tall in the saddle and feeling like a million bucks. A proper suit of clothes did that for a man, he figured. He passed a couple of drinking establishments, but the place that caught his eye was The Joker's Wild Saloon. Shorty figured he'd need all the luck he could muster up, and he'd pretend he had a joker up his sleeve to pull this off.

Shorty tied his steed to the hitching post around the corner in hopes no one would recognize his stolen horse. He wandered into the saloon and stepped up to the bar. He licked his parched lips; robbing a feller of his clothes worked up a man's thirst. A red-headed Irish feller smiled at him.

"What can I get a fine gentleman like yourself?" the feller inquired in a thick Irish brogue, peeking over his wire-rimmed spectacles.

Gentleman.

Shorty could get used to that. He smiled back. "Whiskey. Thank you kindly."

"Aye. Whiskey it is." The Irishman poured a shot and set it on the bar. "Name's Darby O'Dell. What brings ya to town, sir? I haven't seen you 'round these parts before."

"And you probably won't be seeing me again. Just passing through on my way to Miles City, but I worked up a bit of a thirst on the trail." Shorty downed the shot. He'd never tasted anything quite like it in his life. But he'd drunk worse. He passed the glass back.

"Another?" confirmed the barkeep.

"It's a hot day today." Shorty tossed the fellow another coin.

"Here ya go, sir," said O'Dell. "I've other customers to tend to, but

I'll be back in a minute."

Shorty nodded his head. He'd take his time drinking this shot. Many more, and he wouldn't be fit to ride Rex without toppling off.

The barman rushed to the other end of the enormous in-laid mahogany bar and conversed with a pair of customers seated together. The men appeared deep in a heated discussion.

Shorty eavesdropped on several conversations at once.

"Damn hot weather's to blame for that fire out on the Diamond C."

"Dry conditions. We needed rain."

"Are you headed to Miles City like ya planned?"

"Nope. Got a meetin' with that damn banker fellow, Peterman, tomorrow."

"Lightning without rain is bad business."

"Thinking of selling some of my steers. Too dang dry on my land."

"Well, that grassfire was winning. The whole ranch would have been ashes if the rain hadn't started to pour when it did."

Shorty leaned back against the bar. Grassfire on the range threatened some ranch. He could care less. Talk of bankers and cattle. Waste of his time. Maybe Shorty should wiggle his way into one of these conversations. Just a subtle-like observation, so as not to end up with a pistol upside his head. For now, he'd just continue to listen.

"I heard tell that lawyer happened to come to Sunday dinner at the Carlyle place, and he even helped out, fighting the fire."

"Rutherford? The feller the gossips have been saying is interested in Mrs. Barkley?" The man laughed. "If old Barkley ever returns to town, Rutherford will find his britches full of buckshot."

Shorty nearly choked on his sip of liquor. Now we're talking, boys. Give it up. What all do you know about old Barkley.

"I doubt there's any truth to it. Just the gossips making trouble. Ellie being a schoolmarm and all. She ain't likely to scandalize folks by messing with some feller ain't her husband." The old-timer sent a stream of tobacco in the direction of the spittoon, and actually hit the target.

"Heard she's raising Barkley's son as her own. Good of her to step up for the young'un."

"Do ya suppose that lawman will ever return to town? If'n I was married to a fine-looking woman like Ellie, I wouldn't be up and disappearing as he done." The man downed his drink and slammed the glass on the bar.

"Me neither, but maybe Ellie is just friends with Rutherford. I heard she claimed she's got legal dealings with the lawyer, nothing more."

"Ain't no never mind to me. I'd best get home to my own woman. There'll be the devil to pay if'n I'm late for supper." The man slid off his chair, caught his balance, and landed on his feet in one impressive move. Seemed to Shorty that the man had been patronizing the place for a few hours now.

Shorty finished his drink. He'd learned everything he needed to know. The wife's name was Ellie. She was friends with some lawyer named Rutherford. How difficult could it be to find a law office in a town this size? He'd ride up and down every street until he found the place, and then he'd head back to the hideout and share his findings with Billy Bob. This Rutherford fellow could tell them where Ellie lived, and he'd bet that traveler feller's fancy new boots, the woman would know where their money was hidden.

Shorty waved to O'Dell and sauntered out of the saloon. He climbed into the saddle and rode around town for less than ten minutes before he found an impressive old house with a sign stating 'Law Office' nailed above the front door.

"Yessiree," whispered Shorty, reining Rex toward the outskirts of town. He couldn't wait to start spending that money!

CHAPTER 18

Thursday, August 14, 1890

Ellie settled her bonnet on her head, tied the ribbons under her chin, and closed her front door on the way out. As she strode toward the general store, she recalled the evening she slammed the door in Robert's face in order to avoid answering his question.

The man appeared as thick-skinned as a crocodile. For the past week and a half she'd attempted to avoid him, quite unsuccessfully. Every time she'd ventured into the general store, he'd slipped in a few minutes later, claiming he'd run out of sugar, or flour, or coffee, or something. His larder must be filled to bursting by now. And every time he'd insisted on carrying her purchases home.

"The man's impossible," she complained aloud.

Conveniently, the last time she encountered Robert he'd happened to have her divorce application with him for her to sign. At least, the paperwork had been set in motion.

"Hello, Florence," greeted Ellie as she passed by the Jones' house.

"Hello," responded the harried mother of twelve, eight still living at home. She waved while hanging her wash on the clothesline.

As Ellie continued down the wooden sidewalk, heading toward the town's business section, she recalled how mercilessly Elizabeth Waverly teased her about the lawyer's infatuation with her. If she didn't know better, she'd swear the two of them arranged a secret signal that informed Robert of her presence in the store. The gossips hadn't found a new target and rumors about them continued to circulate.

And it didn't stop there.

Last Sunday, Robert waited until the second before Reverend Gerald announced the first hymn before dashing into the church and slipping into the pew beside her and Edward. No mystery where he'd learned that trick. She cursed Sadie Peterman's existence.

Ellie waved to June Davidson busily sweeping the sidewalk in front of the hotel on the opposite side of the street. "Good morning, June," she called.

"Morning, Ellie." June waved back. "Drop in for a cup of tea if you've got the time."

"I'd love to. Thank you," called Ellie just before she rounded the corner.

Admitting her fondness of Robert's company galled her. Her feelings for him hadn't deepened—at least, she didn't think they had—but he remained kind to her and he'd been trying to win over Edward. Her son wanted nothing to do with Robert. Understandable, considering who'd been her son's example for most of his young life. She hoped someday Edward would realize all men weren't like his father, Robert being one of them.

"Good morning, Elizabeth." The bell above the door tinkled loudly as Ellie swept into the general store.

"It's lovely to see you," greeted Elizabeth, smiling.

"Don't you dare inform Mr. Rutherford I'm here," warned Ellie, forgetting her manners in her annoyed state and rudely wagging her finger at the proprietress.

"Whatever are you talking about, Ellie?" Elizabeth stood hands on hips.

"You know precisely what I'm talking about. It cannot be pure coincidence that that man shows up every time I enter this establishment," accused Ellie.

"I have no control over my patrons. If Mr. Rutherford stops in for supplies, it's simply by chance that you are also present at the time." Elizabeth sighed.

"Chance, my foot." She selected several pieces of candy for Edward who was spending the day at the Diamond C with his grandfather.

Her mind wandered while she continued selecting the items she required. Robert never kissed her on the lips, but every time they parted he'd reach for her hand and place the gentlest kiss on each finger. On a couple of occasions, Ellie felt a swoon coming on but recovered her equilibrium in time. Her face warmed with the direction her thoughts had taken. She glanced in Elizabeth's direction, but the storekeeper's wife busily waited on another customer who wasn't Robert.

Usually, he would have put in an appearance by now.

Where was the man anyway?

She examined the new bolts of calico and satin while she waited.

Last night she'd lain in bed, seriously considering whether or not she was falling in love with Robert. The idea thrilled her, but at the same time, a fearful shiver crawled up her spine. He'd asked her to accompany him on a carriage ride next Sunday. His sudden request had taken her by surprise, and she couldn't fabricate one reason to decline his offer. In truth, she looked forward to the outing.

There was a distinct possibility Jimmy George would return before she could successfully acquire the divorce. Robert had warned her that the process could take as long as a year. She dreaded the thought of what the first encounter with Jimmy George would hold for her if he did suddenly pop back into her life. She hoped she would never lay eyes on her poor excuse for a husband again. But for propriety's sake, she couldn't allow Robert to openly court her in the meantime.

Ellie glanced up every time the bell above the door tinkled when Elizabeth's customers arrived or exited. Feeling slightly disappointed it was never Robert, she returned her attention to the bolts of material.

A second later, Sadie Peterman stormed into the store with the skirts of her satin gown bunched around her legs, almost tripping her. She shook out her skirts and adjusted her elaborate hat which she'd knocked askew during the hasty entrance.

"Ellie Barkley, you've stolen my Robert's affections!" she shouted, eyes blazing. "He's declined my invitations to supper every day this week. And he occupied a pew beside you at Sunday services. You're a shameless thief is what you are. And you are still married to the sheriff."

"Now just one minute, Miss Peterman," warned Elizabeth, charging toward the little troublemaker. "I won't have you shouting at my customers. Out with you." Elizabeth guided Sadie toward the door.

Ellie gasped and she felt her face warm.

"You haven't heard the last of this," Sadie admonished Ellie.

"You've said plenty enough." Elizabeth glared at Sadie, standing hands on hips beside the girl at the front door.

"Robert's rejection has shattered my heart. I'll see to it that your reputation is shredded to pieces. I'm telling the gossips what a horrible woman you are." Sadie turned on her pointy-toed boots and slammed the door on her way out.

"That girl couldn't ruin the reputation of a skunk under a schoolhouse." Elizabeth returned to Ellie's side.

Ellie's heart pounded in her chest. How much more of this could she take? At least, everyone important in her life knew the gossips' rumors were absolute rubbish. Thankfully, no other customers were in the store to witness that humiliating display.

Ronald wrapped her purchases while Ellie settled her nerves over a cup of tea with Elizabeth. And he agreed to deliver her parcels after the store closed. Ellie tucked Edward's bag of candy into her reticule, thanked Elizabeth for the refreshing cup of tea, said her goodbyes, and started for home.

As she strode down the street, Ellie realized Robert hadn't put in an appearance at the store the entire hour she'd been there. She silently scolded herself for her erroneous and uncharitable thoughts toward Elizabeth. Obviously, Ellie was mistaken. It had only been pure coincidence that Robert previously patronized the store at the same moment she had.

Unconsciously, Ellie had taken the long way home, the route that passed by the Spirit Creek Law Office. Still at a considerable distance, Ellie watched two strangers ride up to the law office and dismount. Flipping their horses' reins around the hitching post, the pair strode up the stairs and glanced at each other. Ellie stared in shock as one of the men removed a pistol from his holster. And then they stormed through the law office's front door.

Ellie's boots were rooted in place. She opened her mouth to scream, but not a sound came out. What was happening at the law office? Were Robert's and Janie's lives in danger? Who were those ruffians? One fellow appeared relatively well-dressed, but the other wore ragged and filthy clothing and a badly-worn hat. While the questions raced through her head, she argued with herself as to what course of action she should take. She couldn't just stand around and do nothing!

Help. She must find help.

Ellie whirled around and collided with Deputy Jones who was currently serving as Acting Sheriff in Jimmy George's absence.

"Deputy, did you notice those men enter the law office?" asked Ellie, visibly shaking and grasping the young deputy's arm.

"I saw them. I received a telegraph yesterday warning me to be on the lookout. I'd bet my next paycheck they're the two escaped bank robbers believed to have been working with your husband, ma'am." Deputy Jones grabbed her by the shoulders when she teetered.

"I'm all right," she insisted. There was no time for any weak-kneed silliness; she must help Robert in any way possible.

"Look, Deputy, there's Luke and Ned." Ellie pointed down the street. The two men rode together in a supply wagon coming toward them. "They'll help."

Deputy Jones stepped into the middle of the street, waving wildly.

"What in tarnation is the matter, Jones?" asked Ned, pulling up on the reins as the wagon approached. "Get off the road. Someone's likely as not ta run ya over."

"Luke, could you please help?" requested Ellie from the sidewalk.

"What's the problem?"

"I don't like the look of the two men who entered Robert's law office, and one man drew his pistol. Robert could be in terrible danger."

Ernest Jones related the details of the telegram he'd received to

Luke and Ned, while Ellie continually interrupted with observations of her own.

"Please Luke, you have to help Robert," pleaded Ellie.

"I'd appreciate your assistance, Mr. Carlyle," added Jones, removing his pistol from the holster on his hip. "There are two of them, and they're reportedly a mean pair. Gotta admit I'm not certain I can handle both of them on my own."

Luke and Ned drew their side arms.

"Consider yourselves deputized," stated Ernest.

* * *

"What's the meaning of this? You can't just storm into my office!" Robert Rutherford rounded his desk.

He'd smelled the two men before he saw them. The mountainous one had long stringy brown hair, mangy beard, and cold, piercing black eyes. With rags for clothing, he limped as if his boots were a couple sizes too small. The smaller fellow wore clean fashionable clothes, and a like-new bowler sat atop jet-black hair and rheumy blue eyes.

"I'm sorry, Mr. Rutherford," whimpered Janie Jones, being manhandled by the larger of the two men. "I couldn't stop them."

"I'll do the talking, little lady." The enormous man dragged Miss Jones by the arm across the room and shoved her onto the high-backed chair beside Robert's desk.

"Who are you men and what do you want?" demanded Robert, hoping he sounded considerably braver than he felt at the moment. There hadn't been a lecture in law school that he could recall regarding the proper handling of gun-toting scoundrels, like the pair that just busted their way into his office. Foremost, he must remain calm and protect Miss Jones. From there, he hadn't a clue how to proceed.

"None a yer business who we are. We want some information, and you're gonna give it to us." The fellow grabbed Robert by the front of his white shirt, almost lifting him off his feet. His hand was the size of a grizzly's paw, and he smelled about the same. He toted a gun in his other hand.

"We're lookin' fer a woman. Name's Mrs. Jimmy George Barkley." The smaller man spat a stream of tobacco juice in the general direction of the spittoon kept beside Robert's desk for his clients' use. The man aimed as accurately as a cross-eyed coyote.

"All we want to know is where Ellie's house is." The first fellow's grin exposed yellowed and chipped teeth. His breath could curl a steel pipe.

"I'm afraid I can't be of any help, gentlemen. I'm not acquainted with a woman bearing the name Ellie Barkley. Perhaps you've got the wrong town." Robert hoped the man didn't notice the sweat on his brow. There was no way on earth he would ever tell these men anything about Ellie, and certainly not where she lived.

"Now I believe yer lyin' to us, lawyer man. Shorty here overheard a couple fellers discussin' the woman. Heard you were 'good friends' with her." The ruffian bobbed his eyebrows suggestively, cackling and tightening his hold.

"That's a true fact, Billy Bob. Heard it with my own ears."

"Ya continue unco-operatin' and it won't be healthy fer ya. If ya git my meaning," growled Billy Bob.

"I've told you I don't know anyone by that name. Now, please leave. Miss Jones and I will forget we ever saw you." Robert's voice rose in proportion to the grip on his shirt slowly cutting off his air supply. He prayed he wouldn't pass out and embarrass himself.

"Perhaps Miss Jones here can help." Shorty moved toward the frightened girl.

"Leave her alone!" shouted Robert, squirming wildly.

To his surprise, Billy Bob lost his grip, freeing Robert. Without thinking, he grabbed for the gun and wrestled with the fellow for several seconds.

"Get him off me, dammit." Billy Bob shouted at his partner.

"Dang it all. You're twice his size. Can't you do nothing right?" Shorty bore down on them.

The sound of a gunshot exploded in the room, and Robert crumpled to the floor.

"We'd better get outta here, Billie Bob!"

The two men headed for the door, leaving Robert bleeding profusely on the floor and Miss Jones screaming at the top of her lungs.

CHAPTER 19

"That was a gunshot!" Deputy Jones quickened his pace, Luke and Ned glued to his side.

"Robert!" screamed Ellie, racing past the men on her way toward the law office.

Ernest and Luke overtook her in two strides. "Stay back, Mrs. Barkley," ordered the deputy, grabbing her by the arm and guiding her toward Ned who wrapped his arm around her waist, waylaying her.

"You stay put, ma'am," Ned ordered, planting his feet in the dusty ground. Ellie struggled for a second and then collapsed against him. Ned shuffled over to the wooden sidewalk, taking Ellie along with him. "We'll wait right here where it's safe."

"Keep alert, Luke," warned Deputy Jones, on the run. "We don't know what we're going to find in there." Pistols drawn, Ernest and Luke reached the wooden sidewalk in a dozen strides and leapt up the steps two at a time.

The first ruffian slammed the building's front door back against the wall as he made his escape. Rushing out the door, the mountainous fellow collided with Deputy Jones. Ernest immediately decided being hurled against an oak tree would have been less painful, but before the fellow realized what had happened, he lay on his belly on the sidewalk, in handcuffs.

Luke tripped the second man as he plowed past the deputy, creating a loud thud as he hit the ground. Ernest tossed the rancher a second set of handcuffs. Luke caught them handily and had his prisoner immobilized alongside the other one within seconds.

"That went rather well," observed Deputy Jones, grinning from ear to ear.

"Very well indeed," agreed Luke.

Ellie wiggled free of Ned's hold and raced up the steps, carefully avoiding the two outlaws sprawled on the rickety wooden sidewalk. "I hope you two hooligans are full of splinters," she spat at the two men.

Miss Jones dashed outside, her clothes askew and her hair in disarray but appearing otherwise unharmed. "Help me, please. Mr. Rutherford's been shot." Hoarse from screaming, her plea was no more than a whisper.

"Robert!" Ellie disappeared inside with Deputy Jones and Luke right behind her.

Miss Jones slumped onto the wicker chair situated outside the law office, while Ned held a gun on the two men sprawled on the boardwalk.

"What the hell happened, Billy Bob?" muttered Shorty, shaking his head. "I think my head's concussed. Musta hit a post or the boardwalk when that bastard tripped me."

"Shut up, Shorty. Ya ain't dying."

"Both of ya shut up. Ya best be aprayin' Mr. Rutherford's not dying in there." Ned kicked the one named Shorty with the toe of his boot.

* * *

Robert Rutherford's office floor resembled a bloody battlefield.

Deputy Jones crouched, examined the lawyer, and then met Luke's eyes. "He's breathing, but his pulse is weak."

The lawyer lay in a pool of his own blood, and Ellie collapsed beside his still body. "Hang on, Robert," she pleaded, placing his head in her lap. She bent forward and whispered in his ear. "I need you. Don't you dare die on me, you hear?"

"I'll be right back." Luke charged outside.

"Ned, I'm going to fetch Doc. It doesn't look good." Luke raced down the street in the direction of Doc Benjamin's house and clinic.

* * *

Deputy Jones ensured the two outlaws were securely locked behind bars in the Spirit Creek Jailhouse, but he kept the front and back doors wide open to air out the place. The pair of them smelled worse than a week old slop pail.

Ernest had felt nervous at first, facing down the two escaped prisoners. But with Luke Carlyle there for support, he'd handled himself with confidence. Offering the two fools special favors had proven a stroke of genius since the dang idiots had believed him. Reportedly, both of the prisoners were meaner than a pair of grizzlies with a sore paw, but for the past two hours, they'd been singing like a pair of pretty yellow canaries, admitting to all manner of crimes in hopes of saving their hides.

After he was riled to the point of distraction, Billy Bob blurted out a confession to killing Jimmy George. The rest of the details regarding the matter flowed from his partner's mouth. Ernest even figured out Shorty was the fellow who'd ambushed Stan Wakeman on his way to Miles City a couple days ago. Stan had ridden his horse back into town. The poor fellow was barefoot, wearing a pair of faded red long johns and a look of disgust, madder than a hornet with a headache. Doc had fixed up Stan's bruised face and wrapped his sore ribs, the result of getting walloped with a substantial tree branch.

After completing the interrogating, Ernest poured Luke and Ned a cup of strong coffee. "How long has this mud been sittin' on yer back burner?" inquired Ned, spitting his mouthful of coffee back into the tin cup.

"I reckon since yesterday afternoon," answered Ernest, not particularly fond of coffee anyway. But his ma had taught him waste not want not, and a pot could last him a couple of days. "Why? Is there something wrong with it?"

Luke chuckled. "Nothing I can detect."

Ned huffed. "Yer taste buds up and died years ago, Sonny Boy."

"Just like my coffee strong," confirmed Luke, grinning at Ernest.

"When do you suppose we'll hear something? Doc's been working on Mr. Rutherford for a spell now." Ernest sipped his coffee which tasted same as always.

"Surely we'd aheard if the feller passed," suggested Ned.

Luke finished his coffee and set the empty tin cup on the desk. "I'll go see if there's any news."

"Ned, please stay and watch the prisoners while I send a telegraph to Sheriff Sanders in Miles City." Ernest leapt to his feet, smiling broadly. "He's gonna be real pleased to hear from me."

"I dare say you're right," added Luke, slapping the young lawman on the back. "With Barkley out of the picture, we need a replacement. Perhaps we don't need to advertise for a new sheriff. Could be I'm looking at him."

"Thanks, Mr. Carlyle. If you recommended me for the job, I'd rethink that business with the Pinkertons." Deputy Ernest beamed. "Heck, I helped solve a missing person case and got a fellow to admit to murder right here in Spirit Creek!"

"I'll drop by the Land Titles Office and suggest it to Mayor Barker before I go check on Robert at Doc's clinic. Tomorrow too early to swear you in?" asked Luke.

"No, sir!" Deputy Jones shook Luke's hand enthusiastically and then settled his crumpled old hat on his head. "Not too soon at all, sir. Ma's going to be right proud of me."

"Ya did good today, son. We're all proud a ya. Now git!" encouraged Ned. "The sooner these varmints are sent back to that prison in Californie the better."

Deputy Jones raced out the door, and Luke followed close behind.

* * *

Ellie Barkley felt someone watching her and she opened her eyes. Luke Carlyle stood in the doorway, removing his Stetson. Ellie had curled up on an uncomfortable piece of furniture which Doc Fitzgerald, the old doctor who passed on about a year ago, had dubbed the clinic's waiting-to-hear sofa. Doc Benjamin Johnson inherited it along with the entire medical practice.

"Has there been any news at all?" asked Luke.

"Doc told me he removed the bullet and patched Robert up, and then Doc disappeared again." She swung her legs off the side and stood. The muscles in her back ached, and she stretched each side in turn. She felt groggy and disoriented; she must have dozed off for several minutes. No doubt her eyes were red from crying; she probably looked a sight. She arranged her skirts and attempted a smile, but a sob escaped her lips.

"He's young and strong and healthy. He'll pull through, Ellie." Luke strode across the room, pulled her into a quick brotherly embrace.

"If Robert still hasn't regained consciousness. That's a bad sign," assumed Ellie, sniffling.

"We don't know that for a fact. Could be his body's way of dealing with the pain." Luke patted her hand. "Let's just wait and see."

"I'm glad you're here, Luke. Makes the waiting easier. And thanks for bringing Robert to Doc's clinic in your wagon."

"Don't mention it." He waved away her thanks with his hand. "Are you up for some news about those men we arrested?"

Ellie flopped back onto the sofa. "Were they the escaped bank robbers?"

Luke settled onto the opposite end. "Sure were. Ernest offered them special treatment in a local prison instead of shipping them back to California in exchange for their co-operation. Soon, they started spilling their story."

"What did you learn? Was Jimmy George involved with…?" Ellie couldn't finish the thought. But she wanted to learn the truth. At least, she felt fairly certain she did.

She'd already accepted the fact that Jimmy George wasn't the man she'd believed him to be, and she never doubted for a minute that he'd committed those robberies. But did one of those despicable men know where Jimmy George was? Had he left Montana? Headed back to

California? Had Jimmy George ever killed anyone? Had he killed his wife? She shivered just thinking such things.

"Yes, Jimmy George was involved with them, using the name Theodore James when they met him. As Theodore, he spent his days gambling and his nights chasing women, reportedly more successful with the women. Always short on cash, it didn't take a lot of arm twisting to recruit him into the gang of bank robbers. According to them, the train robbing was Jimmy George's idea." Luke shifted slightly when a metal spring poked him in the backside.

"And all this occurred in San Francisco?"

"Initially. As they continued pulling off more robberies, they moved farther north to avoid capture." Luke leaned back and crossed one leg over the other, grasped his ankle. "And it worked, for a while."

"But they were caught. Why wasn't Jimmy George imprisoned, too?" asked Ellie.

"Jimmy George convinced them to keep their mouths shut by promising them he'd hide the loot before someone else stumbled upon it. Then they'd all meet up again once the other fellows were released from prison, and they'd divvy up the spoils." Luke shook his head. "Barkley must have been some talker to convince them he meant it."

"So when the other two escaped, they arranged to meet Jimmy George in Miles City."

"Apparently, they sent a cryptic telegraph to your husband a week before he left Spirit Creek."

"I had no idea. But what happened when he met up with them?" Ellie shifted forward.

"According to their version, Jimmy George showed up empty-handed, intending to kill them and keep all the money himself. They wised up to his plans. According to them, they had to kill him in self-defence," scoffed Luke.

"You can't be serious?" Ellie's jaw dropped.

"No judge would believe your husband was shot in self-defence, especially on the word of those two. A prairie dog might have been the only witness to the whole conversation, but I don't imagine he'll talk."

"So with no witnesses and only their word for it…" Ellie left the thought hanging.

"Ernest and I are fairly certain they killed Jimmy George like they claim in their signed confessions. But they wouldn't tell us what they did with his body."

"But without a body, we can't be certain the two of them aren't lying. Maybe Jimmy George lit out for Texas, or even Mexico." Ellie frowned.

"I'd speculate they dumped his body out on the range somewhere.

We'll just have to hope his body is found to provide absolute proof." Luke touched her arm. "In the meantime, we'll consider him dead according to their signed confession."

"I suppose we don't have a choice. But why did they shoot Robert?" asked Ellie.

"According to Janie, they stormed his office to find out where you lived, figuring you'd know where Jimmy George hid the money, being his wife."

"Robert was shot because of *me*," she whispered, incredulously. The full impact of Luke's words slowly filtered through her brain, and her heart almost stopped. "Robert could die because of *me*?"

"Robert refused to tell them where you lived. The robbers didn't know that the money they'd stolen with Theodore James had been deposited into the same banks they'd robbed, in new accounts under the name Jimmy George Barkley. Takes more nerve than brains to do such a thing, and the bankers will feel like fools when they're informed where their money is."

Ellie caught her breath. "Are they on their way back to prison? Deputy Jones didn't make a deal with them to let them go, did he?"

"Made the whole thing up about the special favors, and they fell for it. Pretty convincing young man. Our soon-to-be new sheriff telegraphed Sheriff Sanders to have them transported back to California."

Ellie's jaw dropped. "Mayor Barker is hiring Ernest to replace Jimmy George?"

"He's young, but he couldn't do worse than Jimmy George Barkley." Luke grinned.

"*Anyone* would be an improvement."

"My thinking runs along the same lines." Luke patted her hand. "Donald Jones is interested in following in his brother's footsteps so Barker intends to hire him as the new deputy. All of the Jones children are honest to a fault. The Jones boys will make good lawmen."

"At least, you can trust these home-grown young men. I've taught several of the Jones children and they're all extremely intelligent." Ellie leapt to her feet.

Luke swung around, hearing footsteps behind him.

"What's the word, Doc?" asked Luke, rising from his seat as he spotted the doctor approaching in the narrow hallway.

"He's regained consciousness. Asked about Miss Jones. He's in a lot of pain, and he's lost a lot of blood. Weaker than a newborn kitten. But I think he'll pull through." Doc Benjamin smiled. "He also asked about Ellie, but I told him I hadn't seen her all day."

"You what!"

"Just joking, Ellie." Doc Benjamin smiled. "I told him you've been planted on my waiting-to-hear sofa since Luke brought him in. I've come to fetch you. You can see him now, if you want."

"Of course, I want." Ellie dashed down the hallway.

"First door on the right," imparted Doc, grinning.

"Ellie Barkley truly loves that man, whether she knows it or not," said Luke, shaking his head. "Thanks for patching him up for her, Doc."

"Just doing what I do, Luke. Let's go see if Pearl has the coffee on." Doc Benjamin slapped Luke on the back.

"I could swear I smell apple cobbler, too." Luke grinned.

"Let's check on Robert first. See if Ellie is kissing him silly yet."

CHAPTER 20

After waiting what seemed an eternity, Ellie rushed down the narrow hallway leading to Robert's room. She paused outside his door and grimaced; she must look a fright. Can't be helped, she decided, patting her hair, pinching her cheeks, and pasting a smile on her face. Taking a deep breath, she slipped into the room.

A pristine cotton sheet covered Robert to his chest. He lay so still on the narrow metal bed she felt tempted to check for a pulse. She barely recognized him as she moved closer. A huge multi-colored bruise covered most of one cheek, and a swollen left eye distorted his features. A thin strip of red seeped through the yards of white bandages wrapped around his left shoulder.

A sob escaped her lips and Robert's eyes fluttered open at the sound.

"Hello," he whispered, attempting a smile as he grimaced in pain.

Ellie rushed across the room, skirts rustling, and reached for Robert's hand. "You frightened me near to death!"

"Was a bit frightened myself," he admitted.

"Your poor face." She reached out to touch his bruised cheek, but stopped herself in time.

"Struck my head on something when I hit the floor." Robert closed his eyes and grimaced again. "Maybe it was the floor."

"How are you feeling?" she asked, and then blushed. Any fool could see the answer. And it was all because of her. He should have just told them what they wanted to know.

"I feel like someone shot me." He shifted position on the narrow bed while attempting to remain discreetly covered by the sheet.

"At least, you've retained your sense of humor." Ellie rearranged the sheet for him. "Would you like me to fluff the pillow?"

"Don't fuss, Ellie." The words came out a whisper, and he cleared his throat. "I'll be fine. Can you help me with a sip of water?"

Ellie held the glass to his lips. She set it down again after he'd swallowed a mouthful.

"Thank you." Robert eased himself back on the pillows. "Where's Edward?"

"He's with June Davidson at the hotel." Ellie rested her hand on the shoulder that wasn't bandaged. It felt wonderful seeing him, hearing his voice, knowing he was alive.

"At the hotel?" Robert's voice sounded stronger. "You should have found a safer place for him."

Ellie frowned. "I'm certain she wouldn't allow any harm to come to Edward."

"June has little control over the goings-on. Unsavory characters stumble in from the saloon. An argument over a card game could spill out into the street. There's always the possibility of a stray bullet…"

"All right. I understand," muttered Ellie, controlling her temper which threatened to surface. "Speaking of bullets, why didn't you just tell those men what they wanted to know?"

Robert paled and he appeared to be tiring. "Because they wanted to know where you lived. Do you think I'd tell them? Not on your life!"

"What about your life?" She took a deep breath to calm herself.

Robert reached for her hand. "I would never save my own hide at your expense. And I'm insulted you'd believe me capable of doing such a thing!"

"You almost died because of me!"

"Doesn't matter. I'm no coward. Even with a gun to my head, I never would have told them where to find you." Robert grimaced from the exertion of his statement.

Ellie yanked her hand away. "I just learned I'm a widow. Those despicable men killed Jimmy George over the money they'd stolen together."

For a second, Robert closed his eyes. "Then it's over. No need to label yourself as a divorced woman. You're free."

"Free to pursue a relationship with you? Ha! If we were married, you would have left me a widow again today," accused Ellie. "I don't want a hero, if he's a dead one."

Luke and Doc entered the room, and the grins on their faces told Ellie they'd heard them arguing. She felt her face redden.

"Ellie, you shouldn't have been anywhere near my office. Doc told me you spotted those men and Ned had to restrain you from coming inside. You demonstrated very poor judgment and foolishness."

Ellie stood hands on hips. "Me? Foolish? *I* wasn't the one refusing to tell them what they wanted to know. *I* wasn't the one getting shot! *I* wasn't the one lying half dead on my office floor. It wasn't *my* shoulder that Doc removed a bullet from."

"That is a totally different matter." Robert reddened.

"Different, my foot!"

"What if those men rushed out of my office and spotted you there? What if they shot Luke and Ernest and hauled you away with them. I just…" began Robert.

"But that didn't happen, did it? Good day." Ellie waved at Luke and Doc and then stomped out of the room, strode down the hallway, and slammed the clinic door on her way out.

"Robert, I detect a definite bump in your road to happiness," Luke drawled.

* * *

Elizabeth Waverly entered the Spirit Creek Hotel and searched the dining room for Edward Barkley. She spotted the little boy sitting by himself stacking wooden blocks at a small table in the far corner. She strode across the room toward him.

"Hello, Edward. I was out for a stroll. A bit of brisk evening air is the best cure for a headache. May I join you?" she asked, smiling.

Edward shrugged his shoulders; she interpreted the gesture as a 'yes'.

"Would you care for something to eat?"

"Mrs. Davidson gave me a bowl of stew." Edward continued playing with his blocks, but his tipsy tower suddenly crashed onto the table.

"Then would you join me for a piece of pie and a glass of milk?" Elizabeth bent down and touched his arm.

Edward met her eyes and smiled. "Sure, Mrs. Waverly, but don't tell Mama. She's not in favor of a lot of sweets."

"It will be our little secret." Elizabeth settled onto the chair across from Edward and waved at the young waitress.

When the girl approached their table, Elizabeth ordered two pieces of berry pie, a glass of milk and a cup of hot tea. The girl disappeared into the kitchen.

"Are you looking forward to attending school with Miss Paterson? Classes will start soon." Elizabeth removed her gloves and set them atop her bag.

"Mama helped Miss Paterson clean up the school. I helped, too. My job was dusting all the books. Miss Paterson stepped into a bucket of water when she was scrubbing the floor. I laughed really hard, but she never scolded me," said Edward. "I figured I'd be in a heap of trouble, but she was laughing, too. Miss Paterson is a nice lady."

"That she is, or my husband wouldn't have hired her as your teacher." Their order arrived and Elizabeth thanked the girl before she wandered over to another table where four cowboys hunched over plates of stew. "Eat up, Edward."

He abandoned his blocks. "Yes, ma'am."

"Did you have fun at the ranch today?"

"I love playing with Sam and Rags. And Grandpa taught me how to ride a pony this summer." Edward beamed, as much pie on his face as in his stomach. "I'm a good pony rider."

"I'm certain you are. Your mother is very proud of you." Elizabeth sipped her tea.

"Where's Mama? Mike brought me here and said Mama would come fetch me." Edward's eyes glistened and his lower lip quivered slightly. "She didn't come yet. I think she's mad at me."

"Edward, honey bun, your mother is over at Doc's place. Mr. Rutherford had a bad accident, and your mother is checking on him." Elizabeth wiped the pie off his face. "Your mama's not mad at you. She's just a tad busy right now."

"She'll come get me?" Edward's face brightened.

"Of course, she will. And I'll wait with you until she does," promised Elizabeth. "Now finish your pie, darling."

"Yes, ma'am."

At that moment, Ellie entered the hotel's dining room and immediately spotted them.

"Here's your mother now, Edward!" Elizabeth smiled as her friend approached.

"Mama!" Edward leapt off his chair and flung himself at her, wrapping his thin arms tightly around her body. "I thought you'd left me here."

Ellie met Elizabeth's eyes, and then she returned her attention to her son. "Why would you think I'd ever leave you?"

Edward's eyes filled. "I got scared that you were missing like Pa."

Ellie stroked his hair and lifted his chin. She winced at the fright and uncertainty she saw in his eyes. "I'm not going anywhere. I'll never leave you alone. You believe me, don't you?"

"Yes, Mama," said Edward.

Ellie recalled Edward's words when his father went missing. *I don't care if he ever comes home.* She knew that regardless of her son's feelings toward his abusive father, learning he'd been killed would still hurt. "Collect your toys, Edward. We're going home now. And there's something you need to hear from me."

CHAPTER 21

Tuesday, August 22, 1890

News of Robert's progress had spread by word of mouth. Doc Benjamin insisted Robert remain at the clinic where he and his wife could oversee their patient's recovery. And Ellie certainly couldn't have permitted Robert to stay with her and Edward considering the impropriety of it.

Doc Benjamin cornered Ellie at the general store this morning and insisted she drop into the clinic at her earliest convenience to visit with Robert. Neither Doc nor Robert had summoned her for a visit until now. But considering they'd argued on the day Robert was shot—her cheeks flamed at the memory—perhaps Doc considered it prudent to allow her and Robert a cooling-down period.

The man infuriated her no end. And yet her heart almost stopped when she saw him lying half dead on his office floor. Did she care for him more than she was willing to admit? Was she falling in love with him? Now that the mystery surrounding Jimmy George's disappearance had been solved, she could permit Robert to court her.

Ellie readily agreed to the visit, eager to apologize for her part in their unseemly argument. And for her own peace of mind, to assure herself that Robert was on the mend. Ellie strode into Doc's clinic, tripping over a rug in her haste. She caught her balance and straightened the rug before continuing on her way. As she stood outside his room, she took a deep breath, patted her hair, and pinched her cheeks. As she reached for the doorknob, she heard the cross between a cackle and a guffaw that was Janie Jones' unmistakable laugh drifting through the door left slightly ajar.

"You're such a treasure, my dear. I couldn't survive without you," said Robert, laughing.

His words slammed Ellie in the chest like a wooden battering ram, and she froze in place.

My dear? A dozen questions raced through her mind. Had Robert's affections for her changed? Ellie recalled the ordeal Robert and Janie had shared in his office two weeks ago. Had almost dying together brought the two of them closer?

"Ellie, you've come to visit with Robert!" exclaimed Pearl, Doc's wife.

Ellie almost jumped out of her bloomers. She whipped around and glared at the nurse. "I've changed my mind," she responded through clenched teeth. And then she turned on her heel and charged out of the clinic.

For the past two hours, Ellie had scrubbed the kitchen floor and ironed two baskets of laundry for a neighbor who'd recently given birth to a baby. She'd alternated between bouts of unexpected jealousy and an unexplained urge to cry. She had no claim to Robert's affections, and the townsfolk expected her to be in mourning for her dead husband. Why was she reacting so strongly to discovering Robert and Janie together?

A loud knock on the front door startled Ellie, pulling her from her troubling thoughts.

"Coming," she called and strode down the hallway. She flung the door open and discovered Luke Carlyle standing on her veranda.

"Come quickly," ordered Luke, stepping aside. "Robert's taken a turn for the worse. And he's asking for you."

Ellie stood, speechless. Her heart in her mouth. What could have happened? He sounded fine when she'd lingered in the hallway outside his room.

"What happened?" she choked out the words after a few seconds. "A couple of hours ago…"

"Grab your bonnet and let's go." Luke held the door open for her. "There's no time to waste. Where's Edward?"

"He's playing at Robbie Wakeman's house."

"Come on then. It didn't look good when I left Robert a quarter hour ago."

Ellie grabbed her hat and reticule as she raced out the door. She assumed Luke closed it behind her, but she couldn't have cared less. What if Robert didn't make it? What if she didn't reach him in time to say goodbye? Tears blurred her vision as she stumbled along attempting to match Luke's longer stride.

Luke shortened his steps and reached for her hand.

"What if I don't arrive in time?" Ellie sobbed.

"We'll make it in time," said Luke, as they charged through the clinic doors. "I'll wait here and give you a few moments alone with Robert."

Ellie met his eyes and smiled weakly. "Thank you for rushing over and fetching me."

She swept down the clinic hallway, paused outside Robert's room to pat her tear-stained cheeks and dry her eyes with her handkerchief. She couldn't hear any noise coming from within through the closed door.

Was she too late?

Had someone notified Janie Jones of Robert's changed condition? She realized this was no time for petty differences, and she'd gladly share Robert's final minutes with Miss Jones. Bracing herself for the worst, she straightened her spine, turned the doorknob, and entered Robert's room.

Ellie froze in her tracks.

Robert Rutherford was sitting up in bed, sipping tea, and reading Dickens.

"You're not dying?" blurted Ellie.

"Not unless there's something Doc isn't telling me," answered Robert, setting his teacup on the bedside table.

Before Ellie realized what was happening, Pearl charged into the room. "Mr. Rutherford, I see you have another visitor! First, Miss Jones and now Ellie. My, you're a popular fellow today."

"Hel…lo, Pearl," stammered Ellie. And then realization dawned. "Where is Luke Carlyle? That sneaky…"

"Luke dropped by a half hour ago, said he had something important to take care of and dashed out of here," replied Robert. "I mentioned to Luke that you hadn't been around, and now, here you are. How are you doing?"

Robert sounded genuinely pleased to see her, and concerned about her, too. How was she doing? She hadn't narrowly missed the grim reaper. She wasn't the one Doc dug a bullet out of two weeks ago.

"I'm fine," she managed.

Robert closed the book he was reading and set it on the bedside table. "I've been waiting for you to visit me. Come sit beside me here." He patted the bed.

Ellie stepped closer. "You're looking so well. You must be receiving the best of care."

"Excellent care. In fact, I'm bored to death, but Doc refuses to allow me to set foot outside the clinic. Miss Jones has dropped by a couple of times to deliver important papers for my perusal and to bring several documents requiring my signature. My secretary is an absolute gem; I couldn't survive without her help at the office."

"So that's what you meant by…" Ellie clamped her jaws shut. Robert wasn't aware of her eavesdropping earlier.

Robert appeared confused, and he shifted position on the narrow bed.

Before he could question her, she asked, "Have you been overdoing it? Is Doc aware that you're working during your recovery?"

"Now, Ellie, before you start scolding me for working instead of resting…"

"I wasn't about to scold you." Ellie interrupted him, and then took a deep breath. "In fact, I must apologize for my inexcusable behavior two weeks ago."

Robert interrupted her with a wave of his hand. "No need to apologize."

"There was no call for it."

"I was equally argumentative. My only excuse is severe pain and excessive laudanum use at the time."

"I suppose my only excuse is the adrenaline rush when I found you lying on your office floor, bleeding to death." Ellie shivered with the memory of how close she came to losing him. Although she wasn't certain of her feelings for Robert, she certainly didn't want him dying. And especially not if he was protecting her at the time.

"I don't remember any of that, which is probably for the best." Robert smiled. "But I recall how shamefully I criticized you. Please forgive me."

"Apology accepted." Ellie placed her hand on Robert's arm. "I should go now. I don't want to tire you."

"Heavens, no. You've just arrived." Robert grabbed a file off the bedside table, set it on his lap, and flipped it open. "And you must sign these papers before you go anywhere."

Ellie stammered, "But…what…I don't…" She swallowed hard. What papers could possibly require her signature?

"Is something wrong?" asked Robert.

"Yes…no…I don't know," stammered Ellie. She felt the blood drain out of her face. "What must I sign?"

"Nothing to be concerned about," answered Robert, soothingly. "We've been apprised of Mr. Barkley's demise and his part in the bank robberies. I've withdrawn the petition for divorce, so there will be no record of that following you around for the rest of your life. These papers authorize the transfer of the stolen funds in Jimmy George's accounts. The money will be totaled, pro-rated, and then distributed to the banks they were stolen from."

Ellie smiled, broadly. "With pleasure! I can't wait to end this. Show me where to sign."

Robert instructed Ellie to remove the quill pen and ink bottle from the drawer in the small table beside the bed. Under his direction, Ellie signed the legal documents in all the proper places.

"You have no idea how happy and relieved I am, giving all that money back." Ellie playfully wiped her brow with her hand.

"Everyone is pleased about it, except Old Peterman. His bank is about to lose a substantial account." Robert blew on her signatures to dry the ink.

"Doesn't he realize the funds were stolen?"

"Yes, but his only concern is how the withdrawal of funds affects the bank." Robert carefully slipped the signed papers back into the file.

"Well, I'm certain those California bankers are delighted." Ellie beamed, pleased that she'd come running when Luke summoned her. Even if he'd trick her into it. Finally, she could put the whole matter behind her. A new day hovered on the horizon. Time to make plans for her future with Edward.

"The banks are only recovering about eighty cents on the dollar, but it's better than nothing." Robert rubbed his shoulder while he spoke.

Ellie wondered if he was aware that he was doing it. Was the shoulder itching or paining him? Was it a sign of healing? Or did it mean something was wrong and he was experiencing complications? She decided an inquiry would be in poor taste. Hopefully, Doc would put in an appearance and offer them an update on Robert's condition before she left.

She lowered herself onto a bedside chair. "What about the train company? Are the owners recovering what was stolen from them?"

"A substantial amount of gold was stolen from the Santa Fe Railway. None of it has been recovered, and no one has any idea what happened to it." Robert shrugged and then grimaced slightly. "Several bags containing mine payroll money are missing, too. We may never know what happened to it. Jimmy George could have hidden it anywhere."

They sat together in silence for several minutes, each lost in their own thoughts.

"I have to thank you for coming today. I was so worried that you wouldn't speak to me again." Robert's pained expression tore at her heartstrings. "I wouldn't have survived losing your friendship."

"Hopefully, today is the end of our troubles. Signing those papers ends my business and all connections with Jimmy George. And you appear to be on the mend so I needn't be worried about you," she said, smiling.

Ellie studied Robert as if seeing him for the first time. Robert's straight nose had never suffered an injury or his strong chin taken a punch during a fist fight. Being a lawyer, he worked indoors and although he wasn't tanned like Luke Carlyle or his ranch hands, Robert's complexion appeared healthy, not pasty. Then there were his eyes, smoldering pools that drew her to him like a magnet to metal. Robert exuded confidence, an invisible strength that she found so comforting.

Robert stared at her without uttering a word. Was he reading her thoughts? Ellie blushed and fidgeted in her chair. Suddenly, she leapt to her feet. "I should go."

"Ellie," whispered Robert. "I hope you know how much I love

you. I realize you don't share my affections, but I'm praying that someday you might come to love me."

"I'm exceedingly fond of you, Robert. But Edward and I have experienced so many changes in our lives in recent months that we require some time to just take a deep breath."

In truth, Ellie suspected if she allowed herself to admit it, she probably did love him. Otherwise, why would she have become so disturbed when she'd believed he'd turned his affections toward another woman? Somewhere she remembered hearing that we don't realize what we want until it's taken from us. Truer words were never spoken.

But Ellie was reluctant to share her true feelings with him. If Robert learned that she loved him, would he insist on courting her immediately? Or just propose to her? Whisk her off to the altar? Edward had lived in a boiling caldron of change and uncertainty the past few months. And this was no time for further disruption in her son's life. Her sweet young son had adjusted to a stepmother, a grandpa and his family, a new town, new friends. She would continue to care for the orphaned boy, and she couldn't wait until the adoption was final. But motherhood seemed so new to her. She refused to add a new husband for her and a new father for her son to the mix. At least, not yet.

"I can see the turmoil you're in every time I look into your eyes. And it angers me that I lie in this bed unable to help you." Robert thumped the blanket with his fist.

"Robert, you must heal and regain your strength." Ellie grasped his hand. "Don't fret over Edward and me. We'll be fine…financially, emotionally, physically. The two of us will care for each other." Ellie kissed his cheek.

"Whenever someone tells me 'don't worry', that usually means I definitely should be worrying." His hand touched the spot where her lips brushed his face. "There's trouble in the wind, sweetheart, I can feel it in my bones."

"Nonsense," she insisted on her way out the door. "Get some rest. Perhaps your mind is playing tricks on you."

CHAPTER 22

Saturday, August 30, 1890

"Good morning!" Robert Rutherford knocked on Ellie's open back screen door. "Is everyone ready for a picnic?"

Edward filled Captain's food dish with breakfast scraps, completely ignoring the man at the door when he opened it to set the old chipped bowl outside.

"It's almost September. My goodness, where has the summer gone?" Ellie smiled at her son. She wouldn't be surprised if he purposefully left some of his meal for the dog. Her son's attitude toward Robert hadn't improved despite her assurance she wasn't marrying anyone. "We're almost all packed. I'm just waiting for my pies to finish baking." Ellie smiled at Robert.

"Could we please partake of a glass of lemonade on the back veranda while we wait?" Robert wiped his face with his handkerchief. "I'm about ready to melt from the heat in this kitchen."

Ellie patted her face with the corner of her apron. Even on a hot Saturday afternoon, Robert arrived impeccably dressed in a suit and white shirt. He'd been allowed to go home alone just yesterday. "An excellent suggestion. A cold drink while my pies bake, a minute to fix my hair, and another minute to change my dress, and we'll be off to the Diamond C."

A few minutes later, the trio sat together on the back veranda sipping lemonade while Ellie fanned herself with an old newspaper.

"Grandpa says a Carlyle picnic is more fun than anything in the whole world." Edward gulped his lemonade and wiped his mouth with the back of his hand.

"That's the truth, my dirty-faced boy." Ellie tweaked his nose.

Edward idolized his grandfather, and Ellie thanked God such a wonderful man had entered her son's life when the child needed him most.

Since his pa's death was confirmed, Edward smiled constantly, conversed with everyone. Well, he wasn't fond of Robert. Her son shared his thoughts, his joys, and his fears freely with her. He seemed more relaxed, enjoying just being a little boy. She couldn't love him more.

"Finish your lemonade and then wash your face so you're presentable for the picnic."

Robert leaned back in the old rocking chair and cupped his hands behind his head. "Why is Captain so intent in his digging over there?

"Where?" Ellie's gaze roamed the yard. She'd scolded that hound for digging nearly every day. He'd dug up several flowers she'd finally gotten around to planting in front of the house.

"Over there beside your shed?"

"Mama, Captain's digging a hole to China." Edward giggled.

"He'll be digging for years." Ellie dipped her handkerchief in the water pail and patted her face and neck. "But better China than my flowers."

"Captain's been digging back there all week," added Edward, carefully pouring himself more lemonade.

"Let me take a look, Ellie," offered Robert, winking at Edward. "Perhaps you have a skunk living under your shed."

"What?" shouted Ellie, leaping to her feet.

"I'm just teasing, sweetheart," chuckled Robert, motioning for her to seat herself again. "You'd know by now if a skunk had caught Captain's attention."

* * *

Robert set his glass on the top step and sauntered across the back yard.

"Captain, what have you got there?" he called, rounding the corner of the shed, impressed with the substantial hole the hound had dug. Almost two feet deep at one end, the hole proved the dog's tenacity.

Robert crouched down for a closer inspection, mindful of his tender shoulder. The surrounding ground had been dug up recently while the remainder of the yard remained hard-packed and sparsely covered with grass. A pointy-edged rock poked out from the far corner and reflected in the sun. On closer inspection, Robert determined it wasn't a rock at all, but a chunk of metal.

"Ellie, do you own a shovel?" asked Robert, calling over his shoulder.

"Look in the shed!" she answered.

When Robert poked his head into the shed, he heard the unmistakable sound of mice scattering. He paused for a few seconds until his eyes adjusted to the dark interior. An assortment of tools hung from hooks on the far wall, and a grass push mower hung on a hook to his left. Robert grabbed the shovel and headed outside.

"Move aside, Captain, and let me give you a hand." Robert gently urged the dog aside with his leg.

"What in blazes do you think you're doing?"

Robert nearly jumped out of his skin; he hadn't heard Ellie approach.

"There's something metal buried in here, and I'm giving Captain a hand with the digging," answered Robert.

"The Devil you are. Hand over that shovel this minute. You'll damage your shoulder." Ellie wrestled the shovel out of his hand and swatted his good arm before plunging the shovel into the loosely-packed dirt.

"Dang it, Ellie, I could have done that."

Ellie glared daggers at him.

"All right. Closer here," directed Robert, as she tossed aside a substantial shovelful of dirt. "Goodness sakes, you're a strong woman, Ellie."

"Thank you. Women can do more than cook and clean if necessary."

Robert's excitement grew as the metal corner of the box revealed itself with the removal of each shovelful. "I cannot believe our good fortune, Ellie." Robert dropped to his knees beside the hole. "Do you know what this is?"

"A big metal box in the ground," grumbled Ellie, tossing aside another shovelful of dirt. "My back's sore and my hands are starting to blister. Why is it so darn important that we uncover this thing?"

"It's a strongbox. Look closely here. The ink is very faint, but I believe it says *Santa Fe Railway*." Robert brushed more dirt off the top of the box.

"Oh, my goodness!" Ellie dropped the shovel in her excitement. "Are you saying this could be the stolen gold from the train robberies?"

"I'm almost certain. Help me dig it out, Edward," encouraged Robert, clawing and loosening dirt with both hands.

Robert and Edward worked frantically until they'd uncovered most of the box.

"A fellow with a gimped shoulder, a woman, and a small child can't dream of hauling this find out of the hole," stated Robert. "But I'm convinced we've found the missing gold. Do you suppose the missing payroll is buried nearby?"

"Mama, if there's a reward does Captain get it?" asked Edward, beaming.

"Hush, Edward. No one gives reward money to dogs." Ellie ruffled his hair.

"But if there is a reward, Captain earned it," mused Edward.

"You and Edward remain here, Ellie, while I fetch Sheriff Jones and his brother." Robert brushed the dirt from his trousers, raced across the yard, and disappeared around the corner of the house.

* * *

Once the sheriff and deputy left, Robert returned home to change into another suit. Edward and Ellie changed into clean clothes and finished packing their contribution to the potluck supper.

"This crust is slightly darker than I would have preferred. I almost forgot my pies in the oven with all the excitement," complained Ellie.

"No one will notice." Robert set the pies into the picnic basket with the rest of the food.

They climbed into Robert's newly-acquired carriage and headed for the Diamond C.

The annual Carlyle Community Picnic was in full swing by the time Robert, Ellie and Edward rode up, decidedly late. Several members of the community swarmed them, inquiring about the delay.

"Was there an accident?" asked Wilma Wallace, the liveryman's wife.

"We'd convinced ourselves someone took ill," reported Ivy Paterson, the schoolteacher who'd begin classes next week.

"Did Captain run off again, Edward?" asked Elizabeth Waverly.

"Nope. We found gold!" proclaimed Edward, grinning broadly.

Everyone stared, dumbstruck.

"Well, we did," confirmed Robert, standing behind Edward and resting his hands on the boy's shoulders. For once, the young lad didn't slip away from his touch.

Robert, Ellie and Edward related the story, each adding new bits of information.

"Not only did Ernest and Donald Jones haul the strongbox of gold bars out of the ground, but underneath the box they recovered several pouches filled with the missing mine payroll from the train robberies," explained Ellie.

"Our new sheriff will be sending the Miles City lawmen a telegraph." Robert smiled. "I predict Sheriff Sanders and his deputies will drop by in a few days to collect the strongbox and money pouches."

"Where's the gold and the payroll money now?" asked Ronald Waverly.

"Safely locked up in the bank vault. We just caught the Peterman family before they left town, heading out here." Robert patted Edward's shoulder. "You run along and play, son. You've had enough excitement for today."

"Okay, Mr. Rutherford." Edward raced across the yard toward his friend Sam.

"Robert, I'm going to help the ladies set out the meal," said Ellie, smiling.

"I'll bend Luke's ear for a while." Robert handed her the picnic basket.

"Come find me at supper time, please," requested Ellie. "I'd like you to sit with Edward and me."

"I'll do that." Robert smiled, and then turned his attention to the owner of the Diamond C Ranch and the host of today's event. "Luke, please accept my apology for arriving so late."

"The ladies are just setting out supper. Your timing is perfect." Luke shook hands with Robert, and then they strolled together toward the cookhouse where more than a dozen tables were laden with platters of meats, vegetables, and all the fixings. Desserts covered two tables; coffee, tea, and lemonade were served at another. Robert and Luke filled their plates and settled on a blanket under a cottonwood tree.

"How are things with Ellie? You've obviously resolved your issues since the night you argued at Doc's clinic." Luke dug into his meal.

"Yes, we've declared a truce," chuckled Robert. "Doc told me about the scheme you and Pearl cooked up, or should I call it the little white lie, to lure Ellie to my bedside."

"Desperate times…"

Robert chucked. "If you'd seen Ellie's face when she discovered me the picture of health sitting up reading in bed, instead of taking my last breath…"

"I'm not apologizing for our somewhat underhanded ploy," stated Luke. "Pearl insisted the two of you were meant for each other, but she couldn't get away from the clinic and enlisted my help. The end justifies the means."

"I've taken a few steps toward something more permanent with Ellie," confided Robert.

Just then Elizabeth Waverly approached with her husband in tow. "Luke, Robert, may Ronald and I join you?"

"Of course. Please sit with us," invited Luke, making room for the newcomers on the blanket.

"What were you fellows discussing so intently?" asked Ronald. "We aren't interrupting a private conversation are we?"

"Robert says he's making plans for his future," said Luke.

Robert sighed. "Sarah Grayson is moving to Philadelphia to reside closer to her sister."

"Sarah mentioned something about her sister in Philadelphia after church last Sunday." Elizabeth passed her plate to her husband, carefully lowered herself onto the blanket, and settled her skirts around her. She balanced her plate on her lap while her husband settled himself beside her.

"I bought Sarah's mansion," announced Robert.

"You did?" Elizabeth patted her chest. "My goodness, does Sarah intend to leave us forever?"

"She mentioned returning for a visit on occasion, but she intends to make Philadelphia home." Robert stuffed a forkful of meat into his mouth.

"That's wonderful for Sarah's sister, but Spirit Creek won't be the same without Sarah." Elizabeth frowned.

"I invited Mrs. Grayson to stay at the house as my guest whenever she returns for a visit. And I'll check into the hotel for the duration of her stay in town." Robert raised his fork to his mouth again, paused. "Of course, if I was a married man there would be no impropriety."

"So you intend to fill that house with a wife and children." Luke winked at him.

Robert chewed his mouthful of food. "I intend to fill it with Ellie and Edward for starters. Ellie's been hurt so badly by that Barkley fellow. My work's cut out for me, but I'm hoping I can convince her to marry me someday."

"You'll have young Edward to contend with, too. Seems to me, he's not of a mind to share his new mama with another fellow."

"Perhaps he'll change his mind eventually." Robert recalled several incidents when Edward displayed dissension toward him. Perhaps Ellie would intercede on his behalf.

Hoping a change of subject would deflect the attention from himself, Robert observed, "This is delicious beef, Luke."

"Been cooking underground for hours," advised Luke, smiling. "Somehow delicious doesn't do it justice, does it?"

"Tastes better every year." Ronald moaned, closing his eyes in obvious bliss.

Sheriff Ernest Jones approached the group. "Evening folks," he greeted everyone, removing his Stetson.

"Good evening, Sheriff." Luke set his fork down and extended his hand.

Ernest shook the rancher's hand. "I'm still getting accustomed to the 'sheriff' part. But I do love the new job. Thank you very much for recommending me to Mayor Barker."

"You're the right man for the job, Ernest. I hear you've earned your wages today. Help yourself to some supper."

"Yep, we had a bit of excitement all right." Ernest glanced over at Robert. "I'll dish up a plate in a minute. I couldn't help overhearing your conversation. If your house in town is going to be available for rent once Robert marries Ellie and she and Edward move out, I'd be honored to rent it from you."

"Dang it, Ernest," groaned Ronald Waverly. "Don't tell me you're fixing to get hitched? I wish the dang sheriffs would quit marrying my schoolteachers. I suppose I'll be advertising for another one now."

"I'm not marrying any schoolteacher," insisted Ernest, turning crimson.

"I bet Ernest has his eye on one of the twins working for June at the hotel," suggested Elizabeth.

"I don't have my eye on any female." Ernest stood, hands on hips. "My brother Donald and I want to rent the house, Mr. Carlyle. We're too old to be living with our parents. If we moved out, it would free up some room for the rest of the family. With my wages as sheriff and Donald's earnings as deputy, I believe we can afford the rent."

"Don't see any reason why you and your brother shouldn't rent the place, Ernest." Luke extended his hand again.

Ernest shook hands to seal the deal with Luke, and then he glanced at Robert. "I'd appreciate you getting your lady to the altar real soon, Rutherford," he teased.

"I'm working on it," muttered Robert.

CHAPTER 23

Ellie had enjoyed the Carlyle picnic immensely, but her elation wore off quickly when Robert requested she meet with him at his office in the morning. He dropped off Ellie and Edward at her house and then headed home without explaining the purpose for the meeting. She'd fretted about what he needed to discuss with her well into the wee hours of the morning, and she woke up at six o'clock with a throbbing headache. She still felt absolutely rotten.

On her way, she stopped at the Wakeman house to drop off Edward to play with his friend. Now, she turned the corner and strode up the walkway leading to Robert's office. She promised herself she'd face head on whatever issue Robert intended to drop in her lap.

Janie Jones, Robert's secretary, escorted her into Robert's office immediately.

"Good morning, Ellie. Would you like a cup of coffee?" he asked, smiling.

"No, thank you. I'd like to hear what you have to say though." Ellie settled into the chair across from Robert. "I hope this isn't more bad news. I've had my fill for the year."

Robert chuckled. "No, nothing like that. I wanted to show you these papers that arrived on Friday. Edward's adoption has been finalized. He is now legally and officially your son."

Ellie leapt to her feet. "Thank you so much! Oh, my goodness. I can hardly believe this."

"It's true." Robert grinned, broadly.

Ellie swatted his arm. "You knew about this all weekend and you never told me?"

"I wanted to wait until my first day back in the office to share the good news and present the papers to you. Doing so from that dang hospital bed wouldn't have felt right."

"I wouldn't have cared where you did it."

"Oh, I know. But this way will be special." Robert waved off her comment. "You and Edward are expected at the newspaper office at four o'clock this afternoon. I've arranged and paid for your picture to be taken together."

"Thank you again. What a perfect gift. I'm just delighted that…"

Just then, Sheriff Jones slid the pocket doors open and poked his head into the office.

"Sheriff, what's the meaning of this?" demanded Robert. "I'm meeting with a client."

"Pardon the interruption, Mr. Rutherford." Sheriff Jones removed his Stetson. "I have a few questions for your client."

"Hello, Sheriff Jones." Ellie greeted the man who entered the office. And then she noticed Banker Peterman and the gray-haired bank clerk, Mr. Jackson, following behind him as he approached the lawyer's desk. Her heart leapt into her mouth. What on earth was going on?

"Mrs. Barkley." The lawman acknowledged her with a pained expression.

Ellie immediately sensed something amiss. "Sheriff, what is it? Is something wrong?" she asked, holding her breath.

"I'm hoping we can clear up the matter without a lot of fuss," stated the sheriff. And then he quickly added, "Unless, of course, you can't prove yourself innocent of this little problem."

"Are you serious? I haven't done anything wrong," protested Ellie

Robert leapt out of his chair and raced around his desk. He stood beside the chair Ellie occupied. "What problem?" he demanded.

"It must be a mistake, Robert," Ellie pleaded, standing and reaching for his hand.

"I know. Don't worry. I'll get this straightened out in no time." Robert patted her arm. "Sheriff Jones, I represent legal counsel for this woman, and I demand an explanation."

"Mrs. Barkley has been implicated in the deposit of stolen funds into a Spirit Creek Bank account bearing her husband's name."

"That's impossible. Mrs. Barkley was not privy to her husband's illegal doings." Robert huffed. "And those funds have been returned to the banks they were stolen from."

"I'm sorry. Mr. Peterman has implicated Mrs. Barkley in the deposit of the stolen funds. If you wish to dispute these accusations, we'll discuss the matter at the jailhouse. Now, kindly step aside," the sheriff ordered.

"No. I will not have my client paraded through town like a common criminal. We will discuss it right here, right now," insisted Robert. He met Ellie eyes. "We'll clear up this matter, Ellie."

Robert spread his arms wide, and she rushed into his embrace. After savoring the brief moment of comfort, Ellie stepped back and took a deep breath. "I'm all right. But I insist this misunderstanding be settled now. I refuse to allow Jimmy George Barkley to control my life for another minute," vowed Ellie, straightening her spine.

"That's the spirit," Robert whispered in agreement.

"Very well. Mrs. Barkley, we've received a complaint from Mr. Peterman who claims he possesses a document that bears both your signature and Jimmy George's signature," began Sheriff Jones.

"What document?" demanded Robert.

"A deposit slip which proves you were aware of the substantial sum of money that your husband deposited into his bank account." Sheriff Jones' expression suggested her explanation had better be a good one.

"I don't recall signing any documents during the entire time I was married to that despicable man. If this document has a signature on it, then Jimmy George signed my name, not me." Ellie shivered, and Robert slipped his arm around her shoulders. She met his eyes and smiled weakly.

Mr. Peterman stepped in front of her and waved a slip of paper in her face. "Are you familiar with this?" he demanded.

Ellie reached for the paper and glanced at it. "This is a deposit slip. I've signed these whenever I deposited a portion of my pay into my account at the bank."

"Are you denying that that is your signature?" accused Mr. Peterman.

"Please look closely, Mrs. Barkley." Sheriff Jones waved her closer, encouraging her to take a second look.

Ellie held the document near the lit lamp on the desk. "That is not my signature. I never sign my entire name. I've only ever signed my deposit slips and any other important documents as E. Thomas, or E. Barkley after that unfortunate marriage ceremony."

Robert stepped forward. "I can vouch for Mrs. Barkley. Any legal documents she's signed in my presence have been signed exactly as she claims."

Mr. Peterman sneered. "You're certainly in no position to vouch for her. You've been courting the woman!"

Ellie's eyes dropped to the bottom line on the deposit slip, and her eyes flew to the banker. "Oh, my word! I've never signed a deposit slip with this huge sum on it! If I had, I certainly would have remembered."

"Mr. Jackson, you're employed as a clerk at the Spirit Creek Bank," confirmed Sheriff Jones, turning his attention to the older fellow.

"Yes, sir. Worked many years for Mr. Grayson when he owned the bank. A fine gentleman he was." Mr. Jackson nodded toward Mr. Peterman. "Working for this fella now."

"Please take a gander at this deposit slip and tell me if you believe this is Mrs. Barkley's signature," demanded Sheriff Jones.

Mr. Jackson extracted a pair of wire-rimmed eyeglasses from his pocket and settled them on his nose before grasping the paper in slightly trembling hands. He glanced at the signature.

"Nope, Sheriff. Not hers," he declared, passing the paper back to the lawman.

"Are you certain?"

"You barely looked at the damn thing. How can you be sure?" demanded Peterman, sneering.

Ellie stifled the urge to say something to the pompous fool who clearly considered himself superior to his clerk.

The old fellow waved off the matter. "Miss Ellie only uses her initial. First day she opened her account, I questioned her decision. Suggested it might be better to sign her entire name, but she insisted she'd never used more than her first initial. And that was that." He sighed loudly. "She's never signed a deposit slip with more than the initial E, ever."

"Dammit to hell!" exclaimed Peterman.

Sheriff Jones glared at the banker. "You dragged me over here without first checking with your clerk to ensure the signature was valid?"

"I…I thought that…I never…" stammered Peterman, reddening with embarrassment.

"Mrs. Barkley, please accept my apologies." The sheriff grasped her hand. "Clearly, we were wrong in our assumptions."

"Just a minute. Let me see that deposit slip again," requested Jackson.

Sheriff Jones passed him the deposit slip.

"Mrs. Barkley might have signed this the day Mr. Barkley deposited these funds." Jackson rubbed his chin, deep in thought. "Yep. I'm almost certain Mrs. Barkley accompanied him into the bank that day. I remember, because I've seldom seen a fellow depositing so much money at one time. Mr. Peterman was out of town, and I handled the transaction myself."

"You must be mistaken, Mr. Jackson." Ellie stumbled across the floor and flopped onto an empty chair. "I never signed that deposit slip."

The next half hour was a blur for Ellie as she listened to bits of garbled conversation. None of it registered in her mind. Her temples throbbed with a worse headache than before.

Finally, Robert approached and squatted down to her level. "Do you recall ever entering the bank with Jimmy George? Do you recall signing any papers while you were in the bank with him?"

Ellie lowered her head, straining to remember. Suddenly, she gasped and her eyes flew to Robert's. "I remember now. There was one day. Jimmy George told me he'd arranged to open a trust fund account for

Edward. Jimmy George said Edward had inherited money from his mother and the papers required both of our signatures with our full names. He stuck some papers under my nose to sign, but I never inspected them or asked any questions. I just signed where he told me to." Ellie's hands grasped her handkerchief in a death grip. "How could I have been so stupid? So trusting?"

Robert patted her hand. "Ellie, this should only take another minute or two."

"That scoundrel tricked me into signing that deposit slip, didn't he?" Ellie grimaced.

"Let me handle this." Robert retreated to the other side of the room.

Ellie observed Robert and the other gentlemen from her seat. The men appeared to be arguing about something, accompanied by a generous amount of head nodding and head shaking. What was going on, she wondered?

She overhead Sheriff Jones exclaim, "You cannot be serious!"

* * *

Robert explained his theory for the second time. "Mrs. Barkley never looked at the document she was signing."

"Do you know this for a fact? Or are you just taking her word for it?" demanded the sheriff.

"Most women don't have a head for business. They don't understand legal documents and the like. Place any piece of paper in front of a woman, and tell her to sign it, and she will." Robert stood, arms crossed. "In my profession, I've seen it dozens of times. Why wouldn't a woman sign a document without looking at it first, if someone she trusts, perhaps her husband for example, asked her to sign it? In Jimmy George's case it might have been more an order than a request."

"I'd have to see it for myself," said Sheriff Jones, skepticism apparent in his voice.

"If I submit a bogus document to Mrs. Barkley and she signs it without hesitation and without a second glance at its contents, as she claims happened in the bank, will you agree to forego any charges against her?" asked Robert, challenging the lawman.

"Between you and me, I truly don't believe she's guilty of any wrongdoing," admitted the sheriff. "But we have to prove this beyond doubt. If you can prove to me that her story is undoubtedly the truth, there will be no charges."

Robert rummaged through his desk for a blank piece of paper. He scribbled on it for several seconds and then passed it to Sheriff Jones. The lawman quickly perused the document. "If she signs that without a moment's hesitation and without reading the dang think, I'll drop the whole matter."

Banker Peterman's eyes widened as he read what was written over the sheriff's shoulder.

"Prepare to do some dropping, sir," whispered Robert, smiling.

The sheriff scowled.

"Ellie, please come here for a second," requested Robert, waving the woman to his side.

Ellie stood and shuffled across the room. "What is it?"

"We're almost done here, Ellie." Robert handed her a pen and set the piece of paper down on the corner of his desk. "We just need you to sign this paper first, and then we'll finish up as soon as possible."

"Thank you so much for coming to my rescue, Robert." Ellie bent forward and signed E. Barkley on the hand-drawn line on the bottom of the paper. She set the pen down beside the sheet of paper and returned to her chair.

"Dammit," cursed Sheriff Jones. "I cannot believe she signed that thing."

"She trusts me, explicitly. And I'm not even her husband, just a friend." Robert smiled.

"Mrs. Barkley, please come over here again, ma'am." The sheriff waved his hand.

Ellie rose from her chair, strode across the room, and met Robert's eyes. "Was there something else you needed?"

"Is it common practice for you to sign documents that you haven't read?" demanded Sheriff Jones.

"Well, I suppose…sometimes…" stammered Ellie.

Banker Peterman threw up his hands and glared at her. "I don't believe this."

"Robert, did I do something wrong?" she whispered.

"Would you please read the document you just signed?" demanded Sheriff Jones, passing her the piece of paper.

Ellie quickly read through the three sentences and gasped.

"That's right, Mrs. Barkley. You've just agreed to purchase from Mayor Randy Barker the Town of Spirit Creek for the sum total of ten thousand dollars." Sheriff Jones took the sheet of paper from Ellie and ripped it into a dozen pieces.

"Ellie, I suggest from now on you read every document placed before you and then sign it," advised Robert.

"I'm sorry. I didn't…" Ellie blanched. "I just wanted the whole business over with."

"You did exactly what I knew you would do." Robert hugged her shoulder. "You did exactly what you did in the bank that day when Jimmy George demanded you sign that piece of paper in order to implicate you in his unlawful deeds."

"I won't be charging you with anything, Mrs. Barkley," confirmed the sheriff.

Ellie smiled and her eyes filled. "Thank you, Sheriff Jones. And thank you, Robert."

"You're welcome," replied Jones.

Robert smiled. "My pleasure. Of course, I wanted to help."

"The full impact of this business is finally coming to roost," said Robert, noticing Ellie's tears. "I'll escort Ellie home and make her a nice cup of tea before we go fetch Edward at his friend's home."

"This has been one of the worst days of my entire life." Ellie headed toward the door. "At least, I hope it's been the worst day of my life. I'll never survive another one like it."

CHAPTER 24

Sunday, September 14, 1890

Reverend Gerald fired up his congregation with a particularly rousing sermon on brotherly love. Afterward, Robert and Ellie joined the other small groups of parishioners that formed in the churchyard to discuss the sermon's encouraging words and exchange the weekly gossip. Ellie loved Sundays since Robert could spend the entire day with her and Edward.

Luke Carlyle approached and shook Robert's hand.

"Sheriff Sanders informed the incarcerated robbers that all the stolen money has been recovered and returned to the rightful banks," explained Robert. "And he advised them that the gold bars have been found and returned with the payroll sacks to the Santa Fe Railway company. I love being the bearer of good news."

Luke smiled. "That is good news."

"If those scoundrels escape again, they'll have no reason to come after Ellie," said Sheriff Jones.

"Thank goodness for that," added Elizabeth Waverly, standing in the group with her husband.

"Sometimes I wish they'd just hang the pair of them." Ellie felt her face redden. "Thankfully, the reverend wasn't nearby and heard that. It sounded rather uncharitable."

"Secretly, I wished for the same thing, dear," Robert whispered in her ear, and then he turned to their circle of friends. "Why don't we all meet at my home for a picnic on the back lawn?"

Robert recently moved into Sarah's mansion, but he still came for supper at Ellie's house almost every night. Afterward, he helped Edward with his sums or listened to him read while Ellie relaxed in her rocking chair beside the fire and knitted socks and sweaters for the coming winter.

Edward was warming up to Robert, realizing he wasn't at all like his pa had been. Robert left for home promptly at eight o'clock when Edward headed off to bed, refusing to fuel the fires for the gossips.

Robert never asked for more than her friendship, and Ellie loved him for respecting her feelings. One day soon she planned to confess her reasons for marrying Jimmy George. But not yet. The loss of her baby was still a bit too painful.

"A picnic is an excellent idea, Robert." Maggie smiled. "Elizabeth and Ronald, Luke and me and the children."

"Ellie, Edward and myself. And Reverend Gerald, of course," added Robert. And then he smiled, wickedly. "Ernest, would you like to join us? Bring your lady friend along. Wasn't her name Ivy?"

"Dang it all. A fellow dances with a pretty girl once, and you've got them married off." Ernest kicked the ground with his boot. "I don't have a lady friend."

"Bring your brother then." Robert grinned.

Ellie swatted his arm for teasing the young lawman.

"You get a powerful pleasure riling me up over the womenfolk, don't you," accused Ernest.

"I do indeed," admitted Robert. "It's one simple pleasure in life that I truly enjoy."

Ellie waved Edward over to her side. "Robert, share the news about the money," she suggested, waiting for her son to join them.

"A substantial sum was put up as a reward for the return of the gold. Since the gold was found on the property she inhabits, Ellie will be receiving the reward from the train company owners." Robert clasped her hands in his.

"Actually, I've declined the reward money," announced Ellie, straightening her spine.

"What?" exclaimed Robert.

"I requested an alternate recipient." Ellie loved surprising Robert who was always so serious and in control of every situation. Throwing an unexpected development his way made her smile.

"Ellie, what have you done?" inquired Robert, wagging a finger at her.

"The reward funds will be forwarded to the nuns operating the orphanage in Boston where I was raised." Ellie chuckled and clasped her hands to her bosom. "I'd love to see the expression on Sister Margaret's face when she receives that money."

"Ellie, dear, your generosity warms my heart." Robert brushed her cheek with a kiss, and then blushed profusely realizing he'd kissed her in public.

"The reward equals several years' worth of operating funds. But

I've stipulated that the funds must be spent solely on college educations for the brighter students, to be chosen at the nuns' discretion." Ellie paused for a moment and took a deep breath before continuing. "I don't want anyone struggling to pay their way through college like I was forced to do at the normal school."

"I wish I'd heard about this earlier, before today's sermon," observed Reverend Gerald, stepping up to the group. "What a marvelous example of brotherly love! Or should I say sisterly love! Ellie, you are truly one of God's children."

Ellie blushed profusely. If the good reverend knew the extent of her sins, would he be so generous with his praise? Would her financial assistance to those unfortunate children make up for her past indiscretions in some small way? She hoped she deserved Edward, deserved a man's love. That she deserved Robert.

Would her beloved Robert wait much longer before seriously pursuing her affections? She felt ready for courting. And putting the past behind her. Robert was such a fine man, not an imposter like Jimmy George had proven himself to be.

Saturday, September 27, 1890

Ellie entered the dance hall connected to the Spirit Creek Hotel, on Robert's arm. Mayor Barker had planned a celebration in honor of Arthur and Lily MacDonald and their successful newspaper, *The Spirit Creek Chronicle*. The entire population of Spirit Creek and surrounding area were invited.

Ellie wore a new store-bought, rust-colored silk gown which looked stunning with her red hair. She refused to wear black, despite the fact the entire town had discovered her husband indeed was dead. If the gossips hadn't been apprised of what a nasty individual Jimmy George was, and in turn, they hadn't reasoned that he didn't deserve her mourning complete with the customary black widow's weeds, then that was just too bad. Let them gossip!

Robert looked quite dashing in a new charcoal gray suit and waistcoat. She proudly walked beside the handsome gentlemen as they wandered among the crowd. Edward skipped along beside them, dressed in new party duds. The child grew an inch every other week it seemed.

Ellie noticed Luke and Maggie Carlyle slipping into the room. Edward and Sam spotted each other and immediately disappeared in the crowd.

"Aren't you the delightful couple?"

Ellie turned and came face to face with Rebecca Simpson, soon-to-be retired midwife.

"Hello, Rebecca," she smiled and they shook hands. Rebecca was training Agnes Armstrong to replace her, and the young lady was excelling as a midwife. Ellie prayed someday she'd require Agnes's services.

"Hello, dear." Rebecca grazed Ellie's cheek with a quick kiss.

"Good evening, Mrs. Simpson." Robert smiled. "Shall I fetch us all a glass of sherry?"

"Yes, thank you," answered Ellie.

"None for me, young man," Rebecca declined, smiling. "But thank you for asking."

Robert disappeared into the crowd.

"I'm surprised to see you here." The words were out of Ellie's mouth before she could stop them. But Rebecca was a renowned homebody and seldom attended social functions in town.

"Wilber insisted we attend, as a show of support." Rebecca wore a plain brown dress and arthritic fingers nervously patted her gray hair swept up in a bun. "Everyone is delighted Spirit Creek finally has a newspaper."

"Robert and I couldn't be happier," added Ellie, and then she blushed. "About the newspaper, I mean."

"Every lady in the community was so concerned about you, marrying the new sheriff so unexpectedly. Sometimes crippling grief causes folks to make rash decisions. And the man turned out to be such a despicable fellow." Rebecca patted Ellie's hand.

"Thank you for your concern." Ellie was so thankful she was accepted by the community, rash decisions and all. If the true reason behind her unexpected marriage had revealed itself, she doubted the ladies of Spirit Creek would have been so understanding. But everything happened for a reason, even painful things.

"I'm pleased you're making sound decisions once again, stepping out with a wonderful fellow like Mr. Rutherford." Rebecca smiled at the approaching gentleman.

"I'm coping well. And Mr. Rutherford is a true gentleman and a good friend," said Ellie, accepting a glass of sherry from Robert.

"Rumor has it…the two of you are getting married," whispered Rebecca, partially covering her mouth with her hands.

"That, I can assure you, is strictly a rumor...for now," Ellie whispered and winked.

Arthur and Lily MacDonald strode toward them. The guest of honor wore a dark blue suit and striped waistcoat, polished boots, and a broad smile. Slightly balding and portly in stature, he appeared several years older than his wife. Lily MacDonald wore a pale pink satin gown with ivory silk trim, and her blonde hair shone in a youthful upsweep. If Ellie wasn't mistaken, she detected a thickening of Lily's middle. Was she with child?

Ellie hoped so and she couldn't be happier for the couple.

"We can't thank the community enough for such a wonderful celebration," gushed Arthur.

"This is truly a splendid evening," added Lily, squeezing her husband's arm.

"It's not every day someone starts up a newspaper in our little town." Robert shook Arthur's hand. "The mayor insisted upon a demonstration of our appreciation."

"We are delighted that *The Spirit Creek Chronicle* has been so well received. And we're running a special edition on November 5th the first anniversary of Montana's statehood," announced Arthur, beaming.

Ellie smiled. "Something to look forward to."

"Sounds like a wonderful idea," agreed Rebecca.

"Shall we dance, Ellie?" asked Robert, setting their sherry glasses on a nearby table.

"Are you certain you should be dancing?" cautioned Ellie.

"I was shot in the shoulder, not in the foot," explained Robert and whisked her onto the dance floor.

Several minutes later, the waltz ended. Robert felt a definite tug on his trouser leg and looked down into Edward's smiling brown eyes.

"Do you intend to cut in?" asked Robert, with a raised eyebrow.

"I need a drink of water," pleaded Edward, his face flushed from rambunctious play.

Ellie discreetly patted her brow with her handkerchief and announced, "I could use a drink of water myself, sweetheart. I'll be right back."

* * *

Robert watched Ellie disappear into the crowd and turned back to the little boy he was towering over. He guided Edward off the dance floor, settled himself on a chair skirting the room, and patted the chair beside him. "Can we have a man-to-man talk, young fellow?"

Edward met his eyes and whispered, "Am I in trouble?"

"No, no, no," chuckled Robert, ruffling the boy's hair. He took a deep breath. "It's just that…so many confusing events have occurred in rapid succession. Your life has been quite a muddle lately, hasn't it?"

Edward crawled onto the empty chair.

"First, your dear mother died, and I know it hurts your heart still when you think of her. A fellow never recovers fully from losing his mother. No matter how old he is when she passes."

Edward hung his head.

Robert patted the boy's arm and continued, "And then you were uprooted and plopped down in the middle of a new town. Left in the care of total strangers more nights than not. Mind you, Mrs. Waverly at the store and Mrs. Davidson at the hotel are lovely ladies. You won't find any better. And then your pa suddenly up and married Miss Thomas."

Edward met his eyes. "I was surprised when Pa told me my teacher was my new ma."

"No more surprised than I was!" Robert spoke the thought a little more harshly than he'd intended. He cleared his throat and continued. "I still don't understand your ma's reasoning behind the marriage, but it turned out well for you."

"She's a real good ma," agreed Edward.

"That she is. And with your pa gone…" Robert left the thought hanging in the air between them, awaiting the little fellow's comment.

"Pa was a bad man," whispered Edward, searching Robert's eyes.

"Yes, son, your pa did some bad things." Robert wondered how much the boy understood about Jimmy George Barkley's escapades. Without a doubt the scoundrel had abused the little fellow's ma, and probably contributed to her passing. Had Edward witnessed his pa's abuse? Had his pa physically hurt the little boy, too? "Please remember, Edward, your pa's actions don't reflect on his kin. You are a very good boy. And your pa probably loved you in his own way. How could he not love such a wonderful little boy, like you? Any man would be proud to claim you as his son."

Edward's mouth hinted that a smile lurked near the surface. Was Robert finally winning him over? He swallowed hard. The time had come to show his cards. Would Edward accept a new man in his ma's life? Would the little boy share his ma with him?

"Do you love your new mother?" Robert tilted his head, awaiting an answer.

"I love Mama a lot."

Robert smiled. "Do you treat your mama kindly?"

"I give Mama a hug and a kiss every night before I go to bed."

"Well, Edward, I love your mama, too. And I treat her kindly."

Edward met Robert's eyes, appeared deep in thought. "Do you ever get angry?" he whispered.

"Sometimes," admitted Robert, recalling his argument with Ellie after his surgery. "But not very often."

"When you get angry, are you going to hit my mama?"

"I would never hit your ma or any woman. And I wouldn't hit you either, son." Robert rubbed the boy's back as he spoke. "I'm not like your pa, Edward."

"Are you going to marry my mama?"

Robert felt the child's small body stiffen.

"That depends. Not unless you give me your permission. But I'd be beholden to you if you'd allow me to marry your ma and become your new father. What do you say? Can we share your mama?" Robert extended his hand and awaited the child's reply.

Edward smiled and shook his future pa's hand. "You can marry Mama. She likes you a lot. I bet she likes you as much as I like Captain."

Robert chuckled and pulled the boy into a quick hug. "Thank you, Edward. I love your mama very much, and I love you, too, son. I promise you, the three of us are going to be a happy family."

"Four of us," corrected Edward, squirming out of the embrace.

"You want a little brother or sister?" whispered Robert, searching the boy's eyes, feeling his face warm.

"No! Babies are noisy." Edward frowned and crossed his arms. "Captain is part of the family, too."

Robert threw back his head and laughed. "Of course you're right, Edward. Captain is definitely a member of the family. And the four of us are going to be very happy."

"Edward, here's your water," said Ellie, approaching and handing a glass to her son.

"Thank you, Mama," said Edward before he gulped the contents.

Robert bent forward and whispered into the boy's ear. "Let's keep this conversation our little secret for now."

"I can keep a secret," whispered Edward and handed the glass to Robert.

"Good boy." Robert patted his future son's head and set the glass on a nearby table.

"What are you two whispering about?" asked Ellie, looking suspicious.

"Nothing." Edward disappeared through the wall of onlookers watching the dancers swirling around the floor.

"I watched you from across the room. What were you and Edward discussing so intently?" asked Ellie, hands on hips.

"Just things a couple fellows discuss at a dance." Robert kissed her cheek and guided her onto the dance floor. "Don't worry your beautiful head about it. Just dance with me."

Robert was dancing on air. Now he just had to find the right time to ask the most important question of his life.

CHAPTER 25

Robert waltzed Ellie around the festively-decorated ballroom—a waste of money in Mrs. Davidson's opinion at the time, he'd heard, but included in the blueprints at her late husband's insistence—with graceful, fluid steps while keeping a respectable distance between them. The lawyer and widow remained the favorite topic of discussion among the townsfolk, and there was no reason to incite a frenzy of gossip with an unseemly display on the dance floor.

While they danced, Robert noticed two gentlemen enter through the main door. He recognized Pinkerton detectives when he saw them. Both wore the requisite Pinkerton garb: dark suit, white shirt, polished boots and bowler, which they'd removed when they'd arrived inside the door. The detectives wore their hair cut short and slicked down. The older fellow wore wire-rimmed glasses and a bushy mustache, while the younger man was clean-shaven.

Robert wondered if the detectives concealed their pistols in shoulder holsters under their suit jackets, or in their boots, or if they were unarmed which he thought highly unlikely considering their line of work.

The detectives wandered the perimeter of the room and gravitated toward Luke Carlyle. Hand shaking and a great deal of gesturing followed. And then finger pointing, directly at him.

Robert tightened his hold on Ellie while he swung her around the dance floor. He considered himself an accomplished dancer, but momentarily distracted, he missed a step and whispered an apology into Ellie's ear.

Out of the corner of his eye, he watched the two detectives as they descended upon him like hawks on a mouse. Matching we-mean-business expressions appeared on their faces, and Robert was curious as to what brought them to Spirit Creek.

"Are you Mr. Robert Rutherford?" inquired the older of the two gentlemen, blocking Robert and Ellie's way and preventing further progress across the dance floor. Both men produced a Pinkerton Agency badge.

"Yes, I'm Robert Rutherford. What can I do for you gentlemen?" he asked, smiling. He extended his hand to the older man, intending to shake hands.

"Robert Rutherford, I'm placing you under arrest." The older fellow reached for Robert's hand, and in an instant he'd slapped a pair of handcuffs on him.

"What the hell…" cursed Robert, forgetting that Ellie stood at his side.

"Come with me, please, and kindly refrain from making a scene." The older detective grasped Robert's arm and lead him toward the door. The younger man followed.

"What is the matter with you fellows?" protested Robert.

Ellie followed them, almost tripping over her skirts in her haste.

"Have you lost your minds? I've done nothing wrong. I'm an attorney and a respected citizen. You must have the wrong person."

"We're just doing our job," stated the older detective.

"Quite poorly, if you believe I'm guilty of any crime." Robert attempted to dislodge his arm from the man's iron grip, unsuccessfully.

At that moment, Luke Carlyle stepped in front of the two detectives. "Where are you taking Robert?" he demanded.

"To the train station in Miles City, sir. We have orders to arrest this man to stand trial."

Ellie gasped and her tear-filled eyes met Luke's. "There must be some mistake."

"This whole business is preposterous. What are the charges?" demanded Robert.

The two Pinkerton men forged ahead without looking back.

"Luke, I'm innocent. Contact my former colleagues in Boston, please," called Robert over his shoulder, his hands in cuffs secured behind his back. "Janie has their names at the office."

In another moment, the two detectives and Spirit Creek's esteemed lawyer disappeared out the door.

* * *

"Luke, what's happening?" pleaded Ellie, patting her tear-stained cheeks with an embroidered handkerchief.

"I haven't the foggiest notion what this is about, but I certainly intend to find out." Luke's hands fisted at his sides; he was annoyed with the embarrassing disruption to the town's celebration. Mayor Barker hadn't even given his speech yet. "What possible reason could the Pinkerton

Detective Agency have for arresting Robert?"

Ellie shook her head. "It's happening all over again, Luke. I trusted Jimmy George, believed him to be a good man, but he fooled me completely. I considered Robert to be a pillar of the community, and he's just been arrested by Pinkerton detectives!"

"I'm certain there's been a mistake, Ellie. There must be a reasonable explanation..." Luke placed his hands on her shoulders, but she thrust off his attempt to console her.

"When will I ever learn?" Ellie struck off across the room toward Maggie.

Luke charged out of the Spirit Creek Hotel and searched the dark street. There was no sign of the detectives or Robert. Horses or some means of transportation must have been waiting for them.

He intended to investigate this further. He'd bet his ranch that Robert Rutherford was innocent of any wrongdoing.

* * *

Hours later, Robert settled onto the train seat. His wrists burned where the handcuffs chafed. The older Pinkerton detective removed the handcuff from his left hand and attached it to the sturdy metal train seat frame.

"That ought to hold you until we arrive at our destination." The detective settled into the seat across from Robert where they were joined by the younger detective.

"Would one of you kindly explain to me the reason for all this?" Robert rattled the handcuffs locked on his right hand. "I have absolutely no idea why you believe I'm guilty of something unlawful."

"Is that so? Is it a short memory you have? Or just a selective memory?" asked the younger man, sounding skeptical.

"No memory of any wrongdoing is more accurate; I've done nothing wrong. I'm an attorney operating a respectable law office in Spirit Creek, employed by a prestigious Boston firm prior to relocating to Montana." Robert straightened in his seat. "So, gentlemen, kindly enlighten me. What are you so certain I'm guilty of?"

"The charges will be read at your preliminary hearing, sir."

"Why aren't I just facing a judge at the Custer County Courthouse in Miles City?" asked Robert.

The older man lit a cigar and blew a smoke ring heavenward. "Your trial isn't being held in Miles City."

"Then where?" demanded Robert.

"San Francisco," replied the older gentleman, speaking around his cigar.

"San Francisco!" Robert attempted to leap to his feet, but the handcuffs restrained him, pulling him back into his seat. Robert felt the blood drain out of his face. "Why on earth are you taking me there? I've never set foot in San Francisco in my life!"

"Then how do you explain the fact you've been positively identified as the individual who deposited stolen funds into the Mutual Savings Bank of San Francisco?" asked the younger detective.

"That's impossible."

"Are you acquainted with a Sheriff Sanders from Miles City?"

"Yes, I know Sheriff Sanders quite well. I worked with him on a case recently that involved the lovely woman I was dancing with before our evening was so rudely interrupted." Robert fought to control his temper, realizing it wouldn't bode well to provide these gentlemen with further ammunition for their case against him. He was totally innocent of any charges, but the pair of them didn't appear to be of a mind to believe him.

"Earlier today, we presented the sheriff with a sketch of the gentleman who deposited the stolen funds, as drawn by the bank clerk who's apparently quite the artist. Sheriff Sanders positively identified you as the person in the sketch."

"But that's impossible, I've never…" Robert gasped, overcome with a sick feeling in his stomach. "Richard! Damn that twin brother of mine. Could he have been released from prison already?"

"Suddenly, he recalls a twin brother on the family tree. Isn't that convenient. He has a twin brother, boss." The young detective scoffed. "As if we haven't heard that one before."

"It's true." Robert slumped in his seat.

Luke Carlyle was his only hope. Unless Luke contacted his former business partner in Boston to help him out of this pickle, he could be in for a long stint of incarceration Lord knows where.

Suddenly, it occurred to Robert that no one, not even Luke, knew he was headed to San Francisco. His stomach flip-flopped, and he almost lost the delicious supper he'd shared with Ellie earlier this evening. Would anyone bother to locate him, help him? What if every citizen of Spirit Creek believed him guilty?

Ellie. Dear, sweet, Ellie. What must she think of him?

Robert silently prayed that someone in Spirit Creek considered him an innocent man.

* * *

"Robert Rutherford has a knack for breaking up a party," mused Luke, removing his white shirt and tossing it onto his wife's chaise longue in their bedroom.

"I can't help feeling sorry for Ellie. Suffering the humiliation of watching while her good friend—although I believe he's more to her than just a friend—is arrested in the middle of a public gathering." Maggie hung her party dress in the armoire. "I would have been purely mortified if that had happened to you, Luke."

"Well, my dear, I hope it never does. I just can't understand why those fellows believe someone like Robert could be guilty of anything illegal. And they wouldn't divulge the charges against him."

"It's absolutely ridiculous." Maggie wrapped her arms around Luke's middle. "Please assure me you're going to do everything in your power to help the poor man. I've never heard him mention any family or siblings. Perhaps he was raised an orphan like Ellie. Robert must be feeling very alone in the world right now."

"I'm sending a telegraph to the head of the Pinkerton Agency first thing in the morning." Luke kissed his wife, running his hands down her sides. "There must be a logical explanation for all of this."

Friday, October 10, 1890

Ellie answered the knock on the front door, anticipating a visit and news from Luke or Sheriff Sanders. She was shocked to discover Buddy Maxwell standing on her doorstep.

"Mr. Maxwell! What are doing here?" she exclaimed. Her face warmed as she stepped to the side. "Come in please."

"Call me Buddy, Mrs. Barkley." Buddy removed his Stetson and stepped over the threshold.

"And I'm Ellie. Would you like a cup of coffee? There's a pot warming on the woodstove." Ellie stood wringing her hands. For the life of her she couldn't imagine what the rancher wanted.

"No, thank you kindly." Buddy twisted his hat in his hands. "Could we sit for a spell? I need to talk to you."

"Certainly." Ellie noticed the older gentleman didn't look well at all. He appeared ready to collapse from exhaustion. She immediately ushered him into the parlor and guided him to her comfortable rocking chair.

"I suppose you're wondering what brings me by." Buddy leaned back in the seat and heaved a sigh.

Ellie smiled. "I admit I'm a bit surprised. Are you working on a community committee or a new project? Is there something I can do for you?"

"No, ma'am. Nothing like that." Buddy cleared his throat. "There's no easy way to tell you this, Ellie. One of my cowhands was out looking for strays on the far corner of my land this morning. He…well, he…"

"Yes?" Ellie held her breath, almost certain she knew what was coming. And praying he'd say what she hoped he would. Buddy's news could end the matter once and for all.

"My ranch hand came across your husband's remains, ma'am." Buddy grimaced. "The incident frightened the daylights out of the poor fellow. I thought he'd pass out while he was relating his story to Sheriff Jones."

Ellie's breath came out in a whoosh. "And you're certain it's Jimmy George?"

"Yes, ma'am. We brought the body into town, and the coffin maker found this in the fellow's trouser pocket." Buddy stuck out his hand.

Ellie inhaled sharply. "That was his tin star?"

"Sheriff Jones confirmed it. Told me to bring it with me when I spoke to you, and then he instructed me to take it over to the blacksmith's shop and have it melted down and destroyed. No true-and-proper lawman alive would wear this dang thing on his chest." Buddy twiddled the piece of tin in his fingers.

Ellie whispered. "It hasn't much meaning now, does it?"

"No ma'am. It's a mite tarnished, in more ways than one." Buddy stuck the useless piece of metal back in his pocket.

Ellie rose, refusing to detain him any longer. It appeared he should be home in bed, recovering from whatever ailment had him looking so poorly. "Thank you for dropping by with this information. Now, I can move forward with my life. That unfortunate chapter has been closed, forever."

"I thought you'd feel that way. That's why I made a special trip to town to tell you myself. I reckoned it was my place, being that the feller was discovered on my land and all." Buddy clambered out of the rocking chair and touched Ellie's arm. "I've heard all about your troubles with him. You put it all behind you, girl. Git on with your life and don't look back."

Ellie's eyes swam with tears. "Thank you for saying that. I appreciate it more than I can say. And that's exactly what I intend to do."

"Glad to hear it. Now, I'll be heading on home." Buddy lumbered to the front door. Stuck his Stetson on his head and slowly descended the two stairs to her walkway. "You take care now, missy. Maybe I'll see you in church on Sunday."

"Yes, you will. And thank you again for dropping by." Ellie waved to the old fellow as he climbed into his buggy and drove the rig down the street.

Finally, it was truly over.

CHAPTER 26

Monday, October 13, 1890

Luke and Maggie repeatedly assured Ellie they were attempting to discover Robert's whereabouts and the reason for his arrest. He hadn't been in contact with anyone and even the local lawmen had no idea where he was. To Ellie's way of thinking, Robert had fallen off the face of the earth.

Until the initial shock of Robert's arrest had worn off, she'd believed history had repeated itself and he'd tricked her. In the light of day next morning, she convinced herself the idea that Robert could commit a crime was preposterous. And she was prepared to stand behind him no matter what. If she only knew where he was.

Luke had fired off several telegrams to the Pinkerton Agency headquarters in Chicago demanding information regarding the matter, but he hadn't heard a word back. Ellie knew Luke well enough to realize he was rapidly losing his patience. Luke left for Miles City early this morning to request Sheriff Sanders' help, and he'd even hinted that he'd travel to Chicago to the Agency's headquarters if necessary.

Ellie's emotions had run wild for the past two weeks. In Robert's absence, she realized not only did she miss him, but she loved the man with every fiber of her being. She'd welcome Robert back into her life in a heartbeat.

She hadn't heard from the man since the night he'd been arrested and hauled away in handcuffs. Her teeth clenched, recalling the memory of that embarrassing scene at the hotel. Surely, if Robert could have contacted her, he would have by now. Wouldn't he? Or was he simply too humiliated by the whole unseemly affair?

She'd never believe him guilty of any wrongdoing.

But would the authorities believe it?

If Robert was found guilty of something illegal—although she doubted that would be the case—it could be years before he returned to Spirit Creek. She imagined there were several persons convicted of crimes when they were innocent but unable to prove it. Knowing Robert was the man she'd searched for all her life, was she now willing to wait for him?

Yes. Definitely, unequivocally, yes!

Ellie turned the corner, strode down the wooden sidewalk, and paused outside the front door of The Spirit Creek General Store. Suddenly, the Deadwood Stage rumbled down the street heading toward her. A few citizens lined the sidewalk anticipating passenger arrivals. And there would be mail from all parts of the country. And probably goods that Ronald ordered to restock the store. Ellie slipped inside without giving the matter another thought.

A few minutes later, Ellie departed the store having purchased the black thread she required to patch the torn pocket on Edward's trousers. She headed down the wooden sidewalk, intending to stop at the hotel on her way home, making good on her promise to drop by and share a cup of tea with June Davidson. Gazing across the street, she stopped dead in her tracks.

She blinked to ensure she wasn't hallucinating.

There stood Robert Rutherford on the wooden boardwalk.

"Robert!" screamed Ellie, sprinting across the street without heeding the dirt and horse manure. Fortunately, no horses, buggies or carriages raced by at that moment, or she could have been seriously injured or worse.

"Ellie," whispered Robert.

Ellie's heart beat wildly in her chest. "Robert! I can't believe it's you."

"Hello, sweetheart." Robert grinned.

"Why didn't you send a telegraph to let me know you were all right, and free, and on the way home?" she chastised him.

"I wanted it to be a surprise, darling."

"I'm not dreaming, am I? You're really here?" She searched his eyes and touched his cheek.

"Yes, I'm here, sweetheart. I can't tell you how much I've missed you." Robert embraced her, swinging her off her feet.

And then he kissed her full on the mouth!

In front of God and everyone!

Robert never condoned public affection, but today's reunion was special, she supposed. The townsfolk simply had to forgive such an unseemly display. She felt like a ninny, questioning why she hadn't heard from him. Robert had simply wanted to surprise her. And he'd certainly succeeded!

"Come to my house for tea. I want to hear all the details." Ellie wrapped her arm around Robert's and tugged him toward her small house. "Why on earth were you arrested?"

"Ellie, let me just look at you for a minute. There's plenty of time for talking about it later." Robert smiled at her.

Suddenly, Ellie's world clicked back into place: Robert was free. Robert had returned home where he belonged. Everything bad was behind her.

* * *

Robert begged off afternoon tea, but he promised Ellie he'd come for supper. He needed a few hours to rearrange his life after his lengthy absence. His first order of business found him at the telegraph office.

"Well, look what the cat dragged in!" teased the aging, sickly telegraph operator when Robert walked through the door.

"Good afternoon, sir."

"How ya been, young feller? Heard all about your arrest. Caused quite a ruckus at that MacDonald fellow's party, so I've been told." The old fellow coughed up a storm, and then settled down to business. "Ya sending someone a telegraph, Mr. Rutherford?"

"No, actually, I've come to ask a favor." Robert pulled several bills out of his pocket and handed the money to the old fellow. "There's a chap falsely using my name for the most unimaginable things. I wouldn't put it past him to send Ellie a telegram telling her all manner of foolish lies and signing my name to it. If you receive any telegrams intended for Ellie, would you please direct them to me instead? I don't want the lovely lady upset by all this nonsense."

"Mr. Rutherford, I will surely honor your request. I imagine Miss Ellie's been a mite distressed by your troubles already. I'll let you take a gander at any telegrams before she sees them." The old fellow stuffed the money into his baggy pants pocket. "I'm delighted you're home safe, and I'll let you know the minute any telegrams arrive for your lady friend."

"Thank you. I knew I could count on you to help me watch over Ellie." Robert tipped his hat and smiled at the old fellow.

"My pleasure," added the telegraph operator, patting his pocket where he'd tucked the money. "My pleasure indeed."

Robert strode down the sidewalk in the direction of the Spirit Creek Law Office. His pocket watch indicated a few minutes past five o'clock, but he hoped someone would still be at the office. Luckily, he arrived just as his secretary was clearing her desk in preparation to lock up for the day.

"Mr. Rutherford!" Miss Jones clasped her hands to her cheeks.

"You're back!"

"Just arrived on the stage, and I can't tell you how delighted I am to be home." Robert removed his hat and tossed it onto his desk. "Is there anything pressing, or would you prefer to wait until tomorrow to help me catch up with business?"

"Most everything is under control, sir." Miss Jones opened a file on her desk. "These papers require your signature, but other than that… Let's wait until tomorrow morning. I won't keep you from your homecoming celebrations. I'm certain Ellie is delighted to have you back."

Robert grabbed a pen off the desk and scribbled his signature on the papers his secretary placed in front of him.

"Don't you intend to read those first, sir?" she asked, frowning.

"Heavens no, dear. I trust you've handled things admirably while I was away. Let's do the rest of it in the morning. Ellie invited me to supper, and I certainly don't want to be late."

"Ellie and Edward will be thrilled to see you. Poor little fellow was so confused when you disappeared. He's become quite fond of you, sir." Miss Jones winked. "He confided the secret with me after church last Sunday. He was just busting to tell someone, and I assured him as your secretary I could be trusted with a secret. I couldn't be happier for you."

"Secret?" asked Robert, knitting his brow.

"About your intention to ask Ellie to marry you?"

"Oh, right. I've been under so much stress with the arrest and all. I shall propose when the perfect moment presents itself." Robert smiled at his secretary and handed her the signed documents.

"Don't wait on me, Mr. Rutherford. I'll file these documents away until tomorrow. You go on ahead and I'll lock up." Miss Jones glanced at her boss. "Did you purchase a new hat, sir?"

"You are a real gem." Robert settled his bowler on his head. "And you are exceptionally observant I might add. Yes, I required new clothes after my lengthy turn in that jail. I couldn't return home to Ellie looking like a street urchin."

"Of course not, sir. What was I thinking?" Miss Jones tapped her forehead.

"Good night then, miss. I'll see you tomorrow." Robert strode out the door.

After a quick trip home to check the house, he arrived at Ellie's home at six o'clock on the dot for supper. He strode up the steps, crossed the veranda, and knocked on the front door.

Edward threw the door open and smiled. "Hello, Mr. Rutherford. Mama told me you'd come back."

"Good evening, Edward." Robert smiled at the lad. "How are you?"

"I'm good, and so is Captain."

Just then the huge dog charged into the front entryway, barking and growling. He stood between Edward and Robert with his hackles raised. "Captain, what's gotten into you? Stop that growling this minute." Ellie flew down the hallway from the kitchen.

"Mama, what's wrong with Captain?" asked Edward.

"Hello, Robert. I don't know what the problem is. You've only been away a couple of weeks. Surely, he hasn't forgotten you already." Ellie chuckled nervously. The animal was acting so strangely.

"Hello, Captain," said Robert, bending to pet the animal.

Captain bit his outstretched hand.

"Ouch," yelped Robert and kicked at the animal's hindquarters. "That beast is dangerous."

"He's normally a big softy. I don't understand what's gotten into him." Ellie grabbed Captain by the scruff of the neck and hauled him down the hallway and out to the backyard. "Bad dog, Captain, bad dog!" she scolded their pet.

When Ellie returned to the kitchen, Robert was pumping water at the sink and holding his hand under the cold stream.

"Mr. Rutherford kicked Captain, Mama," sobbed Edward, crying uncontrollably. "He told me he didn't hit anybody."

"I didn't hurt the dog. I just wanted him to release my hand," explained Robert, attempting to defend his actions. "Captain just startled me. I won't kick him again, Edward. I promise."

The reunion continued downhill from there.

Supper was burnt, the cook being distracted while nursing Robert's hand with ointment and a bandage. Ellie wasn't certain about dog bites and suggested he visit Doc in the morning. Edward didn't exchange one word with Robert who choked down the meal. Ellie could tell from his expression he wasn't enjoying the food. She couldn't blame him. It was hardly the celebratory meal she'd envisioned in her mind this afternoon.

After she tucked Edward into bed, Ellie poured Robert and herself a cup of coffee. Sitting together on the parlor sofa, sipping the steaming brew, she demanded, "Please tell me everything. Most importantly, tell me why on earth you were arrested?"

Robert set his coffee cup on the side table and reached for Ellie's hands. "Sweetheart, where do I begin?"

"Anywhere. Just tell me what happened."

"Do you recall me mentioning my twin brother, Richard?"

"Yes, you told me he's in a prison in Boston. The authorities had blamed you for your brother's illegal shenanigans, but you'd cleared your name and then moved to Spirit Creek." Ellie searched Robert's eyes.

"All of that is true. What we didn't know…Richard was mistakenly released from prison. The prison workers confused him with another prisoner. By the time they realized their mistake, Richard was long gone."

"Oh, my heavens," whispered Ellie.

"Apparently, while on the lam, he executed several robberies that netted him a substantial sum of cash. He foolishly deposited the money in a bank in San Francisco, assuming no one would investigate."

"San Francisco! He was in a Boston prison! He travelled from one coast to the other without being recaptured?" asked Ellie, incredulously.

"Apparently so." Robert released her hands and leaned against the sofa back. "The clerk became suspicious after the depositor left the bank. Apparently, the fellow is a crack artist, and he sketched a remarkably accurate picture of the man. The Pinkerton fellows called in on the case had helped arrest Richard Rutherford and send him to prison in Boston, so it never occurred to them to verify that he was still in custody. Thus, they assumed the drawing was a picture of his twin brother. Me."

"How did they track you to Spirit Creek?"

"The Pinkerton sons were hired. As I heard it, their father was a lifelong friend of the bank manager where the funds were deposited. Anyway, the detectives telegraphed my former boss at the Boston law office and discussed the matter with him. He informed the detectives that I had moved to Spirit Creek." Robert sighed. "When the two detectives arrived in Miles City, Sheriff Sanders identified me as the person in the picture, and thus I was arrested."

"How did you manage to prove you were innocent?"

"At the preliminary trial, the authorities learned that Richard had been mistakenly released and was most definitely the guilty party. They cleared me of all charges and sent me on my way. And now I'm home."

"And thank goodness you are." Ellie's eyes misted. "I imagined all manner of terrible things happening to you."

"Well, I'm home now. We can carry on with our lives, and hopefully, put all this unpleasantness behind us." Robert smiled, reached for her hand and kissed the back of it.

Ellie thought it strange that Robert didn't kiss each of her fingers as was his habit before the arrest, but she was delighted to have him back in Spirit Creek and didn't give it a second thought.

"I should head home, Ellie," announced Robert, standing and taking her hand as he led her to the front door.

"Thank you for coming to supper, and I apologize for the ruined meal. I was concerned about your poor hand, and I totally forgot about everything else."

"There will be other suppers."

"Thank you, Robert. You're very gracious and forgiving." Ellie patted his arm.

"The past two weeks have been a nightmare, and I'm looking forward to sleeping in my own bed tonight." Robert smiled, wickedly. "Unless you invite me into your bed?"

Ellie gasped.

"I'm only joking, sweetheart. Please forgive me. I'm so exhausted I'm not thinking straight." Robert embraced her and kissed her on the mouth.

Robert quickly released her. "Goodnight, dear. I'll talk to you tomorrow." Robert disappeared out the door into the night.

While Ellie prepared for bed, her thoughts centered on Robert. He'd survived the two week ordeal, but he'd changed in so many ways. Firstly, he was extremely affectionate, even in public. Before his arrest, she'd received sweet kisses on her hand, one finger at a time. Since his return, he'd kissed her passionately on the mouth. Mind you, she wasn't complaining; she loved Robert with all her heart. Ellie felt ready for their relationship to advance to the next level, and she prayed he would propose to her.

She was stymied, however, as to why Captain reacted so strongly to Robert. As far as she knew Captain had never bitten anyone in his life. Why would he bite Robert? She'd never seen Robert kick an animal, and she was trying very hard to forgive his kneejerk reaction when bitten by the dog. Edward wouldn't forgive him any time soon. Of that she was certain.

Ellie brushed the day's tangles from her hair, seated at her vanity table. Thinking back, she realized the whole evening puzzled her. She recalled how close Edward and Robert had become just before Robert's arrest. But tonight Robert paid little attention to Edward, and he'd provided a lame apology for kicking Captain. Robert never offered to read her son a bedtime story which had been their nightly ritual before the arrest. Of course, Edward had shown Robert a cold shoulder all evening. She loved them both, and Ellie hoped the two of them could patch up their differences in a day or two.

Ellie laid the hairbrush on the table and then slipped between the sheets. Recalling Robert's remark about her welcoming him into her bed, she blushed. That comment was so unlike Robert who always presented himself as a gentleman. He seemed a totally different man as a result of his arrest and trial. What he must have endured!

But the man she loved was home now, battle scars and all. Hopefully, in the long term, he was none the worse for it. Ellie drifted off to sleep praying that after a good night's sleep, the man she'd fallen in love with would be himself again tomorrow.

CHAPTER 27

Wednesday, November 5, 1890

"Ladies and gentlemen, may I have your attention for a minute, please?" Arthur MacDonald stood beside his wife in the front area of his newspaper's offices. For a moment, they looked into each other's eyes, and Arthur wrapped one arm around Lily's shoulders. They were dressed in their Sunday best for the newspaper's grand opening in conjunction with this special day. Arthur beamed proudly and his wife appeared decidedly with child.

Ellie's gaze wandered across the gathered crowd. There was still no sign of Robert and he'd assured her he would meet her here.

"Today, we've printed a special edition of *The Spirit Creek Chronicle*, celebrating the first anniversary of Montana's statehood," continued Arthur, holding up a copy of the edition. "My wife and I are delighted to welcome such a splendid turnout to tour our offices. Although we've been operating for a few months now, today is our official grand opening. I'm certain all of you are as happy as Lily and I, recognizing Montana's anniversary and celebrating our little corner of this great United States of America."

"Hear, hear," shouted a fellow from the back of the room.

Randy Barker stepped up beside Arthur and shook his hand. Spirit Creek's mayor turned his attention to the crowd. "Good day, folks. I would like to remind everyone about the potluck celebration at The Spirit Creek Hotel tonight. As I announced at church on Sunday, the entire town is invited. And Reggie and his pals have volunteered to play some fiddle and guitar music for a dance after the meal."

Thunderous applause followed the announcement, and Ellie clapped enthusiastically.

"I'm hoping for a good turnout tonight!" Randy raised his voice to be heard over the noisy crowd.

"Now, everyone is invited to tour the newspaper facilities and don't be shy about asking questions." Arthur waved forward the first group of folks to tour the building while other citizens enjoyed coffee and cookies in the main entry while they waited their turn.

"Are you enjoying yourself, dear?" asked Robert.

Ellie swung around, hearing the familiar voice. "Yes, I'm delighted to share in the MacDonalds' success. This newspaper was exactly what Spirit Creek needed."

"No argument here." Robert handed her a cup of coffee. "Miss Jones has been extremely helpful in bringing me up to speed at the office. There are still a few folks here that I don't recall meeting before. Perhaps you could remind me of some names, dear?"

"Are you still forgetting names?" asked Ellie, frowning. Wilber Simpson mentioned Robert had forgotten his name at church last Sunday, and Ellie thought it odd. But her beloved explained that he'd survived a terrible ordeal in that prison until he'd cleared his name. She'd become quite concerned about his memory loss. Robert had seen Doc Benjamin and the physician believed it was only temporary.

"I won't forget too many more, now that I'm resting up and receiving nourishing meals again. And I have you to thank for that, my dear." Robert kissed her cheek. "I couldn't have recovered from that nasty business without your tender care. I promise you, my memory keeps improving with each passing day."

"No one could blame you for blocking out portions of your past, along with the deplorable conditions at the jail, and fearing no one would come to your aid." Ellie smiled and patted his cheek.

"It's behind me now, so let's not dwell on any of it." Robert tucked her arm around his and patted her hand. "Let's just enjoy today. A special day to remember for both of us."

After the celebration at the newspaper office, Ellie rushed home to feed and water the dog and bake two pies for her contribution to the potluck. When Edward arrived home from playing with his friend after school, he and Ellie changed into their party duds for supper at the hotel.

"Mama, why do I have to wear my Sunday clothes when it ain't Sunday?" complained Edward.

"Because it's a special celebration supper tonight. Please hurry or we're going to be late," explained Ellie, through her open bedroom door across the hallway.

A few minutes later, Ellie rushed out of her room toward the front door. Robert suggested they meet outside the hotel dining room at six o'clock sharp, and the hallway clock indicated it was already ten minutes past.

"Hurry, Edward, or Mr. Rutherford will believe something is

wrong." Ellie stood at the front door, holding the box containing her pies, waiting for Edward to tie his shoes.

Finally, they were on their way.

* * *

"Ellie! Edward!" Robert spotted them hanging their coats on the rack inside the door of the hotel's dining room.

"Please forgive our tardiness." Ellie accepted his kiss on her cheek while handing the box of pies to one of the young girls collecting food items at the door. "Edward is hopeless when it comes to donning his fancy clothes, especially when it's not Sunday. You could dress a pig in a petticoat quicker."

Edward grinned, sheepishly. "Pigs don't wear petticoats, Mama."

Robert ruffled the little boy's hair and chuckled. "Well, you're both here now."

In the past few weeks, Ellie noticed that Robert and Edward had patched up their differences although she doubted they'd ever share an amicable friendship again. She suspected Edward attempted to get along with Robert solely to appease her.

"Can I go find Sam?" asked Edward.

"Of course, you…"

"Before you disappear on me, might I have a word with you, Edward?" interrupted Robert.

Edward met his ma's eyes.

"Listen to what Mr. Rutherford has to say, Edward, and then you may play with Sam." Ellie smiled at her son. "If you need me, I'll be right back. I'm absolutely parched, and I'm going in search of something cold to drink. And then I'll say hello to Rebecca Simpson over there."

"This will only take a minute or two, Ellie," imparted Robert, as Ellie disappeared into the crowd.

Robert clasped Edward's hand and led him to a private corner by the kitchen.

"Am I in trouble?" asked Edward, looking way up into Robert's eyes.

"Not in the least. I'd like to ask you something." Robert crouched down to the little boy's level. "I intend to ask your ma to marry me tonight, and I need to confirm that you're still in agreement."

"You told me it was a secret, and I never told anyone." Edward blushed with his lie, and then confessed. "Except Janie. She's my friend Billie's sister. But she promised not to tell."

"Miss Jones kept our secret. And I'm proud of you for keeping it, too, because it was a big one." Robert smiled. "I just wanted to double check that you didn't change your mind."

"Are you gonna be my pa soon?" whispered Edward.

"If I have any say in the matter," affirmed Robert. And then he rose to his full height. "Now, go play with Sam."

"Okay." Edward streaked across the floor and disappeared out of sight.

"So you're going to propose to Ellie?"

Robert's heart nearly stopped. He swung around and came face-to-face with Luke Carlyle, grinning broadly. "Good Lord, man. You nearly caused me heart failure."

"A big secret, huh? The fact that you intend to marry Ellie Barkley someday is about the worst kept secret in Spirit Creek." Luke chuckled.

"I spent a lot of time in that jail cell, thinking about my life and Ellie. I intend to propose marriage and whisk that fine woman to the altar as soon as possible." Robert smiled.

"Do you think she's ready to marry again?" inquired Luke.

"I believe it's exactly what we both need." Robert straightened, raised his head a fraction. "Separated from loved ones, you realize life is too short to delay what your heart desires most."

"Perhaps you're right. But I've got to ask you a question before you propose." Luke glanced away for a moment, and then met Robert's eyes. "Did Ellie ever reveal to you her reason for marrying Jimmy George Barkley?"

Robert swallowed hard.

* * *

As Ellie approached the two gentlemen, she overheard Luke's question. She stopped in her tracks and ducked into the corner. For some reason, it seemed important to hear Robert's answer.

Robert shifted from one foot to the other. "I suppose she had her reasons, but it doesn't really matter. I love the woman dearly, and I intend to marry her at the earliest possible date."

Ellie's jaw dropped open. Robert intended to propose? Soon?

"You're not concerned or curious about that marriage?" asked Luke, persistently.

"Should I be?" Robert tilted his head.

"Well, it's just…" began Luke.

"There you are, gentlemen!" Ellie stepped into view from behind her hiding place.

"Good evening, Ellie." Luke greeted her with a kiss on the cheek.

Ellie patted her friend's arm. "Luke, what a wonderful celebration and such a splendid turnout. The room is positively bursting at the seams."

Luke chuckled. "Some wonderful aromas are coming from June's kitchen, too. I can't wait for supper."

"Would you like some sherry, sweetheart?" inquired Robert. "I'll fetch us each a glass while we wait for the call to supper."

"That would be lovely," agreed Ellie. "Perhaps Luke would like a glass, too."

"No, no, I'm fine." Luke waved Robert away. "You go ahead. I'll keep company with Ellie in your absence."

"Be right back, dear," whispered Robert, and he was gone.

"Did you hear Robert's reply to my question?" inquired Luke, frowning. "His back was to you, but I noticed you hiding in the corner."

"I almost fainted when he said he wasn't concerned." Shock evident on Ellie's face, she continued, "For weeks, he spoke of nothing else and constantly badgered me to explain myself. And now, it doesn't matter to him?"

"I don't understand it at all." Luke glanced away for a second.

"He's changed so much," added Ellie. "He's like a totally different man. What do you suppose they did to him in that prison? He's hinted that it was absolutely dreadful, that he feared for his life at times. He's even claiming to have suffered memory loss from it all."

"I've heard his explanations," whispered Luke.

"I've formed a theory about Robert, but you'll probably consider me daft." Ellie searched her friend's eyes. "The whole idea is so far-fetched…I think that man is actually Richard."

"Richard?" asked Luke, frowning. "Who's Richard?"

"Of course, you wouldn't know. Robert has an identical twin brother who has been known to impersonate him," explained Ellie. "I think my Robert is still in jail somewhere, and Richard is here impersonating him."

"Good heavens, Ellie. That's a bit of a stretch," whispered Luke.

"I know, but he's so different. Nothing else explains it. Captain even bit him the first night he returned."

"Dogs are a better judge of character than people." Luke appeared deep in thought for a minute. "Dang it, Ellie. You've almost got me convinced you're right."

"I know. I've been rattling the idea around in my head for a few days now." Ellie grimaced. "The very thought of that man living in this town, eating at my table, talking to my son… It gives me chills. Robert told me he was a very dangerous man."

Luke placed a hand on her shoulder. "I don't mean to upset or frighten you. Please keep an eye on the man. I'm going to contact Sanders in Miles City about the matter."

"I'll keep a list of everything strange or unusual he's done in case

Sheriff Sanders requires evidence to pursue my suspicions." Ellie peeked around Luke to ensure Robert hadn't returned. She gasped, seeing him approaching. "Here he comes."

"Contact me immediately if you find irrefutable proof," whispered Luke.

"Ellie, dear, here's your sherry. I'm sorry I took so long. I stopped to chat with Ernest Jones for a moment." Robert handed Ellie a small glass of sherry.

Ellie grasped the glass with slightly shaking hands, but thankfully no one noticed.

Robert continued, "That young fellow is thoroughly enjoying his new position as sheriff."

"Ernest and his brother are doing an admirable job in the short time since Randy Barker hired them." Luke smiled at Ellie. "If there's any illegal activity going on in or around Spirit Creek, I'm certain those two fellows will unearth it."

"Impressive," muttered Robert.

Just then, June Davidson, owner of The Spirit Creek Hotel, called everyone to supper.

"Remember what I said," Luke whispered in her ear while Robert was momentarily distracted by Edward and Sam who'd popped up beside them.

Ellie walked arm in arm with Robert toward the supper line, her head swirling with her suspicions. Was Richard escorting her to supper and not Robert? The whole idea seemed totally preposterous. Or was it? It certainly would explain a lot.

* * *

Ellie hoped Robert hadn't noticed how quiet she'd been during supper. They were seated at a circular table with Luke and Maggie as well as Wilber and Rebecca Simpson, chatting about how Montana's statehood had benefited everyone the past year. The group discussed the inevitable influx of sodbusters that would turn the free-range ranching industry on its ear. And everyone sympathized with Robert, concerning his recent ordeal and how he'd fortunately cleared his name and returned to Spirit Creek.

"Yes, I feel extremely blessed," admitted Robert, smiling at Ellie.

That evening, Robert danced every dance with Ellie, and then he escorted her and Edward home in his carriage. The hallway clock chimed eleven o'clock as they entered her house, and Ellie immediately saw Edward to bed while Robert waited for her in the parlor.

When she returned she discovered he'd poured himself a generous shot of whiskey. On previous visits, he'd complained that she didn't keep spirits in her home. She'd dumped out every bottle of liquor she found after Jimmy George left. But Robert had brought a supply of his own a few days ago. Just another thing out of character to add to her list.

Robert invited her to join him on the sofa and handed her a glass of sherry without first inquiring if she even wanted one.

"A toast to a wonderful day is in order," he declared, raising his glass.

Ellie clinked glasses with him and took a sip. She was surprised that Robert had poured them another drink after such a whirlwind evening. Normally, neither of them would partake of more than a single drink.

"I'm hoping we'll have something else to remember about this day." Robert dropped to one knee beside the sofa. "You know my feelings for you have grown steadily since the moment we met. While incarcerated, my only thoughts were for the lovely woman waiting for me back in Spirit Creek. I've discussed my intentions with Edward and he's given me permission to ask you this question."

Ellie's hand flew to her chest. After overhearing his conversation with Luke, she knew what was coming. But she hadn't expected it to happen tonight.

"Ellie, dearest, will you please do me the honor of becoming my wife?" Robert removed a small velvet box from his waistcoat pocket. With a grand flourish, he flipped the lid open.

"Robert, I never dreamt you intended to…tonight, I mean…" Ellie feigned surprise and decided it best to play along, especially if the man actually was Richard. He might become suspicious if she suddenly refuse his proposal. "Of course I'll marry you."

Robert slipped the diamond and sapphire ring on her finger. It fit perfectly. "This was Mother's ring. She removed it from her hand only hours before she passed, with strict instructions that someday I present it to the woman I loved when I proposed."

"Robert, it's beautiful." Ellie gazed at the magnificent ring's brilliance shimmering before her eyes. She truly wished it was Robert proposing to her. She should be sharing this moment with him, and not fearing it was his brother. And she was almost certain it was Richard who'd just proposed.

"Wear it in good health, my dear." He smiled broadly and kissed her hand.

"I haven't the words to express how happy I am." Ellie forced herself to smile. Goodness, she could make a living acting with a traveling theater show.

"No happier than me." Robert kissed her hard on the mouth.

Ellie felt light-headed, no doubt from the stress of her suspicions. And then she sobered. "There's something I should tell you before we say our vows." She swallowed hard. This would be the ultimate test. "I know you've badgered me for months to explain myself. To reveal the reason for my sudden marriage to Jimmy George Barkley..."

"Not another word. It doesn't matter, sweetheart." Robert covered her lips with his finger. "That fellow and all the trouble he caused you are in the past."

"But…"

"It's not important. I don't want to hear another word about it. Now, I believe we should set a wedding date. Is tomorrow too soon?"

"After the last fiasco, I insist on a proper wedding with a beautiful gown, and flowers, and guests. Everything should be perfect, and I require at least six months to prepare." Ellie didn't add that it would buy her the time she required to clear up any doubts about his true identity.

"Six months! I'd thought perhaps a Christmas wedding would be nice. Would December 20th be too soon?" Robert grinned.

"December 20th would be perfect." Ellie hoped it would be sufficient time to hear back from Sheriff Sanders. "I can't wait, and thank you for this lovely ring. I'll talk to Maggie; I'm certain she'll be my witness. She'll help me with the preparations, too."

"Wonderful." Robert gulped down the rest of his drink. "It's very late, and I'll leave before the gossips notice my carriage outside at this unseemly hour."

"There's no stopping them from ripping one's reputation to shreds without a moment's hesitation. Whether it's justified or not."

"Well, we won't supply an ounce of meat for them to feed upon. Only the utmost discretion until we are well and properly wed." Robert kissed her again as they stood on the veranda. "I've never been the subject of the gossips' poisonous tongues, and I have no intention of starting now."

Ellie gaped.

"Goodnight, my sweet," called Robert, waving as he climbed aboard his carriage.

"Goodnight," whispered Ellie, glancing at her beautiful engagement ring sparkling in the moonlight.

She slipped back inside the house, closed the door, and slowly slid to the floor. *I've never been the subject of the gossips' poisonous tongues?* The true Robert wouldn't have forgotten all the weeks that the gossips' tongues wagged about the two of them before he was arrested. All of the speculation about his interest in a married woman whose husband was missing. Considering the names he'd forgotten and other things she'd had to explain since his return, she realized she was right. There wasn't an ounce of doubt in her mind.

She glanced down at her hand and the ring's brilliance dulled at once.

Richard Rutherford had proposed to her.

CHAPTER 28

The next morning, Ellie Barkley walked Edward to school and then drove a rented buggy out to the Diamond C Ranch. She felt justified in bringing her concerns to her friends' attention since there were other citizens' safety to consider as well. Like Janie Jones who worked with the man every day in his office.

"Ellie, what brings you out our way?" asked Luke, meeting her as she pulled up to the house.

"Do you have a few minutes? I have some news to share," stated Ellie, handing the reins over to Luke's ranch hand. She smiled at Mike, her former evening student. "Are you still enjoying reading?" she inquired.

"Yes, ma'am," Mike informed her, beaming.

Ellie patted his arm. "I'm glad to hear it."

"For you, Ellie, I have all the time in the world." Luke smiled. "While you're watering that horse, Mike, please tell your pa I'll join him in a few minutes."

"Will do, sir." Mike headed off toward the horse barn with the buggy and mare.

"Ellie, come on in. Maggie has the coffee on."

Luke and Ellie entered through the back door and hung their coats on a peg.

"Maggie, look who dropped by," called Luke, removing his Stetson.

"Ellie!" Maggie entered the kitchen, carrying her son, Willie, on her hip. "What on earth brings you out our way this early in the morning?"

"I have news to share." She stuck out her hand to draw attention to her ring finger.

"You're engaged!" Maggie flopped onto a kitchen chair, settling her son on her lap. "Robert popped the question?"

"I'm engaged," confirmed Ellie. "Last night after I tucked Edward into bed, Robert proposed and I accepted."

At that moment, Willie began wailing at an unheard of decibel.

"Someone's hungry. Please hold Willie for a moment, Ellie, while I prepare his breakfast." Maggie shoved her eleven-month-old son into Ellie's arms and disappeared into the pantry. The child settled, staring at this new person holding him.

"So, he proposed last night," stated Luke, pouring Ellie a cup of coffee.

Ellie bounced the child on her knee. "If I hadn't overheard you talking with the man, I'd have been absolutely shocked. But I didn't ruin the fellow's surprise."

"Did he mention Jimmy George at all?" Luke poured himself a cup of brew.

"He didn't bring up the subject, but I did. Again, he insisted an explanation wasn't required. He reiterated that my troubles with Jimmy George were in the past." Ellie sipped her coffee and her mood sobered. "Robert was so adamant before, demanding an explanation for my sudden marriage. But now he's unconcerned about the whole thing? This is Richard, not Robert."

"From the moment Robert returned, I've felt there was something different about him, too." Luke shook his head. "All the forgotten names. His claims about memory loss. Initially, I'd believed the arrest could have done him in, but…"

"The man I'm engaged to is Richard! Last night, he mentioned something about never being bothered by gossips. My goodness, do you remember all those months that Robert and I were fodder for the local gossipmongers! What do we do now?" pleaded Ellie.

"The fewer people who know about this, the better. We tell no one of our suspicions, not even Maggie." Luke whispered while his wife worked at the far end of the kitchen. "Continue your usual routine. And that includes inviting your betrothed to supper and making wedding preparations with my wife. I'll get Sanders checking into this immediately."

"All right," Ellie replied in a soft voice. "Richard Rutherford is a dangerous man, and I don't want to be around him any longer than necessary. And I hate that he's anywhere near Edward."

"I wish I could say we're probably way off base here, but I can't. Ernest Jones is too inexperienced to handle this," whispered Luke. "I'll be in contact with Sheriff Sanders in Miles City. I trust him completely to help us."

"Thank you, Luke." Ellie smiled and leaned forward in her chair. "We have to find Robert. He must be in a jail somewhere."

Luke patted her hand. "We'll find him. In the meantime, just play along with Richard. But be careful."

Ellie nodded.

"Here's your breakfast, darling. What are you two whispering about?" asked Maggie, seating herself at the table and reaching for her baby boy.

"Nothing important, dear," answered Luke.

* * *

On Monday morning, Luke and Maggie rode to town, seemingly for the purpose of purchasing wedding paraphernalia with Ellie who met them outside the store at ten o'clock. In no time, Elizabeth and Maggie were fussing over dress material and patterns while Ronald finished stacking canned goods.

Luke stepped up beside Ellie who was looking at dress patterns. He whispered near her ear, "After our little chat at the ranch on Thursday, I headed into town and sent Sheriff Sanders a telegraph requesting a meeting to discuss a sensitive matter at his earliest convenience."

Ellie met his eyes. "What did he say? Does he believe me?"

"I never mentioned the reason for the meeting. Didn't want the wrong people reading that telegraph besides the sheriff," explained Luke.

"Have you heard from him?"

"The old fellow in the telegraph office slipped me Sheriff Sanders' reply before church yesterday. The sheriff advised me to expect him in Spirit Creek on Monday morning. That was why I insisted Maggie and I say hello after church yesterday. And why I suggested you meet with us here today."

Everyone turned, as the little bell above the door tinkled a warning that someone entered.

"Sheriff Sanders," greeted Luke, grinning. "What brings you to town?"

"Good morning, folks," replied the Miles City sheriff, smiling. "Just passing through town, and I decided to look you up and enjoy a bit of a chinwag."

Luke and Sheriff Sanders shook hands. "Why don't we wander over to the jailhouse? I'll introduce you to our new deputy, and you can say how-do to Ernest." Luke winked at the sheriff.

"Actually, I'd like a palaver with Mrs. Barkley." The sheriff shook Ellie's hand. "I've been wondering how you're doing, ma'am?"

"I've never been better, sir," answered Ellie smiling. "I've just become engaged."

"Well, then, congratulations are in order." The sheriff tipped his hat.

"Maggie and Elizabeth, please excuse me for a few minutes." Ellie glanced over her shoulder. "I believe I'll accompany Luke and Sheriff Sanders to the jailhouse, but I'll return as soon as we've caught up on our news."

"That's fine, Ellie. We'll be waiting." Maggie waved her on her way.

* * *

Ten minutes later, Luke and Ellie were seated on a couple of rickety chairs inside the jailhouse, sipping a cup of sludge and explaining their suspicions. Sheriff Sanders leaned against one wall and Ernest Jones sat behind his desk, speechless.

"Have you two been drinking?" asked Sheriff Sanders. "That's a tall tale if I've ever heard one."

"Ya reckon?" scoffed Ernest, finally finding his voice.

"Son, you require a lesson in brewing coffee," muttered the visiting sheriff, setting his tin coffee cup on the corner of Ernest's desk. "Where is this Richard fellow now?"

"Probably over at the law office," suggested Luke.

"Lord knows what Richard is doing to his brother's law practice," whispered Ellie. "Robert's secretary is smart as a whip, and she'll keep things on an even keel over there with any luck at all."

"And you're convinced he's Richard not Robert?" The sheriff stared at the accusers.

"Don't look so surprised. Richard Rutherford has impersonated his brother on several occasions. For unlawful reasons, not just childhood pranks. Robert told me so himself," insisted Ellie. "The Robert who returned to Spirit Creek is a night-and-day-different man from the one who was dragged out of town by those Pinkerton detectives."

Sheriff Sanders glanced away for a moment and then met her eyes. "Mrs. Barkley, I've got to admit I identified Robert myself from a sketch the Pinkerton fellows showed me."

"What?" asked Luke and Ellie in unison.

"That dang sketch was the spitting image of Robert. This is the first I've heard about any twin brother." Sheriff Sanders started pacing the narrow strip of office floor. "I've no reason to believe Robert Rutherford isn't the man currently living in Spirit Creek."

"You're entitled to your opinion on the matter." Luke leaned forward in his chair. "But could you check into this for us, as a favor for Ellie? If we're wrong, then we'll apologize for wasting your time, but if we're right…"

"Does the term 'wild goose chase' mean anything to you folks?" asked Sheriff Sanders, standing beside their chairs. "But if it's that important to the both of you, then I'll make some inquiries."

"Keep us posted, Sanders. I'll be making several trips to Spirit Creek, looking for a telegraph from you. I can come up with no end of excuses to come to town: attending a cattlemen meeting, ordering supplies, meeting with the mayor, you name it. My wife knows nothing of this and I intend to keep it that way."

"I'll work on this and you'll hear from me. Soon as I know for certain that fellow is Richard, I'll have Ernest arrest him," instructed Sheriff Sanders. "Meanwhile, Ernest, he's Robert."

"I understand," said Sheriff Jones.

"I'm convinced it is Richard I'm engaged to, but I'm going ahead with these wedding plans so he doesn't become suspicious," said Ellie, leaping out of her chair. "But as soon as you can prove his true identity, one way or the other, please let us know."

Sheriff Sanders touched the brim of his Stetson. "If at all possible, you'll be the first I tell."

Friday, December 5, 1890

Sheriff Sanders yawned, reining the horse he'd acquired at a local livery through the streets of San Francisco. He'd decided several days ago that he was getting too old for this investigation nonsense. Late nights and missed sleep, skipped meals, and hours traveling on a train. Next time, he'd leave it all to a younger man.

He'd spent weeks retracing Robert Rutherford's steps since the night he'd been hauled out of the Spirit Creek Hotel ballroom after being placed under arrest by the Pinkerton detectives. He could wallpaper half the Miles City jailhouse with the number of telegraphs he'd sent and received.

The trail led him here to San Francisco where he'd spent the past day learning the details of the case against Rutherford, reading all the paperwork on the charges and his final judgment in court, and then learning where the man was incarcerated.

The House of Correction on Ocean House Road. At least the poor bastard hadn't been sent to San Quentin. A judge had instructed Saunders to talk to Superintendent Dore when he arrived at the institution.

As the sheriff approached the facility, he stared in wonder at the brick building which appeared cold and massive. Sanders figured it might take a while to find one man in the huge place.

Soon, he was introduced to the superintendent and escorted into the fellow's office in his lavish living quarters. Sanders marveled at the expense. He'd been invited to some exquisitely-appointed homes in his day, but few compared to this fellow's lodging in the main building.

Sanders removed his Stetson and shook the superintendent's hand.

"My name's Sheriff Bob Sanders from Miles City, Montana. Retired Texas Ranger, now frontier sheriff."

"Pleased to meet you, sir. Take a seat," said Dore, indicating the chair opposite the leather one behind his black walnut desk.

Both men seated themselves.

"Can I offer you…" began Dore.

"No thank you. I've traveled a long way and I'd like to settle this matter as soon as possible."

"Very well. My sheriff's deputy told me you were looking for someone."

Sheriff Sanders cleared his throat. "I believe you had a prisoner here by the name of Robert Rutherford. It's my understanding he was sentenced, sent here, but later proved his innocence and was subsequently released."

"Rutherford," muttered Dore, digging a file out of a pile on the corner of his desk. "Yes, I'm familiar with his case. Deposited stolen funds into a local bank."

Sanders nodded. "That's correct."

"Why would we release him?" Dore leaned forward and rested his arms on his desk. "Prisoner Rutherford is not innocent. He's still here at this facility."

"Robert Rutherford."

"Yes."

"Not Richard Rutherford."

"Who is Richard Rutherford?"

"Oh, hell," muttered Sanders. "We've got a problem, sir."

"I don't believe I have a problem, but what is your complaint?" inquired Dore, folding his arms across his chest.

"First of all, Robert Rutherford is an esteemed attorney working in Spirit Creek, a small town south of Miles City. He worked for a prestigious law firm in Boston before he moved to Montana. Robert has a twin brother named Richard who also hails from Boston. Anyway, Richard operates south of the law most of the time unless he's incarcerated for one crime or another." Saunders shifted in his chair.

"Go on," said Dore, leaning forward and resting his arms on his desk.

"I read the details of the charges and the trial proceedings against Robert Rutherford."

"So have I," added Dore.

"Could we speak to Mr. Rutherford, please? After reading those documents, I know for a fact that he's innocent. With Robert's help, I'd like to prove it to you."

Dore scowled at Sanders, rose to his feet, and left the office without a word. Several minutes later, a pale and emaciated Robert Rutherford, clad in prison garb and handcuffs, shuffled inside ahead of the superintendent who closed the door behind them.

"Sanders!" blurted Robert the second he spotted him. "Thank the Lord. Finally, a familiar face."

"How-do, Robert." Sanders smiled. "Hear you've gotten yourself in a peck of trouble."

Robert grimaced. "Not of my doing, that's for sure."

"Quiet, prisoner. You will only speak when spoken to. All right, Sanders. Prove to me why you believe this man is innocent," growled Dore.

Robert gasped. "Sanders, you believe I'm innocent?"

Dore glared at him.

"You've read all the paperwork concerning this case, Dore. Correct?" asked Sanders.

"That I have," confirmed Dore.

"Then you're familiar with the charges that Robert Rutherford deposited stolen funds into that San Francisco bank," explained Sanders.

"Yes. The clerk sketched a remarkable likeness. There's no doubt in my mind that Rutherford is guilty." Dore leaned back in his chair.

"Me either."

"What the hell!" Dore leapt out of his chair. "I thought you told me…"

"Rutherford is guilty. You've just got the wrong Rutherford." Sanders twirled his Stetson in his hand. Could this actually work? Could he prove Robert was set up, once again, by his despicable twin?

"What makes you say that?" asked Dore, sounding skeptical.

Sanders glanced over at Robert, standing on the rug. "Robert, were you told what day you allegedly deposited those funds?"

"I may have. I don't recall. My mind's been a little fuzzy lately. Does it matter?"

"August 14 was the day," informed Sanders.

Robert's mouth dropped open. The sheriff smiled, knowing the prisoner realized exactly why he was innocent.

"What difference does the date matter?" asked Dore. "The clerk identified him."

"Well, now, I hate to admit it, Robert, but I was the one who identified you from that dang sketch." Sanders grimaced. "Of course, nobody had told me about your twin brother."

"I can understand your mistake," replied Robert.

"Back to this twin brother business," scoffed Dore. "Why are you so certain the twin brother is to blame?"

"Because I know for a fact, Robert Rutherford was not in that bank on August 14."

Dore glared at the prisoner. "Then where were you?"

"I was lying in a pool of my own blood on the floor in my law office. A couple of escaped bank robbers named Billy Bob Newberry and Shorty Jenkins attempted to scare some information out of me. I refused and a subsequent scuffle resulted in me being shot."

Dore appeared to be pondering this bit of information.

The sheriff continued, "There is no way on earth Robert Rutherford deposited that money since he was miles away and busy bleeding to death at the time. The local lawmen telegraphed me and I traveled to Spirit Creek and arranged for the escaped bank robbers to be returned to California myself."

Dore scoffed, "Can you prove this?"

The sheriff pulled a telegraph out of his pocket. "I've been in contact with Spirit Creek's physician, a Doctor Benjamin Johnson previously from Philadelphia. He confirmed that on the afternoon of August 14th, he was performing surgery, digging a bullet out of Robert Rutherford's shoulder." He handed the telegraph to Dore. "Care to show him your scar, Robert?"

Dore gazed at the paper and then rubbed his chin. "Appears we both have a problem after all." He crossed the floor. "Which shoulder?"

Still in handcuffs, Robert nodded his head to indicate which one.

Dore pulled down Robert's clothing to expose the shoulder in question. "Appears recent but healing nicely. I bet it hurt like the Dickens at the time."

"That it did," Robert confirmed, a hint of a smile twitched at the corner of his mouth.

"Robert believed his brother was in a Boston jail, but I've been in contact with the authorities in Boston. Richard Rutherford was discharged from the prison in error in early July. A mix-up with two prisoners with similar names. By the time the prison superintendent realized the mistake, Rutherford was long gone."

"So where is this Richard Rutherford fellow now?" demanded Dore.

"I believe he resides in Spirit Creek, having assumed his brother's identity."

Dore's head whipped up. "Are you serious?"

"What?" Robert's face reddened. "I'll have his head…"

"He even proposed to Robert's lady friend." Sanders shook his head.

Robert gasped and his hands fisted. "Ellie? He proposed to my Ellie?"

Sanders continued, "It's imperative we release Robert and recapture Richard. I have no idea when the wedding date will be. Don't brides believe June is the perfect month for a wedding?"

"I don't imagine it's pleasant traveling to Montana this time of year, but this matter must be rectified now." Dore leapt out of his chair. "I'll talk to a judge immediately."

"Thank you, Superintendent." Sanders shook the other fellow's hand with great enthusiasm. "I cannot tell you how thankful I am that you've agreed to help."

"Would you send a telegraph to Ellie for me, Sanders? She must be warned…" pleaded Robert.

"Absolutely not," insisted Dore. "We haven't convinced a judge of your innocence yet. Besides, we cannot risk tipping our hand. If this Richard fellow is dangerous, it's best if we just show up and arrest him. If he travelled clear across the county without detection, anything is possible with this character. Should anyone let our news slip, he'll disappear and it could be years before we find him again. "

"I agree. I don't want to put my friends in danger." Sanders stuck his Stetson on his head. "Where do we start?"

"Have the sheriff's deputy take me back to my cell for now," suggested Robert. "You fellows do what you need to do."

Sanders slapped Robert on the back. "We'll have you headed back to Montana in no time."

"Let's talk to a judge, Sanders. Bring that telegram with you." Dore grabbed Robert's file off his desk and led the way out of the office.

CHAPTER 29

Saturday, December 20, 1890

Luke Carlyle pushed his breakfast plate away and leaned back in the chair. A toothpick whipped back and forth from one corner of his mouth to the other while one booted foot tapped impatiently on the plank floor. He hadn't heard a word since Sheriff Sanders left to investigate.

A few weeks ago, he would have bet the ranch that Richard Rutherford was impersonating his twin brother. Had Ellie's suspicions been proven wrong? Had their imaginations simply been running amok? Was no news good news? Uncertainty troubled Luke, and he couldn't stop worrying.

Was something amiss?

Was Sanders still searching for answers?

Had Sanders himself gotten into trouble?

Ellie would be exchanging wedding vows with this fellow, whoever he was, in a few hours, and although Luke felt honored to be giving the bride away, he couldn't help feeling concerned for Ellie. She'd endured so much pain in recent months: losing Franklin and then the baby, marriage to that abusive Barkley fellow. And then their suspicions about Robert. He imagined she was on pins and needles, today. Wondering. Concerned. Worried.

"Was Richard impersonating his brother? Or was Ellie about to marry Robert?" whispered Luke aloud.

"Did you say something, sweetheart?" asked Maggie, sweeping into the room, holding an elaborate wedding dress in her arms.

"Just talking to myself." Luke rose from the chair and pecked his wife on the cheek. "How's Ellie holding up?"

"Nervous, as is expected of any bride." Maggie chuckled. "Agnes pressed a few creases out of her wedding gown, and I'm on my way upstairs with it."

"I've enjoyed Ellie and Edward's stay with us these past few days." Luke carried his breakfast dishes to the kitchen counter and sank them into a pan of soapy dishwater.

"Their visit has been an absolute joy. Ellie is like the younger sister I never had," added Maggie, smiling.

All of Ellie and Edward's possessions had been moved from the modest house Ellie had rented from Luke into Robert's elegant new home, formerly Sarah Grayson's mansion. Propriety dictated that Ellie and Robert refrain from co-habitation until after the wedding, so she and Edward had moved to the ranch in preparation for the big day.

"When are we holding Willie's first birthday celebrations?" asked Luke, arms crossed, leaning against the kitchen work station.

"We're opening his gifts at ten o'clock. Ned and Morning Star, and Agnes and Mike are coming up to the main house for a cup of coffee and cake. And then they're staying for the wedding at eleven." Maggie sighed. "Willie is one year old today, Luke. The time has just flown by. I'll turn around any day now, and he'll be heading off to school."

"Don't despair. The little fellow just started walking. He won't be doing his sums for another week or so," teased Luke, chuckling.

"Goodness, this house is a beehive of activity," commented Aunt Penny, Maggie's only living relative from Philadelphia, as she tottered into the kitchen.

The elderly matron arrived yesterday in time for the wedding and an extended stay through the Christmas holidays. Once again, against everyone's better judgment, she'd made the long journey unescorted. But once again, she'd arrived safe and sound, wondering what all the fuss was about concerning her travels.

"Take a seat, Aunt Penny, and I'll pour you a cup of coffee." Luke pulled out a chair for her. "You appeared exhausted when you arrived. How did you sleep?"

"I'm getting my legs under me." Aunt Penny patted Luke's hand. "Thank you for your concern, Luke, but I'm recovering nicely from my journey. And I don't begrudge one stiff muscle or aching bone if I'm able to celebrate the holidays with everyone again."

"And to celebrate Willie's birthday," Maggie reminded her aunt.

"Don't forget there's a wedding to attend as well," beamed Aunt Penny. "I just love weddings."

"Well, we're delighted you've come again." Luke poured the coffee from the pot warming atop the woodstove, and then set the steaming cup of brew in front of their visitor.

"Thank you, young man." Aunt Penny beamed up at him. "A good strong and hot cup of coffee is exactly what I need to mobilize these old bones."

Smiling, Luke crossed the floor and whispered in his wife's ear, "Didn't you mention Willie was growing up too quickly for your liking? If you desire another baby in the house, we could start making a sister for him." Luke wiggled his eyebrows, suggestively.

"Perhaps we already have…" Maggie purred under her breath.

"Are you?" Luke whispered, feeling slightly faint.

She whisked out of the room, leaving Luke with his mouth hanging open.

"Is everything all right, young man?" inquired Aunt Penny, peeking over her spectacles as she set her cup down. "All the blood drained out of your face, dear."

* * *

"Here's your gown, Ellie," proclaimed Maggie, sweeping into the second-floor guest bedroom.

Ellie swung around and her eyes rested on the beautiful dress. Until she'd met Maggie, the term 'friend' held no meaning for her. Now, she realized the other orphans she'd been raised with were merely acquaintances. None of those girls had ever made her feel special or cherished like Maggie did. Ellie could tell her anything, even her most intimate secrets, and vice versa. No matter what, Ellie could count on Maggie standing at her side through all of life's challenges. And Ellie did the same for her.

"My dear friend, how will I ever thank you," whispered Ellie, her eyes filling.

"No tears today," ordered Maggie, handing the dress to the bride. "Not on your wedding day."

"I'll try." Ellie blinked away the moistness in her eyes. Her hands caressed the delicate wedding dress: yards of white silk and lace, hundreds of seed-pearls, and a wide satin sash that would settle just under her bosoms. "I never dreamed of ever wearing such a beautiful gown. I might drown in all these voluptuous skirts."

The elaborate creation had arrived with Aunt Penny. Ellie had almost fainted when she opened the box and extracted the contents. And then she and Maggie christened the gown with a deluge of tears. Ellie wasn't certain which of them was more pleased with it. But thanks to her substantial funds, she could certainly afford to spoil herself with such a beautiful wedding dress. Hopefully, her last.

Sheila Bennett has certainly outdone herself, proclaimed Aunt Penny when she saw Ellie wearing the gown for the first time. Aunt Penny's custom dressmaker and owner of Bustles and Bows Dress Shop in

Philadelphia created the gown especially for Ellie.

Maggie smiled. "This gown is absolutely wonderful."

"I believe I've died and gone to heaven," whispered Ellie, clutching the gown to her bosom. If only she could be certain it was Robert and not Richard she was marrying. Her doubts were spoiling the day. And what if she went through with the ceremony? Would the marriage be legal if it actually was Richard she said 'I do' with?

"Just return from heaven in time for the marriage ceremony," warned Maggie, laughing.

"I've definitely waited long enough for happiness to knock on my door again," observed Ellie, for her friend's sake. She'd never divulged her suspicions to Maggie at Luke's insistence.

And she hadn't forgotten her doubts about Robert's identity for a moment. For weeks, she'd played along with the man she believed to be Richard, for safety's sake. Neither she nor Luke had heard anything from Sheriff Sanders, however, and as much as Ellie wished she could just relax and enjoy her special day knowing she was indeed marrying Robert, she couldn't. Ellie was convinced, more than ever, that the man preparing to marry her today was Richard.

"Now, I must celebrate my baby's first birthday. I suggest you lie down and rest for a little while. You have a big day ahead of you. I'll return in an hour or so," said Maggie, kissing her friend's cheek before dashing out the bedroom door.

* * *

The Diamond C's main house parlor was decked out for the holidays, and Maggie wandered inside for a final peek. She'd changed into her matron of honor dress of sky-blue silk with matching lace trim and swirling skirts. And she'd styled her hair in a flattering upsweep of auburn curls with an intricately-designed blue bow that matched her dress.

A huge pine tree, resplendent in Christmas baubles and other finery, stood in the turret. A few colorful paper ornaments, home-made by her children, hung on the lower branches. Sunshine poured in through the trio of windows and reflected off the shiny blown-glass balls which contrasted wonderfully with the dark evergreen boughs.

Red ribbons and bows decorated the doorway leading into the parlor. Identical ribbons and bows and evergreen swags covered an archway, situated at the far end of the room, under which the bride and groom would exchange their vows. Candles stood ready for lighting, and the parlor furniture was relegated to the corners of the room to accommodate the wedding festivities.

Maggie peeked into the dining room. The enormous table was set with rose-patterned china, silverware, and sparkling crystal, awaiting the guests and the sumptuous meal that would follow the ceremony. Red ribbons topped the posts on the dozen ladder-back chairs, surrounding the table. And an elaborate centerpiece of pine boughs decorated with white candles and white ribbons and bows ran almost the entire length of the table. She inhaled deeply, and a mixture of holiday scents including pine boughs and apple cider tickled her nose.

Returning to the parlor, Maggie spotted a large straw basket beside the tree, holding an assortment of wrapped presents for the birthday boy. Willie wouldn't comprehend the reason for all the to-do, but Maggie couldn't allow such an important day to pass without some celebration. Especially since her son's birthday was being seriously overshadowed by her best friend's nuptials.

"Here's the man-of-the-hour," gushed Agnes, rushing into the parlor with Willie in her arms. The baby clapped his hands in a game of patty cake as he was passed to his mother.

"How's my little man?" cooed Maggie, inhaling his clean-baby scent. Agnes had dressed Willie in a navy blue and white woolen suit and little black leather shoes. A small matching woolen hat perched atop Willie's head. Maggie was amazed her son hadn't already tugged it off and tossed it on the floor. She wanted her son to look his best. Arthur MacDonald and his wife planned to attend the wedding and also promised to record Willie's big day with a photograph.

"I'm exhausted! And it's only quarter of ten in the morning," complained Agnes, flopping onto one of the sofas. "This is too much excitement in one day."

"I'm tired already, too. But I'm fairly certain I know the reason." Maggie sat down beside her mother's helper.

"Pray tell. I'm all ears." Agnes sat up a little straighter.

"I suspect I'm with child again," whispered Maggie. "Perhaps we share the same reason for our tiredness?"

Agnes gasped and began counting on her fingers. A flabbergasted expression appeared on her face. "I think…I think you may be right. I've been so busy with the Christmas preparations and the wedding planning and running the household…I never suspected a thing."

"My lips are sealed until you've had an opportunity to share the good news with your husband. Mike is going to be delighted." Maggie set Willie down between them and reached for Agnes's hands. "Kindly keep my secret for a while longer, too."

"Certainly." Agnes giggled. "*This* is so exciting."

"Let's check with Doc Benjamin after the holidays to confirm our suspicions, before we start counting chickens." Maggie hugged Agnes. Squished between them, Willie attempted to push the two women away with his chubby hands.

"That's a good idea. I wouldn't want to build up Mike's hopes and then shatter them afterwards."

"My thoughts exactly," she agreed, patting Agnes's knee. "A young man is celebrating his birthday today, however, so let's get busy."

Ned and Morning Star burst into the room. "Where's that little whippersnapper?" asked Ned, toting a carved wooden rocking horse in his arms.

Willie spotted the present and clapped his hands in approval. Ned and Willie wore matching ear-to-ear grins.

* * *

Ellie tossed and turned atop her bed for more than an hour. A thousand questions and troubling thoughts competed for attention in her mind, making napping virtually impossible. Only Sheriff Sanders could set her mind at ease for certain.

Why hadn't she or Luke received any word from the Miles City sheriff? Surely the local lawman must have learned something by now. For the millionth time she asked herself, was her fiancé telling the truth? Was he Robert? Or were her suspicions true and she was actually engaged to Richard?

Ellie sat upright in bed. That man was Richard! She'd bet her life on it! Perhaps she was.

"I cannot marry that man!" she declared aloud. But what excuse could she use? Claim she'd gotten cold feet? Pretend she'd come down with an illness? Maybe it would be best to just slip away and hide out somewhere until she heard from Sheriff Sanders.

Ellie leapt off the bed and strode to the door. She paused with her hand on the doorknob. Sheriff Sanders' departing words popped into her head. His warnings that she not say a word to the dangerous man, play along with him at all costs. But, was actually going through with this blasted wedding too much to ask of her?

"What should I do?" she whispered aloud.

Suddenly, the doorknob turned and Maggie whipped the door open. Ellie's heart almost stopped. "It's you!" Ellie crossed the floor and dropped onto the bed.

"Who were you expecting?" asked Maggie. "Robert's been warned that he's not to set foot upstairs. Ned and Luke are keeping him company out in the bunkhouse until the wedding."

"No…I thought I would…never mind. Has Willie opened his presents?"

"Yes, and he would like to thank you for the new sweater," replied

Maggie, smiling. "He's taking a much needed nap after all the excitement of presents and cake."

"Willie is very welcome." Ellie smiled. "I'll give him a big birthday kiss when he wakes up."

"Ned built him the most precious little rocking horse, painted a half dozen different bright and sunny colors. That was a huge success, but Willie enjoyed gnawing on the rope mane as much as he enjoyed sitting in the saddle. I suspect there's another tooth on the way." Maggie settled herself in the rocking chair beside the bed. "It's so quiet and peaceful up here. I'm enjoying this escape from the hubbub downstairs."

"I suppose I should finish dressing. Just need to slip into my dress and put my shoes on." Ellie rose from the bed.

"Arthur finished taking Willie's picture and he's setting up his photography equipment in the parlor to take a picture of you and Robert after the vows are spoken." Maggie rose to her feet. "Do you need some help?"

"I should use the indoor convenience while the opportunity presents itself, and then I could use some assistance slipping the dress over my head." Ellie dashed out of the room.

A couple of minutes later she returned with Aunt Penny in tow.

"Look who I ran into in the hallway." Ellie beamed.

"I'm loaning Ellie a little *something borrowed*," explained Maggie's aunt.

"That's not necessary…" began Ellie who was immediately silenced by a wave of the elderly lady's wrinkled and age-spotted hand.

"I insist, dear." Aunt Penny rummaged around in a small wooden box with a spray of lilacs painted on the top. "I wore these earrings and this necklace the day I married my dear Theodore, and these baubles brought me many happy years with my husband, rest his soul. You must wear them today to ensure you live a long and happy life with your young man."

Ellie gasped as Aunt Penny extracted a set of diamond earrings and a matching diamond necklace. "These baubles?" exclaimed Ellie. "They must be worth a fortune. I couldn't possibly."

"I'm not giving them to you, dear, this is simply a loan." Aunt Penny grinned. "I doubt you've invited a jewel thief to your wedding, so these will be quite safe around your lovely neck and clipped onto your delicate ears. Now, not another word…let me see them on you."

Ellie held her breath while Aunt Penny clipped the earrings on and closed the clasp on the necklace. She tiptoed over to the cheval mirror and peeked at herself. "Oh, my, they're so beautiful," gasped Ellie.

"They're perfect for a bride." Aunt Penny patted her on the shoulder and grinned, mischievously. "Wear them in good health, dear, but I insist you return them at the end of the day."

"Thank you so much." Ellie hugged the generous matron. "I'll be exceptionally careful with them."

Someone knocked at the door and Agnes peeked inside. "We have the bride's bouquet here, if anyone's interested." Agnes and Belle walked into the room, smiling broadly.

"A bouquet?" asked Ellie. "It's December! Every flower in the garden is dead."

"Don't need fresh flowers for a bouquet," insisted Agnes, and she pressed the creation of evergreen sprigs with dried white roses tied together with blue ribbon.

"Isn't it wonderful?" gushed Belle. "Agnes is so creative."

"I dried the roses to freshen my armoire, but including them in your bouquet serves a better purpose."

"Thank you for your thoughtfulness."

"No trouble at all," insisted Agnes.

"I left Third downstairs with the other fellows for a few minutes. He's minding Matilda, so I can't stay long, Ellie. But Third and I wanted to wish you all the best on your special day." Belle leaned over and kissed Ellie's cheek.

"Thank you, Belle. I appreciate your good wishes."

Belle headed toward the door. "I'd better go fetch my daughter, but I'll see everyone downstairs."

"Thanks, Belle," said Ellie, smiling.

"Dash downstairs, Auntie and ensure everything is ready for the bride's arrival," instructed Maggie.

"All right, dear. Although these old legs haven't dashed anywhere in years," chuckled Aunt Penny.

"Let's get you dressed, Ellie. The hallway clock indicated five minutes after eleven when I came in. You'll be more than fashionably late if we don't get a move on." Maggie shooed the bride toward the armoire where the wedding dress hung.

"I'll await your grand entrance downstairs, Ellie. Good luck today, dear. You deserve all the happiness in the world." Aunt Penny waved on her way out the door.

Ellie smiled at her friend.

"Nothing can ruin this day for you, Ellie," gushed Maggie.

If only that were true, thought Ellie.

CHAPTER 30

The wedding guests conversed in small groups in the spacious parlor, a few folks spilling out into the entryway where the groom stood awaiting his bride. Fragrant evergreen boughs were tied around the staircase posts and at measured intervals on the railings. Their pleasant pine scent drifted throughout the entire house.

Ellie appeared at the top of the staircase, and the groom smiled when he spotted her.

"Are you ready?" Maggie touched Ellie's arm.

"I suppose so," she answered, clasping her bouquet in her hands.

Luke stepped to the groom's side, smiling as Maggie preceded the bride down the long staircase.

As Ellie descended the stairs, her eyes remained riveted on her groom. Trembling hands grasped the small bouquet, and she carefully placed one foot before the other, no doubt mindful of the abundant skirts on her gown that could cause a fall if she hurried. The groom extended his hand toward her, smiling. Her heart pounded in her chest. Oh Lord! It was really happening.

Ellie continued downward, reaching the halfway mark without tripping. Suddenly, the front entryway's heavy wooden double doors flew open. Startled by the unexpected intrusion, Ellie stopped in her tracks and gaped in disbelief.

"There are two of you," she gasped.

The groom turned and the blood drained out of his face.

Sheriff Sanders charged into the house a second later. Taking in the scene before him, his expression soured. "Stop this farce!" he shouted.

"Sanders, where in hell have you been?" demanded Luke, stepping forward. "We've waited ages to hear from you."

"I've been exceptionally busy proving your theories weren't so absurd after all." Sheriff Sanders removed his Stetson and pointed to the gentleman who'd accompanied him across the threshold. "Let me present the real Robert Rutherford. This fellow," he accused, pointing at the gentleman standing at the bottom of the stairs awaiting the bride, "is Richard Rutherford."

Ellie teetered on her feet and Luke raced up the stairs, steadied the bride before she fell.

"I knew it!" she exclaimed.

Sheriff Sanders grabbed the groom by the arm and spun him around to face him. "Richard Rutherford, you are under arrest."

"This is ridiculous…" he began, taking a step back. His eyes darted from one person to the next, like a caged animal.

"Don't even attempt to convince me you're Robert. I know otherwise." Sheriff Sanders dug a pair of handcuffs out of his pocket.

Richard's expression confirmed he realized he'd been discovered. He raced toward the kitchen with Sanders and Luke in hot pursuit.

"Don't let him escape!" shouted Robert.

Richard rushed into the kitchen and headed for the back door. As he sailed past the laundry room, Captain bounded out of the back porch, tripping Richard and sending him sprawling across the plank floor.

"Damn that stupid mutt," cursed Richard, his feet flailing at the animal.

Captain yelped when one boot connected with his hindquarters. The dog growled and latched onto Richard's leg.

Richard howled in pain.

"I'm placing you under arrest for the impersonation of your twin brother, for possession of the deposited funds which you no doubt stole, and for leaving a state prison knowing you were released by mistake. And for any other damn thing I can come up with, including kicking that dog." Sheriff Sanders hauled Richard to his feet and slapped the handcuffs on him. "You are the worst excuse for a human being I've ever come across."

Robert dashed into the kitchen and took in the scene.

"Thank goodness he didn't escape," said Robert, approaching his brother.

The two men eyed each other up for a moment and then Robert's fist connected with Richard's jaw. Richard collapsed on the floor with a thud. "I'm real sorry, Sanders. My hand slipped," confessed Robert.

"I didn't see a thing," replied the sheriff, smiling.

Luke chuckled. "Me neither, Robert."

Sanders hauled Richard to his feet and the men all headed out of the kitchen.

Ellie had made her way down the staircase by then, peeked into the kitchen and witnessed the entire thing. She stood staring at the real Robert. Disheveled from traveling and gaunt and pale-faced from his ordeal. She barely recognized him. What had happened to the man she loved?

"Oh, my poor sweet. How are you?" Robert took her hand in his and placed a soft kiss on each finger.

Ellie burst into tears; this man was truly her Robert!

"I'm so sorry," she whispered, tears streaming down her face as they followed the others down the hallway and into the entryway.

"Oh, darling. You have nothing to apologize for." Robert reached out and wiped her tears away. "Even the authorities were totally fooled."

Robert turned and grabbed Richard by the shirt. "Why did you do it?"

Richard sneered. "I needed to get even for you sending me to prison when you lived in Boston."

"You deserved to be incarcerated. You're a thief, a criminal. You always have been since we were children." Robert shoved Richard away. "You'll never change. There isn't an honest bone in your body."

Richard met Sheriff Sanders' eyes. "How did you figure it out? Did my esteemed brother lend a hand in your investigation? Robert has always been the righteous one in the family."

"I'm not answering any of your questions. I can't wait to haul you back to jail. You won't be released in error again. Of that I can assure you." Sanders slapped his Stetson back on his head.

"Goodbye, sweetheart." Richard smiled wickedly at Ellie who was shaking slightly. "I regret we weren't together long enough to enjoy the honeymoon."

In a blurred movement, Robert's fist connected with his brother's jaw again, sending the fellow sprawling on the entryway floor.

Richard shook his head to clear his senses. "Sheriff, are you going to allow that? I've been assaulted. Arrest him!"

Sanders chuckled. "Robert just beat me to it. Sorry for the interruption, folks," apologized the sheriff and then hauled Richard to his feet and dragged him outside.

Ned slammed the door behind them. "Good riddance."

"I agree," said Luke.

Ned slapped the new arrival on the back. "Tarnation, Robert, what a close call. Yer darn fool brother nearly married yer bride."

Robert returned his attention to Ellie. "Thank goodness we arrived when we did."

"Why didn't you telegraph me? Warn me I was engaged to that imposter?" demanded Ellie.

"Richard had been on the run for months. He'd been playing at being me for weeks and the lawmen knew where he was." Robert dragged his hand though his hair. "I begged them to let me contact you, but they deemed it too dangerous. They required the element of surprise when they arrived to arrest him. Couldn't risk him getting wind of their plans and disappearing again."

"That makes sense, but I've been so frightened I'd say the wrong thing. And then knowing I was about to marry the wrong man today…" Ellie heaved a sigh. "Thank goodness it's over."

"I can't believe this." Robert slumped onto the bottom stair. "We never dreamt the wedding would happen so soon."

"Dang good thing ya got here when ya did…" repeated Ned.

"What if I'd married that man?" Ellie's eyelids fluttered and she wavered on her feet.

Robert caught her in his arms when she fainted.

* * *

Fortunately, Doc Benjamin and Pearl were invited to the wedding. Witnessing Ellie's collapse, Doc grabbed his medical bag off the hallway table and raced upstairs on Robert's heels. Maggie led the way to Ellie's guest room and a few minutes later, Ellie was revived with a bit of assistance from smelling salts.

"What…what happened?" she mumbled, pushing herself up on her elbows. Overcome with dizziness, she fell back against the pillows.

"Just relax," instructed Doc. "Get your bearings before you try to sit up again."

"Do you remember anything?" asked Maggie, patting Ellie's hand.

"I descended the stairs. Robert was waiting for me, but there were two Roberts. I…" Ellie clasped her hand to her mouth. "I could have married Richard. I think I'm going to be sick!"

Doc sat beside Ellie on the bed. "You'll be fine. Just lie back and relax. You only require a few minutes to recover from the shock."

Ellie closed her eyes and took a deep breath. Her stomach stopped roiling, and she patted her chest.

"No one knows better than me what Richard is capable of," whispered Robert. "Would you actually have married him?"

"I need to explain everything to you," began Ellie, attempting to swing her feet over the side of the bed.

"Stay put," ordered Doc.

Ellie's cheeks reddened, and she met Robert's eyes. "What you must think of me…"

"We can discuss this later." Robert met Doc's eyes. "Is Ellie all right? Just suffering from the shock?"

"She'll be fine once she lies here and relaxes for a while." Doc patted her arm and stood. He stuffed his instruments back into his bag. "We'll leave you two alone for a few minutes."

Maggie, Pearl and Doc left the room.

Robert stared at Ellie for a few seconds. Without saying a word, he walked out right behind them.

Ellie burst into tears.

* * *

Luke charged up the winding staircase, stopping on the stair second from the top when he spotted Robert closing the spare room door, muttering to himself.

"Are you all right?" whispered Luke.

Robert looked up, eyes dazed. "I need a drink. Do you have a whiskey handy?"

"Follow me." Luke led Robert down the stairs, toward his study. "Ned is relaying apologies to our guests, but I insisted he didn't send anyone home until we sort this out."

"That's good I suppose," replied Robert.

After settling the badly- shaken gentleman in one of the chairs beside his desk, Luke poured a generous portion of whiskey into a crystal glass and passed it to his friend. "Drink that," he ordered. "And then I'll pour you another if you need it."

Robert tossed back the drink and then handed Luke the empty glass.

"What the hell happened to you?" asked Luke.

"There's plenty of time for explanations later." Robert accepted the refill. "Was Ellie actually going to marry that imposter?"

"You told Ellie yourself how dangerous Richard was. He did a wonderful job of fooling everyone else." Luke settled into the leather chair behind his desk. "Sanders headed out searching for you weeks ago, assuring us he'd stay in touch. But we never heard a word."

Robert paused to down a healthy swig of his drink. "Sanders informed me Ellie figured out my brother's deception in the first place."

"Ellie became suspicious, and I encouraged her to pursue the matter. When Sanders was apprised of our suspicions, he agreed to either prove or disprove them." Luke folded his arms. "When we never heard from Sanders, I wondered if we'd been wrong. But Ellie was adamant, it was Richard she was engaged to. And she insisted in going along with him for her own safety, as well as others. There was Edward and Janie to consider."

"Didn't the lack of contact with Sanders suggest that something was definitely wrong?" snapped Robert. "It's my understanding he promised to be in touch."

Luke heard the disgust in Robert's voice. Or was it

disappointment? Either way, he realized Robert felt betrayed by the woman he'd loved for so long.

"Richard bamboozled all of us. For a time, I even believed the bastard was you." Luke rested his elbows on the desk. "Do you still love Ellie?"

Robert bolted out of his chair. "Of course, I still love Ellie. For Pete's sake, I've loved the woman for years. I'll always love her. Why would you ask such a foolish question?"

"Because you're acting like a horse's behind." Luke stifled a grin. "If I loved Ellie, I'd be charging back up those stairs. I'd be…"

"All right! I get your point." Robert dragged his hand down his face. "Walking into the house, discovering Ellie dressed in a wedding gown, holding a bridal bouquet…"

"Received a bit of a shock?"

"My heart damn near stopped." Robert grimaced. "I'd planned this grand entrance to surprise the trousers off that miserable brother of mine. Instead, I wanted to kill the bastard when I realized what was happening."

"A line was forming. When I realized it was you, I could have throttled Richard myself." Luke stood. "So what are you doing about Ellie?"

"I'm going to marry her," stated Robert, without a moment's hesitation.

"Marry her," repeated Luke.

Robert contemplated what he'd shared a minute ago. Then he laughed, smiling broadly. "Yes, I'm going to marry her. There's no sense wasting that pretty dress, and all those nice folks are waiting in the parlor for a wedding. I bet the women prepared enough food to feed a small army."

"All true," confirmed Luke, grinning.

"I'm going upstairs and propose to Ellie. Keep the reverend here. I'll carry her down to the parlor, kicking and screaming, if I have to."

"Well, good luck to you." Luke extended his hand, and they shook on it. "I'm all duded up. Let me know if any best man services are required."

"There will be, if I have anything to say about it," called Robert on his way out the door.

* * *

Robert knocked on the door and poked his head inside.

"Could I please have a word with you, Ellie?" he asked.

"Yes, of course, come in, Robert." Ellie leapt off the bed. "I'm so happy you came back."

"How are you doing?" he whispered.

"I'll be all right now that you're here. How have you been?" A pained expression crossed Ellie's face. "Of all the stupid things to ask you…"

"Pardon my language, but I've been to Hell and back." Robert couldn't meet her eyes, jammed his hands into his pockets. "I'll tell you about it, someday."

"After you were arrested, I worried myself sick for days. I hadn't an inkling where those men hauled you off to, or even why. I cried all day, awoke from the most frightening and confusing nightmares." Ellie sighed. "And then you appeared out of nowhere, stepped off the stagecoach and assured me everything had been a huge mistake. I was such a fool…"

"My brother is a polished liar, among other things. I imagine he was exceptionally convincing." Robert reached out and tucked a strand of hair behind her ear.

"He seemed so like you, except for little things: suddenly kissing me in public, forgetting people's names. I'd convinced myself that being incarcerated had caused these small changes in you." Ellie gulped. "But Captain growled every time you entered the house, and the dog had never done that before. He actually bit Richard the first night he came to supper."

"Good dog," whispered Robert, grinning.

"I started to wonder if perhaps it wasn't you when I remembered you mentioning a twin brother. The whole idea seemed so absurd that I started to question my own sanity. But I shared my suspicions with Luke and Sheriff Sanders."

"I'll thank God every day that you did." Robert leaned over and gently kissed her cheek. "Otherwise, I'd still be incarcerated because of Richard, and he'd be living here, laughing heartily. Worst of all, he'd be married to you."

"Please, that scenario is beyond contemplation." Ellie shivered. "I'm feeling much better now. We really should go downstairs and apologize to everyone."

"Ned and Luke are explaining what happened, answering all of the guests' questions." Robert added, in a remarkably accurate imitation of Luke, "*That lawyer is a real pistol, isn't he? The old chap maneuvers himself into a heap of trouble on a regular basis.*"

Ellie smiled. "At least you see humor in all this. It will take every bit of willpower I can muster up to face those folks again."

"You have nothing to be embarrassed about. You're a victim here, as much as I am." Robert kissed her cheek again. "We could announce some good news."

"Your being rescued and brought back to Spirit Creek safe and sound is all the good news I need."

"There could be more," alluded Robert.

"Such as?" inquired Ellie.

"There's no reason to waste such a pretty wedding dress." Robert reached for her hand.

"That, sir, is the most pathetic attempt at a proposal I've ever heard." Ellie tilted her head to one side, grinning.

"Loving you and dreaming about the day we'd be reunited were the only things that kept me sane while I rotted away in that jail cell all those weeks." Robert grasped her hands, kissing each finger in turn. "A few times I thought I'd never see you again, questioned why I was bothering to be brave. And then I realized you'd horsewhip me if I succumbed to the feelings of hopelessness that were threatening to overtake me."

"Oh, Robert, I can't imagine how unbearable your ordeal must have been. I should have realized Richard wasn't you the moment I spotted him after he stepped off the stagecoach. I should have questioned him point blank. I should have ordered him out of my life, out of Spirit Creek."

"No, Ellie." Robert reached out and touched her cheek. "You did exactly the right thing. Richard can be extremely dangerous, especially when he's cornered. I'd trust a wounded grizzly more than I'd trust Richard."

"But I feel so stupid for not…"

"It's over, for all of us. And we've been presented with the opportunity to celebrate our happy ending." Robert dropped to one knee. "My dearest, please say you'll marry me?"

"Yes," whispered Ellie, smiling and tearing up at the same time. "Let's celebrate with a wedding. I'm ready to marry you right now. But first I must explain why I married Jimmy George. You've waited long enough…"

"I figured it out, sweetheart. While I was wasting away all those days in jail." Robert whispered, "You were with child, weren't you? Smith had gotten you in the family way."

Ellie's eyes welled with tears and she nodded her head. "I lost the baby the night of Luke and Maggie's party."

"I figured that out, too. The influenza story." Robert wrapped his arms around her. "Sweetheart, you've been through so much. But the past is just that. It's the past. Today will be the first day of the rest of our lives together. Our future begins now. Give me a half hour to beg, borrow or steal a decent suit of clothes from Luke, and I'll meet you downstairs."

Ellie smiled. "There's something you need to do first."

"What's that?"

"This." Ellie tightened their embrace, rose up on her toes and kissed him on the lips.

Robert's heart almost stopped from the sheer pleasure of being in Ellie's arms again. Kissing her madly. His hand rested on her breast and she pressed her body against his. No doubt, she'd feel the evidence of his love for her. Soon, this delightful woman would be his wife. Forever. Thoughts of how he'd greet her when he returned to Spirit Creek had kept him hopeful all those nights alone in that jail cell. But nothing he'd conjured up in his imagination even came close to the reality.

By sheer willpower, he stopped himself from burying his hands in her beautiful hair. He wouldn't muss it before the wedding though. Her lips parted, permitting his tongue to explore her delectable mouth. If he died this second, he'd pass away a happy man.

"Thirty minutes, starting now," whispered Ellie, laughing, when they finally came up for air.

When the bedroom door flew open, Robert and Ellie broke apart.

Edward rushed into the room. "You're back, Mr. Rutherford! Is it really you?" he asked, incredulously.

"Yes, Edward, it's really me."

"I'm happy you're back. That other Mr. Rutherford kicked Captain," complained Edward. And then a broad grin creased his face and he giggled. "Captain bit him though."

Robert burst into laughter and lifted Edward into his arms, squeezing him tightly. "Son, I've missed you so much. And your mama, too. Your mama and I are getting married just as soon as I can get cleaned up."

"Yippee!" shouted Edward, clapping his hands.

Robert set him back on his feet. "Come along, Edward. You can help me get ready for the wedding."

"Can Captain help, too?"

Robert chuckled, kissed Ellie on the cheek, and followed his soon-to-be new son out the door.

CHAPTER 31

The wedding guests milled around the parlor in groups, discussing the day's events and awaiting the bride, once again.

"Let's attempt this a second time, folks," announced Luke, chuckling as he strode into the room. The nervous groom stumbled along beside him, fidgeting with his tie. "Your tie is fine, stop it."

"Dang thing don't feel right." Robert glared at Luke and then grinned, sheepishly. "I've never taken a bath so quickly in my life, but I imagine I smell considerably better. And thank you kindly for lending me this suit, shirt, and tie. At least I'm wearing my own boots."

Luke dug a comb out of his pocket. "Fix your hair. You forgot to comb it."

"Dang it," muttered Robert, grabbing the comb and racing toward the nearest mirror.

"A bit nervous about saying 'I do', is he?" inquired Aunt Penny, stepping up beside Luke. "I don't understand why. The fellow had a full thirty minutes to get accustomed to the idea."

Luke chuckled. "Thirty minutes, thirty days, tying that noose around your neck…"

"Oh, pooh," interrupted Aunt Penny, slapping Luke on the arm. "You love being a married man and you know it. And this young fellow will, too. Ellie is an absolute treasure."

"I agree wholeheartedly, ma'am." Robert passed the comb to Luke, and then extended his hand. "I don't believe we've been introduced."

"Aunt Penny…" began Luke.

The spunky older gal took over, sticking out her bejeweled hand. "Mrs. Penelope Margaret Williamson. I'm Maggie's aunt, visiting for the Christmas holiday. I brought Ellie's lovely wedding dress with me, all the way from Philadelphia."

"I'm delighted to meet you. I'm Robert Rutherford, the true

groom." Robert kissed the matron's hand. "What an exquisite ring, Mrs. Williamson."

"Please, just call me Aunt Penny. Everyone does. And thank you for noticing the ring my late husband presented me with on the day we wed." The elderly matron beamed. "I'm no spring chicken mind you, but I insist you save me a dance. They'll be dancing after the meal, you know."

"Top of the list, ma'am, after my bride," said Robert, grinning.

At that moment, Ned lumbered into the room. "Bride's on the way, folks."

Everyone found a chair and then turned toward the doorway. Maggie entered, followed by a blushing Ellie on Luke's arm, walking slowly toward Robert. Maggie assisted the bride with her skirts, and Ellie passed the lovely bouquet to her friend to hold during the ceremony. Luke stepped up beside the groom, exchanging giving-away-the-bride duties for best man duties.

"Good afternoon." The reverend greeted everyone after positioning the bride and groom together under the arch.

"You're the most beautiful woman on earth," whispered Robert and kissed Ellie on the cheek.

"We usually wait until after the ceremony for that part, Robert," observed the reverend.

The bride and groom blushed profusely as everyone in the room burst into laughter.

"My apologies, Reverend." Robert winked at Ellie.

Reverend Gerald raised his hand for silence. "Dearly beloved, we are gathered here today…"

"Sorry, I'm late, Mama," called Edward, racing into the room while tucking his shirt into his trousers. He hopped onto a chair beside Sam. "I had to go real bad."

Folks smiled and glanced at each other. Then everyone in the room burst into laughter. Edward sat on his chair, a confused expression on his face.

"What's so funny?" he whispered to Sam. His best friend just shrugged his shoulders.

"As I was saying," continued Reverend Gerald. "Dearly beloved, we are gathered…"

* * *

Ellie recalled Maggie confiding that she hadn't heard a word of the marriage ceremony when she'd wed Luke. Couldn't even recall saying 'I do' or recall the moment when Luke placed the ring on her finger. And such a magnificent ring it was, too.

Ellie vowed she'd listen to every word of her own wedding ceremony and remember every precious moment. And she did. When it came time for Robert to place the ring on her finger, he whispered, "I'm sorry, sweetheart. The ring belonged to my mother, but it's locked in my safe at home."

Ellie stuck out her hand. "You mean this ring?"

Robert gaped. "That bugg…brother of mine cracked open my safe, too?" he asked, in disbelief.

Ellie removed the ring and discreetly handed it to him.

Robert smiled and reached for her hand. "With this ring, I thee wed," he repeated after the reverend, and slipped the ring back onto her finger.

As soon as the ceremony ended, Ellie's nerves evaporated and she felt the weight of the past few weeks lift from her shoulders. Everything in her world aligned as it should. Robert became her husband, and Edward their child. A family at last.

The succulent roast beef wedding meal tasted delicious, and Ellie ate heartily. She even enjoyed two glasses of wine with the dinner, which left her feeling slightly tipsy. But in a good way.

Afterward the chairs were cleared to the edges of the room and a local fiddler played dance tunes while Aunt Penny accompanied him on Maggie's beautiful piano. Almost everyone took a turn dancing around the parlor floor. Luke served apple cider or sherry when the musicians took a break.

Ellie hooked Maggie's arm. "I'd like to change. Would you help me out of my wedding dress?"

"Certainly. I can only imagine what that dress weighs. You've done well to last this long." Maggie chuckled, and the two women strolled arm in arm out of the parlor.

As they entered Ellie's guest bedroom, Ellie turned and whispered, "Could you please pinch me, to assure me I'm not dreaming?"

"No need for pinching. You just married the love your life." Maggie quickly unbuttoned the row of buttons running down the back of the dress.

"It should be illegal to feel this happy." Ellie helped Maggie guide the dress over her head. "Oh, that's a relief. We should weigh this dress for fun someday. Sheila Bennett described this gown in a telegram, and I purchased it based on her description. But actually seeing it…her description didn't do it justice."

"She certainly does beautiful work." Maggie hung the dress in the armoire. "And to think at one time we considered purchasing material and a pattern in Elizabeth's store!"

"I have to confess something. After the real Robert proposed and I was waiting alone in this room, I almost took it off. And then I realized that the dress was bought for my wedding to Robert.

"You only made it halfway down the stairs the first time. And it wasn't even Robert waiting for you." Maggie smiled.

"Robert saw the dress when he proposed. But I don't believe all that fuss about the groom seeing the bride in her dress before the wedding." Ellie laughed. "Only if this marriage doesn't last until death us do part will I consider there might be something to the superstition."

"Good for you. You narrowly escaped the need for one divorce. I'm certain there'll be no need now. When you're a white-haired granny celebrating fifty years of marriage, I'll remind you of this day," added Maggie, chuckling.

"Fifty years! Good heavens, I'd be seventy-five years old!" Ellie laughed.

"Aunt Penny is seventy-two and she's not showing any signs of slowing down."

"No, but she lost her husband." Ellie slipped her navy woolen dress over her head. "We've shared many cups of tea together the past couple of days. She related so many stories about 'her dear Theodore', that I feel like I know the man."

"The kindest, most generous man ever." Maggie sighed. "When my uncle passed I cried more tears than when my father died. That sounds terrible, doesn't it? But my uncle and aunt doted on me when I was a child, much more so than my parents ever did."

"Some folks shouldn't be parents." Ellie grimaced. "Jimmy George…"

"Oh no, we're not going down that road." Maggie grabbed Ellie's arm. "Edward's adoption is final. He has the best set of parents he could ever hope for. Now, let's go. It's time to open the wedding presents."

"Give me a few minutes, please," requested Ellie, seating herself at the vanity table and grabbing a comb to fix her hair mussed while changing dresses.

"Take all the time you need," whispered Maggie, closing the door behind her.

Ellie smiled, contemplating everything that had brought her to this moment.

Time. While awaiting Robert's proposal, she'd finally found the time to properly mourn Franklin, taken the time to mourn the baby she lost. And then she'd put that time in her life behind her. She'd concentrated on helping Edward adjust to his new home and his new mother. In so doing, Ellie learned that bad choices didn't always ruin your life. Horrible situations would improve. Conflicts could be resolved. Time healed wounds and new beginnings were possible.

Patience. She felt so thankful that Fate stepped in and removed Jimmy George from her life. And by sharing her suspicions with Luke and Sheriff Sanders, Richard's masquerade had been uncovered, sending him back to prison where he belonged. Ellie had learned that no matter how bad things become, no matter how hopeless the situation appeared, she should never give up. By trusting friends, taking the necessary steps to rectify a bad situation, and with a bit of patience, circumstances could be altered and things eventually would end well.

Change. Ellie realized she'd accepted change, even learned to welcome it. Change could be very good, especially when it arrived in the form of a man who truly loved her and her adopted child. Thankfully, her sins were forgiven and she wouldn't question why she'd been granted these blessings. Life was all about change. Hopefully, it would always prove to be change for the better. One thing she hoped would never change: Robert's love for her and Edward. She would love them both for the rest of her life, and she hoped her family would grow someday, filling her home and her heart with more children to love.

No regrets. One future day when she and Robert were white-haired and content to spend their days in rocking chairs on the veranda, Ellie would reflect on everything that had happened to her family since this day. Despite the hardships they would undoubtedly endure, the happy times they would surely share, and the changes they would face head on and successfully overcome, there would be no regrets.

Ellie rose from the vanity chair and headed downstairs to share the remainder of the day with her new husband, her son, and her friends. There was no time like the present to welcome the future with all of them at her side.

The End

You can find Brenda at:

Website: http://www.brendasinclairauthor.com

Facebook: http://www.facebook.com/brendasinclairauthor

Twitter: https://twitter.com/bsinclairauthor

Email: mailto:brendasinclairauthor@gmail.com

SPIRIT CREEK SERIES

historical western sweet romance,
NO MORE
NO TIME
NO CHANCE
NO TIES
NO WAY
NO HOPE

Contemporary Romance Titles

Available on Amazon.com
by Brenda Sinclair
http://www.amazon.com/-/e/B007OXHMES

LOVE TO THE RESCUE
ebook and print book available
50% of the author's royalties will be donated to Humane Society shelters

A BANDIT CREEK MIRACLE
ebook and print book available

WHEN DREAMS COLLIDE
Sequel to A Bandit Creek Miracle

Escape to Alaska Trilogy
NOT WHAT IT SEEMS
ALMOST DOESN'T COUNT
NEVER A BRIDE

COOKING FOR COWBOY
(A Stampede Sizzler)
Warning: some adult content

SECRETS FOR COWBOY
(A Stampede Sizzler,
Sequel to Cooking For Cowboy)
Warning: some adult content

ABOUT THE AUTHOR

Brenda Sinclair is a writer of historical American West and contemporary romance, a member of her local chapter of Romance Writers of America, a healthy lifestyle advocate and past leader of her TOPS weight-loss group, a gardening enthusiast and dog lover.

Brenda was raised on a farm in southern Manitoba and taught school on a semi-remote reservation in northern Manitoba where, during frequent visits to a nearby town, she met her husband, a Treaty Cree member of the local First Nations band. She worked in the accounting field for over twenty-five years. A few years ago, she retired and traded in numbers for words when she decided to be a full-time writer.

Brenda and her husband have been married for over forty years, and during that time they raised two sons. She is extremely proud of her three wonderful grandchildren.

During writing breaks, Brenda enjoys walking the beautiful Fish Creek Park trails near her home in Calgary, Canada with her little dog, Kelly, checking out what Jack Abbott is up to on today's installment of The Young and The Restless, or snuggling with Kelly on the sofa and enjoying a good book.

Brenda believes life is good, and for days that life isn't so good, just get over it. There's always tomorrow.

32910692R00139

Made in the USA
Charleston, SC
29 August 2014